GENES

AN INTERNATIONAL SENSORY ASSASSIN NETWORK NOVEL

Other Books by Mary Ting

ISAN, International Sensory Assassin Network, Book 1
Helix, International Sensory Assassin Network, Book 2
Jaclyn and the Beanstalk

Awards

ISAN—International Sensory Assassin Network, Book I
GOLD MEDAL—Science Fiction & Fantasy
2019 Benjamin Franklin Awards

GOLD MEDAL—Science Fiction—Post-Apocalyptic
2018 American Fiction Awards

GOLD MEDAL—Science Fiction
2018 International Book Awards

GOLD MEDAL—Young Adult Thriller
2019 Readers' Favorite Awards

GOLD MEDAL—Young Adult Action
2018 Readers' Favorite Awards

SILVER MEDAL—Young Adult Fiction—Fantasy / Sci-Fi
2019 Moonbeam Children's Book Awards

FINALIST — Action Adventure
2019 Silver Falchion Awards

Jaclyn and the Beanstalk
BRONZE MEDAL – Juvenile / Young Adult Fiction
2019 Illumination Book Awards

GENES

AN INTERNATIONAL SENSORY ASSASSIN NETWORK NOVEL

MARY TING

Genes
An International Sensory Assassin Network Novel

This is a work of fiction. Names, characters, places, and incidents either are the
product of the author's imagination or are used fictitiously.
Any resemblance to actual persons, living or dead, or locales is entirely
coincidental.

ISBN: 978-1-64548-010-5

VESUVIAN BOOKS

Published by Vesuvian Books
www.vesuvianbooks.com

Printed in the United States of America

10 9 8 7 6 5 4 3 2 1

TABLE OF CONTENTS

CHAPTER ONE – MY TWIN

AVA

I sprinted to Zen's office at the rebel base, my pulse thumping along with my footsteps. When I'd learned I had a twin from my father's journal, I was possessed by the need to find her.

I had not found her through my own efforts but by fate. Well, by Zen's blood test.

Zen didn't say a word when I entered, but his wary eyes followed my every anxious step.

His old, rickety desk was empty. No TAB. No monitor. Just a scratched-up metal surface that had seen better days.

Chairs were lined to the side. The dilapidated wall of plaster and metal beams were to my left—destruction long ago untouched, unrenovated. So not his office then, but a place for a debriefing?

I gave Zen a tightlipped smile as I slid into my seat. *Do I speak first?*

The news Zen held would be life changing for me. No longer alone. I had a twin. A sister I could confide in, trust, with whom I could share the loss of our mother. The thought set my heart dancing.

Let's get on with it.

I inhaled a deep breath and tucked my hands under my legs to keep them steady.

1

"Zen." I gave him a curt nod.

I have information about your twin. I believe this is a topic I should share with you first. That was what he'd said to me when he'd ended the debriefing fifteen minutes earlier.

"Ava." Zen raked his hair back, his brown eyes gleaming darker.

He seemed to have aged ten years.

Zen placed his hands on the table and then set them back in his lap, parting his lips to say something, but didn't. He did that several times as if unable to make up his mind.

I would be nervous, too, if I were the messenger for something like this. He wasn't talking to me about the weather.

"You've given us a lot of information to process, but I'm ready to find out who my twin is," I said, still processing the torrent of mind-blowing news he'd thrown at us at the meeting. "I still can't believe all the girls in ISAN have special natural abilities—they don't need HelixB77 serum."

"It was the reason why the protein drink was created. The drink not only suppressed their gifts, but it was a form of birth control as well."

"I don't know which is worse. On top of the unfathomable list of crimes, ISAN had taken their memories and given them a new narrative, one that would ensure they stayed obsequious."

Zen rolled his shoulders and stretched his neck to the side to ease his tension. "Yes, that's why I left. Anyway, let's talk about the reason why I asked you to meet me. Rhett told me you read your father's journal. And I did, too. So, I know what you know. But your twin has no idea about you. In fact—"

"I know she doesn't. She couldn't unless she was told about me here, or if she read the journal." The metal chair legs scratched the floor as I scooted closer and crossed my arms on his desk.

"You keep saying *she*. Is there a reason why?" He unbuttoned the top button of his long-sleeved shirt.

I cracked my knuckles and flexed my fingers. "You took samples of our blood, and then you said you found my twin. So it must be Brooke or Tamara. Don't keep me waiting, Zen. Who is it? I'll be fine with either one. I just need to know."

I shoved away the thought of Brooke, who hung onto life by a thread. I could only deal with one thing at a time. Right now I needed to know who my twin was.

Brooke or Tamara.

His throat bobbed. "I'm afraid it's neither. You don't have a sister. You have a brother."

I struck back against the chair breathlessly, the momentum almost tipping me back.

"But you said you tested our blood. Me. Brooke. Tamara. And … and … Oh, God."

No. It couldn't be. But yes, it could. He had beautiful silver eyes. He looked part-Asian like me. But …

Gene is my twin?

Zen said, "Fraternal twins don't always look alike and don't have to be the same gender. Sometimes, they have differently colored hair. One may look more like the mother, and the other the father. Twin only means you shared the same uterus."

"Yes, I know." I didn't mean to snap at him, but his words gave me no comfort. He was explaining something I already knew adding more fire on the blazing torch. I inhaled a deep, calming breath. "I-I don't know what to say. All this time, I assumed … I was sure I had a sister. Does Gene know?"

He already answered that … I can't even think.

3

Zen relaxed his shoulders, looking less rigid than when I first entered. "I told you first. However, I did question him to find out what he knows."

"What did you ask?"

"I asked him if he had siblings. If his parents were alive. The usual. How do you feel about Gene being your brother?"

I tapped my foot like a drummer in a rock band. "Are you sure? I mean, are you sure you didn't make a mistake?" I already knew the answer.

Zen rested his folded hands on the table and hiked an eyebrow. "If it'll make you feel better, we can run another blood test. But it will have to go at the bottom of the list of things I need to do."

At the bottom. My needs are not important to you. I get it.

Though his face was a portrait of a calm scientist, his sharp tone suggested I'd dented his ego. He had a lifetime of experience in a lab and I had none.

"I would like that, if it's not too much trouble."

After going back to ISAN and risking my life to get a sample of HelixB88 as he'd asked, I had at least earned a second blood test. I had to be sure. And no matter how confident he sounded, there was always human error.

"All right. Not a problem." Zen relaxed his clenched fingers on the table. "You've spent some time with Gene. Have you seen him do anything special?"

I fixated on the clean wall behind Zen. "If there is something special about him, he never showed me and none of his supervisors said anything. Even during our training, he didn't stand out. Why do you ask?"

Zen rubbed his temple and frowned. "His DNA indicates he's

4

different from other males in ISAN. Though his genetic signature and yours are similar, his test shows something unique, as does yours."

"Maybe I can ask him? Can I see him?"

Zen closed his eyes, and then opened them, the lines on his forehead deepening. "I'm not sure if that's a good idea. He's not cooperating."

Was he worried?

I gave him a sidelong glance. "You've got him locked up. I would have an issue, too."

"No. We're treating him well. I did explain we needed to evaluate him before we set him free."

"I'd like to see him now, please." My voice was clipped, leaving no room for disagreement.

Zen released a swift breath. "Fine. But don't expect much."

"I don't expect much from people in general. It's a habit I can't seem to break."

"I'm sorry, Ava. I know how much you've been through."

Do you? Do you really? I didn't know Zen well. I hoped he didn't throw those words around lightly. He looked and sounded sincere, but could I trust my senses?

I leaned back and crossed my legs. "It is what it is. I don't think about the past much."

Zen nodded once and rose. "Come with me. He's behind the wall."

I almost ran into him when he stopped well away from the door. Instead of leading me into another room, he placed his palm on a panel.

Red light zigzagged over his hand. Then a section of wall to his right slid up, along with a thick steel door behind it. A descending staircase materialized in the dim light.

A hidden room.

"You had that built?"

"Yes. For this specific reason. We are at war, Ava. I have to prepare for everything."

I understood his reasoning. Going against a network such as ISAN would require resources and creative planning. And secrets.

Zen tilted his head. "Go ahead. I'll be right here. He might not welcome you if he sees me. Just a warning. Two of my men are down there. They know who you are. I already informed them you might be visiting."

I trusted Zen, but the assassin in me hesitated. A narrow stairway would make a good trap.

Stop the nonsense thoughts. You're fine. Rhett is right outside waiting for you. Zen is on your side.

The door clicked shut behind me when I descended the steps. A cool draft and a sterile scent greeted me. Two men waited next to a long, rectangular table equipped with high-tech machines.

"Ava." The sandy blond lowered his Taser. "We've been expecting you."

The second man with dark, buzzed hair pushed a button on a TAB, and the other half of the room lit up, revealing a thick glass panel dividing the space between guard and prisoner.

Gene lay on a cot, the only thing inside his polished, clean cell. He sat up cautiously when he spotted me, his gray eyes bright and wide. His hair a bit disheveled but he looked healthy. Not battered or bruised. No mark of being mistreated.

Gene wore the same clothes he'd had on when Tamara had kidnapped him. She'd needed his help to carry Brooke out to safety.

Poor Gene. He was a means to an end.

I would say he was at the wrong place at the wrong time, but it was fate. Good fortune for the both of us.

Gene had been there all along and I had missed it. My obstinacy had cost us time. Better late than never.

My heart skipped a beat when I approached him.

Aside from having the same color eyes, Gene and I shared no similarities. He had a prominent forehead, a sharper nose, and a square jawline.

Gene met me at the glass wall, his gaze hard as if I had disturbed him. "What do you want?"

I flinched. There was nothing friendly about his tone, and his expression had changed, too. Gone was the affable smile he'd given me when we'd trained together. Still, I understood. I would be unhelpful too if I were held captive.

But he was my brother. I had to accept that fact and hope he would accept it, too. I had much to tell him, so much time to make up for.

Something told me not to tell him just yet.

"Nothing." I recoiled a step.

He eased his frown and tempered his tone. "I can't believe you're alive. How? You were dosed with HelixB88."

Whether he was concerned or surprised, I couldn't tell.

"Do you want me … dead?" I was almost afraid to hear the answer.

Gene drew his face closer until his nose touched the glass. "No, of course not. I don't want you dead."

Relieved, I relaxed, but the way he slowly craned his neck from side-to-side, examining me as if I was some kind of science experiment, left me unnerved.

"No, not dead. Of course not," he continued, his voice taking on a cruel edge. "HelixB88 would have been an easy death. Not the kind for a traitor who deserves a long one."

What?

I took a step forward, raising my chin. Surely, I had misheard him. "What did you say?"

He cocked his head and met my stare with astute boldness. "You heard me, *Ava*. You're nothing but a traitor. Traitor to your team. Traitor to Mr. Novak. Traitor to ISAN."

It took me a moment to register, and when the words sank in, hurt was a ball of flame in my chest. Meeting my brother was not going the way I hoped.

Gone was the passive boy who didn't look like he could hurt anyone. Tamara had disliked him at first. She'd said he was too arrogant. Well, I would have preferred someone cocky over this hate-filled monster.

Brother or no, if he stood in my way, I would kill him.

I slammed the divider with my palm. An icy ache piercing through my hand.

"You have no idea what you're talking about." I gritted my teeth with fresh anger surfacing. "You have no idea how much we've been through, you and I. Taking away our memories was just a small part of the whole picture. So don't say things you'll regret. You need to know everything before you pass judgment."

Gene placed his palm over mine, still on the glass, and for a second I thought he was going to apologize. But his blazing eyes could have burned me to ashes.

"I know *everything*. Everything ISAN did to you, to the other girls, to me. Novak trusted me because I understood it was all necessary for the future we were building."

8

I dropped my hand, my ears burning. "And you believe him? You don't think what he's doing is wrong? To take away our choices, our lives. We're not robots."

Gene lowered his finger and traced an X on the glass. The moisture from his skin left a faded mark. "For the good of science and for the future, sacrifice is necessary. If I were Novak, I would have dissected your brain just to see that chaotic mind of yours. What else can you do, Ava?"

He pressed his forehead to the glass and gave a malicious grin, a promise he would act on his words if given half a chance.

I shuddered in disgust. Sick sycophant. A Novak and ISAN lover. There would be no changing his mind. He had fallen too deep.

He believed in ISAN. How many felt the same? How many knew the inhuman things Novak had done—was still doing—and didn't fight back because they believed in his cause, too?

I slowly retreated, one step after another, still facing him. He looked like a wild animal ready to unleash his hunger upon me, the prey. So different from the boy who'd been on our unit. No— ISAN's team, not mine. We had been training against the rebels, my friends.

When I didn't answer his taunt about my abilities, his jaw clenched. He rounded his fist against the glass.

"Come back, Ava. Don't you want to stay and tell me all the horrible things you've been through? What ISAN did to you? You weak, pathetic freak."

Freak? I loathed that word.

"Shut up. You"—I pointed at him—"are dead to me. I'm done with you." I was glad I had listened to my instincts and withheld the news of us being twins.

He laughed without humor, a dry sound. "Your rebels are going to die. We have big plans. Perhaps when you're caught, Novak will let me dissect your brain. And then the rest of your body. I would love to see what's inside you, how everything connects. You're a traitor, Ava. A traitor. Do you hear me? A traitor. A *traitor* ..."

I gave him my middle finger and faced the guards. My indignation swelled, ready to explode. "Make sure you have twenty-four-hour surveillance on him. He's a high risk and highly trained. For Christ's sake, sedate him."

The two men sitting behind the table gawked at me.

"Do you not hear him? Do you not see him?" I raised my voice to emphasize the urgency and pointed at Gene, who was still yelling and whacking the wall like a lunatic. "Trust me. You can confirm with Zen. I'll let him know what I told you to do."

They rose quickly to do what I said.

As my feet pounded up the cement stairs, Gene continued his tirade, bellowing *traitor* and rapping at the glass.

When I stepped on the heat sensor, the steel door and the wall slid open.

Zen waited for me at his desk with his TAB open. "Well, how did it—"

"You could have prepared me better." My heart raced. "'I'm not sure if it's a good idea' and, 'He's not cooperating' doesn't give me the whole picture. He's a monster. I told your men to sedate him."

He sighed. "I thought maybe he would be different with you. Did you tell him?"

"No. I'm not going to. And I don't want you to. He doesn't deserve to know. It won't change him." I rubbed at my chest, fighting the pang there.

I had longed to find my twin. I'd gone back to ISAN after I'd been out and completely free. I'd risked other people's lives for him. Not a sister but a brother. A brother who was too deep in the world of ISAN. So deep in the darkness, he couldn't even see a sliver of light.

If I had told him I was his sister, I doubted he would care. No, he wouldn't give a damn.

But, there was always a little hope he'd find his way. I had. People could change.

I thought of Justine. I couldn't change anyone's mind. They had to want it. Gene wanted nothing but to give me pain. He wanted to cut me open.

Fear rippled through my body. I'd thought Justine was horrible. Obviously, I hadn't seen the worst of ISAN soldiers.

"If you don't have any questions for me, I need to get some air." Acid filled my stomach. Not how I'd thought my reunion would fare.

This sucks big time. I wanted to cry, but I refused to drop a single tear for Gene, the psycho.

"That will be all. I'm sorry things are not what you might have expected. But before you go to the black market, please test out the special effect I had implanted on your chip."

"Yes, I will. And like I said before, people disappoint me. I'll be fine. I've been on my own for a long time. Nothing has changed."

No, Ava, something has changed. You have Rhett and your friends. You have a family you never expected. Family is not just by blood, but the people you build a home with in your heart.

CHAPTER TWO – EAST COMPOUND

JUSTINE

"*Justine, come with us. ISAN is bad.*"

Ava's plea repeated like a mantra in Justine's mind all the way back to ISAN headquarters from a mission they had failed. A mission Ava had initiated as a way to get out of ISAN with the help from the rebels.

How long had Ava schemed?

Good riddance, Ava. You made your bed with the rebels. Now sleep on it.

Footsteps clicked on the polished floor.

Russ offered a warm smile. "How are you feeling?"

Russ had the most beautiful green eyes Justine had ever seen. His gentle tone soothed her anger.

Justine shifted in Dr. Machine, self-conscious in the thin robe. The glass case enclosing her made her feel both claustrophobic and exposed. She wanted out.

"I've been better. Almost done." Justine jerked her chin to the mechanical hand stitching her up. "Tamara shot Payton, and then she shot my hand. She tore through flesh and bone. I was bleeding all over the place."

"I know." He dipped his head, his way of sympathizing.

Justine's nostrils flared. "She's an excellent shot, so she meant for me to spill blood. If I ever run into her, I'm going to make sure to pay her back."

Justine curled her fingers into a fist and imagined punching Tamara in the gut. If she hit hard enough, she could rip right through internal organs. Justine had never tried before. Tamara could be her first.

"Did you know Brooke and Ava were injected with HelixB88?" he asked.

Is Ava the only one he—or anyone—cares about? How about 'I'm glad you weren't affected, Justine.'

Justine shrugged and faced the flat ceiling, annoyed he'd changed the subject. She was the one who had gotten hurt. He should be asking about *her*.

"Payton debriefed us about their escape," he added.

Justine bared her teeth, heat warming her neck. She didn't care what Payton had said. She wanted to talk about the question he had brought up earlier. "I hope Ava is dead. She deserves to die. She's clearly been a traitor for a while, but Brooke … I never saw that coming. Tamara, I'm not surprised. She followed Ava like a lost puppy. Goes to show you can't trust anyone. Not even your own teammates."

As much as Justine had wanted Ava out of ISAN, seeing Brooke and Tamara leave with Ava had twisted something sharp in her gut. They were *her* troop as well. Sure, they'd liked Ava more than her, but it wasn't her fault.

Russ stiffened and he looked away.

Did I say something wrong?

Russ met her eyes again. "Did you ever hear Ava say anything suspicious? Did she mention a location? Names? Places?"

He knew Justine wasn't close to Ava, so basically he was asking her if she'd ever overheard some juicy information he could use.

13

"No. We didn't talk much. She didn't like me and I didn't like being around her. She ... she was kind of a bully."

Did he just roll his eyes?

A soft sigh deflated his chest, and his posture seemed less rigid, as if he was glad Justine knew nothing. Then it dawned on her—maybe he cared for Ava as more than a friend.

Justine stared at him, trying to read his suspicion in his body language, but a sound caught her attention. A pair of hard-soled shoes and another, soft-soled pair had stopped in the hallway outside her door. Even without Helix, she'd heard. She had never told anyone about her super senses, not even her father.

Justine craned her head to the door and wondered if Russ had heard it, too.

Everyone fawned over Ava, but Justine was the special one. She didn't need Helix for her enhanced strength. Sometimes she didn't even finish her protein drink. On occasion, she dumped half of it into her soup. At first, Justine had just been trying to keep her weight down, but she always felt better when she didn't finish it.

Justine had wondered if her teammates experienced the same, but she'd never asked. She didn't want them to think she was a freak and she liked having a secret advantage.

When the door slid open, Russ flinched and turned, indicating he had not heard their steps.

"Mr. Novak. Payton." Russ gave a curt nod and backed away to give them better access to Justine.

Justine's father always looked debonair—clean shaven with his hair sleeked back. His tailored suit framed his tall, muscular body well. *So* not fair. Their attire consisted mostly of training outfits. The only time they got to wear anything remotely fashionable was on missions.

"Justine. You're healing well."

Never a speck of warmth in his razor-sharp tone or in his cruel gaze—not even for his daughter.

Justine supposed he couldn't give her special treatment. No one knew she was his daughter. Well, Ava, Brooke, Tamara, and Gene did now, since she had foolishly told them. A mistake on her part but they were gone, maybe even dead. Her secret might be buried with them.

"My wound wasn't bad." Justine would never admit vulnerability, never show him she had been beaten, especially by someone as timid and pathetic as Tamara.

Justine's father shoved his hands in his front pockets, studying her. "Payton managed to dodge the bullet."

It was then she finally looked at Payton. His expression stoic, amber eyes dull. He was the perfect portrait of her father. He might as well have been his son.

Payton flashed a glance her way at his name and remained quiet, like Russ.

Justine's father's words stung. His way of pointing out she hadn't been fast enough. Justine could reveal Tamara had purposely missed Payton, so technically, he hadn't done any better than she had.

"Tamara hated Payton less." As the comment slipped out, Justine heard how silly it sounded. Childish even. "But it doesn't matter. You won't have to worry about Ava, Brooke, and Tamara. Due to HelixB88, they're probably already dead."

Justine's father retreated a step when Dr. Machine tilted up and released the lock. The glass door opened but she stayed put.

"Perhaps Brooke and Tamara are, but we'll see about Ava. Her DNA is unique." Justine's father rubbed his chin with his forefinger and thumb. "I wonder how they were injected with the wrong serum."

How should I know? Maybe you did it. You're the only person insane enough to do it.

Justine scoffed. "I don't know. Mitch gave us the serum. Did you ask him?" When her father didn't reply, she continued, "Ava had the nerve to ask me to join her. At least you know where my loyalty lies."

Justine's father cast a glance at the pretty boy and then back to her, straight-faced with no warmth. Payton stood like a robot, his gaze fixed on his gray shoes.

Payton had become her father's lackey, but why him?

"Tell me, Justine ..." Justine's father's lips curled a bit. Not a smile, but a challenge. "Payton told me his side of the story. Do tell yours. How did the other three of your unit escape when they were weakened by 88?"

Justine swallowed a hard lump and stepped out of Dr. Machine. She shivered at the cool surface under her bare feet. Then she put on a thick white robe and shoved her trembling hands inside the pockets. Her father always made her nervous.

If Payton's narrative was different from hers, her father might take *his* side.

"To be honest, I don't remember much. I-I got shot, so Payton took me out of the line of fire. We had to leave. There was no other choice."

Justine's father tilted his head, considering her. She stopped breathing.

"Payton said the same thing. I wanted to make sure your story matched."

Justine blew out a breath of relief. Her father had a bad

temper, especially when people deceived him. She was telling him the truth, but she didn't trust anyone else to do the same. Not if they had something to gain.

"I wouldn't hide anything from you, Mr. Novak."

Justine wanted to call him Dad. No one was supposed to know. He said it was for her benefit, so people wouldn't treat her differently.

Sometimes Justine wondered if he was ashamed of her. Justine wasn't a star like Ava. Maybe if *Ava* was his daughter, he would tell the world.

"I know." He grinned, sliding his knuckle down her cheek.

Although his smile was small, it was just for her. It was something he rarely did, and it emboldened her.

"Since Ava is no longer the team captain, will you be putting me in her place?"

Say yes, please. It would mean so much to me. I want to make you proud.

Now that Ava was gone, maybe her father would pay attention to Justine, especially if she replaced Ava as the team leader. Justine just had to convince her father. He had no reason to deny her. She deserved it.

Justine's father's eyes grew wider. Perhaps he was surprised she'd asked. But he said gruffly, "No."

The answer struck a blow to her heart. She had been absolutely sure he would put her as a team leader. She had worked as hard as anyone else. Harder. It had better not be Payton.

Russ, who had been checking his messages, jerked his head up at this. Payton did, too.

"Why?" Justine beseeched, matching his stern tone.

She shouldn't question him, but after all she'd been through, after having faced many refusals, resentment burned through her caution.

What would it take for him to see her as worthy? She didn't know how much more she could endure, being pushed aside as nothing but a mindless soldier.

He hiked up an eyebrow. "You know why. And you might want to stop there unless you want to make a fool of yourself."

The urge to laugh and spit in his face consumed her. At least she'd get his anger if not his approval.

Although, he wouldn't hesitate to throw me in solitary detention, or worse. Daughter or no, he would kill me if I defied him.

Justine inclined her head, her voice timid. "Sorry, Mr. Novak. You above anyone else would know what's best for the unit." A hint of sarcasm. She hoped he felt it.

Justine's father rocked on his heels. "Why don't you take the day off and think about what went on here. How to choose your words better next time in front of company." He pivoted and swaggered toward the door, his pet behind him. Then he paused to throw another verbal punch. "Payton will be leading Ava's team."

Ava's team. Not just *team*, he had to say *Ava's team*. Ava's, even though she was gone. The ghost of Ava still haunted her.

The door slid open, then he was out of her sight.

Russ released a heavy sigh, reminding me he was there. "I'm sorry, Justine."

Aghast, Justine stood paralyzed. Heat flooded her face. Humiliation. Anger. She didn't want his pity. It was her fault for asking her father the question in front of these idiots. She had been sure he would give her the answer she wanted.

Who was she kidding? She would never live up to his

standards, and she would never be the Ava he'd lost.

Justine dabbed at the stinging liquid easing from the corner of her eyes.

Suck it up, Justine. Don't take crap from anyone, just throw shit back. And don't you dare cry.

"It's fine." She waved a hand. "I'm going to enjoy giving Payton what he deserves, just like I did Ava. Let's see how long he can hold up."

That time, Russ *did* roll his eyes, and he meant for her to see it.

CHAPTER THREE – RELEASE

AVA

Infuriated with Gene, I almost didn't see Rhett and Tamara when I stormed down the walkway from Zen's office. Engaged in a heavy conversation, they stopped talking when they saw me.

"Ava, who is it?" Rhett asked.

I almost keeled over and threw up but clutched my stomach to keep steady. So much I wanted to say at the moment, but not in front of Tamara.

"I never thought …" I gnawed my bottom lip. "Can we talk somewhere private?"

I flashed a quick smile to Tamara so she wouldn't think I didn't trust her. I would tell her later, but first I had to cool down. My nerves frayed, I wanted to punch the wall, clobber anything.

Of all people—Gene!

Rhett coiled his arms around my waist, like an anchor steadying a ship, and guided me to his cozy room.

I sat on the queen-sized mattress, shoving a blanket to the side. With my knees apart, I clasped my face and breathed.

Inhale. Exhale. Inhale. Exhale. Again and again.

"Here, drink this." Rhett handed me a stainless-steel water container.

I finally looked up at him. "Thank you." After taking a few sips, I placed it on the cement surface next to a woven basket stuffed with clothes.

Rhett plopped next to me. "I'm guessing your twin isn't Brooke, but Tamara?"

I blurted out a short laugh. I would gladly take Tamara over that monster. Even Rhett had thought my twin was Brooke or Tamara. He was going to flip when I told him.

I shook my head. "Not Tamara. Not Brooke."

He twisted to the side to face me wholly and furrowed his brow. "Then who? He only took blood samples of you, Tamara, Brooke, and … ohhh. You don't have a sister. You have a brother." He took a moment to absorb the information. "Okay. Brothers aren't bad. Well, Mitch is a different story, but … Gene. Wow, okay."

"Yeah, wow." I clawed my fingernails deeper into the mattress to release some of my frustration. "I thought, okay, so I have a brother. What's the big deal? But when I spoke to him …" I gasped for a breath. My chest caved inward and I needed more air. "He's a monster, Rhett. He wishes I was dead. He called me a traitor and I don't want anything to do with him. He—"

Rhett pulled me into his arms and held me tight. As if his embrace was a tranquillizer, my muscles eased and my labored breathing became smoother.

The disappointment.

"Babe." Rhett's warm breath brushed against my ear. "He doesn't know about ISAN, that's all. Besides, he's been kidnapped and he's locked up. I would say terrible things, too. Just keep in mind how you felt when I kidnapped you. He'll change his mind. You'll see."

Still in his arms, I murmured, "I'm glad you kidnapped me. Thank you for never giving up on us."

So don't give up on your brother.

Rhett drew back, his callused hands cupping my face. "I love you more than anything in this world. I needed you to see, to believe me, you are the reason why I took every risk and every gamble. Everyone has a reason for living. You are my reason, Ava. I did some crazy things and I would do it all over again. I would move mountains for you. I would shatter the world to bring you home to me. Love is a powerful thing."

Oh, my heart, fluttering like a hummingbird. My throat tightened and my inside exploded with bliss.

I lowered his hands and threaded his fingers with mine. "I would have done the same for you. I promise to make it up to you, to fix what I'd broken and make up for the lost times."

Rhett kissed the back of my hands and pressed them to his chest. "Every beat of my heart was yours. Every breath you took was mine. Every moment we spent together was a gift, until it was gone. Even if you can't remember all that we've shared, that's fine. You're here with me and that's all that matters. You don't need to fix anything. We were never broken. You were lost but I found you."

Yes, we were never broken, but until I got *all* of my memories back, I was not whole.

"And as for your brother—he just needs time. Remember, ISAN was not just his life but his world. That was all he knew."

Of course he was right. All of his reasonable thoughts should have gone through my mind when I'd faced Gene, but I acted hastily. I'd only thought about what ISAN had taken from me.

"There is one little detail I should add to the story." I winced at the possible lecture coming. "Gene doesn't know I'm his sister. I never got to tell him. I wish you had seen the look in his eyes. He wanted to kill me."

"Hmmm …" Rhett twisted his lips. "Well, let's not wait too long. But I think you should be the one to tell him. I'll come with you if you'd like."

I stroked a hand across his cheek and stared into those beautiful sunrise irises. "I don't know what I would do without you. And I never want to find out."

He captured my dried hand and kissed the back of it. "Neither do I."

A photo caught my attention. I picked it up from a stack of books he used as a table. It was a photo of me, wearing his black cap and a jacket zipped up to my neck.

"How did you get this?" I asked.

A soft laugh escaped Rhett as his eyes gleamed. "Remember when we went to the city before you went back to ISAN the first time? We took a hydro glider to get there."

"Yes," I drawled. "We stopped by Cleo's bakery."

"Zen was watching a video clip of you through the surveillance camera I had hidden there. I asked him to print a photo from the still image he had captured."

"Why?" I snorted. "I look terrible."

"I love that picture of you. It took every fiber of my willpower not to kiss you that day. I almost did. You probably would have slapped me."

Heat seared my face, and I suddenly felt bashful. "I'm sure I would have. No, actually, I think I wanted you to kiss me. So you missed your chance, boy." I poked his chest.

Rhett snatched the picture from me and set it back on the table. His amber eyes darkened. "Did I?"

I waggled my eyebrows, pinching my lips. "Maybe—"

Rhett tackled me. My back bounced on the mattress with his body lightly pressed on mine. He regarded me with a devilish grin and then padded his fingers along my side.

"Rhett." I wiggled and laughed, trapped in the cage he had created with his arms. "You're going to get it."

Then he stopped.

Our eyes locked, playfulness dissipated. When he traced my collarbone, the simple touch shot hot tingles through my veins.

"Zen made space for you, Tamara, and Brooke. A room close to mine. You can stay there with your friends or you can stay with me. It's your choice."

I crinkled my forehead. "What do you want me to do?"

"You know what I want. I'm not going to make you do anything you're not ready for. I'll understand."

One of the many reasons you make my heart full.

I pursed my lips, trying not to smile. "I think you'll miss me too much. Besides, you need my protection. I'll think about it and let you know."

Rhett grinned bright enough to light up the room. "I do need your protection, though. Who's going to save me from all the other girls who want in my bedroom?"

A low, predatory growl escaped me, and Rhett laughed.

"That sound turns me on, Ava."

I did it again.

Rhett dove in and kissed me, his mouth wild and demanding. *Oh, God.*

He rolled over with me in his arms until I was on top of him, panting. A cowbell echoed down the hall, and he dropped his head on the pillow with an agitated sigh.

"Dinner soon," he said. "That's the bell to tell the kitchen duty group to set up, and that's us. We should get going. If we keep at this, I won't be able to stop."

"Okay," I breathed, but I didn't want him to stop as I recalled the night we'd shared in our make-believe house.

I rolled halfway off him, but he brought me back into his arms. "Not so fast. One more kiss." His soft, warm lips met mine, and then he pulled away. "To carry me through dinner until we meet like this again."

"Is that all you can do? I think I've had better." I faked a yawn.

He scowled. "That better be from me and only me."

Then he gave me a toe-curling kiss, the kind that would not last me through dinner, but would make me beg for more.

"Okay. Much better." My back thumped onto the mattress. The warm, electrifying sensation of his kiss still lingered.

"Time to go." Rhett pulled me up and ran his fingers through his hair. "Oh, I almost forgot. I have something for you." He fished something out of his pocket and let it dangle.

"It's—it's beautiful." I watched the silver chain swing.

The pendant was a small, pressed dandelion, encased in a flat see-through locket.

"I bought it at the black market when you were still in ISAN. It reminded me of you and I had to have it. I thought it was a sign that we would be together again. I know it sounds silly, but it gave me hope."

"Rhett." I shuddered a breath, my heart cracking at what he had been through. I moved closer, the tip of my toes bumping his. "It's not silly at all." I paused to take in his melancholy grin, which I mimicked as I caressed his cheek. "I'm here now. You brought me home and I'm never leaving you again."

"I know," he said softly.

I felt the ache in his voice. He glanced at the hole in the wall like that part of the memory was stored there. It's one thing to move on, but it's another to forget. Like Rhett had said, you can't forget emotions.

"Well, aren't you going to put it on me?" I said with a playful bite.

Rhett blinked, his focus back to me. "Of course." He looped it around my neck. "It's perfect on you."

I rubbed at the pendant and closed my eyes, then opened them. "Thank you. This is thoughtful of you and I'm never taking it off."

Rhett planted a tender kiss on my forehead. "You're welcome. It was made for you. It found its home."

"Rhett." My heart blossomed with joy for being with him, though a part of me felt guilty.

"Yes, Ava."

"Brooke?"

I didn't need to say more. He knew what I was asking.

"Tomorrow. We'll get what Zen needs for Brooke."

"Thank you. After dinner, I'd like to see her."

"Of course. But before dinner, let me take you to meet Momo and her friends, the group I was telling you about earlier. The ISAN rebels from the south."

"Perfect. I can't wait." I dodged an office chair, its leather seat stained and old.

Rhett pushed it back against the pitted sheetrock wall but it didn't provide more space. "We need to find a bigger room if you're moving in."

With my hands in my pockets, I rocked from side to side. "Who says I'm staying with you? It's kind of"—I took in the low

26

ceiling and the snug space—"small in here."

"Oh," he said, sounding surprised. "I thought—"

"I'm kidding, Rhett." I leaned into him, my hand over his heart, and repeated the words he'd said to me back in our makeshift home. "My favorite place in the world is next to you. I wouldn't want to be anywhere else. This place is perfect. Anywhere with you is home. Just you and me." Then I pushed back the fabric used as a door after I planted a kiss on his cheek.

His lips lifted into a crescent, beaming like the moon, melting me into the dirt, and he led me out with his hand in mine.

CHAPTER FOUR – MEET AND GREET

AVA

"**M**omo? That's a strange name." I followed Rhett down a slope assembled from chunks of broken concrete.

"Momo is her nickname." Rhett extended a hand and I graciously took it. "Monet is her real name. They all have cute-sounding nicknames. Must be a kid thing or a southern rebel thing."

He gathered me in his arms, swung me around, and placed me on a wooden platform.

"Ava. Rhett." A familiar male voice greeted us.

"Oz. Hey." I patted his shoulder when he caught up to us.

"Good evening, Oz." Rhett gave Ozzie a high five.

Ozzie smiled. "What did you do to him, Ava? He's not a grouch anymore."

With the intent of making Ozzie blush, I said, "I heard sex cures a lot of sicknesses."

Ozzie flushed a bright shade of red and cleared his throat. Unable to look me in the eye, he said with a squeak, "Oh."

Rhett gawked at me. Then he took on an extra swagger. "I like Ava's answer. And I like seeing Oz flustered."

"I bet you do." Ozzie scowled at the walls.

"Where's Reyna?" Rhett glanced about.

Ozzie pointed to his left. "She's there with the rebels from the south."

Rhett hiked up a small pile of debris, a substitute stair leading to a bigger heap of rubble.

Feet shuffled, pounding faster. Closer. Then three slim people sprinted into the light from the back corner toward the meeting area. The little Asian girl jabbered away to Rhett.

They looked familiar. Where had I seen them before? Two girls and one boy. They all wore a black cap with a word I recognized—*Renegades*—in white print.

"This is Ava." Rhett waved a hand to me.

When they turned their attention to me, they froze. Their eyes widened at the same time I realized who they were. The kids who'd kidnapped Palmer. The ones who made me look like a fool.

"You." I pointed, giving the talkative girl a death glare.

"See you later, Rhett. Run, guys!"

She took off, her friends behind her, but then they scattered like trained ISAN soldiers. A tactic we'd learned to employ if we were being chased.

"Come back here." I ran after the girl, presumably the leader, as dirt kicked beneath my boot. "You little—if I get a hold of you, I'm going to—"

She soared over a firepit, knocked a pot at me while passing through the kitchen, and weaved through the tents. Then she scrambled up the wall to the second level, ran across the provisional bridge, and slid down a slope near the front exit.

The girl was fast. Faster than I'd ever seen anyone run. Her long dark hair flowed like a cape behind her.

I recalled Rhett's words: *She doesn't need Helix. She has natural ability. I saw her in action.*

I didn't need an extra dose of Helix either. Technically I never had. Those of us with special genes never had. The Helix serum was based on what our bodies produced naturally. Instead of something I injected, it had been with me all along.

Girls had been recruited into ISAN because their DNA indicated special abilities. The aftermath of the meteor radiation changed women, and only women, at a cellular level.

But ISAN had told us none of that. They'd said our DNA showed we could use HelixB77, which we'd all thought gave us our abilities. Instead, it gave an adrenaline surge that provisionally overrode the inhibitor ISAN administered—the protein drink. It made us feel invincible.

I could have pushed Helix through my veins to catch up to her, but I slowed when she hid behind an old woman. The other renegades followed suit, panting.

Smart kids. Brave kids. But stupid for messing with me.

"Don't touch these innocent kids." The old woman glowered at me with a cane ready to defend the younglings.

I raised my hands, a peace offering. "I'm not going to hurt them. I just want to talk to them."

Going around the old lady wouldn't be a problem. I was just about to strike when arms coiled around me.

Rhett spun me around. "What's going on?"

"They, these brats, they ..." I closed my mouth.

They what? Went against ISAN? Why was I mad, ready to pounce on kids, for crying out loud? They hadn't done anything wrong besides messing with my ego, but ...

Grow up, Ava. There are more important things to deal with.

My breath eased enough to speak. "I ran into them during a mission. They interfered."

Rhett looked at Momo and then back to me with pinched

eyebrows. "Let me guess—they snatched a political figure named Roth Palmer out of your hands."

I shoved my fists to my hips. "How do you know about that?"

"Jo, their captain, told me. They knew ISAN was going to try to capture Palmer, so during their last mission before they escaped, they kidnapped him and took him to safety. Jo is working for Chang, a double agent like Mitch. Palmer didn't actually have the list. Chang put the word out he had a list of Remnant Council representatives, undisclosed to the public, and he planned to sell it to the highest bidder. Palmer was sent to capture the buyer who Chang thought might actually have other names on the list. Her goal was to get to Verlot's reps."

"Oh, I see." I puffed out my annoyance.

The kids flashed innocent smiles at Rhett.

"Come here." Rhett crooked a finger at them. "This is Ava. You know who she is. She won't hurt you."

They scurried and huddled behind Rhett.

Oh, please.

I rolled my eyes. Sure, look all cute and harmless. I knew their manipulative ways. Then something tugged at my heartstrings.

They were young, about the age I was when I'd been sent to my foster parents. I remembered being a child, naïve, and innocent, too. They had likely been forced or manipulated to be in ISAN. I would get their story one day. And perhaps they were truly scared of me.

There were stories of me floating around in other territories. They said I was a ruthless, cold assassin bitch. They exaggerated the rumor of course, but I supposed I wouldn't want to be near someone like that.

"Come on. She won't bite, right, Ava?" Rhett's eyes widened

as if to say, *Help me out here.*

The way he protected these kids gave me a warm fuzzy feel, so I eased my frown.

"This is Momo." Rhett set his arms around the Asian girl's shoulder and pulled her to his side.

Pretty little thing.

"This is Coco and Bobo." He gestured to a girl with auburn hair in a tight French braid, and then to a lanky, dark-skinned boy.

"Hi." I extended my hand. "We got off on the wrong foot. It's nice to meet you. Any friend of Rhett's is a friend of mine."

One by one, they shook my hand and bustled away as if afraid I would bite them.

Rhett stroked Momo's hair. It seemed the girl had weaseled her way into his good graces.

"We're all good now." Rhett patted Coco and Bobo's shoulders. "No bad guys here. Just a happy family. We all need to get along or we'll drive—"

"Get back here. Stella. Jasper. I mean it!" Reyna's scolding echoed down the hall.

"—each other crazy," Rhett finished with a roll of his eyes.

Stella and Jasper were the oldest among the kids I'd met the first time I'd come here. Jasper skidded to a halt in front of me while Stella waited for him a few yards ahead, gasping for breath.

"Hey, Ava. I didn't know you came back. You're looking fine." Jasper gave me a once-over. Then he scrammed before Reyna could catch up to him.

Rhett snarled softly.

Momo watched Jasper zoom up the debris, her eyes bright as the sun poking through the solar panels. Someone had a bit of a crush, it seemed.

"Whoa. Whoa. Whoa." Rhett snagged Reyna's arm and stopped her from advancing. "What's going on?"

"Look at me." She waved a hand down her body. "I'm soaked. Those brats splashed water on me."

Reyna's hair was dripping and a huge wet spot spread over the front of her sweatshirt.

"Where's Oz?" I looked over my shoulder, and then near the tents. He had been with us until I'd run after the kids.

"Where do you think?" Reyna hiked a thumb behind her. "You know he doesn't wait for food for *anyone*."

"Come on. I'm starving." Rhett met my eyes and grinned.

I stepped beside him, and the trio of kids lagged behind. Reyna swore and continued her chase.

We picked up our plate of food—canned brown beans, bread, spinach, and carrots—much of the produce grown there. Water, in recyclable plastic bottles, was already set on the table.

Instead of eating at the adult table, we joined the trio, surrounded by little folks wearing *Renegade* hats.

Twenty pairs of eyes fixed on us—people most likely wondering why we'd sat with them.

"Here. Utensils are allowed during dinner only." Rhett passed me a worn basket filled with warped metal spoons and forks.

"Thanks." I took out a fork and passed the basket to Coco.

After a few bites, Rhett cleared his throat. "Momo, why don't you tell Ava about what you can do?"

Next to Rhett, Momo lit up, slowly relaxing but still cautious of me.

"I can do things a normal kid can't do."

"Like?" I smiled, not to intimidate her.

She was fast. I knew that much.

She finished chewing a piece of carrot. "I can beat five men's freakin' asses to a pulp on my own." Her pitch rose with elation and pride.

The kids at the table snickered. Coco spat out a mouthful of beans, which made the kids laugh even harder. Bobo elbowed her arm. I almost sprayed out my water, but pursed my lips and held it in.

"Momo. What did I say about cussing?"

Momo's shoulders curved inward at Rhett's scolding. "*Freakin'* and *asses* are not bad words. Everyone says it."

Rhett sighed and shook his head. "There are little ones at the table. Anyway, go on."

I smiled at Rhett's parenting skills.

"I can do these things without Helix. Coco is like me, too, but Bobo can't. Only the girls but I don't know why. I know there are others like me, like you out there. I heard the news."

"Yeah." Coco nodded reverently, her long braid bobbing.

Bobo only shrugged and scarfed down a piece of bread.

I jabbed my fork into my spinach and scooped up a mouthful. "When did you know you can do these things without Helix? Do you know the extent of your abilities?"

Momo scratched the left side of her head. "I knew before I was sent to ISAN. Well, more like I was sold."

I stopped my fork halfway to my mouth. "What do you mean, *sold*?"

"My foster father. I don't know his name. When he found out what I could do, he called someone. I heard him talking about selling us to a network and I would make him rich. I figured ISAN would be a better place. I had no idea we were going to be trained to be assassins."

34

"Why didn't you beat the crap out of him and run?"

I wasn't judging her. My foster father had been bad, but he'd never threatened to sell me to ISAN. I wished I had done something then, but I'd had no idea what I was capable of. I had been scared and without options. When I had run, I'd landed in juvenile detention.

Her eyes dulled until no spark of cockiness remained. "There were too many of us. I thought I was the only special one. Even knowing about me, they were afraid to leave. Kids like Bobo, they couldn't fight back against guns pointing at them. Back then, before training, I probably couldn't either. Our foster father was not alone. We weren't in a regular foster home. It was a group house with a bunch of scary men and a couple of women. So I stayed. I stayed for my friends. I had nowhere else to go. I always used my super hearing to help us avoid getting caught doing stuff we shouldn't be doing."

"I'm sorry. I'm sorry you had to go through all that. I know how you feel."

I meant every word. I sympathized not just with her, but with everyone who'd lived through ISAN.

Momo straightened her spine, and continued to eat.

Rhett gave me a heartfelt smile, the kind that said, *I'm proud of you.*

"Where did you get those caps? ISAN certainly didn't give them to you." I laughed dryly, but the kids stopped eating and lowered their heads.

Had I said something wrong?

Rhett cleared his throat, his face drawn and solemn. "Debbie did. She was their supervisor, like Jo. Like Russ for you. Both women schemed and executed the mission to get the kids out of

ISAN in the south. Not all escaped. There are many still at the base. They split the troop that escaped, which was smart, but Novak found the first group's hideout. They didn't make it out alive. Jo, Reyna, Ozzie, and I were on our way to warn them of an attack. We had no way of communicating. We were too late."

I swallowed, though my throat constricted. "I'm so sorry." It was difficult to say those three simple words.

Mr. Novak had done this. He had told me about it when I'd woken up after treatment in Dr. Machine. *The rebel team in the south has been destroyed.* No remorse. He'd killed innocent children, and he'd been proud of what he had done.

Rhett and my friends had been there in the line of attack. They could have died in that blast. And the kids who died, they'd only wanted a better life. Was that so wrong?

We were supposed to mold our young ones to make a brighter future, not destroy it—or them.

Momo broke the silence. "Anyway, on our scouting day, Debbie found a warehouse full of kids' clothes and accessories. We had a field day picking them out. Debbie found a bag full of hats. She thought the Renegade caps were fate. She told us to never give up, never stop fighting. Because of who we were and our abilities, she always said it was up to us to save others who can't defend themselves. If we didn't, then the gift given to us would be a waste. She believed having powers didn't make you any better. Anyone can be brave. All you need are wits, good skills, and to believe in yourself."

"She's right," I said softly. "I'm glad you had a leader like her." I needed to say more, but nothing seemed remotely enough.

Momo pointed at a two-inch-long scar on her right arm. "See this. Dr. Machine can't touch my scar now that I'm out of ISAN.

I got this on the day we escaped. Debbie said my scar is beautiful. She said a scar tells a story. My story. A story of courage and strength. ISAN can't take this from me."

"I agree with her," I said. "And some scars are internal. It's how we decide to deal with them that defines who we are."

"If it wasn't for Debbie and Jo, we wouldn't be here." Bobo smeared a drop of liquid across his cheek. "I wish our friends could have been here with us. I wish they didn't have to die."

"They died so we could live." Coco's voice was strong and in command. "Like Debbie said, let's not waste our gifts. We have others to help get out of ISAN. Renegades forever."

The kids whooped and banged on the table. "Renegades forever."

All adult eyes turned to our table. Some frowned, but the rest were friendly. When the noise faded, we continued our meal. I scouted how many southern rebel children, and then I realized I didn't know what Jo looked like.

"Which one's Jo?" I took another gulp of my water.

"She's sitting with Oz." Momo pointed over me.

I found Ozzie sitting between Tamara and Jo, eating away. Frank and his men and Cleo were also at the same table. Zen must have eaten earlier. He was nowhere to be seen.

Tamara lifted a fork at me, and I lifted mine back to her. Reyna had finally caught the two pranksters.

"I'm sorry. I'll never do it again." Jasper's voice faded in the distance.

Reyna was never the type to give up. Neither was I.

Hold on, Brooke. Just hold on.

CHAPTER FIVE – THE PLAN

AVA

The next day, we held a meeting by Brooke's bed. She lay still in the glass case, connected to life support through tubes and wires.

Her breathing—regular.

Her pulse—steady.

She'd almost died, I'd found out the night before. Zen had had to shock her heart into pumping again.

I wouldn't have handled it well had she passed away while I slept in Rhett's arms, safe and warm. Perhaps I should consider sleeping here in case she had another episode or—by some miracle—woke up.

Zen had people monitoring her twenty-four hours a day. She was in good hands. But still ...

We stood around Brooke, waiting for Tamara and Zen. I laid one hand on the case as if I could touch her.

Tamara skidded to a halt, out of breath. "Hey. Am I late?"

The last time I'd seen her, Tamara had had shiny black hair as long as mine, but she'd had it chopped off. It barely touched her shoulders.

I did a double take. "No, but you cut your hair. It looks nice."

Rhett, Reyna, and Ozzie stared, but said nothing.

"Thanks, Ava. I wanted a different look. It got in the way."

38

I had thought about cutting my hair short like hers. My hair sometimes got in the way during the missions. It would give me a new look, too, a symbol of a fresh start.

Seeing Tamara in a new light was hard to adjust to at times. I was glad to find out she was more independent and braver without me, but I missed the old Tam. Brooke, Tamara, and I were a band. We'd gotten each other through some rough times.

I wondered if our friendship would change with the new environment.

"Are we all here?" Zen entered holding a small TAB. He looked between Reyna, Ozzie, Tamara, Cleo, Rhett, and me.

"Yes, we are." Rhett leaned away from the wall. With his legs spread apart slightly, he crossed his arms.

"Good. I'm sending Rhett and Reyna the list I need via their chip. It's a short list, so it won't take you long to find the items, but acquiring them might."

"Then we should get going." Ozzie stared at Brooke. Only when he realized I was watching did he turn away.

I wondered what he was thinking.

"Let's not waste time." Dressed like a warrior, Tamara flipped her silver pocket knife. On her back were twin short blades tucked inside black leather scabbards.

Rhett clapped once. "Let's go, then."

"One more thing." Zen put up an arm to stop us and swiped at his TAB. A hologram of an unfamiliar crumbled building appeared. "Take the truck to the north building. Then take the oldest glider. It's best not to draw attention."

"It's a piece of crap." Rhett scrubbed the back of his head, frustration in his tone. "If we're followed? Then what?"

Zen, who was on his way out, stopped mid-stride. "I have a

lead on the girls from the news. I have an ensemble ready to dispatch, and they need the faster transport. I'm sending Frank and his men to that location. Also, I sent you coordinates. Black market is in the east this time."

"Oh, good. We're at least in the same territory and don't have to fly far," Cleo murmured.

Rhett sighed. "Fine. Are we excused?"

"No. One more thing. Try to stay out of sight of the drones. I don't want to hear about the disturbances in the news again."

Rhett glanced at the ceiling. "Are we excused now, Pops?"

Ozzie snickered. "He said Pops."

Zen scowled at Ozzie. "Remember to switch out your chip. Reyna and Rhett, you have 4Qs in your accounts. Be back soon. Councilor Chang is on her way."

"Fine." Rhett rushed out of there.

Everyone headed for the exit.

"I'll be back," I whispered to Brooke, tapping the glass case gently.

She looked so peaceful. My chest caved in.

Hold on my friend. We promised we would make it out together. Don't break your promise to me.

Rhett popped back in to the room, out of breath. "Ava." He'd realized I wasn't with him.

"I'm coming."

A piece of junk was an understatement. The aircraft glided at a snail's pace. Not to mention the rusted interior and exterior.

"Well, here we go." Rhett punched in a location and banked

right. He grabbed my hand and kissed my knuckles. "Brooke is going to be fine. We're going to get what Zen needs and she'll come out of her coma."

I squeezed his hand and stared out the front. I needed something to distract myself from my friend.

Sunlight poked through the dark clouds. We flew over destruction and debris too costly to clean up. Until there was a need for more land, nothing would be done about the mess.

We passed over high tech and gleaming cities. Thanks to the meteors, I supposed. What had nearly destroyed us had also forced us to rebuild and focus resources on advancing the future. For some people, anyway.

Cancer, genetic diseases, and viruses. They'd been virtually wiped out once scientists created vitamin pills—consumed on a daily basis. People not only lived longer but looked younger as well. Less demand for plastic surgery and wrinkle creams.

After a smooth ride, we lined up with other transporters, merging in with society. So many gliders. So many skyscrapers. Such a wondrous sight. I marveled at the high-rise structures, each with a unique design.

Citizens were busy in their daily lives, having never heard of ISAN. However, they'd recently had their first taste of women with superpowers. The world was changing. And the world would fear it. We had to act fast.

"We're almost there. So this is the plan." Rhett switched on autopilot and shifted to get a better view of his cast. I did the same. "Ava, Tamara, and I will head east once we enter. Reyna, Ozzie, and Cleo, go west. We'll communicate through our chips. Once you get the goods, get back to the glider and stay put. Reyna's party is looking for myrrh. Must be oil, not solid. And a few other things."

"Yeah, we know, Rhett." Reyna released the hologram from her chip and showed us a picture of a clear bottle filled with yellow liquid.

"What will you be looking for?" Ozzie reached over and shut down Reyna's image.

"Meteor," Rhett said.

"Meteor?" I shrieked. "What? They sell pieces of that stuff? How did they get a hold of it?"

Tamara placed a gentle hand on my knee. "Black market. They get stuff we have no names for. Some legal and some not. The reason we shouldn't stay long, and the reason black market travels to a different location every week."

I frowned. "How do you know?"

Cleo brushed something off her jacket. "My father knows a lot of people. Don't worry. Rhett knows who to contact."

"Everyone, brace for landing." Rhett flicked some switches and tapped the touchscreen in front of him. Then he tugged on my seatbelt. "Just making sure. Hold on."

The glider jerked violently. I slammed my hands on the dashboard, my head whiplashed frontward. As if we'd run into an invisible wall, the aircraft shoved us forward and slammed us back.

Loud grunts came from behind me and people thudded against the floor.

"Who's back there?" Rhett bellowed as the transporter dove.

I tried to get a better look over the headrest, but I couldn't see anything. Everyone gripped their seats as the glider nosedived.

Drawing on Helix, I used my mental map and spotted three bodies. Harmless, so I didn't say anything. Rhett would deal with them after we landed.

"Can't you do anything about the speed, Rhett?" Reyna squealed.

"I'm going to throw up." Ozzie puffed one rapid breath after another.

Cleo gripped her armrest. "After today, I'm never riding this piece of junk again. My father is going to get a mouthful from me."

Tamara let out a belly laugh. "You're all wimps."

So hard to get used to this new side of Tamara. The real Tamara, actually.

My stomach dropped as we plummeted like a fallen missile before we finally leveled off behind an encroaching tall building. The edifice was intact, but the front face gaped like an open wound, especially toward the bottom.

Abandoned. Wrecked. The whole street was the same. No windows, just metal beams, concrete, and rotted wood.

No other aircraft passed. No sign of life.

The glider landed smoothly, despite the way it had handled the descent. Rhett veered into a dark spot on the second floor.

The door whooshed open and seatbelts unclicked. Without a word, Rhett stomped toward the back, shoving Ozzie and Reyna aside on the way.

"Rhett?" Reyna threw up her hands. "What's the hurry?"

"Did anyone give you permission?" Rhett roared, half of his body behind the divider.

"I don't need permission from you." Reyna shot up from her seat.

"Not you, Reyna. Them." Rhett pointed to the ground.

We rushed over and sure enough, we found the three small stowaways I'd pulled up in my map. Momo, Coco, and Bobo were sitting crossed legged with heads lowered.

"Momo." Rhett's face changed color, his jaw clenching, his tone soft but deadly.

Momo peered up with big, innocent, brown eyes. "We're here to help. The three musketeers at your service."

"What did I tell you about the word *help* and what it means? When I need your help, I'll ask for it. You can't just assign yourself to missions."

"I told you he would get mad." Bobo's lips scrunched together while shifting his *Renegades* cap. "Why do we always listen to you?"

"You never ask." Momo tugged at the hem of her shirt.

A muscle on Rhett's face jumped. "Because I don't need it. What part of *I'll ask* did you not understand? You've wasted our time."

"Fine. I'm sorry." Nothing about her tone was rueful. "But we can help. We can *do* things."

"I'm aware of what you're capable of, but right now, you're excelling at getting on my nerves, understand?"

Wordlessly, Momo dusted grime off her dirt-caked boots.

"What else did I say, Momo?" Rhett sounded more like a father instead of a military commander.

Momo flicked at her bootstrings. "I put not only my life, but my friends' lives in jeopardy when I don't listen."

"Good." Rhett patted Momo's knees. "Please cooperate and let us handle this."

"What are we going to do?" Cleo pulled Rhett's sleeve to get his attention.

He opened a drawer and tossed brown fabric at us.

"Whoa, this is so cool." Tamara flung it around her and buttoned it at the top. "It's a cloak. I feel mysterious."

"Everyone wears one at the black market to hide their identity, even the sellers sometimes." Rhett adjusted mine and snapped it closed by my neck. The simple gesture warmed my heart.

"Leave your weapons. No weapons are allowed." Rhett took his Taser from his holster and shoved it in a drawer.

After he fastened on his cape, he turned to the kids. "Here is your mission, Momo. Stay here and make sure no one steals our glider."

"That's not—"

Rhett held up a palm. "Take it or leave it."

Coco elbowed Momo in the ribs and murmured something.

"Fine." Momo crossed her arms and angled her head to the side.

"Come on. We need to get going." Rhett gestured for me to go first.

We hiked down the ramp leading out into the street. After Rhett caught up, we fell into our diamond-shaped formation— Ozzie and Reyna watching our backs, Tamara and Cleo on either side, and Rhett and me in front—we had all sides covered.

Rhett pulled up the map from his chip and led the way.

The soft breeze carried loose trash along the length of the road. Rusted street signs were bent or flattened. Cars parked on the curbs had been stripped of tires and anything salvageable or outright smashed.

Shops had missing doors, windows, and roofs. Plastic shopping bags, dirty paper envelopes, torn cardboard boxes, and even ripped books lay in the gravel. I felt like I was inside a junkyard.

This dilapidated neighborhood looked like any other abandoned city, with newer rubbish layered over the meteor-created wasteland. Every region had its own pockets of neglect.

We moved lightly and unencumbered among the ruins.

"Looks like death here." Tamara matched my steps, breaking the formation.

Cleo, Reyna, and Ozzie clustered to the left of Rhett, distracted by their group conversation.

"So, Tamara, what's your real story?" I lagged a little behind Rhett, but close enough so he could see me. I needed some space for Tamara to open up to me. It was the first time I'd spoken to her one-on-one after escaping.

"I'm really sorry about not telling you the truth," she said.

Tamara's eyes glistened when the sun escaped long enough to give us warmth. Her hood covered her hair, like mine. I wouldn't have minded her being my twin. But Gene?

I pushed that thought away.

I leaped over an upturned chunk of asphalt. "We're past that. It's fine. I understand. How did you meet Zen?"

"Everything I told you about my ex-boyfriend hitting me is true. And also about my grandmother raising me. I want to get that clear first."

"Okay." A broken glass bottle crunched under my boot.

Tamara flattened a hand on top of her hood when a sudden breeze whipped by. "It's a long story. I'll make it short. Councilor Chang came to visit me in juvie. She told me I had a special gift. She also told me about ISAN and the rebels. I had two choices: rot in juvie or work for her. They faked my death when I agreed, and Zen took me out of juvie like any ISAN recruit. Zen placed me in ISAN as a newbie and trained me in the North where he was stationed. Eventually we worked collectively to get others out—those who wanted out, anyways. Some were like Justine. ISAN was their life and they didn't want to leave. Others were too afraid."

Rhett twisted to check up on me when I fell farther behind. I held up a finger to let him know I needed a moment.

"Well, I'm glad Zen was there for you. And I'm glad you were there for me."

"Thanks." She flashed a quick smile. "When Rhett's group escaped and he told Zen about you, Zen sent me back in right away. Zen knew your father, but he knew Rhett and Mitch's father, too."

"Did Mitch know you were working with Zen?"

"No. Zen didn't tell a single soul and neither did I."

I nudged aside a rusted office trash bin with my boot. "Then how did you get back in ISAN?"

Tamara hugged her cloak tighter. The sun had tucked back into the dark clouds. "Zen did the paperwork. He made it seem like I was a transfer from the North. Don't ask me the details, I have no idea. Zen knows a lot of people in and out of ISAN."

"Wouldn't they have already recorded you had escaped or were missing? They've got DNA records on all of us."

"One of Zen's techs must have overridden the system from the inside. Novak doesn't know every ISAN assassin by name. I was fairly new when I escaped with Zen. Besides, Novak never saw me in person until I went to the East."

"Oh, I see. I almost didn't ask you to escape with me and Brooke. If I hadn't, what would have happened to you?" I felt guilty admitting it, but I knew she would understand.

"I don't think anything would have changed. I would have tagged along, like I always did." She snorted. "Or I would have told you the truth if you didn't trust me. One way or another, it would have worked out. But I have to admit, it makes me feel good you thought of me as your friend and trusted me enough to risk your escape on it."

I smiled. "It's good to know people have your back."

"I agree." Tamara elbowed my shoulder with a goofy grin. "I thought going in I'd be faking my friendship with you, but in the end, I gained two friends. You and Brooke. We both have her back, and we will get what she needs."

It felt good not to have to fight alone, as I had in ISAN until I'd bonded with Tamara and Brooke.

Rhett slowed and we caught up to him.

Conversation halted.

In the heart of what had once been a beautiful, prosperous city, the opening of a dark tunnel emerged.

The black market.

"We're here." Tamara's eyes rounded.

Rhett gripped my hand and squeezed once. "Stay close."

CHAPTER SIX – REGROUP

MITCH

Mitch entered Russ's office. Lydia sat stiffly on a chair next to Russ at his desk. Mr. Novak leaned back on the sofa with his legs crossed, Payton beside him—pale and expressionless.

Poor kid. He had to follow Novak everywhere he went. Payton had indirectly told Mitch he could detect if people were telling the truth. Mitch was surprised Payton had shared highly classified information, but Mitch presumed Payton sensed he could trust Mitch. Payton might have even been reaching out for help behind Novak's back.

Payton had similar genes like the girls with abilities, either through an experimental procedure, or he was born that way. Mitch speculated Payton had been experimented on by Novak's scientists long before he'd come aboard.

Mitch had promised Payton he wouldn't say a word to anyone. And he wouldn't—unless he needed to protect himself. Novak would shoot that boy if his secret weapon wasn't a secret anymore.

"Why are we meeting yet again? Nothing's happened since the last one." Mitch shoved his sweaty palms inside his front pockets, his heels scuffing as he strolled across to the empty chair next to Russ.

Being in the same room with Novak always left Mitch

nauseated. His luck might run out one day and Novak would find out all the things he'd done for the rebels.

Keep your head up. Don't give Novak any reason to be suspicious.

"I've lost my top three assassins from this facility and I don't want that ever happening again." Novak flicked something off his dark-gray suit, his tone calm but lethal.

Silence.

So deadly quiet, Lydia's shuddering breath resonated in the room.

Novak rose and paced, eyeing each of them as he passed. "Tell me. How is it possible my most trusted intelligence agents allowed three teen girls to slip by? The rebels also managed to capture Gene in the process. Is there a traitor in this house or are you just bad at your jobs?"

Russ cleared his throat. "None of us are traitors. There was fire and chaos. We were spread out all over the warehouse. For all we know, all of them could have been kidnapped."

Stupid answer, bro. Just keep your mouth shut.

Novak stopped in front of Russ, his glare piercing. "All? What do you mean by all? I said nothing of being kidnapped, Russ. They escaped. *You* let them escape." Novak pounded a fist on the table and kept it there.

Russ jerked, and so did everyone else, Mitch included.

Never had Mitch seen Novak violent and flustered. Yes, he raised his voice, but not like this. Losing Ava had tested the limit of his tolerance—he hadn't much to begin with.

"I didn't mean—"

Novak spread his fingers on the table and leaned closer to Russ, baring his teeth. "Don't say another word. Being kidnapped is one thing, escaping is a whole different story. Escaping means they schemed with the rebels. And they had help. Surely the girls must have given some indication of their lack of loyalty."

Lydia's skirt rose to her thigh when she crossed her legs. "Don't question me. I wasn't there."

Novak scanned up her legs to her pale face. "Perhaps I need to put you back in the field. Maybe the team needs your expertise, Lydia."

A threat.

Lydia didn't say a word, her cheeks losing their color. She had been a field operative agent, but things had gone wrong during a mission. HelixB77 had failed the males and one of her soldiers had gone ballistic.

He'd killed his troop and left Lydia badly injured with a broken arm, a cracked rib, and a concussion after she'd put a bullet through his head.

After Lydia recovered, she had requested office duty. She wasn't special like Ava, nor did she have the DNA marker ISAN wanted. She had once been a council guard, recruited specifically for her combat skills.

Novak had accepted her request because she could no longer perform under pressure. She'd even freeze during mental missions.

"There's no need to put Lydia back in the field," Russ said. "Her expertise is teaching the girls. But there is something more urgent at hand. Brooke and Ava were injected with HelixB88. I'm not sure about Tamara. We don't know if they're alive or dead."

Novak glared at Russ. "I don't care if Brooke is dead. I knew it would kill her, but Ava is different. Her body will fight it off. Tamara is not affected, though I was quite shocked to hear she had left with Ava. My intention was not to kill Ava, but to show her what I can do to those she cares for. I want Ava and Gene back.

What are we doing to make this happen?"

Nothing. You can go shit on yourself. When the rebels don't need me in here anymore, or I get more information about my father, I'm out of here.

Lydia, Russ, and Payton were stunned silent. Novak had bluntly admitted his attempt to kill Brooke.

Mr. Novak had always been malicious and manipulative, but killing good girls—before he knew they were traitors—was psychotic.

Wanting Ava back Mitch could understand, but Gene? He'd seen Tamara overpower Gene and force him to help Brooke out of the warehouse. What was special about him?

Mitch felt horrible Ava and Brooke had been injected with 88. He'd been careful, but the label must have been wrong.

"I'm missing something here, Mr. Novak. The label was clear on the type of Helix. How were Ava and Brooke the only ones affected? How about Tamara and Justine?"

His lips curled enough to hint at a proud grin. "Let's just say I knew where their loyalties lay. At least I thought I knew about Tamara. I gave them a dose of the remedy in their protein drink before I sent them in the field. They weren't aware of it."

A remedy?

"There's a remedy? And you're just telling us this now?" Lydia never raised her voice at Novak, but she did today. Mitch agreed with her, but he was flabbergasted by her tone.

Lydia shrank in her seat when Novak raised an eyebrow.

"We didn't have one until now. It wasn't ready. I tested it on Justine and Tamara. It worked. So now we do."

He said it matter-of-factly, like it was no big deal. What if they both had died? And he'd experimented on his own daughter.

"Well, at least we know what happened," Mitch said, biting his tongue not to lash out at this psycho.

Novak pivoted slowly toward Mitch, his hard stare questioning his loyalty. "Exactly what did happen in that warehouse, Mitch?"

"It happened all too fast, sir. If it wasn't for the fire—"

"Oh, yes, the fire." Novak gave him a contemptuous glare as he cut him off. "I'm tired of hearing excuses."

Novak had no idea what Mitch knew. Mitch had followed Ava in the warehouse and hidden behind some crates. He lingered to find out what was wrong with her when she'd stumbled like she was drunk. That was when Justine had spilled the details.

Justine wanted Ava to know she had some kind of power over her. She was jealous of Ava, always vying for Novak's attention. When Ava, Tamara, and Brooke had been clear from the fire, Mitch had played his part by taking Justine and Payton back to the glider so they could report the details.

Of course, Justine had fibbed during debriefing to make herself look heroic.

"Do we have access to the remedy? In case of an accident." Mitch tried not to sound too keen and wanted him to focus back to the essential topic.

"Never an accident, Mitch. But I will allow an agent to carry one dosage of HelixB100, as our scientists have called it."

Russ pushed back his shoulders and rubbed the back of his neck. "Our first move is to track down the rebel base. But this may take time. I'll reach out to ISAN West."

Careful with your lies, Russ. Now you have to see it through.

Novak nodded. "Working with Sabrina is a good idea."

Ava said Russ was one of the good guys. Russ and Mitch had

an extensive conversation of what each of them knew about ISAN. Russ didn't know as much as Mitch did, and Mitch was reserved in what he had told him.

The lines on Novak's forehead deepened as he pinned his glare on Mitch. "Seems Mitch has gone on a mission of his own. Tell us why you went to the black market yesterday."

Not a question but a demand. He must have had Mitch followed. But who? He had been careful.

Mitch scooted closer to the edge of his seat and clasped his hands like he had grand news. "I was going to tell you—tell our team at this meeting. I went to the black market to scout for rebels. I figured if the girls fell into a coma like the other B88 females, the rebels would send someone there in hopes of finding an antidote."

Novak regarded him for a moment, then focused on the ground as if considering.

"I planned to go again after this meeting," Mitch added to convince him. "They'll be desperate, and they're bound to show up at a black market because that's the first place illicit or secret tech shows up. If the girls are still alive."

Please let those girls be okay. They don't deserve this.

Novak met his eyes. "Take Russ and Payton's team with you. The three new girls I added to their unit are ready. I'll send guards, too. Bring Ava back with you unharmed at all costs. I doubt Gene will be with them. We'll have to find another way to get him back. But I'm not particularly worried about him. The rebels won't kill him and Gene has my instructions. He knows what to do when the time is right."

Mitch stiffened. Not what he wanted to hear.

"But we've only had a few practices together." Payton's eyes widened in concern. "My squad isn't ready."

Who wasn't ready? Him or the girls? No matter—wrong answer.

Novak clenched his jaw. "Do I need to spoon-feed you leadership skills? You have time this morning. Get them ready."

If Ava were here, she would have said, "We have time this morning for an extra round of practice. I'll get them ready."

Some were just born to be leaders.

Novak strode out the door, shaking his head.

A remedy. Mitch had to get his hands on it before he left and pray Rhett was at the black market at the same time. Novak's confidence hinted there was more to Gene than his innocent face.

CHAPTER SEVEN – BLACK MARKET

AVA

The tunnel led to a building above the ground, giving the inside a night-feel and another meaning to the term, *black market*. All parts of the missing walls and where the windows had once been were boarded up.

A new world of blinking radiant decorations, electric candles, and hovering orb lights emerged. With all the illuminating objects, the black market was like the expanse of the universe. I felt as though I floated within the infinity of the stars. These glowing gadgets made the market seem more mystical than dangerous.

"This is amazing." Tamara peered up to the second, third, fourth, and beyond the fifth level.

"How are we ever going to find the goods?" Ozzie's voice dropped, sounding defeated.

Reyna smacked Ozzie's back. "We ask around, dodo brain. What else?"

Ozzie's lips tilted down at the corner. "Don't call me that."

Reyna ruffled his hair. "Sensitive beast."

"Don't call me that either."

Teddy bear. Ozzie was a big, fuzzy bear with a soft heart.

Rhett tapped his chip and then clapped once. "Okay then. Time to split up. See you at the glider. Let me know if you find yours first. Stay out of trouble."

"Will do, Captain." Cleo pressed two fingers on her eyebrow in a salute, her blue eyes glimmering in the winking lights above her.

With our hoods down, our heads inclined, we went our separate ways.

Our team pivoted left. We joined the line and waited about ten minutes for our turn to enter.

Six men dressed in black uniforms with Tasers flanked an arching body scanner just tall and wide enough for a person to pass through.

Piece of cake, right? Then why was I nervous?

My palms were sweaty, pulse racing. Hot. Too hot. Unbearable heat.

When I scratched an itch on my head, Rhett gently guided my hand down. He said not to give them any cause for suspicion. I wanted to take off my cloak, or at least lower the hood. The guards made me uneasy.

They're not ISAN, I repeated to myself.

Tamara entered first, then Rhett. They waited for me on the other side, the scanner dividing us.

"Next," one of the guards said.

The guard watched me stop at the scanner. I dared not look at him, afraid I might roll my eyes or give him a death glare.

"Name?"

"Julie Lee." I calmed my voice.

"Scan your chip."

When I ran my forearm over a metal square, a hologram of me appeared next to him. He examined me, and then the hologram. Staring and scrutinizing between us.

Come on. You can see the hologram looks exactly like me unless you're an idiot.

One second passed, two, three, four. Finally, after what seemed an eternity, a small panel on the scanner tinted green and beeped.

I released a breath and sprinted to my team without looking back.

Relax. You've got this. You're not going to be thrown back to ISAN.

I eased my muscles and marveled at the atmosphere and the aesthetic.

Green, blue, red, and violet lights on strings sparkled around the front of each shop in an invitation to draw the customer closer. Each tentative store had been created by tents or metal panels.

We passed by fashion districts, high-tech gadgets, fine jewelry, and household goods. I stared open-mouthed at the robotic prostitutes and the booths selling fake chips and drugs.

Too many holograms appeared in my mental map. Sounds and colors fused together until sensory overload caused the building to spin. I shut down Helix, tucked it in at the border of my mind so I could access it easily.

We climbed the stairs to the next floor. From my vantage point, I got a clear view of the night circus. People came here not only to purchase illegal goods but also to entertain themselves.

Various hybrid animals paced in cages. Acrobats walked on tightropes. A man swallowed fire. Women danced on hovering skates, waving ribbons to the music. Gasps and applause boomed through the air.

When we reached the next floor, I smelled spices I hadn't since Mother's kitchen. Rosemary from baked chicken. Cumin on pork. Thyme sprinkled on beef. Fresh bread, chocolate, and sweets churned my stomach and distracted me. My mouth watered. I wanted to taste everything.

"You smell that?" Tamara took a long sniff and licked her lips. "Did we have to go this way?"

I moaned in agreement. This floor was an international food court, with all kinds of cuisine from India, Italy, Korea, Mexico, Japan, and so much more. We had eaten before we left, but our meal had not been flavored and certainly hadn't smelled this good.

Rhett stopped at a Chinese booth. I salivated over shrimp dumplings, eggplant with beans, beef noodle soup, pork and leek dumplings, and mapo tofu. To the left, behind a clear plastic divider, hung cooked whole ducks and chickens.

An old man waved at us, his hair white as the cooked rice inside his bowl. "Great food for cheap price. Try it."

I placed a hand on Rhett's back and leaned closer. "What are we doing here? It smells so good. You're driving me insane."

"I know what I'm doing." Rhett kissed my cheek and tapped my nose. Then he turned to the old man. "Give me one order of xiaolongbao."

The man scowled and fanned a long wooden spoon. "There are three of you. There are only two pieces in one order. You each must order one."

Bad customer service.

The old man's face reddened as if he were standing over a pot of boiling water. With his little kitchen area behind him, he didn't have much space to move about. And his supplies, pots and dishes, were piled high.

Rhett leaned closer to the man. "Fine. We'll go somewhere else."

"What?" The wrinkle on the old man's forehead deepened.

"My food is the best around here. You can't find its equal even in the big city." The man wiped sweat off his forehead with a yellow towel and slapped it over his shoulder.

"Settle down, Mr. Lee. It's me." Rhett pushed the hood back enough to show his face.

Rhett knows who to contact, Cleo had said. *The reason* we stopped at this booth. So much for sampling the food.

"Sniper." Mr. Lee gave a wry grin, reaching out. He clasped Rhett's hand tightly; he looked like he'd have tackled Rhett had the table not been in the way. "I didn't recognize you."

Rhett rubbed his chin. "I shaved."

"Indeed, you did. But my eyes are bad and my hearing not so good." He pointed to his ears.

"You should get your eyes done. Laser would only take ten minutes, or take the vitamins for the eyes."

"Hmmm …" He huffed a breath. "Maybe. But there is something else. Something is different about you." He glanced between Tamara and me.

Rhett draped an arm around me, and that was his reply.

The old man spread his lips wider and nodded in understanding. "Ahhh. So this is the girl you talked about. I'm happy you found her. So, what can I get for you?"

Rhett shifted closer and shared a small hologram of a black rock. Then he swiped an amount displayed on the screen, I assumed the offered compensation. A quick brush of Rhett's thumb over his forearm shut it down.

Wordlessly, Mr. Lee scooped up the dumplings with a slotted ladle and placed them inside a recyclable container. He had given more than Rhett had asked for.

When he passed it to Rhett, he cupped the box with both

hands, bottom and top. Rhett placed a hand on top of the man's hand before taking the box.

"Thank you, Mr. Lee. The transaction is complete." Rhett gave a curt bow and backed away. "That boy ... he's taking more risks these days?"

"I can't control what he does, but I don't mind helping good people like you and Zen."

"I appreciate it. And Zen sends his regards." Rhett pivoted, checking for anything unusual.

"Wait." Mr. Lee chopped off two chicken legs, placed them into a tall paper container, and handed them to me. "For the two beautiful ladies." He smiled, the corner of his eyes crinkling.

Tamara clasped her hands and dipped her head. "*Syeh-syeh.*"

I mimicked her action and words.

"*Bu yong xie.* Be careful." The man inclined his head and attended to the next customer.

I offered Tamara one chicken leg and gave Rhett the first bite of the second.

"What did he say?" I asked.

She chewed on the xiaolongbao Rhett had passed her and swallowed. "He said, you're welcome."

Duh. I guess I should have known.

"Where to next? Why did he give you a coin?" I tore off a chunk of chicken and almost had a food orgasm. He had flavored it the way my mom used to, with some kind of tea bag filled with herbs. The memory tugged at my heart.

Rhett studied my face for long seconds. "How did you know?"

"Fast reflexes." I took another bite. "I catch things human eyes can't."

"Lucky. You'll see. Eat on the way." Rhett stuffed his face with

61

another xiaolongbao and pointed at the words *fifth floor* flashing on the wall screen. "He gave me five fingers for the fifth floor. The people we're looking for move around, even here."

"Let's get going then." Tamara licked her fingers one by one.

We climbed up the dilapidated stairs to the fifth floor. When we passed by a bakery and exotic food I would never eat—things that wiggled and crawled—we rounded the corner.

We halted at the clicking of drawn weapons. Men built like tanks with big guns and Tasers appeared from the shadows.

What now?

Tamara gasped beside me. I assessed the men's gear, how many there were, and charted my map for escape routes. The three of us could take them down, even without weapons. But we had a goal. No showing off here.

Rhett cautiously advanced. He scanned the dimly lit floor and dropped his hood. "Good afternoon, gentlemen. It's been a while."

"Sniper?" a man with tan skin said, shoving the tip of his weapon against Rhett's chest.

The man towered over the others. A crescent-shaped scar stood out over his left eyebrow. His hair fell past his shoulders, some parts braided. Dragon tattoos snaked along both arms.

His men had the same tattoo as well. A cult? Another secret army?

As if Rhett could read my mind, he whispered, "They call themselves the Imugi. Underground faction. I'll explain later. Be nice. We might need them one day."

Fine, but I didn't like the way the man looked at Rhett, like he was about to eat him alive.

I curled my fingers inward, gathering Helix. Tamara flexed and unflexed her fists, clenching her jaw.

Rhett and the man locked eyes without flinching—a stare down. Then the man shoved Rhett lightly, causing him to stumble back. I poised to spring at him when Rhett jumped first.

They clapped each other on the back and laughed.

I hissed through my nose. Tamara did the same.

"A warning next time." I frowned at Rhett.

The man's hand went down, and his team lowered their weapons. "And who are these lovely ladies?"

"Ava and Tamara." Rhett stepped aside. "This is Eben."

Eben kissed Tamara's hand and then mine. The five hoop earrings he had in each ear tinkled like a chime when he bent. "So, this is Ava. I've heard so much about you. I've been dying to meet you."

"I would like to say the same for you, but I have no idea who you are." My irritation hadn't abated, but I faked a smile for a dash of humor.

"I like her." Eben's eyes glistened.

His black eyeliner brought out his hazel pupils under the hovering orb lights. He smiled, showing two golden front teeth.

Were they real gold?

"So, what can I do for you?" His gaze still rested on me, even though his question was for Rhett.

"You can let us in." I shrugged, smiling.

"How about you keep me company while Rhett does his thing?" His eyes wandered the length of my body.

"How about I break your leg?" I offered a coy smile.

Rhett waited silently—he knew better than to step in unless I needed help.

I am not your toy.

"I really like her." Eben gave a nervous laugh, then all

playfulness vanished. "But seriously. Why are you here?"

Rhett sized up at the men on either side of Eben. "I need a rock."

"Do you have an appointment?"

"No, but I have this." Rhett fished Mr. Lee's coin from inside his pocket.

Eben extended his hand reluctantly. "I will honor it. We have been more cautious of who we let in, usually with an appointment, as you have done in the past. But this coin must mean it's urgent. Believe it or not, that old man is highly respected in our community."

"I know. It's too bad he's related to Zeke."

Eben heaved a breath. "I agree with you there." He stepped aside without another word and his men followed suit.

Rhett led us down a corridor alongside a path of floating orb candles. We walked for thirty yards and stopped in front of a black curtain.

"Let me do the talking." Rhett met our eyes to confirm.

At my and Tamara's nods, he pushed aside the curtain.

White mist drifted in the confined space of the canvas tent. Fake candles scattered about the room gave it a romantic feel.

I fanned the fog with my hand and saw a young Asian man in the center, smoking a pipe. Five women dressed in scanty outfits caressed different parts of his body. When we stepped forward, the ladies scurried away behind another dark curtain in the back.

"People have no manners. At least knock or announce yourself before entering." The man pushed up off the seat but fell back down.

"Then get a door, Zeke," Rhett said.

"It stinks in here." Tamara pressed her finger under her nose.

Zeke rose with his hands on his head and then rested one hand on top of a jade Buddha statue. The room must be spinning for him. When he steadied himself, he adjusted his pants, but didn't bother to button his long-sleeved shirt.

Thick silver chains garlanded his neck. A spear shape made from jade hung from one chain. From another, an onyx cross. His eyes traveled from Tamara, to me, and then stopped.

"Rhett. It's been a while. But what lovely company you keep." He shook Rhett's hand, his voice low and thick. Tattooed dragon scales peeked out from under his sleeve, similar to Eben's.

He sounded nice enough. My reservations about meeting him eased.

"I do, but I'm not here to talk about who I travel with. I don't have much time." Rhett's tone was all business.

Zeke lowered himself onto a mattress and ruffled his dark, curly hair. He picked up a clear flask containing bubbling green liquid and took a gulp. He moaned in pleasure as he trembled, and then a lazy smile spread.

"Would you or the ladies like to try this? It's something new. Not for sale yet." He wiped his mouth with the back of his hand.

Rhett cringed. "No, thank you."

Zeke took another drink. "Eben let you in, right? I'm assuming my uncle gave you a free pass, then. Sit. Please. What can I help you with?"

Rhett sat cross-legged on a red, square cushion and we did the same. A dark, low wooden table with a lacquered Asian dragon on top was in front of us.

"Your uncle is a good man," Rhett started.

Zeke puffed from his pipe and blew the smoke upward. "More of a nuisance sometimes, but he's the only family I have. And maybe the only person on this planet who truly cares about me. He never asks me for anything. Not even money."

Probably because it's blood money.

"So ..." He flickered an eyebrow at Tamara and me. "You came here. Must be something important."

"I need a rock—just a small piece."

Zeke considered Rhett for a moment and lowered his voice. "How small? These rocks are expensive."

A muscle twitched on Rhett's face. "Hand size. I'm aware how much they cost. We've done business before. You know we are good on our end. I can do a direct transfer with a click of a button like the last time."

"True. You haven't deceived me yet. Can't trust people these days, can you?" He snorted and his eyes glowed at Tamara, then to me.

His stare made me feel small and naked. I didn't like it one bit, so I stared right back in a silent challenge.

Zeke shifted his attention. "Tell me, Rhett. What happened to the other lovely companion of yours? Got tired of her? What was her name? Oh, yes. Cleo. I'll tell you what. I'll give you double the size if you include these two beauties in the bargain."

Rhett sat taller as Tamara cursed. I almost punched him in the nose, and would've if Rhett hadn't placed his hand on my thigh. For once, I tamed my temper. I tried to relax and let him handle it.

"They're not for sale. I'm attached to them both."

Apparently Zeke didn't know who Rhett was. And he had no idea two deadly assassins with superhuman abilities were in proximity.

"You have to give me credit for trying." Zeke clapped loud

enough to startle me, like he was signaling a maid.

Sure enough, a few long seconds later, a young woman with a tray came in and knelt beside him. On the tray lay a black rock on top of an onyx velvet cloth.

It looked like any other rock except it had many tiny holes with some jagged edges. I shivered. Tamara rubbed her arms beside me. She felt its energy, too.

"The rock," Zeke announced as if it was the most priceless thing. "Just making sure this is what you want. Does the size suffice—or should I get a bigger one?"

A muscle quivered along Rhett's jaw, his eyes stone cold on Zeke. "Is this real?"

Zeke scrunched his lips, offended. "Is this real? Of course this is real. Selling fakes would put me on a hit list even the Imugi couldn't fight. I value my life more than you think I do."

"Fine. The size is fine," Rhett said. "Let's close the transaction and get this over with. Or I can find another dealer who's willing to give us a better deal. The only reason we're here again is because Zen trusts you. If you jeopardize that trust, he will see to it you'll never get a customer again."

Zeke straightened and blinked. His tone changed from challenging to a more cooperative one. "No need to get offensive, Rhett. Let's do this quickly so you can be on your way."

"I couldn't agree with you more." Rhett pulled up the bank account from his chip, and then the hologram of whatever he was looking at disappeared. "Now, hand it to Ava and I'll send at the same time."

"You don't trust me, Rhett?" Zeke carefully shoved the rock inside the large pouch and tossed it to me.

When the item landed on my hand, Rhett said, "Done. You're

welcome to check before I leave. And no, I don't trust anyone. An old habit."

"Well, the feeling is mutual. Besides, I'm sure I'll see you soon." He leaned back and crossed his arms. "Be careful out there. You never know who you'll run into. Give my love to Cleo and that brother of yours. He was here the other day. I think he was looking for you."

"Half. Half-brother," Rhett stressed. "If you see him, don't breathe a word of why I was here or you'll see me a lot sooner." He stood, his lips tight. "And one more thing. Be good to your uncle. Having the same blood doesn't guarantee you'll be taken care of. He took you in when you had no one else. And remember, don't tell anyone we were here."

"Relax, Rhett. Never without your permission," Zeke said, his cool, easy tone dripping like honey. He stood and inclined his head slightly. "It's always a pleasure doing business with you."

"I wish I could say the same," Rhett mumbled under his breath. He met my stormy gaze and tilted his head to the curtain.

"Ladies, I'm here if you change your minds." Zeke winked.

I gave Zeke an I-don't-think-so expression and strutted out.

"We're not property," Tamara hissed behind me.

CHAPTER EIGHT – LIKE OLD TIMES

AVA

The rock was lighter than it looked. I slipped the pouch inside my cape pocket and shadowed Rhett, Tamara behind me. Rhett informed Reyna we had the goods and were on our way out.

Reyna's team had purchased the items and would meet us at the exit. They would arrive there about the same time.

So far, not a hitch.

People were busy buying and selling, engulfed in their daily lives. They all wore different colored cloaks, mostly hooded. Nobody wanted to be seen.

When we neared a booth, I heard a voice stopping me in mid-stride. My skin crawled and I instinctively wanted to hide. I knew that voice. That deep, throaty sound. The reek of alcohol had always accompanied it.

My foster father was yelling at someone.

Stupid me had to steal a glimpse. A huge mistake.

I should have moved on, but I had to see his face. Just a peek.

Maybe I wanted him to see me, to see me healthy and strong. Or perhaps I wanted him to say something, so I'd have an excuse to give him what he deserved. Or the voice might not belong to my foster father. It had been a while and I could be wrong.

I peeked over my shoulder anyway. Identity confirmed. Dark, shaggy curls. Yellow-stained teeth, some missing, and a scar on the right side of his mouth as if someone had sliced his lip.

He was watching me. Our eyes locked for far too long.

Walk away. Don't cause attention. But I wanted him to see me so I could punish him for all his wrongdoing.

I bared my teeth and flipped a finger. His eyes widened with recognition and then narrowed in a death glare.

"You little bitch." He shoved a kid next to him and lunged at me.

I bolted.

Rhett and Tamara knew better than to call my name. I wouldn't respond. So they ran after me.

"What's wrong? Slow down." Rhett's voice disappeared to the roar in my ears.

No more. I was not that scared little girl. Recalling the horrible things he had said and done to me had rendered me almost immobile.

You're stronger than this. Stronger than that weasel of a man. Get him back for all the misery, not just for yourself, but for the other kids.

I had never told anyone there were a bunch of us, all abused and degraded, except for my foster father's two biological children. They had privileges and favor and were as malicious as he was.

"Get her. Stop her," my childhood nightmare shouted.

Glass shattered behind me. More thumps and clanking.

"Come back here and pay for this," a woman bellowed.

"I'm reporting this to the guards."

Screams and shouts continued.

I managed to avoid breaking anything as I raced to stay ahead of him, but just enough to keep him on my trail. The map I had pulled up with Helix showed me a dead end ahead.

Good. I'd corner him there.

Someone grabbed me in a chokehold as I slowed to make my stand. A knife pressed to my neck.

"Stay back or I'll cut her." The husky feminine voice was also familiar.

I could have fought her off easily, but I waited to assess the situation. Helix showed me she was alone, but there could be someone farther away with a gun pointed at me. I worried for my friends as well, and I had to consider the citizens.

I panted out of breath, adrenaline still pumping. My eyes skirted toward Rhett and around him, looking for my foster father. When she pressed the knife tighter, my stomach flipped, hand shaking, unsure if I could remove the knife from my throat. One wrong move, I could die.

"Wait. We've got no beef with you. Just let her go." Rhett raised his sleeve and then pressed something on his chip.

A slick move to alert our other troop.

Then he raised both of his hands, one folded into a fist—signaling Tamara to stay behind.

It didn't matter what he asked Tamara to do. We were surrounded by my foster father and four men pointing Tasers at us.

How in the world had he gotten weapons inside? Well, it was a black market after all. Half the people here were skilled criminals.

The shopkeepers turned their heads, minding their own business.

"You," he snarled at Rhett. "We meet again."

"You son of a b—"

A Taser pressed against Rhett's head, and then Tamara walked out of a shadow with a weapon pointed at her back.

"I wouldn't finish that sentence if I were you. Have a little respect for my father."

The hair on my arm rose. It had been years since I had seen him. A bit taller and bulkier, but he was undoubtedly Cory, my foster father's oldest son. He had the same curly hair and cruel eyes as his father.

"How have you been, *Ava*?" My foster father's eyes beamed at the promise of torture, his teeth still stained the color of piss. "I didn't recognize you at first. I thought you were just a decent piece of ass. But I thought, what girl would be bold enough to flip me off? And of course I thought of you." He moved closer. "I've thought of you plenty. I searched for you, but you were like a ghost. I ran into Rhett and his friends not too long ago. We had some unfinished business, but thanks to you, I have a second chance."

"You're Ava's foster father?" Rhett's nostrils flared. "If I'd known, I would have killed you then."

"So sentimental, lover boy. Too bad you didn't. Showing mercy doesn't get you anywhere. You can call me Vito. And it seems Ava has spoken a great deal about me. She must have missed me as much as I missed her. My, my, Ava. You have blossomed into a beautiful woman." He ran a hand down my hair.

"Don't touch me," I said, recoiling.

I'd never known his name. I had to call him Father, and so did everyone else.

I cringed away from him, and when he laughed, I spat on him. Liquid dripped down from his cheek. A low rumble escaped his mouth and he didn't bother to wipe it.

"You're an animal," I hissed, fury rising in me. "You're nothing but a rat who preys on children."

My head whipped to the side as his palm connected with my cheek. Warm blood trickled from my lip.

72

Rhett growled.

"Have a little respect for your elder, sweetheart," Vito sneered, his alcoholic breath stunk, brushing against my face.

"Don't touch her." Rhett could do nothing but watch, his eyes wide and furious.

Tamara scanned about as if gauging her chances.

No, not yet, Tamara. Don't make a move. I would have never thought to worry about Tamara, but I didn't know what her true self was capable of.

"Ava, do something or I will," Rhett said.

I had ferreted a plan, but I couldn't share it with him. If I didn't act soon, Rhett would, so I winked at him letting him know I had it under control.

"You keep great company," Vito said. "Now I can bring the three of you in for a hefty award. For the bounty on you alone, Ava, I could retire."

I licked the blood from the cut on my lip. "Then what are you waiting for? And before you act, Mr. Novak—I'm assuming he's the one who arranged this bounty hunting stuff—will have you killed if I come back damaged. You see, he has a thing for me, just like you. You're both sickos."

Vito swore. "Let's go," he said to his men.

Rhett looked at me, silently asking why I was taking so long. Tamara looked worried as the men guided us between the shops. I wanted to get to a more crowded area and use our surroundings to create mayhem.

The person holding me at knifepoint lagged and we ended up being last.

A soft, earnest voice brushed the tips of my ears. "Ava. I didn't know it was you. It's so good to see you. It's me, Naomi. I'll help

73

you escape. Tell me what to do."

"Naomi." My heart skipped a beat in elation. I wanted to squeeze her in my arms.

It had been so long since I'd seen her. Naomi and her older sister, Natalie, had always been nice to me. When I'd run, the sisters had decided to stay, too scared of Vito.

"Where's Natalie?"

When she didn't answer, I figured something terrible had happened.

"I wish we had run away with you."

"You can still. Come with me when we leave here."

We banked around a booth of bootleg home appliances. Rhett glanced my way, earning him a thump on the head with the Taser.

"Hey." I tapped the guy's shoulder. "Nobody hits my boyfriend."

"What the he—"

My fist interrupted him.

"It's about time," Rhett said. Then he head-butted the guy next to him, confiscated his Taser, and Tased him.

Tamara whirled on the guy holding her prisoner, twisted his wrist, and flipped him over into a table selling utensils. The owner bellowed and threw himself aside to dodge the onslaught of spoons, forks, and knives.

Tamara picked up a pair of weapons. *Perfect.* I did the same. Then she hurled them one by one to disarm the thugs who were making a break for it. The knives hit their marks with precision. Vito's goons thudded to the ground, flat on their faces. People screamed and raced to get away.

Atta girl. No Helix needed. Away from ISAN, her power emerged on its own.

When Vito tried to bail, I grabbed his cloak and spun him around. After a sharp jab to his nose, I smashed my heel sideways into his shin and brought him down to his knees. Then I gripped his hair, yanked his head forward, and pinned a small kitchen knife under his chin.

Vito scowled. "I should have turned you over when I first took you home. Who knew a scrawny kid would be such a prize? Now be a good girl and let me go."

I seethed. "Naomi. What shall I do with him?"

Naomi came to my side, trembling. She had grown taller, cropped her hair short, and had lost some weight. Her face was pale, as if she rarely saw sunlight.

"I don't know where to start. He's done so many horrible things." Anger and fear were in her voice. "He has more kids locked up. He's going to sell them to someone."

Memories poured into my mind. Wrath burned through my blood. All his cruelness, and all his ugly words, and all the lashes under his belt. No more.

I could end him. Kill him now. It would give me pleasure to see him bleed to death. I had dreamed about it many times. The decision was in my hands.

I pierced the tip deeper into his flesh and nicked him.

"*Ava*. Don't do anything you'll regret." Rhett became the voice of reason, made me hesitate.

I didn't release the weapon even after blood dripped down Vito's neck. But I was no murderer, no matter how badly I wanted to kill him.

Naomi could lead the way to Vito's home and release the kids.

I didn't care we were on the fifth floor of the black market. I didn't care if people watched us. I didn't care we were out of time.

I would end this right here. Shut him down for good, the right way.

Ozzie, Reyna, and Cleo found us but kept their distance. Ozzie chewed something, probably food from a stall. Reyna and Cleo watched the crowd, their posture tense.

Vito spat on the ground. "You're a rat, Ava, and you'll always be one. Nobody cares for you. You're not important to anyone. Your father threw you away. Your mother died because of you. You have nothing. You *are* nothing."

Vito had some balls to talk with such detestation when I clearly had the upper hand. In the past, he'd always known his words held power over me, but not this time.

I laughed, not because his words were funny, but because I wished I had been wiser in my younger years. Enough to realize his words carried no weight to anyone except scared children. He made me feel small so he could feel big.

He was no man, but a rodent himself.

Vito was a nobody who made dirty money by selling children.

He had been the monster under my bed, in my closet, and in my mind. Vito had impaled me with cruel words and those dagger-sharp, hateful eyes. All I'd wanted was basic kindness and to have a sense of a home, and he'd given none of that.

But no more. I was older, wiser, and I knew so much better.

I squared my shoulders. "I'm not a rat. And you made a grave mistake by coming after me. I'm bringing you down, and you can rot in hell. I don't care what happens to you when I turn you in. Nighty-night, *Father*."

"Wait. I can give you—"

"I don't give a damn."

I gestured to Naomi, who had positioned herself in front of

him.

"This is for my sister and for all the kids you tortured, asshole." Naomi's fury was palpable as she socked him in the face. Twice. Then Tased him longer than needed.

Vito writhed spasmodically and collapsed. If we'd had time, I would have tortured him. Being Tased was too quick and easy. He deserved much more misery and pain.

Reyna came closer and grimaced. "Oh, God. Not him again."

"You've got to be kidding me. Him again?" Ozzie shook his head in repulsion.

"Naomi, you all right?" My fingers cuffed around her wrist to get her attention.

Her eyes were trained so hard on Vito I thought she would never look away. I understood the hate she had for this man for all the terrible things he had done to her and everyone she cared about.

She wrapped her arms around me so fast, I almost lost my balance.

"It's so good to see you, Ava." Her voice was soft but jubilant, a complete turnaround from moments ago.

"Likewise." I pulled back to see her teary face, and my own tears threatened to escape.

"We need to help the other kids."

"I can send someone. You should come with me. Would you like to?" I looked to Rhett for confirmation.

We'd never talked about bringing anyone to our base with us, so I didn't know how to go about the procedure with Zen. If there was one.

When Rhett didn't answer, Naomi lowered her voice so only we could hear. "I know about ISAN and I myself have an ability."

Ability? Now was not the time to ask. We needed to get out.

"Rhett?" I drawled.

"Fine. But we have to go now. The guards are on their way." Rhett shoved a Taser he'd taken off one of Vito's men into his waistband.

"What do I do with him?" I nudged Vito with my boot.

"Leave him. He's not worth your time or even a second of thought." Rhett guided me away from Vito. "I'll take care of him. I'll inform Zen of his child trafficking operation. Vito will be out of business and behind bars."

"Guys?" Ozzie called urgently, looking down toward the crumbling second story. "Hurry. ISAN is here."

CHAPTER NINE – OLD FRIENDS

AVA

Ozzie's words impaled me. My muscles tightened as I held onto Rhett's shoulder for a brief moment to collect myself. It would be the first time I had to face Justine and Payton after I had escaped. I didn't want to hurt them.

Why? How?

Stupid questions.

You know why, Ava. They guessed we needed a remedy and this was the place to get it.

I spotted Justine climbing to the second level on the other side of the market. Mitch, Payton, and few new girls sprinted behind Russ.

"Do you see them?" I gestured at them.

"I sure do," Reyna snarled.

"Mitch." Ozzie swore.

"No." Rhett pulled out his Taser. "Mitch comes here when he needs to tell me something since we can't meet at his apartment anymore. The black market is our second rendezvous point. Zeke said Mitch was here yesterday. I need you to distract their squad and get to the glider while I meet up with him."

"No." Cleo wrenched Rhett's shirt as he turned to leave.

Rhett gently peeled Cleo's hand off him. "I'll be fine. Worry about yourself first."

She cared about him still. I didn't blame her. Cleo blinked when she caught me looking at her. I stepped over to Rhett. I didn't need to make this more uncomfortable than it already was.

"We've done this plenty of times." Rhett kissed my forehead. "I'll be fine. We've got Mitch and Russ on our side now, remember? Go. Stay safe. Meet me back at the glider."

"Okay. Be careful." I watched him pivot past the table with mechanical toys.

"I know this place well." Naomi's eyes glinted. "I can show you the faster way out."

"First, I need Justine to see me." Getting her attention was a tactical gambit.

I crept toward the uneven edge as the shopkeepers returned items that had dropped or broken. Justine and her group had split up, moving swiftly down an aisle of booths. I could no longer see Mitch or Russ.

I gave a wolf whistle. "Hey, Justine!"

Though many heads turned toward me and I'd grabbed the interest of the market guards, only one mattered. Justine pointed at me from the ledge facing us.

Just then, Payton pointed a gun-like gadget at me. A thin rope uncoiled from the barrel and slung a brace around a metal beam.

Payton secured his end, soared across, and landed where we had stood seconds before. His unit followed, red beams streaking the air, and pellets raining from their Tasers.

Justine wasn't the captain, despite her boasts.

"Hurry." Naomi looked at us over her shoulder. "I'm taking you to a private exit, but the market guards know the layout."

And so did I. I willed my Helix, but there were too many people and too many doors. I had no idea which exit she had in mind, so I let Naomi be the frontrunner.

Payton's team slowed to avoid the market guards.

Citizens screamed. People slammed into each other. Some got hit by ISAN Tasers and collapsed. ISAN assassins were forbidden to shoot civilians. They must be desperate to catch me. Or they simply sucked.

Payton's team and the market guards gave chase while Naomi steered us to an exit marked for vendors only.

Naomi tilted her head. "Hurry. This way."

"Wait." I gripped her arm. "Why are we going up instead of down?"

For a second, I doubted her. Had I made a hasty decision inviting her with us? No, I had been her captive at first, but after she'd found out who I was, she'd offered to help me escape.

"Ava, trust me. I want to get out of here as much as you do."

At my nod, she proceeded. As footsteps pounded behind us, we ascended.

On the twentieth floor, we exited through a door to the roof, panting. The chilly breeze did nothing to cool the adrenaline pumping through my veins.

A quarter of the roof had been demolished, slanting to a twenty-story fall. Steel and concrete—the foundation of the building—showed through each level below.

My stomach dropped. I dragged my feet backward. The view of the city's destruction was worse up here than on the ground. Half of the building surfaces were missing. As if a giant sword had slashed off the faces and limbs of the edifices.

"What do we do next? They'll be here any minute." Cleo aimed a Taser at the door.

On my mental map, I detected five people coming up the

stairs. "No guards. Payton's team must have taken care of them."

"This will slow them down." White light illuminated from Naomi's hands. Then the light glowed red. She gripped the handle until it warped. "I give off heat." She looked down at her palms and then smiled at me. "And I can burn things."

I gaped at her wordlessly. So this was her ability.

"Wow," Reyna breathed.

Ozzie gawked. "Cool."

"Let's ogle later. They're on the eighteenth floor." Tamara patted the daggers, two strapped into scabbards on her waist and two shoved behind her waistband.

She had stealthily taken more weapons from the booth when we'd fled.

Reyna's eyelashes batted. "Girl, you're dangerous. Four knives?"

Tamara's eyes shimmered. "I'm good with knives. I never miss."

"How does she know they're almost here?" Naomi asked.

"If you know about ISAN," Tamara said, "then you know we all have heightened senses, but some of us have distinctive powers like you. I can sense things through vibration and people's energy. I'm somewhat clairvoyant." Tamara spoke without an ounce of shyness or hesitation. The old Tamara would've been reluctant to share.

"Cool." Naomi looked pensive and then pointed over her shoulder. "This way." She led us to the other side of the door.

A long cable attached to a thick metal hook extended to the adjacent roof, about fifty yards away. Heavy clobbering began on the door, a flurry of blows, followed by a deep boom. Only one person could make such a noise, and only one person was strong

82

enough to break the door down.

"Hurry. Naomi, go first." I patted her back harder than necessary to get her going. "Then Cleo and Tamara, you're next. Ozzie and Reyna, I need you to cover me once you cross. I'm last."

Naomi sat on the edge of the roof, her feet dangling. "Use your sleeve or you'll burn your hands. Unless you have a device like mine." She pushed a button from her belt and a metal hook popped out. She clipped the hook on the cable and soared to the other side.

Luckily, we had similar gadgets in our gear. Our belts, though not as well-stocked as ISAN's, were good enough.

Cleo landed, and Tamara was midway across when the door exploded open and tumbled off the roof.

"Ava." Justine's voice was filled with rage.

"Miss me, Justine? I'm right here." My taunt drew another growl from her.

"Ava is mine!"

The clicks of drawn weapons and more footsteps pattered like raindrops. The ISAN faction filed through the doorway and scuttled behind the stairwell structure for cover.

"Go," I said to Reyna.

I shot one of the newbies with my Taser just as she aimed her weapon at Reyna. Ozzie shot the other one.

The newbies dropped and convulsed. Two down, three to go.

"Oz, go," I ordered, but I heard a swish in the air, one after the other. Not the sound of Taser pellets, but something far more dangerous. A rain of bullets.

We jumped apart to dodge them.

Thanks to Helix, I heard Payton command Justine to put her gun down because Novak wanted me alive.

"Ava. Get Oz."

Reyna's panicked voice sliced through me like a razor blade. I whirled to find Ozzie hanging by one hand off the roof. His fingers were slipping. My pulse lurched, and I acted without another thought.

"Oz. Hold on." I grabbed his arm and hauled him up halfway.

I pushed a button on his belt and flung the hook around the rope, a few yards from us and set him free. Ozzie's eyes were thankful, and then full of concern as he soared backward.

Knowing Novak wanted me alive gave me an advantage. It also meant he knew I wouldn't die from HelixB88 and had only meant to kill Brooke. Sadistic psycho.

All right, Justine. I can play, too.

"Justine, you should teach your soldiers some manners. Don't they know not to shoot unless you give the order?" I clucked my tongue. "Oh, wait. You're not the lead. You were so sure of yourself. What happened? Did your daddy deem you incompetent and unfit, like the rest of us did?"

"Shut up. Shut up." Justine materialized out of the shadows and fired a Taser, unwisely abandoning her shield.

With exact aim, I countered each pellet coming toward me with one of my own. They collided like mini fireworks. Finally, she stopped.

"How can you do that without Helix?" she snarled. "And how are you alive? What about Brooke? I hope she's dead."

It took every fiber of my willpower not to attack, but I had the rock and time was running out.

Don't take the bait, Ava. Keep it together. Think of Brooke.

"She's not dead. So you can give your *daddy* my regards."

"Payton, do something," Justine screamed. "Don't just stand

84

there."

Payton, who seemed to have frozen when he saw me, at last held up his Taser in a trembling hand. "You're surrounded, Ava. Your team is on another roof. You have no help." Payton inched closer, his two-member troop left beside him. "ISAN guards are waiting for you below. They have your glider surrounded and the kids."

His words sounded rehearsed, or maybe it was nerves.

Had he said, *kids?*

He might be playing me, but how would he know about Momo and her friends? Hopefully Rhett would …

No, no time. I had to solve the situation now.

"Fine." I looked over my shoulder at my crew and then back to Payton. "I'll surrender peacefully if you let my friends go."

"No, Ava," Naomi bellowed.

I ignored her. She was new to our band and didn't understand I would never yield unless my teams' lives were at stake. And they were not.

"Put your Taser down, Ava." Justine could have fried an egg on her bright red face.

From her toothy grimace, she didn't know whether to gloat or sulk. Perhaps both.

I dropped my Taser and stood there with my arms crossed. "Come and get me."

"That's Ava? *The* Ava?" The pretty-faced newbie's voice cracked with fear as she approached.

The three assassins came in a straight line.

Justine glared at the newbie. "Shut up, Tessa. She's not unbeatable. She's not God."

"Wait." I raised a hand.

"Why?" Payton's fist went up and halted his unit.

I yawned and stretched my arms to the cloudy sky. "For this. You never knew about Tamara's hobby, did ya? She never misses."

I had given Tamara instructions in case of such an incident. Never hurts to over-plan.

Two daggers tore through the air from the other roof. One speared the newbie's biceps with a fountain of blood, and the second skewered Payton's hand, knocking his Taser over the edge. Both clutched their bleeding wounds while Justine's eyes widened.

"Don't piss me off again or I'll ask them to target you next time. And this is for Brooke."

Willing the strength of Helix, I sprinted to Justine and landed a solid punch in her face. Bone cracked like a beautiful song, and then she smashed into the stairway wall, leaving an imprint in the cracked cement before she flopped down.

I flew across the rope, my squad cheering blissfully in my ears. But my satisfaction died when I spotted the few dozen ISAN guards Payton had mentioned below.

It seemed Novak didn't trust Payton's unit to bring me in. And Payton's words had been no bluff. Or maybe he'd been warning me.

Payton, whose side are you on?

CHAPTER TEN – MEETING MITCH

RHETT

After Rhett kissed Ava's forehead, he rushed off in the opposite direction. He didn't know if Mitch had seen him, but when he split up with his team, he ran to their covert meeting point.

On his way, he hefted Vito over his shoulder and dropped him off at Zeke's tent. Rhett told him to hold the scum prisoner until Zen sent further instructions. He also purchased a few new gadgets, promising him they would return to buy more if he gave him a good deal. Rhett hoped that would help entice him to keep his mouth shut if ISAN came asking questions.

On his way to meet Mitch, he voice-messaged Zen to give him the rundown. "We got the goods. We're bringing a plus-one. Ava ran into her foster father, who is a bounty hunter, and we need to save the kids he's captured before they are sold to ISAN."

Rhett went down to the first floor. At the far end away from the shops, a staircase led down to a small basement. With the stolen Taser by his side, he crept down the dimly lit hallway.

Two sets of footsteps echoed behind Rhett. Then a creak. Heart pounding, he slid halfway into the room and aimed his Taser. Mitch always came alone. Had the guards followed him? Rhett had been sure he had ditched them.

"Rhett?" A soft whisper.

Sounded like Mitch.

"Rhett. It's Mitch." Footsteps approached.

"Here. I'm coming out. Who's with you?"

"Russ. He helped Ava. Ava can confirm. You can trust him."

Rhett sized up Russ without showing himself. Young. Light brown hair. Green eyes. A bit shorter than him.

Ava had told Rhett about Russ, how he had helped her. Rhett had wondered if he had a thing for his girl, then he erased that thought and felt grateful he had intervened. And Mitch wouldn't lie to him.

The two wore black ISAN suits and gear. They reminded Rhett of ninjas. The fabric, cool to the touch, melded to the body as if it were a second skin.

Rhett stepped out of the shadows and offered his hand. "Russ. We met once when you first came to ISAN. Do you remember?"

Russ released his hand after he shook it. "Yes, but shortly after I was sent to ISAN East."

"Yup. So." Rhett faced Mitch. "How are things? And you need to talk fast."

Mitch frowned. "What? No sarcastic remark?"

Rhett hiked up an eyebrow. "Would you like one? You wanted this meeting."

"True. But I don't like going through Zeke. He's so full of himself."

Rhett arched his eyebrow again. "And you're not?"

Mitch scoffed in amusement. "Anyway, since you're not trying to kill me, I'm assuming Ava is fine. I want to tell you I didn't give the girls HelixB88. Russ can confirm this. He was there when Novak confessed he did it."

Rhett kept his lips tight, glancing between Russ and Mitch. "Yeah, Ava is fine."

"What about Tamara and Brooke?" The hesitation in Russ's

voice suggested he cared for them.

"Tamara is fine. No trace of 88 in her blood test. But Brooke ..." Rhett paused and stared at Russ, debating how much information to share. Not because he didn't trust them, but he could safely guess Novak thought she was dead, or as good as. Perhaps that would be an advantage for them, but he wasn't sure how. Before he could finish, Russ continued.

"Listen, Rhett. I know you don't know me, but you need to trust me. Novak told us he gave the girls 88 knowing Ava would survive and not Brooke. He also has a remedy. He gave it to Tamara without her knowledge."

It took Rhett a few seconds to register his words, and then another few seconds to speak. Then he wanted to punch the wall again and again.

"Remedy? A remedy. Where is it?" Rhett's voice was low and full of rage. He knew the answer neither gave him. "Let me guess. Novak is the only one with access to it, and you can't get it."

Russ and Mitch exchanging glances was his answer. It didn't matter. They got the rock and the essentials needed.

"Is that all you needed to tell me, Mitch? I have to get going." Rhett tapped his foot, anxious to get back to his squad.

A muscle in Mitch's face twitched. "Novak is ... he's plotting something. I don't know what it is yet. Novak said, 'Gene has my instructions. He knows what to do when the time is right.'"

Rhett cracked his knuckles, releasing tension. "He's always scheming. I know you didn't give the girls 88, so don't worry. Next time, use our meeting time wisely. Give me something worthwhile. I can't believe I'm going to say this, but you are risking your life, so don't be reckless."

A hint of relief showed on Mitch's face. He cleared his throat.

"Novak will do anything to get Ava back. He wants Gene back, too. I think Gene is special. I don't know what Ava knows, but some males with special abilities are showing up. Gene might be dangerous, but he also might have information that can help us."

"Okay. Thanks for the warning. Don't worry, he can't get out of where he's at." Rhett softened his tone. "By the way, Justine told Ava she's Novak's daughter. You might want to get close to her and use that as an advantage."

Russ's eyes widened. "Well, that explains a lot. She's always looking for attention."

"I'll talk to her," Mitch said.

"We good?" Rhett looked down at his chip in case he missed something.

Mitch perked his lips to the corner. "Yeah, I think."

"I don't have time for 'I think,'" Rhett gritted his teeth. "There's no room for failure." He paused and scrubbed his face. "Oh, God. I can't believe I quoted our father."

"I'm getting close, Rhett. I'm going to find him."

Russ blinked, confusion marked on his face.

"Don't do anything foolish. It's not worth your life," Rhett said.

"Mitch. Where are you? We're on the roof. I've got eyes on Ava," a male's voice resonated through Mitch's chip.

"Who was that?" Rhett wrenched Mitch's shirt. Rhett released him when he realized what he had done. "Sorry. But that's my girl."

Mitch straightened his shirt and rolled his shoulders back. "It's Payton. He replaced Ava as squad leader."

"Tell him not to engage. Tell him to wait until you arrive. I need time to get to my team."

Before Mitch had a chance to respond, Rhett bolted.

CHAPTER ELEVEN – EXPLOSION

AVA

ISAN guards covered all sides of the building. There was no way of going around or avoiding them.

We had momentarily disabled Payton's team, but Payton and Justine might leave their fallen members behind and come for us if Justine recovered enough to fight, even with a broken nose.

I shared a defense plan with my troop. I hoped to rally the guards to one side of the building. It would be to our benefit and ensure the escape would go smoother.

We hiked to the second level and prepared to drop to the first.

Rhett messaged me, asking where I was. I sent the coordinates. He wanted me to wait, but I said we needed to stay on the move.

I didn't tell him ISAN guards had found our glider because if I had, he would have gone alone. One step at a time. We had to work together. It was the safest way.

"Are you ready?" I adjusted my cloak and tied my hair back. My hair was longer and getting in my way. "No matter what happens, you get to the glider and save the kids."

God help me if something happens to them. Rhett would never forgive himself for leaving them behind.

"Here. Zen gave me these explosives before we left." I handed them each a sphere-shaped object, about the size of my thumb.

They fit inside my back pockets but packed enough power to

damage the building.

Tamara rolled them between her fingers like a magician. "I'll make sure these are in position."

Reyna tugged on her rope and I did the same. After I gave my group a thumbs up, I dropped with Reyna. The rest of them would descend behind the structure when all was clear.

Tasers were pointed at Reyna and me when we landed.

"Raise your hands," the man in the center commanded.

They all wore the dark ISAN guard uniform. Helmets with dark face shields obscured their features.

"Hi, boys. I'm turning myself in. No need to get all riled up." I raised my hands in surrender, keeping my tone level and sweet as honey.

"Get down on your knees and keep your arms up," the same man demanded.

I lowered to my knees. "We're just two girls, and there are so many of you. Relax, solider."

He cautiously advanced, five men on either side of him.

"Aren't you going to let the other guards know you've got me?" I said.

Come on. Just let Reyna and me be enough.

"I was told there were a handful of you. So unless you let me know where the others are, you are going to have one massive headache." He pointed a Taser at my temple.

To my horror, one of the guards took out a pistol when I didn't answer and jabbed it against Reyna's head. "Tell me where the others are, Ava, or she's dead. Mr. Novak wanted only you alive."

Reyna shifted her leg to a better position for action. I did the same.

"Wait. Hold on. I'll tell you." I had to stall him.

In the distance, a familiar form emerged, darting from one damaged car to another. I had left my chip on for Rhett so he could hear the conversation.

One thing I loved about being in a ruined city—there were so many places to hide.

"One," the man holding the gun on Reyna said. Then, "Two."

"I don't think you want to say three." I winked.

"Watch me," he said.

"Three." Rhett finished the sequence just as something clattered to the ground in the center of ISAN guards. Smoke fizzed out of a golf ball-sized metal contraption.

My man had come just in the nick of time.

"Sleeping gas," one of the guards closest to the smoke yelled, and then he collapsed.

The guards scattered. Some dropped to the ground unconscious, but the smoke died quickly and the others got away.

The captain holding a gun on Reyna never moved. They weren't near where the sleeping gas had exploded. As his finger tightened on the trigger, he fell back with a bullet to the neck. He got what he deserved.

Peering up, I saw Ozzie still aiming at the captain. He gave me a thumbs up and dove to the side to dodge a blow.

"Ava. Behind you." Rhett's voice alerted me through my chip.

I had already seen the guard flanking me, so I pushed off in a back flip. Instead of landing on my feet, I wedged my legs around his neck and snapped it. As he fell, I jumped off, picked up a Taser, and used it to smack another guard on his skull.

Reyna draped her cloak over the man's head and sent him soaring with a thrust to his gut. He collided with a boulder and dropped.

Reyna and I recovered another weapon each, hid behind an upside-down vehicle, and fired.

Rhett climbed on top of a pile of cement debris. From there, he had a clear view of the whole scene.

I whirled but lost my footing. Naomi gracefully dropped from the second level in front of me and gripped a soldier's arm to burn him. He hollered and jerked free.

Keeping the burned arm against his torso, he pointed his Taser with a trembling hand. Before he could pull the trigger, I drove my fist into his stomach, sending him soaring into another soldier. I tossed his fallen Taser to Naomi.

"Thanks." She gave me a curt nod and launched pellet after pellet. Her aim was dead on, but the pellets didn't even make the guards stumble.

Cleo, Tamara, and Ozzie lowered themselves with their ropes and fired at the ISAN targets. But they didn't make a dent either. ISAN guards were Taser-proof. We had no guns, but they did.

The guards were covered almost from head to foot. Except one spot. I somersaulted to dodge a bullet and shot at one of the ISAN soldier's feet. He fell, his body shuddering. Then I moved on to the next guard and the next, wounding all in the same place.

Pellets bounced off me as I charged ahead. They should have remembered I had an ISAN Taser-proof suit, too.

"Shoot them in the feet," I yelled into my chip. "Boots are not Taser-proof."

Rhett had found Cleo in the pandemonium. They were covering each other's backs while moving toward the glider.

"Come on. This way." I alerted my band through my chip. "It's time for Plan B."

"Got it," each member of my team confirmed.

Plan B was not the best plan but it had to work, or we would be trapped there for who knew how long. And time was not on our side. We needed to get back.

Reyna and I scurried into the empty building from the first level and climbed up the stairs to the second. I hollered at the ISAN guards to get their attention.

"This building is going to collapse in ten seconds. Run." I held up a demolition device. "The counting has begun. Leave while you can. You've been warned."

Some guards took off, while others ran toward the second floor to find us.

Stupid fools.

Reyna and I were no longer on the second floor. I'd used a hologram trick, generated from my chip. Zen had downloaded some new app and I hadn't had time to test it before we left, but thank God it worked.

The guards had guns pointed at Reyna's and my holograms. When I heard bullets pinging against the walls, I knew our diversion had worked.

Then the ground rumbled and the second floor gave way when I tapped my chip to activate the explosives.

"Ava. What did you do?" Rhett ran beside me.

"Zen didn't tell me they were that powerful. I didn't take much. It shouldn't—"

The ground underneath me shook. Then another two booms.

"Run faster," Rhett hollered.

We'd almost reached our glider when the collapsing building roared like an avalanche. Dense, white smoke billowed upward in a dark tower and rolled toward us like rapids. It would engulf us in seconds.

"Here." Rhett ushered us into a space between two buildings.

Too tight to be an alley but good enough. Rhett positioned his body over mine, always watching out for me first. I pressed my face into his shoulder to avoid breathing the toxic air. We stood speechless and waited until the smoke died.

"I didn't think it would crumble like that." I drew my hood lower to cover more of my face. "I didn't intend to kill so many."

"It's okay. It was either them or us." Reyna panted as she rested a hand on my shoulder. "You saw the solider holding a gun on my head. He was going to kill me. We had surrendered and he still wanted to kill me. He didn't care."

"The kids," Tamara said. "Did you tell Rhett?"

"I did." Cleo waved at the lingering smoke, using her cloak to cover her nose.

"Then let's not waste any more time." Rhett led the way through the lingering haze.

When we neared the parking zone, all appeared calm. No gunfire. No red laser beams. And no pinging of pellets.

Too quiet. The guards were most likely waiting for us, with the kids held hostage.

Please, don't let them be dead. I can't handle more deaths. They're just kids.

Instead of going directly to the front, we circled around the back.

Rhett stopped about fifty feet from the glider. "Ava and I will approach from the front. ISAN wants both of us. Let them think we're surrendering. The rest of you hang back and surprise them. Remember, wait until we lure them out."

After the team agreed, we got into our positions.

"Hey. It's us. Rhett and Ava." Rhett waved his hands, edging closer to the ramp. "We're here to surrender. Come out and show yourselves."

No reply.

Something wasn't right. Maybe they'd taken the kids. I surveyed every angle with Helix, high and low. No ISAN guards.

I knew Rhett had the same thought when his eyes grew big and panic flared in his sun-struck irises.

"I'm going in." Rhett dashed up the ramp and pushed the button for the door to open.

I bumped into Rhett's back when I rounded the corner. He had one hand on the wall as if to brace himself and the other hand clutched to his chest. I prepared my stomach for the worst.

Momo, Coco, and Bobo each held Tasers, pointing at the five guards knocked out on the ground.

What in the world?

"You can come in. It's safe," Rhett said into his chip. Then he faced the kids. "Why didn't you answer me?"

"We didn't know if it was you for sure," Coco said.

Rhett let out a frustrated sigh. "Can someone explain what happened?"

Momo raised her hand, looking terrified. "I swear, Rhett. I— we stayed put like you said. We were laughing and sharing stories when they came. They wanted to take us back to ISAN."

Coco's voice cracked as she wrapped her arms around herself. "We didn't know how to reach you."

"We did the right thing, right?" Bobo's eyes widened.

I inhaled a breath, grateful they were alive. "Yes. Of course you did. You stuck up for yourselves and for each other. You do whatever it takes so you don't ever go back. You're not at fault here."

Footsteps thumped up the ramp and the rest of the squad crowded into the back. They looked as shocked as Rhett and I felt.

The harsh lines on Momo's face softened. "We didn't know what to do with the bodies, so after we knocked them out, we Tased them."

Ozzie and Reyna spat out a laugh.

"What do you mean you knocked them out?" Cleo stepped closer.

"These kids are pretty amazing." Tamara peeked over Cleo to get a better look.

"Well"—Bobo pointed at Momo and Coco—"the girls kicked their asses." He covered his mouth and looked at Rhett. "I mean they brought them to their knees. I think they were shocked at how strong the girls were."

"Well, I'm glad you're all fine." Rhett released a long breath and scrubbed a hand over his jaw. "We were worried."

Momo stood up. "So, you're not mad at me, at us?"

Her question was directed to Rhett.

"No." Rhett shook his head and smiled. "I'm just glad you're all safe."

Momo dove into Rhett's arms and shook. She didn't cry, but she seemed to release her fear and panic into that embrace.

"You're okay, kiddo. You did great." Rhett patted her back.

There was some kind of special bond between them I couldn't explain.

"Let's take the bodies out of here so we can get going," I said.

"I'll help." Ozzie dragged a man out the door.

"This one is heavy," Reyna grunted.

"Monet?" Naomi edged forward from the back, calling out

their proper names "Boden, Coraline?"

Momo—Monet—peeled herself away from Rhett, her eyes flew wide. "Naomi?" She jumped into Naomi's arms, followed by Boden and Coraline.

The four of them held each other tightly.

And this time Momo wept.

I almost did, too.

CHAPTER TWELVE – UNEXPECTED REUNION

AVA

"**H**ow are you here?" Momo gaped between me and Naomi. "It's a long story." Naomi smiled at me, and my mind flooded with memories. "But to make it a short one, Ava and I used to live together. And you're not going to believe it, but Ava and I had the same foster father."

"No way. Holy sh—" Momo bit her bottom lip. "I mean, holy cow. We've got a lot of catching up to do."

"Guys. We have company." Ozzie's voice was frantic. "Catch up later. ISAN guards are here."

"Apparently falling buildings won't stop them." Tamara peered over Ozzie's head.

"Everyone, get ready for takeoff." Rhett slammed into his seat and slid his finger across the touch screen.

We settled into our places, Naomi squeezing in the back with the kids. There was no room for her at the front.

In the passenger seat, I waited for the glider to take off, my weapons in my hands. One Taser and one gun I had stolen. My heart thundered in the quiet. Any second now, we would be out of here.

Hurry, Rhett. What's taking so long?

The guards closed in, less than half of the group we'd fought earlier. And in the far back were Mitch, Russ, and Payton's team.

The girls we'd Tased had been revived, and Justine, broken nose or not, was running all-out toward us.

Rhett's eyes were fixed on the monitor, his jaw clenched, and he looked like he was about to burst out of his chair.

Hurry, Rhett. Hurry.

The engine or some part of the glider rattled, like metal hitting metal in a rapid session, and then nothing. Not a good sound.

"What are we waiting for, Rhett?" Reyna socked the back of Rhett's headrest.

"I'm not waiting for anything. It won't start." Rhett's calm voice did not match his unnerved expression.

"What?" several people asked.

"Is this glider bulletproof?" Cleo took her Taser and the stolen gun from her waist.

We got our answer when a hail of bullets rained on our transporter. The glider swayed back and forth as if it were on a stormy ocean.

"What's wrong?" Naomi rushed over.

"The glider won't take off." A sharp sigh released through Rhett's nose. Persistently, he tapped his finger across the screen as he searched for a way out.

"If we make it out alive, my father won't hear the end of this." Cleo stomped to the back.

"What are you doing?" Tamara blocked the panel that opened the door with her hand.

"We have to do something. This piece of junk can't handle a full assault. We won't be able to fly at all."

"I can help."

I wasn't surprised Momo spoke up.

"Well, not me, but Coco can. She has some kind of electric

thing." Momo wiggled her fingers.

It was the first time I'd heard of Coco's power. I was impressed by what these little girls could do. And they had figured out they didn't need Helix long before we had.

Coco placed her palms on the hull of the glider. "I might be able to jump-start the engine."

"Do it. And hurry," Ozzie said.

"While Coco does her thing, we need to get some guards off our tail or we won't last." Cleo snarled at Tamara to move out of the way.

"Cleo is right." Before I could rise out of my chair, Rhett gripped my arm.

"Be careful, Ava. Stay close. And smoke them. I bought these from Zeke." He handed me two metal, golf-ball-sized gadgets.

"I will." I kissed his lips and faced Coco. "Do it now."

Coco's brown eyes darkened, and then went completely silver, like the electric sparks sizzling out of her fingertips. The silver and blue lights stretched and grew. Lightning crackled within the walls of the aircraft.

Riveted by Coco's pure awesomeness, I almost forgot what I had to do.

Instead of the door, Cleo had opened the roof hatch. I led the squad out with an ISAN shield—thick, bulky, and old. It would protect us as long as we stayed low.

Tamara flanked me, while Cleo and Reyna secured left and right, and Ozzie took the rear. Stomach to the roof with the shield in front, I crawled forward to get a better view and access. I flinched as bullets struck the shield, creating sparks.

We returned fire and brought down the ISAN frontline.

My blood heated when I calibrated for Helix. Could I stop the bullets as I had at Mitch's apartment? I hadn't had the chance to practice. When I extended my hand, nothing.

I pushed and pulled, drawing Helix more. Not the result I wanted.

A metallic scent burned through my nostrils from the torrential downpour of bullets. Colors were too vibrant and stung my eyes. To my astonishment, I saw Rhett in the glider below as if I floated on air and there was no metal between us. Helix overloaded my senses, but I'd just gained a new ability.

Suddenly the bullets stopped. Mitch had his hand raised.

Thank you, Mitch.

"Ava. Rhett. You're surrounded. Surrender and no harm will be done to your team."

Rhett didn't answer.

"No thanks," I said, buying time for Coco to finish.

"Ava, think of your troop and not yourself for once."

Mitch was dragging out the conversation to give us time. He also needed to give ISAN a convincing show to prove his loyalty.

"What a crazy idea. I always think of myself first. You should know that about me, right, Justine?"

If anything, I could count on Justine to be a distraction.

Justine came closer, moving from the safety of the broken pillar. "You're a traitor. And you're no leader. You sucked at it. ISAN doesn't need you. We're doing just fine."

"Ouch. Such hard words. But you're no leader, either, are you?"

An animalistic growl escaped her and she sprinted toward me.

Good. Come closer, be a distraction.

"Get back here, Justine. That's an order." Payton rose from a small pile of rubble.

Tamara tugged my pants. "Hurry. Do something."

Justine reached about halfway when I fired my pistol. The bullet nicked the chunk of plaster in front of her. She stopped in an open, wide space. No place to hide.

Stupid but brave.

"Surrender." Justine pointed her weapon at me, her hate unwavering.

"I'm shocked you have the guts to stand alone against me. I'm not going to shoot you, so you'll have to come get me."

"So be it, then. Guards, fire away."

When Justine realized she was the only one acting on her command, she halted, and saw everyone was staring at electric filaments wrapping around the glider, crackling and sizzling.

The fizzing of Coco's power buzzed under my chest, not only vibrating the glider but making it warmer. Tendrils of lightning blanketed the aircraft, visible to everyone. Threatening to shock anyone near it, the electricity kept the guards at bay. It also gave an illusion it would explode or transform into a mechanical beast.

"What is that?" Russ's eyes widened with terror. "Fall back. Fall back. Everyone, fall back."

"Move. It's time to go." Ozzie's bark was hardly audible when a breeze suddenly tunneled around us, picking up speed and debris.

I tossed the two metal, golf-ball-sized gadgets Rhett gave me at the center to buy us some time. Bombs exploded, creating white clouds of dust. I shuffled back down last and closed the hatch.

Coco's body shone like the dawn breaking, blinding in the confined space.

"Go, Rhett. It should work now."

"Okay, kid." Rhett slammed his hand on a button.

"Hurry. I'm getting weaker."

"I'm trying."

The glider shuddered but lifted. Moving but too slow. Too damn slow. A round of bullets hit the windshield. It had held up so far until now.

A crack.

Spidery lines splintered the glass.

Then more. Spreading. Magnifying.

"Move faster. Come on." Rhett punched the panel.

We had to hurry. If that window gave way … I had to do something.

I recalled the despair and agony of seeing the guards shoot at my friends as they glided toward the roof at Mitch's apartment. I could do nothing but stand there and watch, but in the moment of frenzy, Helix had come through with my telekinetic ability.

I will not die today. We will not die today.

Like a dandelion, be resilient.

My mother's face came to mind as I stared at the bulging, vibrating window. Heat rushed through my veins, gathering power, undulating through me.

I had never seen how I looked when energy rushed in, but I saw myself today through the cracked window. My whole body glowed like the birth of a star.

"You're beautiful."

I vaguely heard Rhett as I focused on fostering my energy.

"Coco, send a lightning charge to the window," I demanded.

"But then the window will explode," Coco rasped.

Her weak voice told me she had seconds left.

If they broke down our window, it would burst inside, but I would rather have it play out differently. A little surprise wouldn't hurt.

The transporter rose higher and banked. Its juice had kicked in, but we were still in danger. Bullets continued to fire at us.

"Trust me. Do it on the count of three. One ... everyone down."

Bodies thumped to the floor. Rhett tapped the screen and enclosed his arms around my waist. Not to distract me, but to be my shield if I needed him.

"Two ... Three. *Now.*"

Coco shifted on my command. Streams of blue and silver lights shot out, shattering the window outward in a thousand pieces. On impact, I exhaled deeply and unleashed my power to combine with the lightning bolts, guiding the energy toward the guards.

Screams erupted. Lightning crackled and sizzled anything it touched. The guards who were assaulted seized, while the ground illuminated, electrocuting everyone in the vicinity.

I pushed Helix as far as I could reach and extended my hands as hordes of bullets still came toward us.

Stop. I told them. *Stop.*

What happened next felt like a dream. The bullets seemed to soar in slow motion. The halted ones in mid-air dropped, but I couldn't stop them all. Not like the last time.

Helix failed me. I failed me. I failed the team.

"Drop, Ava. Everyone, brace yourself." Rhett shoved me down and jerked the glider to the right so the glider's hull took the brunt of the assault.

Whack. Plank. Thud. A few had escaped inside and hit the back wall.

At the thought of what almost happened, my breathing quickened. We could have all been dead on a mere hope I could stop all the bullets like I had before. I didn't know how I had done it then and I didn't know it now.

My squad didn't know what I was trying to do. As far as they knew, I had directed the lightning at the guards as planned. But still ...

I'm not special. I'm just a fool.

Rhett veered the glider up. We were safe for now. Down below, guards rushed to help the fallen ones.

One bullet had hit the door. Another had struck the shield Tamara held for me.

And the last ... no. Oh, God no.

Two small bodies lay on the floor, Momo and Naomi on their knees beside them.

"What happened?" I rushed over.

Ozzie checked Coco's pulse on her neck.

Blood soaked Bobo's shirt; Coco was knocked out, blood on her arm.

Momo's lips quivered as she spoke. "Bobo pushed Coco out of the way. The bullet nicked Coco's arm, but the energy bounced the bullet off her, and it hit Bobo's chest."

None of us knew what to do. Everyone looked at each other for answers and waited for someone to take charge. Shock had made us immobile and speechless.

I snapped out of it.

First things first. Stop the blood. I had nothing, so with my trembling hand I pressed down on Bobo's wound. Warm crimson liquid outlined my hand.

So much blood. He had lost so much.

"Get the first-aid kit," Rhett said behind the controls.

A cabinet opened and slammed.

"Here." Reyna spread out the first-aid box and opened it.

Tamara rummaged inside the kit: Ointment, scissors, bandages, gauze pads, antiseptic wipes, plastic gloves, disposable instant cold and heating packs.

She threw them all out. "There's nothing here to stop the blood."

"Rhett, get us home. Please hurry." Momo's whole body was shaking.

Rhett didn't answer, but he tightened his shoulders and rooted his eyes ahead.

"I might be able to stop the bleeding. I've never done it before, but it's worth a try." Naomi looked at me to confirm.

A moan escaped Bobo.

I gently cupped his cheek. "Bobo, it's Ava. Can you hear me?"

"Co ... co. Is she?"

"Coco is fine. Look at me, okay. Stay awake."

Naomi replaced my hand with hers. A gentle light glowed from her hand, getting brighter and pulsing. Bobo groaned and bit his bottom lip.

"Did it work?" Momo stared at Bobo's chest when Naomi pulled back.

"I think so." Naomi released a sigh and rubbed her hand. The creases on her forehead had eased somewhat. "I'll check on Coco's wound."

A cabinet opened and closed, and Ozzie held out two syringes.

"This should dull the pain and help them relax a bit." Ozzie administered the needleless syringe. "Do you need anything else?"

Dr. Machine, I wanted to say. "No. I think that will help."

Another cabinet slammed, and Cleo tossed me a clean beige towel.

"Thanks." I wiped the blood off my hand, though some remained.

"Leave their blood on the floor." Cleo tightened her jaw. "I want my father to see what happens when he thinks more about resources than our lives. I know he was thinking this mission should have been an easy in and out, but he didn't think of ISAN coming after us. I should have fought for a faster glider. No matter where we go or hide, ISAN won't stop until they have Ava back. We have to keep that in mind at all times, or the cost will be too great."

Cleo's intention wasn't to put me down, but her words put a dagger through my chest. She was right. As long as I was with them, nobody was safe.

I dropped from exhaustion and utter failure, my shoulders caving inward as I leaned back against the wall. Bobo's bleeding had stopped, but the bullet had to be taken out soon. Momo held Bobo's head and whispered in his ear to keep him awake.

Coco was still unconscious.

As for me, I stared at the drying blood on my hands. How much more blood would be shed before ISAN fell?

ISAN had witnessed what I had done and what one of the girls could do. They might tell Novak I had produced the lightning. Novak would either want me dead or be even more determined to capture me.

I had to talk to Gene. I had a feeling he knew more than he'd told Zen. It was time to tell Gene the truth.

Rhett phoned in to Zen, giving him an update as we flew safely home.

CHAPTER THIRTEEN – HOME BASE

ΛVΛ

Children from the southern rebels huddled away from the commotion. Rhett carried Coco, and Ozzie cradled Bobo, into the medical room.

The room had been prepped for an operation. Medical tools lay on a metal tray, an IV drip bag hung by the bed, and syringes along with other things I had no names for waited on a cart.

A few of Zen's helpers wore medical masks as they readied for surgery.

The lines on Zen's forehead deepened. "Rhett, place Coco on the mattress, and Ozzie, put Bobo on the table. Ava, do you have the rock?"

"Yes." I handed it to him carefully. "Reyna has the other essentials."

"Good." Zen placed the black velvet pouch inside his white lab coat pocket. "I promise to get to Brooke, but Bobo doesn't have time."

"Of course." I stepped aside and noticed a person with gray hair I hadn't seen before.

Zen caught me assessing the new member. "This is Doctor Crumb, someone I trust. I asked Frank to bring him here. I'm not capable of performing this surgery. He's here only for the procedure."

"Sure." I gave the doctor a curt nod.

I dug through my memories for his face. When nothing came up, I worried less. Zen wouldn't have brought him here if he couldn't trust him. Still, one could never be cautious enough.

Zen rushed to the water bucket and washed his hands. "Frank's unit tracked down the girls from the news, but they gave him a hard time. He couldn't convince them to come to our base."

Rhett handed Zen a towel and stepped to the side. "Frank is not the right person, and neither are any of his men to do the job. They don't know what these girls have been through. You need ... no, *they* need someone they can relate to."

Zen halted mid-stride in the center of the room. "You're right. Ava, I'm putting you in charge of the mission. Why don't you take a team when we find them again?"

I opened my mouth to confirm, but shut it when Rhett shook his head, frowning. Not at me, but at Zen. I placed my hand on his arm to keep him from saying something he would regret but he said it anyway.

"Give her the faster transporter. That piece of trash is the reason these kids got shot. By the way, you're short one air vehicle. We're lucky we made it back in one piece."

Zen met Rhett's eyes. Kind and soft. "I'm sorry. I didn't know the glider's condition was bad. It hadn't been reported. What's done is done. We need to move forward and fix what we can."

Rhett's taut expression eased, but his fists remained clenched.

"Fine," Rhett said softly. "We'll wait outside."

Jo stopped pacing when she spotted us on our way to join her.

"How are Coco and Bobo?" She rubbed at her arms, as if to soothe her anxiety.

"Coco will be fine," Rhett said. "We just need her to wake up.

Zen is ready to operate. Bobo is in good hands." Rhett gave her the rundown of what had happened at the black market.

Jo cupped her mouth, her gaze moving to Momo. "I should have kept a tighter leash on these three. I'm so sorry." Her tone changed to motherly. "It's not like mental missions. This is real. Bad things can still happen, even for those with powers. Please, just listen next time."

"This is my fault. I'm so sorry." Momo lowered her head and sniffled.

Jo kept her expression hard but her voice tender. "The world is cruel, as you already know. There are too many bad people out there. We're just trying to keep you all safe. We have to work together."

Momo nodded, wiping tears on her sleeve.

"It's going to be a while," Rhett said. "Jo, why don't you take the kids to wash up and give them something to eat? We should all do the same."

Dragging my feet next to Rhett, I headed to the washing quarter with our team. Buckets of lukewarm water were always available, thanks to the cleaning crew. An orderly stack of hand towels waited on a rock. The material wasn't soft like at ISAN, but I would never complain.

I took a cup from inside the larger bucket and ran it down my arm. Red water puddled on the dirt and slowly soaked through. Bobo's blood.

Roxy's team, Chelsea, and her unit—other faces flashed through my mind, all dead. Never to be seen again. Nobody cared. Nobody talked about them. Their parents, if they had living relatives, didn't even know they were gone.

If Bobo died, it would be the same for him. But we would

remember. I would recall how I couldn't stop all the bullets. How I had failed him.

Not my fault. Not my fault.

But this guilty demon inside me nagged. *I should have tried harder.*

My father had written in his journal I was special. I'd thought he meant I was the only one who didn't need the special serum to generate the power, but that wasn't the case at all. There had to be something else.

Telekinesis? Well, I sucked.

I just need to practice. Learn how to use and hone that power first. Perhaps other abilities will emerge in time.

I dipped out more water and thought about my mother. My beautiful mother who should have had more time in this world. If she were alive, things might have played out differently for me. Although, I might not have met Rhett. He might be with someone else—like Cleo. Or maybe fate would have brought us together anyway.

"Ava. You okay?"

Rhett's tender voice brought me back to reality.

"Yeah." My shoulders sagged with a long sigh. Not convincing.

The stubborn, caked-on blood needed a good scrubbing. I looked down and realized I had been rubbing at the same spot, my skin red and raw.

And we were the only two left.

Rhett cupped my hands from behind, the warmth of his body lulling me still. He scrubbed between my soapy fingers. It was difficult to think of anything else but him and his motions.

"It's not your fault. It's nobody's fault. It is what it is."

113

How did Rhett know what I was thinking? When you really know someone, you can guess their thoughts, I suppose. We were two souls and minds intertwined.

"What if Bobo doesn't—"

"Still not your fault. None of our lives are in your hands, Ava."

Rhett gingerly massaged each of my fingers, starting from my knuckles and moving up.

I stifled a moan.

God, that felt so good.

"I need to practice. I need to be ready for next time."

Rhett swung me around to face him and entangled our wet fingers in front of his chest. "You will when we have a chance. But we have much to do today. Councilor Chang is coming, remember?"

I sighed. "Yeah."

Rhett twirled me, my back facing his front again, and his embrace made my muscles go weak. Holding the same position, he guided me down to my knees and placed our hands over the small bucket as he trickled the water over my palms. Then he moved his hands to my head.

I moaned, feeling the tension fade away. I didn't know how long he made circles on my temple with his thumb, but I didn't want him to stop. His touch was a lullaby, coaxing me to a state of euphoria.

"Do you like that?" His voice dripped like honey and his breath brushed hotly against my ear. "Relax, Ava. We don't have time to feel guilty. There is no such thing when you are at war. We do the best we can. Sometimes we have to make decisions in that split moment. Whatever the outcome, it's all fate. I know you tried to stop all the bullets. You gave it your best shot. It would have been a lot worse had you not tried. Think about the good you have done. How many you have saved. No one, not even you, can be perfect. You can't save everyone."

"Okay," I breathed, tilting my head back and resting it on his shoulder as my eyes closed.

"Good," he drawled, his word smooth like butter.

"I still need to practice, though. But first I need to check in on Brooke."

"Practice can wait until you get something to eat. Finish washing up. I'll prepare us something while you go see Brooke." After planting a kiss on my neck, he backed away slowly to not overbalance me.

The cold replaced his warmth, and he left me feeling flustered, wanting more.

CHAPTER FOURTEEN – MY FATHER

JUSTINE

Justine hated Ava. Hated her with a burning rage in her core.
Ava had punched Justine in the face. She was furious with herself for allowing it to happen. Justine almost wanted to laugh. Ava had guts after all. And here Justine had thought Ava was a pathetic weakling who had constantly vied for Russ's attention.

Justine recovered fairly quickly. Thanks to Helix, the pain was bearable, but she wasn't sure if she had a broken nose.

She stormed out of the medical room after Dr. Machine had fixed her up. Her team was already situated in Russ's office. She sat at the empty chair beside Payton as second in command.

Lydia and Mitch sat on either side of Russ. The trio scanned through their handheld TABs, ignoring her. They didn't bother to look at her when she entered or ask how her procedure went.

Yes, it was a simple fix for Dr. Machine and not life threatening, but still, she'd been injured in the field. If Ava were in her shoes, they would have doted on her.

Bethany, Alice, and Tessa hardly blinked, their bodies rigid and expressions stony. Justine kind of missed her old squad, just a tiny fraction. At least they had made her laugh, even if the joke was on her sometimes.

Justine's father walked in, his expensive shoes annoyingly loud, and he commanded the room like his own stage. Even his voice oozed with authority, causing her to bristle.

"I want to know how this happened." Justine's father's glacial expression made her hold her breath.

Because you should have assigned me as the leader and not Payton. Your mistake.

Why did he look at Justine? Payton was the leader. Justine's father began pacing when she turned away.

"Ava's presence confirmed she was not harmed significantly by HelixB88, but what about Brooke? Did you see her?"

Ava, Ava, Ava. Justine's father only cared about Ava.

Payton pressed his lips together and rubbed at his thigh. "There was no sign of Brooke."

Justine's father exhaled and directed his attention at the door as if he could see someone there. "This confirms the unusual mutation I detected in Ava's DNA works the way I predicted. Then they need the items from the black market to create the remedy for Brooke. She would be in a coma if she's still alive." He trailed off and looked sharply at them, as if he'd just noticed other people in the room. "Explain how nearly all the ISAN guards were electrocuted by a few rebels inside a glider."

Justine had expected that question sooner or later. Later would have been preferable since they had no answer.

Payton shifted in his seat and folded his hands, his voice cracking a bit. "There was a girl I'd never seen before with the rebels. She might have an ability—"

Justine's father slammed his hand on Russ's table, not hard enough to hurt himself, but enough to startle them. "*Might* is not the word I want to hear, Payton. Either this girl has the ability or not. There are only two possibilities. You had one job." He held up an index finger. "You all failed. Ava is just one girl. The rest of her team members are useless."

"We had them surrounded, but—"

Justine's father focused on Mitch, cold and calculating. "No *buts*. After the meeting is adjourned, I want you to work the girls harder. Double up the mental missions and physical practice for every group. I need them ready for a war. As soon as Gene accomplishes his mission, we'll have what we need."

Justine squinted up at him. "Gene? He's either partying with the rebels or he's locked up. How is he going to help? He might soften up like Ava."

Justine's father flashed her a dirty look, and she shrank in her seat.

"Gene is loyal. Do not underestimate him. If he doesn't pan out, Dr. Hunt will have to make an appearance."

Mitch and Russ exchanged a glance. It was subtle, but unmistakable. What were they thinking?

Lydia crossed her legs and swiped across her TAB. "Are you sure it's a good idea for Dr. Hunt to make an appearance? I believe most assume he's dead. No one I know, except you, has seen him in person."

Justine's father heaved a breath. He glared at everyone and then at last, at Justine. "I don't care what needs to be done. Ava is coming back home and I don't care who dies to make it happen."

Does that include me, Father?

CHAPTER FIFTEEN – MORE TRAINING

AVA

An hour had passed. One excruciating hour felt like a lifetime. No word from Zen about Bobo. Instead of sitting around waiting, Rhett and I went running on the outskirts of our home.

I sprinted with the cool wind, my feet pounding the earth. I raced against thoughts of Brooke, Gene, my father and mother, Justine, and even Mr. Novak.

Sometimes Rhett jogged beside me. Sometimes I ran ahead, wishing things were different, pushing Helix and myself as if ISAN guards followed.

When I could no longer keep the brutal pace, I slowed to bring my heartrate down.

I hoped Mitch and Russ wouldn't be reprimanded for failing to bring me in. Justine, on the other hand—I didn't care if Novak punished her team. No, wait—Payton's team. They deserved whatever was given to them.

I laughed to myself for breaking Justine's nose. Justine's body makeup was nothing like mine, or any other ISAN girls. Her genetics made her stronger, resilient, and difficult to break. Her strength far exceeded anyone else. So Helix had served me well.

Panting, I rested my hands on my knees when we had circled back to the opening to the medical room. Rhett did the same.

Piles of debris—steel rods, chunks of concrete, twisted wires,

119

rotten wood, broken glass, and weathered office supplies—littered the area near the entrance. It was designed to distract drones or curious scavengers from entering the crumbled building. Toward the back of the pile, the entrance was barely wide enough for a medium-sized person to squeeze through.

Rhett extended his arms to the sky and yawned. "That felt good. We should do it more often."

I stretched my legs and rotated my neck from side to side. "Yes, we should. I need to train. We all need to train. We can't stop until—"

Rhett gathered me in his embrace. "Slow down, babe."

With his steady arms around me, I inhaled a deep breath. Then exhaled just as long.

"You can't seem to sit still," he said. "We can start training now. How about it?"

I retreated a step, taking in Rhett's handsome features. Sometimes, it felt like I'd always been here with him, and all I had endured in ISAN was a fading nightmare.

Rhett crinkled his eyebrows. "What? Do I have something on my face?" He scrubbed the corners of his mouth. When I didn't respond, he rubbed his forehead.

"No, silly. Stop." I took his hand in mine. "Let me try something."

"Okay." He waved a hand at the piles of waste in front of us as if it were my kingdom.

My lips twisted at the corner. I scanned for something to move, something small. Rhett beat me to it and bent to pick up a broken pen.

"Here." He rested the pen in his open palm. "Try to move this."

I fixated on the item and called Helix at the same time. Warmth flooded through me, and a soothing sensation coaxed me to use its power. Helix was not just a serum. It was a part of me, a living entity.

Some women who possessed the Helix gene were unaware, but those who had discovered Helix's power were able to use it. Like the girls in the news. Like Naomi, Momo, Coco, and Tamara.

I closed my eyes and opened them with a new focus. An ultraviolet tendril, the size of a thin ribbon, projected from my fingertip to the object in Rhett's hand, similar to Coco's lightning.

Had those tendrils been present at Mitch's apartment? I hadn't seen them, but I might not have noticed the phenomenon. I had been too distraught over the possibility of my squad not reaching the roof of the next building.

What I saw left me breathless with awe. My body produced this energy. Rhett gave me a sidelong glance as if asking me what I was waiting for, confirming he couldn't see the dark-purple filaments.

I curled my lips in a wicked grin. Then, with a flick of my finger, the pen flew out of his palm.

Rhett rewarded me with a huge grin, his eyes beaming as bright as the sun. Timing couldn't have been better.

He rubbed his hands and picked up another object—a chunk of cement about the size of a tennis ball.

I went through the same routine with the same victorious result. Rhett moved on to something bigger and heavier. From a block of wood to a metal rod. So far, a promising start.

"Great. You're able to easily move one item, but can you stop a bunch of things in motion?"

"Well, if I could have, I would have stopped all the bullets.

Then Bobo wouldn't—"

"Nah-uh-uh." Rhett waggled a finger at me. "We're not going there. You are not responsible for anyone's life."

I gripped my hair and muttered through gritted teeth. "What's taking Zen so long? If only we had Dr. Machine."

"I know, but Zen and his staff are doing the best they can. Bobo got shot in the chest. It might have ... You know what? We're going off on a tangent here. I'm going to throw things at you and you have to stop them, okay?"

"Fine." I sighed.

Rhett picked up a singed notepad, a plastic cup, and a small, rusted metal container. "Ready? I'm going to throw these up in the air. Your job is to stop them from falling on me."

I burst out a laugh. "You have such faith in me. I would move out of the way if I were you."

Rhett's solemn expression replaced his grin. "You did save me that day at Mitch's apartment. You saved our team. If it hadn't been for you, who knows what would've happened."

I dropped my gaze to stare at the ground. "I don't ever want to know."

"Hey. You have to remember your ability has been suppressed and manipulated. From the age of thirteen, you held all that power inside you. ISAN contained it through that damn protein drink, day in and day out. You've been through a lot. I'm not sure how your body took it in stride. You need to give yourself a chance to adjust and learn to call upon your abilities when you want them."

"Okay, I guess you're right. Let's do this and go back inside. Everyone will be wondering where we are."

Rhett nodded, his eyes fixed on me. "On the count of three. One ... Two ... Three."

He tossed everything in the air. I focused on the items over his head. When no ultraviolet tendrils appeared, I knew Helix had not obeyed me.

"Rhett, move out of the way." I leaped for him, feeling ridiculous. The worst damage would be the small metal container hitting his head, and it wasn't deadly.

I knocked him down, my body on top of his. An *oomph* left his throat as his arms secured me around my waist.

"Well, that's one way." Rhett chuckled and then flipped us over, his chest pressed to mine. "We'll train in one-on-one combat later tonight. You need to release some of your energy."

"I'm so sorry. Sometimes I forget my own strength. I didn't mean to ..." I perked my lips, a laugh almost escaping.

"I don't mind it at all. I like it when you play dirty." His eyebrows twitched, and his amber eyes darkened with desire.

"I bet you do." I returned his smirk, lost in this precious moment with Rhett, reality gone for a fragment of time.

"Be a dandelion, Ava. Be resilient. You can do this—you just need to want it bad enough. You need to believe. Something is holding you back. Want to talk about it?"

I looked out into the distance. "I wish I knew."

"I could stay here all day and stare at you, but ..." Rhett gripped my shoulders and tugged me up. "We have things to do and you need to keep practicing. I've got a good guess at what's holding you back."

I dusted off my pants. "You do, do ya?"

Rhett brushed his hands over my jacket and then his. "Two reasons. One is Brooke. And whether you want to admit it or not, Gene is the second. You need to talk to him. He needs to know. I'll come with you. I need to talk to him, too. Mitch thinks Gene knows something crucial that could either help us or destroy us."

"You're right. Let's talk to him after we speak to Councilor Chang."

"Good. I'm glad you agree."

A shuffling sound caught both of our attention. A figure appeared at the opening.

Naomi froze, her eyes wide. "I was looking for Ava, but if this is a bad time ..."

"No. I was just leaving." Rhett looked at me to confirm.

I squeezed his hand. "Thank you."

He planted a light kiss on my cheek and took off.

"I didn't mean to—" Naomi watched Rhett disappear through the entrance and smiled at me. "So, Rhett is your—"

"Yeah. A long story." My cheeks flushed with warmth. "I needed some air. I didn't mean to leave you alone."

She hugged herself. "No, no. It was good to catch up with Momo."

I kicked the metal container Rhett had thrown in the air, and it clattered in the dirt twenty feet away. "So, fill me in with details after I left."

Naomi tucked her hair behind her ear and shivered. "Things got crazy when you bailed. Vito lost it and searched for you for days. Those men with him at the black market, you never saw them when you lived with us. One of them was Tristan—he was in charge of the little ones. Vito hated kids. He didn't even want to talk to them. So Momo and her friends got lucky. They didn't have to deal with Vito, but Tristan wasn't much better. He didn't smack them around at least."

I kicked a metal handle, a part of a desk drawer. "Funny, the juvie director told me no one came for me." I didn't tell her ISAN

124

had purposely kept me locked in juvie to ensure I would be compliant. A subject willing to compromise out of gratitude to be out of jail, to fully submit and be under their control.

"So, what happened to your sister?" I asked. I knew I'd touched a sore topic when she lowered her gaze.

Naomi squashed some bug under her shoe and nudged the dead insect aside. "To make a long story short, one of Vito's men took Natalie and me to a room and ..." She glanced up to the ominous clouds, which were thicker and darker than they had been an hour ago. "He tied us up and ... he assaulted my sister first."

"What?" Rage flashed through me. Bits of debris by my feet trembled. Astounded by what I had done, I tamed my resolve and said, "I'm so sorry." I guided Naomi to a block of cement and sat beside her.

"I was furious." Her pitch rose with fervor. "I wanted to kill him. I looked for anything to try to cut the rope around my wrists. I was struggling so hard that it cut into my skin. The next thing I knew, the rope caught fire. I got free, but the fire spread to the carpet. I didn't know what was happening to me, but without thinking of the consequences, I tried to slap it out with my bare hands. The flames didn't extinguish and they didn't hurt me."

"Must have been the shock of your life." I knew that firsthand.

"It was. The man slapped me and said it was my fault. I jumped on him. My punches didn't hurt him, but he caught fire and fell on my unconscious sister. I pushed him away and tried to save Natalie, but I couldn't put out the flames. I only made it worse when I touched her."

I rubbed her back, sympathizing.

As tears pooled in her eyes, she pulled her knees to her chest and held them. "The smoke was unbearable, and though the fire spread through the room, I walked out untouched. I got the rest of the kids out, and Vito came home shortly after. The firefighters put out the fire, but by then the place was unrecognizable. When they asked me what had happened, I told them I didn't know. I lied because no one would believe me, and I was afraid of what Vito would do to me. It was then I knew something was different about me."

I copied Naomi's pose and imagined what burning power felt like. "It wasn't your fault. What happened after?"

"Vito took us to a new place. Not an actual house, but an abandoned warehouse. It wasn't as run-down as the dump we stayed at before, but run down nevertheless. He had gathered more people, women and men, to join his trafficking ring. Shortly after, he blackmailed me and a few other older kids to be part of his gang. He said if we didn't, he would have Tristan hurt the little ones. I had no choice. I figured I could at least learn to fight and plan an escape. I talked my way into Tristan's company to get away from Vito, and then I met the kids—Momo and the others. Vito still doesn't know what I can do. I kept it a secret, but I practiced every day, even if it was just turning it on and off, like a light switch. With practice, using this strange ability came easier."

I tried to think of words to comfort her. "Must have been hard for you to go through it alone. Nobody to confide in. And with your sister being gone ..." I really sucked at this. "I mean ..."

"Yeah. It was hard." Naomi picked at the rock with her nails. "I would have taken off, but I had no place to go. Besides, I was like a big sister to Coco, Bobo, and Momo. I couldn't leave them. I thought maybe I could protect them in a way I couldn't help my sister."

What kind of friend was I? I left you.

If I hadn't left, would Natalie be alive today? Would I have been able to prevent her assault?

Rhett's words entered my mind. *Think about what good you have done. How many you have saved ... You can't save everyone.*

I examined the dried cracked earth. A few seedlings had taken root and pushed up through the packed dirt. Hope. A small hope. Then I gazed beyond to the snow-capped mountains, so beautiful from afar. Perhaps I was searching for brightness, as I knew Naomi's story would get even darker.

"About six months ago, Tristan sold Coco, Bobo, and Momo to ISAN, who had deep pockets and an interest in kids. Can you believe I'm even saying the word *sold*?

"After the lessons from our past, the devastation from the meteors, we haven't learned a thing. It seems history has a way of repeating itself. Anyway, I was getting ready to leave myself, planning to take the remaining kids with me but you came along."

I admired Naomi more than ever. She was a true hero.

There were all different kinds of heroes. Some enjoyed the spotlight. Others helped from the shadows.

I draped an arm around her shoulder, liking how natural it felt, like old times. I'd never gotten close to her back then. The only thing on my mind had been survival. Having friends meant more heartache, more responsibilities. After my mother had died, I'd only looked after myself.

I felt differently now. Brooke and Tamara were the only reasons I'd made it through ISAN. Having friends could make the darkest time brighter. Sometimes, they carried your burden with you. Plus, I'd seen firsthand the power in numbers. Fighting together made a bigger difference than standing alone.

I squeezed Naomi tighter. "I'm sorry for the things you had to endure. But you are safe now. Zen sent a troop to get those kids out and send them to someone he knows. They will be taken care of. If they have any special abilities, they'll have the option of coming here."

Naomi leaned her head on my shoulder. "Thank you, Ava. Not just for today, but when you left, you gave me the courage to be better. Sure, having fire power helped, but courage had to come from within. You set an example for all of us. You showed us we can make a difference in any circumstances. When you tried to defend us, Vito beat you with a belt and belittled you by calling you a rat, but you never cowered. You had to be scared, but I saw the strength in your eyes. I knew you were different. Actions speak louder than words. You didn't know it then, but your actions screamed."

I didn't know what to say as my own tears threatened to fall. I had felt like I had failed everyone I'd left behind with Vito, even pushed the thoughts of them aside, pretending they never existed. Out of guilt, or maybe shame, I'd never wanted to revisit my past. But hearing Naomi's words choked me up.

Mom would be proud of me.

Did you hear what Naomi said, Mom? I made a difference.

CHAPTER SIXTEEN – OZZIE

RHETT

When Naomi showed up, Rhett could tell she wanted to talk to Ava, so he left the girls to themselves. As soon as Rhett entered, he searched for Ozzie.

Sometimes Ozzie liked to examine the equipment in Zen's lab, so he peeked in there.

Zen's team was dressed in white lab coats. One of Zen's men held a lab notebook, reading and comparing notes to something in a petri dish. Two other men held up vials filled with pale liquids, talking to each other, while a woman melted a tiny portion of the meteor over a burner.

Rhett decided not to interrupt to ask for an update regarding Brooke's remedy. He didn't want them to stop on account of him.

Rhett sought out Ozzie in his room. No Ozzie. He looked for him at the dining room. Sometimes he asked for snacks. Rhett spotted Reyna with Jo, Tamara, Cleo, and the kids, but no Ozzie.

Strange. Very strange.

Rhett went to the main office and made a call to Nick and Katina from the mountain rebel base to give them an update. Afterward, he decided to check up on Brooke. Rhett found Ozzie hunched over the life-support casket, watching her with a frown.

Rhett strode in and checked the monitor to ensure Brooke was stable. Nothing had changed from the last time.

"Everything okay?" Rhett stood opposite Ozzie and waved his hand in front of his face.

"Rhett." Ozzie flinched and pushed back his shoulders.

"What are you doing?"

Ozzie didn't look at Rhett. He looked about the room like he was reeling and couldn't rest. Probably trying to figure out how to tell Rhett why he was acting like a stalker.

It wasn't the first time Rhett had found him alone with Brooke. He hadn't asked about it, because it was none of his business.

Ozzie puffed his cheeks like a chipmunk storing food and then exhaled a long breath. "I feel like I know her."

The anguish in his tone cracked Rhett's heart.

"What do you mean? You do know her, sort of. You met her at ISAN when Mitch captured you, remember?"

Ozzie placed a hand over his heart, a grave expression replacing his confused one. "When I saw Brooke at ISAN, I felt something, a connection. I don't know how to explain it. But seeing her here, the feeling is stronger. I thought I was going out of my mind. I don't want to go crazy. I still remember the serum and how it made me lose control until I hurt people."

Ozzie was talking about two different subjects. He wasn't making sense. And his defeated tone pierced Rhett's heart. His pain, his self-reproach, had Rhett worried.

"You're not insane, Oz." Rhett squeezed his shoulder and shook lightly. "You're having these feelings for a reason. You can work it out. Just talk to me."

"Do you think ISAN took away my memory? You heard Zen. If they took away some of the girls' memories of their life before ISAN and gave them fake ones, isn't it possible they did the same to me?"

"I suppose." Rhett crossed his arms and braced for what Ozzie would spill. "Your memories are true from when you started ISAN. Everything you know and who you know from that time is real. I'm sorry, but I can't be sure about your past. Until we are, let's not jump to conclusions."

Rhett tried to reassure him, but even the possibility Ozzie's memories had been erased killed Rhett.

"I didn't volunteer like you. I had foster parents like Ava. What if I knew Brooke then? What if she meant something to me?" Ozzie touched the case and stared at Brooke.

"What do you feel when you look at her?"

Ozzie swallowed, the hand on the casket trembling. "I just can't ... I don't know." He clutched at his chest. "A longing for someone. I don't have a name for it. I hate this feeling. I don't want it."

"I promise you we'll figure it out together." Rhett wanted to punch the wall. Novak and Verlot had to pay for everything they had done.

I know your pain, my friend. I know it well.

When Ava hadn't remembered who Rhett was, he'd gone ballistic. Rhett had hit just about anything and anyone in his path. Ozzie and Reyna had been there for him when nothing else helped, and he would help him through this.

Brooke needed to wake up, not just for herself, but for Ozzie and Ava. If she died, he would never know the truth and might fall in the pit of his own darkness. And Ava would drown in guilt.

"You told me your mother gave you up when you were born, so you lived with your foster parents all your life?"

"Yes. That's what I've been told by my foster parents. But

maybe they lied to me."

"Remind me why or how you got to ISAN," Rhett said.

"I wanted to be a council guard. So, after I turned eighteen, my foster parents signed me up. They thought it would be good for me. ISAN doesn't exist to the world. How did my foster parents know to sign me up?"

"Maybe they got a private letter like Mitch and I did."

"Or maybe they thought they were signing me up to be a council guard, but it was for ISAN."

"That's a possibility, given ISAN's record of lies and manipulation. But it doesn't explain why you think you knew Brooke before ISAN. Unless …"

"What? What are you thinking?"

Rhett leaned his back against the wall. "Perhaps you were trained somewhere else and Brooke was there as well. But then what purpose would they have to erase your memory?"

Ozzie's eyes gleamed. "Maybe Brooke and I had a thing and they didn't like it. After I escaped from East, they sent in Brooke. Brooke wasn't there when we were, right? Do you remember anything?"

"No, she wasn't. Your theory seems plausible, but don't hold on to it. There's still a lot of room for you to be wrong."

Ozzie tilted his head against the glass and released a long sigh. "If I'm right, and Brooke and I loved each other, I swear to God, Rhett, I'm going to kill Novak. I'm going to blow up ISAN." His words were muffled against the casket.

Rhett patted his friend's back. "I know how you feel. Ava and I will help you."

"I don't know. I don't know anything anymore. I'm so tired. I put on a smile and go day by day like we all do. But I want a normal life." He stood upright and rubbed the spot on his forehead where he'd rested on the glass. "I know you want the same thing. Just about everyone here does. I didn't mean to make it all about me."

"It's fine, man. You're allowed to express your thoughts. If you can't to me, then who, right? I do think about it a lot. I wish Ava and I could live among the citizens and have a mundane life." Rhett snorted and kicked a pebble by his feet. "Unfortunately, it is what it is."

"Yeah." His eyes lowered to Brooke.

"I stopped by Zen's lab. They're working hard. They're going to help her. Don't give up hope."

"Yeah. It's all we have left. And, I thought I overheard Cleo telling the girls one of her employees dropped off some pastries. Want to join me?"

Rhett had no appetite for sweets, but he didn't want to leave his friend alone.

"Come on, Einstein. Let's get you all fed and happy again."

Ozzie hiked up an eyebrow. Unable to hold onto an annoyed expression, he let out a goofy laugh.

It was a relief to see him lighten up. Life was too short for what-ifs.

CHAPTER SEVENTEEN – THE NEWS

AVA

Naomi and I practiced until my chip dinged with a message from Rhett.

Where are you? I miss you.

I smiled and something warm tugged my heart.

I'm with Naomi. I'll be in shortly, I sent back.

"Let's rest a bit and practice later," Naomi said.

"Sure. We should go in."

Instead of regrouping with the others, I took Naomi to meet Brooke. Seeing her in that awful casket broke me every time I visited.

"I'm sorry about your friend, Ava." Naomi caressed my arm as she looked at Brooke.

I sighed, my heart filled with rocks. "She's going to be fine. She has to."

"She will be." Naomi gave a tightlipped smile. "Tell me more about your friends."

I told Naomi about Rhett, Brooke, Tamara, Ozzie, Reyna, Zen, and about ISAN.

Life might not have treated Naomi well, but it hadn't for any of us. Now war was brewing, and we were in the dark. The more our side knew about the ISAN network, the better for all of us.

"Well, I'm glad you're here now, or I might not have found

you," Naomi said.

"Me too." I smiled and examined Brooke's IV bag. Someone had given her a new one.

You're a fighter, Brooke. We got what Zen needed. Just hang on.

"There you are." Rhett strode in with a lazy grin. "Your assignment group is preparing for dinner, but I told them you need to be excused."

"Oh ..." I tapped the heel of my palm on the bridge of my nose. "I'm sorry. I forgot."

"It's fine. You need the rest anyway."

"I should probably find Momo." Naomi glanced between Rhett and me and headed out before I could stop her.

"Wait. We should be out there, too." I linked my arm through Rhett's and escorted him to the waiting area.

All the remaining south rebels had positioned themselves outside the medical room. Some sat on the ground—others stood or leaned against the wall. They all had on their caps. A mark of a solid team.

Two hours had passed, but they still waited to hear news from Zen about Bobo.

"Hey." Reyna smiled when we approached. She was standing next to Ozzie and Cleo.

Tamara weaved around them to stand next to me. "You okay?"

"Yes. I was catching up with Naomi."

"Oh, I see. Good." Tamara smiled at Naomi.

"Naomi, I want to let you know that the foster kids are in good hands now." Cleo showed her a hologram photo of the kids with a woman I'd never seen before. "She works for Councilor Chang. Chang's soldiers stormed the coordinates you gave me. They charged in this morning. All the kids they found are safe and well."

Naomi's shoulders slumped and tears formed in her eyes. "Thank you so much. I'm so relieved."

"Vito will get what he deserves," Ozzie added. "He's still detained with Zeke, but he's scheduled to be taken to Councilor Chang. Zen wants to interrogate him first and find out if there are more bounty hunters. No doubt there are. He can't be the only one making tons of 4Qs selling kids to ISAN."

Rhett crossed his arms and rocked on his heels. "Good. All good news."

Coco waved, awake and sitting on the ground next to Momo. The overuse of her power had left her eyes a bit puffy and her cheeks flushed, but otherwise she looked fine.

"Coco, I'm glad to see you well," I said. "You feeling okay?"

She hugged Bobo's cap like it was her teddy bear. "Yes. Thank you. Exhausted, but well. But you shouldn't waste your time worrying about me."

Oh, Coco, you are worth worrying about.

"You were brave and so strong. Thank you for helping us."

"I was glad to help. I wish I could've done more." Her long eyelashes lowered.

Poor kid. I knew her guilt like it was my best friend.

"You did all you could have done. Whatever happens to Bobo is not your fault. You don't get to choose who lives or dies."

I should take my own advice—or Rhett's advice.

Rhett cleared his throat and whispered, "Sounds like someone took my two cents to heart."

"I did, didn't I?" I scoffed playfully. "Well, look at that. I do listen … sometimes. And your two cents are worth hundreds."

"Bobo is going to make it, right?" Coco asked. "On missions

with ISAN, getting hit by bullets didn't affect us much. I mean, Dr. Machine fixed everything faster. We did have gear on, but ..."

I stroked her hair. "Zen is doing his best."

"What's taking so long?" Momo shot up from the ground and paced to the end of the hall and back.

I'm thinking the same thing, kid.

"Does that mean it's bad?" Another kid, sitting with her knees tucked into her chest, peered up at Jo.

"I don't know. Bobo is a fighter." Jo rubbed at her temples, and then the nape of her neck.

Silence filled the air. Some of the kids rested their heads on each other's shoulders. A few wrapped arms around each other. I found comfort in their closeness.

In East ISAN, it was all about competition, which faction would beat out the other for rewards. There was no room for the friendship or support these kids showed one another.

ISAN molded competitors. Robotic, cold, killing machines. Justine was a prime example. But these kids, they were different. When they had been at the most vulnerable age, they had not surrendered to the system. ISAN hadn't broken them down.

Kudos to them.

I tried to think back when my mother had died. I'd been scared, needed reassurance everything was going to be fine, and I'd wanted a sense of home. Perhaps, somehow, these kids found security in each other. Like I had found with Brooke and Tamara.

Gasps and murmurs rippled down the hall when Zen came out. Feet shuffled. Kids gathered around Jo, holding tightly to each other like a lifeline.

Zen faced the gathered crowd, his expression unreadable. His Adam's apple bobbed as he swallowed. "We did everything we could under the circumstances. The bullet had a sharp tip. Either the bullet hit his heart, or it moved, as that kind of bullet does. I'm so sorry, but unfortunately Dr. Crumb and I could not save Bobo. You can say your goodbyes once the medical staff finishes cleaning up."

A cruel joke. It had to be a cruel joke. But nobody laughed.

It felt like a dream. No one spoke. No one moved.

Would Bobo's death sentence become Brooke's?

The softest crunching of pebbles from Zen's retreating steps sounded like a roar in the quiet. Then Momo screamed. And screamed. Ear-piercing wails filled the space. People came out of their tents, looking worried. Even Frank and his men ran from their office.

This couldn't be happening.

This is war, Ava. People get hurt. People die. But not kids. Not the kids.

Rhett enveloped Momo in his arms, but her screaming did not yield. Then one by one, as if the news washed over them in a wave, the kids wept.

Tears trickled down my cheek. They had been through so much. First the deaths of the other half of their crew, and when they'd thought they were safe, one was taken from them.

Guilt crashed through my resolve. If only I had stopped the bullets.

My fault.

No. You do not get to choose who lives or dies.

But still ...

As self-reproach circulated through my mind, I told myself never again. I would not be vulnerable again. I had to fix this. I had to learn how to will the gifts in me. All of them.

Father had experimented on me, said I was special. I had to find out how, exactly, or Father was one big fat liar and a fool.

Jo released Coco's trembling body, and she too wept as she spoke, each word coming harder. "It's not your fault. You were doing your duty. The bullet bouncing off your light doesn't make it your fault. You had no control. It could have ricocheted off a wall with the same result. Do you understand?"

"We shouldn't have been there." Coco shook her head frantically, wiping her tears with her sleeve. "But we wanted to help. We wanted to make a difference, to stop ISAN from doing the things to other kids they did to us. But we ended up killing Bobo. Bobo is dead. He's dead. He's never coming back. Why? Why does it have to be another one of us to die? Why doesn't ISAN die?"

Oh, my heart. Air left my lungs in gasps. I fought back the sting in my eyes and sank to my knees.

"Coco." I stroked her hair to get her attention. "If you weren't there, *none* of us would have made it out. Though there is nothing we can do to bring Bobo back, you can do something for him."

"What? I'll do anything." She sniffled.

I caressed Coco's hair, the way my mother had once caressed mine. "You start by forgiving yourself. He would have never blamed you, as you wouldn't have blamed him if things were reversed. You honor his name by moving forward and continuing to fight. Fight to stop ISAN, and fight for your future, and for every one of your friends. You have a special gift. It wasn't given to you just to give up." I leaned in closer so only she could hear the rest. "You are a leader now. If you fall apart, so will your friends. They need you to be strong, to give them guidance and hope. It's okay to cry. It's okay to grieve, but afterwards, be like a dandelion. Be resilient."

Coco straightened her spine, and her tears stopped flowing. Though young, she became the portrait of a soldier.

A renegade.

"Thank you," Jo said when I rose. "You've been an inspiration to all of us. We're lucky to be here."

I parted my lips to speak, but my tongue knotted. I never handled compliments well. My speech to Coco hadn't just been for her—it was for me, too. So I simply smiled.

I never had the chance to tell Jo I gave her a lot of credit for all she had done. The kids were well-behaved and mature for their age under her guidance. She was an inspiration, whether she knew it or not.

"Everyone." Jo's voice boomed with authority. "We're going in together as one family to say goodbye to Bobo. Please walk and stay behind me."

I would give my last respects to Bobo after his friends. My squad stayed behind, indicating they would do the same.

When Jo and the kids disappeared into the room, I turned to my friends. "Brooke."

Rhett nodded. "Zen's crew have been working on it. We should hear back from them soon."

"Okay." I sighed.

Ozzie gazed toward the dining area. "Dinner is almost ready. I know we don't have much appetite, but you should all keep up your strength."

I almost laughed, but I could only produce a faint smile. He was always thinking about food.

Even though I hadn't had lunch, I didn't feel like eating, but my stomach protested with the aroma of baked chicken.

"Someone is hungry." Tamara snorted, but it died quickly.

No one laughed. No one spoke. No one moved. We all stared into the gloom of despair.

"Well, if you're going to eat at all today, do it before Councilor Chang arrives," Reyna said.

Cleo narrowed her eyes. "Are you sure she's coming? She canceled twice before. I didn't want to say anything to my father, but ..."

"It's been confirmed," Tamara said. "I spoke to Frank earlier. She'll arrive later tonight."

"You guys go on ahead to the dining hall." Naomi tipped her head to the side, tears pooling in her eyes. "I'm going to wait until they come out."

"I'm so sorry." I caressed Naomi's arm, knowing it would not comfort her.

"I can't believe I got to see him again and now he's gone."

"I know. It's ..." This was so hard. No words could make this better. I felt my heart tearing, not just for Bobo, but from missing my mother. Fresh tears pooled in my eyes no matter how hard I tried to hold them back.

"Anyway, I'm going with Ozzie. He's hungry." Tamara tugged him lightly, backing away. "We'll all meet up soon."

Ozzie looked confused but didn't protest.

"Sure. I'll see you guys in the dining hall. Rhett and I need to take care of something."

Rhett frowned and then understanding played on his face. As we left, I took a peek at the kids. Their heads were inclined with their caps to their hearts. Then I heard the somber voices, cutting my heart into pieces.

"You will always be remembered, Bobo. Renegades forever. The fallen will never be forgotten."

CHAPTER EIGHTEEN – BROTHER FROM HELL

RHETT

Ava took Rhett to the basement, where a cool draft greeted him. With a curt nod, he told the guards they were there to see Gene and asked them to wait upstairs.

When the other half of the room lit up, Gene appeared behind the thick glass divider, sitting in a cool, relaxed manner on a cot. Leaning back, he crossed his legs and folded his hands.

Rhett studied Gene's face. His eyes were the same color as Ava's, but Gene had a sharper nose and squared jawline.

Gene also had an angelic face, the kind you would trust easily. He was a handsome guy, but the way he glared at Ava made Rhett feel aggressive.

"You're back. And who is this … Ahh, the one and only Rhett. You look taller and younger than I expected. So you're the one who fed Ava lies. You made her into a traitor. So, what can I do to entertain you both? That is why you came here, isn't it?"

Gene's tone was calm and nonthreatening, but Rhett's anger built as Gene talked. Not that he hadn't believed Ava when she told him he was stubborn and hard to deal with.

Ava rolled her eyes and approached the glass. "You were boring then and you're boring now. I'm not here because I want to be. I'm here for your sake. I need to tell you something because I feel like you have the right to know."

Gene twisted his lips at the corner and flicked something off his fingernails. "I'll only listen if you let me out of here. I want to be up there, to feel the sun in my face."

"Maybe later. *If* you behave," Ava said with a hint of sarcasm.

Be nice, Gene. Ava needs you.

"If *I* behave?" Gene laughed dryly. "I've been nothing but a perfect prisoner. Do you see me trying to escape? Besides, there is nothing you can tell me. I know everything I need to know."

You're in for a shock, asshole.

Ava slammed her hand on the divider. "Gene, I'm not going to beat around the bush, I'm just going to say it. You're my twin brother. I'm your twin sister." When he stared at Ava blankly, she continued. "Dr. Hunt, our father, is the scientist who created HelixB77 that jump-started ISAN."

Gene rose and stood with his eyes locked on the polished floor.

A few seconds later, a strange sound burst out of him. A dry, humorless cackle.

Rhett flinched.

"You're so desperate to have me on your side, you'll tell me anything. I'll admit, you had me there for a second." Gene sat back down and spread himself across the cot, all casualness.

"I'm not lying." Ava raised her fist as if to punch the barrier, but stopped herself and lowered her arm. "Why would I? I've been looking for my twin, but you're the last person I expected. Zen did a routine DNA test when we brought you in and there's no doubt. Do you think I want you to be my brother? Even the thought repulses me. But because you're my brother, I need to tell you something. Maybe it will open your eyes."

Ava started from the beginning, from the day her mother died. From living with her foster father to landing in ISAN with Russ.

She explained how she met me and our escape. She left out names, but gave enough details to offer a believable truth.

After she was done, Gene's face went neutral, but Rhett knew the wheels were spinning. Gene stayed quiet and absorbed. Then he rose. One slow step at a time, Gene walked toward Ava, never taking his eyes off her.

Please say something good for Ava's sake.

Ava waited in silence. She crossed her arms, and then uncrossed them several times, unable to make up her mind.

Gene's eyes darkened and his facial muscles tightened into a sneer. "You're a disgrace to ISAN. I'd rather die than be your brother. I don't care what the DNA says. It's a lie. You're lying. Zen's lying. You're all lying."

Ava covered her face with her hands and shook her head. "Idiot. You're infuriating." She looked back up at him. "What kind of proof would it take for you to believe me?"

The pleading in her voice cracked something inside Rhett. He wanted to take Ava out of here. Whether Gene would believe her had always been in question, but Ava had frantically searched for her twin.

She was hoping he would come around. The disappointment must be eating at her.

"I need to think about it, but I already told you once. I want to feel the sun. Get some fresh air. It's a simple request. What could go wrong? It's all of you against me."

What could possibly go wrong? Those were dangerous words.

Mitch's warning nagged at Rhett. *Gene might be dangerous, but he also might have information that can help us.*

Rhett saw none of that possibility.

Rhett gave Ava credit for trying. He would have already

stormed out of there. Trying to tame his rage, Rhett sat behind the monitors and read the words on the screen. *Front light. Back light. Open door. Close door. Sleeping gas.*

"Fine." Ava threw up her hands. "If you want to see the sun, then fine. I'll have to get Zen's permission, but I don't see why not."

Rhett didn't challenge her decision. He wasn't sure if she was serious or not.

"Good." Gene strode back to the cot and sat with his legs spread out in front of him, as if they were having a pleasant conversation. "Now, what do you want to ask me? Obviously, there's a reason you haven't left yet."

Ava shifted on her feet. "I want to know your abilities. You and I are supposed to be genetically extraordinary, but I never saw anything unique about you."

"Well, neither did I about *you*." He chuckled. "So, what's so special about you, Ava?"

Ava inhaled a deep breath, then sighed. "We're here to talk about you."

Gene was a blink away from Rhett shutting down the barrier and punching him in the face, so he focused back to the screen. *Volume. Air vent. Temperature control.*

"Well, in that case, *sister,* I'll tell you this and see if you can figure it out. ISAN took a bunch of samples of my blood. Then they came up with a new serum called HelixB88. I was told never to tell anyone."

Ava's jaw dropped, and she looked dumbfounded. "What?" She slowly backed away as if she feared he would break through the thick glass.

Rhett hoped she realized letting him go outside was out of the question.

"You heard me." Gene dusted something off his shirt and rolled the sleeves up on each arm. "HelixB77 was too strong for the other males, but I never had any of the side effects. So they used my DNA to create HelixB88."

Holy shit.

If he was telling the truth, he could have the strength to punch a hole through the concrete wall and escape. But wouldn't he have done it already?

"Go on." Ava began pacing.

Gene gave her an insufferably cocky grin. "If you're wondering why I never led a team, don't. I'm going to tell you all about your so-called lost brother. I suck at giving orders, but I'm good at getting things done. I have no patience with people, but I'm patient when it comes to plotting rebel deaths."

Ava's nostrils flared and she slammed her fist against the barrier. "What's wrong with you? Why can't you see ISAN is using girls, and now boys, and children? They're using us as weapons to take over our nation and then the world."

Gene tapped his shoes and peered up to the florescent panel ceiling, and then back to Ava. "There's only one answer, and no one is going to change my mind, *sister.* I've told you once, and I'm going to tell you again. I agree with everything ISAN is doing."

"What about taking our memories and implanting new false ones? How do you know if your memories have been taken from you?"

"*My* memories are just fine. I know one thing for sure, ISAN manipulates the girls' memories, but had a problem with some guys—something to do with our chemical makeup. I suppose we men are superior."

146

Ava shuddered, veins protruding from her neck.

Gene stood and ambled to the glass. His gait—confident and predatory—reminded Rhett of someone. Who? Gene stopped two paces from the glass.

Touch the glass. I dare you to touch the glass.

Gene's eyes roamed over Ava's body. "It's too bad you don't agree with me, sister. We could take over the world together."

Ava closed her eyes, clenching and unclenching her fists. Rhett could see how much she was holding back and how disappointed she felt.

Ava opened her eyes and smiled. "Well, too bad you can't fulfill your dreams. You can forget about your fresh air and the sun, you freak. You're going to be staying in that tiny square for the rest of your pathetic life."

Gene moved another step forward, his face fuming with hot steam.

Come on. Touch it. Just one more step.

"You. Bitch." Gene's chest rose and fell rapidly as if he couldn't get enough air, and in those eyes, hatred was a living thing. Then like Dr. Jekyll and Mr. Hyde, his expression softened. His lips curled, then grew wider as if he was thinking of something funny. "I can't wait to show you my little surprise." He tapped his fingertips together. "Boom. Boom. Boom. All gone."

"What do you mean?" Ava banged on the glass repeatedly.

Rhett was about to go over and stop her when Gene positioned his hand on the glass for a second. She lowered her fist. His action caused Ava to steady.

"Easy, sis." He winked. "I wouldn't want you to die from a heart attack before you got to witness the boom." He threw his head back with boisterous laughter.

"I'm done with you. You're insane. You're never getting out of here." Then like a true leader, she pivoted and walked away with her head held high.

"Come back here. You can't leave. I'm not done with you. You don't get to—" Gene hammered the glass with his fist.

Perfect.

Rhett had enough. He switched on the speaker so Gene could hear him nice and loud. "Have a taste of your many *booms* to come."

Gene's steely eyes flashed to Rhett's with a promise of revenge. Then a red laser centered on Gene's chest. His body went rigid with terror as blue and silver light engulfed him. Rhett had given him enough of a shock to hurt like hell and render him unconscious.

Rhett caught up to Ava halfway up the stairs. Draping his arm around her shoulders, he led her away from the douchebag.

"I'm not sure why I didn't think about giving him shock therapy myself," Ava said lightly, as if it were no big deal, as if it hadn't caused him pain. "Thank you for acting on my behalf. I feel so much better. I'm surprised at how well I'm dealing with the need to choke him."

"I'm so sorry, babe. I thought if you told him you were his sister, he would come around. Any *normal* person would."

"He's something else." Ava shook her head. "Definitely not normal. It's like he's been brainwashed. You think if I hadn't escaped, I would have become like him?"

"No. Never. Even when you had no memories of me, you felt something was off, didn't you? You questioned why there were only female assassins, right? You were searching for more, am I not mistaken?"

"True. I did question many things. What do you think he meant by *boom*?"

"I'm not sure, but I'll make it up to you. I'll show you a different kind of *boom*—one that will make you forget the world."

Ava smacked Rhett's ass as they ascended back to reality and whispered in his ear. "Show me tonight."

Rhett wished it was night already. When the world slept and Ava was alone with him, their secluded room was his favorite place to be. Right beside her was where he belonged. Anywhere with her was home.

CHAPTER NINETEEN – COUNCILOR CHANG

AVA

I f Rhett had not been with me, I might have killed Gene myself. I walked out of the basement feeling unfinished.

What had he meant by *boom*? *Boom* to me meant explosion. A bomb.

Surely ISAN didn't know about this base or they would have already destroyed it. But they wouldn't risk Gene's life, would they?

Come to think of it, they would. ISAN didn't care about Gene. He was a dedicated soldier who would someday die on a mission anyway.

Loyalty be damned.

After Rhett and I reported to Zen about the incident with Gene, we went to pay our last respects to Bobo. Bobo's slender body had been covered with a white sheet, his face exposed. His eyes were closed, and his chest so still—the only visible evidence he was dead.

My heart splintered when Rhett's voice cracked.

"I'm sorry, Bobo. You should have had a better life, but you're safe now. I know you'll watch out for your brothers and sister from the afterlife." Rhett turned away with his hand pressed to his forehead.

I hadn't gotten to know Bobo well, but he had been part of our fight against ISAN, and he'd only been thirteen-years old.

"Rest in peace, Bobo," I said softly. "You will always be remembered."

The sun had set and the moon had risen. Gone was the daylight, replaced by lanterns and dim lights powered by the solar panels. In contrast to our grief, the compound was peaceful, even beautiful. There was something wondrous about the lights in the darkness.

Rhett and I were about to grab something to eat when an annoying horn bellowed through the air. Councilor Chang had landed.

The fighters gathered by the entrance and waited. Her appearance was top secret, and only a handful would be invited to the private meeting after the greeting.

Seconds turned to minutes, and then finally Zen walked in. Next, a cloaked figure strolled in the middle of a dozen guards clad in dark uniforms. Their boots clanked in unison.

Chestnut hair spilled over her shoulders when Councilor Chang lowered her hood. Her incandescent dark eyes sparkled amid the lanterns.

When I'd seen her at the gala, I'd been on the second floor, which might be the reason I'd imagined her taller. Unlike at the fundraiser, she wasn't wearing makeup now, which made her pretty face look younger, almost innocent, even if it was public knowledge she was in her upper forties.

Chang waved like a princess, smiling as applause filled the cool air.

"Good evening, everyone. I'm humbled and honored to be here." She kept her hand raised until the noise ceased. "I know you have many questions. Let's get comfortable and we can proceed."

The guards surrounded her again when Zen guided us to the back corner by a campfire. Rickety chairs surrounded the flame.

151

I edged closer to the fire. It had been unbearably cold at night. The only thing I missed about ISAN was it was always the perfect temperature.

"Please have a seat," Zen said. "Councilor Chang, please take the center one." He ushered her to his brown-leather office chair, the finest condition relic I'd seen so far.

The best for our councilor.

She'd better be worth the trouble.

After a quick introduction, Jasper and Stella appeared with a tray of steaming, recyclable paper mugs. Councilor Chang grabbed one with a polite nod, as did a few others. But the guards standing behind her did not even flinch when Stella offered them a drink.

"They're fine," the councilor said. "They're not allowed to drink while on duty." She took a slow sip. "Chamomile tea with honey. My favorite. Thank you."

Zen drank from his cup and sat beside the councilor. Frank and his men—Hansh, Miguel, and Owen—sat on the other side of Zen. Rhett, Ozzie, Reyna, Tamara, Cleo, and I sat on the opposite side, facing Chang.

Frank bent lower and rubbed his hands close to the blaze. "Councilor Chang, as Zen informed you earlier, we need more support, weapons or at least more funds if you're unable to supply us. Also, do you have any updates?"

Chang crossed her legs, showing long black boots as her cloak cascaded beside her. "I'm doing the best I can. All the councilors' accounts are being monitored, especially our personal ones. We're all being watched. I'm not sure how Verlot is funding ISAN. He must have other resources and people behind him. It's the only explanation. This Mr. Novak you speak of, I can't find him in our system. No surprise there. However, I'm being creative and finding ways to provide you with what you need, thanks to my trusted advisor. In a week, you will get arsenal supplies, food, and items on the list to make your stay here more comfortable."

Several people murmured *thank you.*

"I have a question." I raised my hand. When Chang gave me a curt nod, I laid it out. "Zen told me he informed you about a group formerly called SAN, an acronym for Superhuman Advocacy Network, but now called ANS—Advocacy Network for Superhumans. They were aggressive. Demanded either we surrender or die. Do you know anything about this group?"

Chang stroked a hand down her hair. "I know of them, but I don't have any details to share with you. They are not my main concern. If memory serves, ANS demanded you surrender when you were with ISAN, correct?"

"Yes."

"So then you have nothing to fear. They will not hunt you or the rebels."

"But they will go after people still in ISAN who were coerced into joining and are only doing what they must to survive. What about them?"

"I'm sorry, Ava, but we can't help everyone and stop every armed group out there trying to destroy each other. We can deal with them later. Our main priority is ISAN because they are well funded and technologically advanced. Perhaps once they are down, the other independent networks will fall on their own. Our country is still rebuilding. We finally have a good system, but it's not good enough. We may never find a perfect system, but we must all try toward a better world."

I supposed she was right. ANS had gone after me because of my connection with ISAN.

"Was Thomax Thorpe one of your men?" I asked.

Thomax had been the first person to tell me ISAN was corrupt. His name would always stay with me, especially since I had killed him.

"No. That name doesn't sound familiar. Perhaps he was working for ANS? But I do have someone working for me undercover in ISAN East."

Who? Mitch, I already knew. But he'd stayed behind to be a spy in an agreement with Rhett. So he couldn't be the one. Lydia? Diana? One of the guards? Russ? But Russ would have told me, right? Knowing Chang wouldn't share, I didn't pursue my curiosity.

"Zen has informed me one of your escaped agents is in need of a remedy for HelixB88." Chang reached into her pocket and pulled out a sheet of folded paper. "My trusted spy has given me the formula. The reason for my delay. I was hoping to give you something to earn your faith. Know that your dedication and hard work sometimes pay off."

I about fell off my chair. Rhett draped an arm around my shoulder. I smiled at him, grateful.

"Thank you," I said to Chang. "This means a lot to me."

But you still don't have my trust—not all of it.

"Thank you." Zen shoved the paper inside his pants pocket. "This is going to help. My team and I have almost analyzed the formula, but something was missing."

"You might want to look into Gene's DNA." I recalled Gene's words. "When Rhett and I went to see him, he said they'd used his DNA to create HelixB88."

Murmured curses came from around the fire.

Zen flickered his eyelids. "When I ran his blood test, it was to confirm whether he had 88 in his system. I haven't drawn blood from him after the first round. I'll do it again to see if it's any different. Let me take yours as well. Perhaps I can find something in your genome that explains why you were less susceptible to the 88. However, it could be your makeup is naturally resilient but not specifically resistant."

"Perhaps." I scrunched my nose and glowered into the crackling fire.

Sparks flickered like tiny fireworks when Rhett poked a metal rod into the logs.

"Interesting." Chang fixed her eyes to our people passing in the distance and took a gulp of her tea.

"Did Gene tell you anything else?" Frank tapped the rim of the cup in a steady rhythm. "I tried to ask him questions, but he's—"

"He's charming, isn't he?" Rhett flashed his teeth, disdain in his tone.

Frank scoffed. "To say the least."

I wanted to tell Frank to stop tapping at the cup, but thankfully Zen placed a hand over his arm.

"Gene has known ISAN all his life," Zen said. "We don't know how he was raised or the people who raised him."

"How about us?" Reyna shifted in her seat and tossed a pebble into the fire. "We are all victims, but we're not ISAN-crazy."

"He might come around—"

"No, not him." Rhett jabbed the metal rod into the dirt by his feet. "He can't be trusted. Don't let your guard down around him. He knows something. Mitch told me so, but he doesn't know what. He might want to show us when we least expect it. If he has HelixB88 in his system naturally, who knows what he can do? I'm surprised he hasn't escaped."

"It's impenetrable," Zen said matter-of-factly.

I ran a lazy hand down my face and yawned. Today had been one long day. "I agree with Rhett. Don't give him any leniency. Don't let him out of your sight. He's up to something."

Zen scratched the back of his head. "Fine. But I'm going to have to see him to draw more blood."

"When you do, let us escort you." Cleo's voice was soft but persistent.

"Let us continue to the next topic on our agenda." Chang scrolled the screen she'd pulled up from her chip. "I'm afraid I'm running out of time. We clock in and we clock out. Yes, we keep a log of each other's whereabouts. Not a trusting system, I'm afraid. As far as the rest of the councilors are concerned, I'm visiting my sister. Unfortunately, my sister knows more than she should. I had no choice but to tell her—I need all the allies I can get."

"Of course." Zen pulled up a hologram list from his chip. "The last topic is regarding the group of girls causing attention in the news."

"Yes." Chang shivered and tugged her cloak over her lap. "I've got my guards tailing one group and patrolling for suspicious activities that could indicate others. It is all I can do without causing alarm among citizens. I am also concerned about Verlot's scouting team. They have most likely captured some we weren't aware of. I'm afraid of the worst—if they didn't comply with his demands to join ISAN, what happened to them? I also know he's been paying families to take their children."

She was right. Drew had confessed to me his family had been paid.

"What about the other councilors? Martinez and Jones."

Ozzie finished his last drop of tea and placed the mug on the small flat rock he used as a side table. "Do they know what's going on?"

"My reps are trying to find out. This is a sensitive matter. If one of them is allied with Verlot, we'd face an unfortunate dilemma. If none of them are, they might not believe me."

Owen leaned back and smoothed his hair. "So I guess there is nothing to do but wait."

"I'm afraid so." Chang rose and adjusted the hood over her head. "I flew here with two gliders so I can leave one behind. She's fast and high tech, the latest model. She was licensed to my sister who has graciously reported it stolen. I'm sorry, but I had no other choice."

"Thank you." Zen gave her a curt bow. "We'll just have to be careful."

"Oh, one more thing." She handed Zen a zip drive, about the size of my thumb. "Upload this to all your people's chips. This tech will prevent drones from identifying your faces. The drones will pass you as if you didn't exist."

"Cool," Tamara squealed, and then shrugged sheepishly when everyone looked at her.

I laughed inwardly. Her excitement was infectious.

Chang buttoned her cape and lowered her hands to the pockets. "Well, then. I think we've covered all bases. Please be careful and I'll be in touch. Unless you have any questions, I should leave."

When we'd been told Councilor Chang would visit us, I had a list of questions I'd wanted to ask. We had barely escaped ISAN, Brooke was in a coma, and I'd had enough of Novak. I had been hot headed, full of myself, thinking I would give her my two cents. I'd wanted to know what she was doing to help.

I'd hoped she wasn't one of those leaders that was all talk. Had she even risked anything for us? Did she have anything to lose?

Seeing Chang in person and hearing her dedication to stop ISAN and make our world a better place, I found my questions regarding her motives had lessened somewhat, but I still didn't trust her.

Yes, she'd provided us with the formula for the remedy to Brooke's B88 poisoning, but would it be effective? She'd risked her sister's life. How could I know she was telling us the truth?

She'd flown late at night, risking her own life, and was leaving behind a glider. Such tasks were easily done.

"Thank you for taking the time to visit." Zen shook Chang's hands. "It shows we are united."

"I wanted to see the faces of the rebels. Those who were taking a chance with me." Chang looked at each of us in turn. "It takes a team to get the work done."

"Yes, it does." Zen patted Frank's back, but also looked at us proudly.

Chang weaved around the fire to stand in front of me and placed a gentle hand on my arm. "Zen has told me so much about you, Ava. I feel like I already know you. I just want to say thank you." Then she looked at my squad. "You're all so young, but you're so brave. I commend you all for your sacrifices for a better future. We were born in the land of the free. Our country pulled through after perilous devastation, but we are still divided. Our collapse won't come from Mother Nature, it will come from human greed. I will not stand and watch our nation fall after we've worked so hard to rebuild. I know you won't do the same. As our forefathers have said: United we stand, divided we fall."

Then Chang's guards clustered around her and Zen led them out.

CHAPTER TWENTY – HELIX

AVA

Councilor Chang left one glider as promised. They would fly in complete darkness until high in the sky to avoid detection by the drones and anyone else.

The next morning, Zen and his team rose early to mix and test the formula Chang had given them. They planned to give Brooke a dose of the remedy as soon as they created one that would work. I needed to do something before I went out of my mind, so Rhett and I finally had something to eat.

In the late afternoon, Ozzie, Cleo, and Reyna decided to train with the kids. I opted to meet up with Naomi and Tamara at the campfire where we'd held our meeting the night before. While Naomi and I waited for Tamara to join us, we picked up countless pebbles and rocks and put them in a pile.

"What are you guys doing?" Tamara flipped her pocket knife in a steady cadence, rotating her wrist.

Tamara had told us she did it to calm herself. She must be worried about Brooke, and like me, anxiety made her restless.

"You'll see." I gave her a wicked smirk.

Tamara scowled and shoved her pocket knife inside her back pocket.

"So, let me try to understand. Tamara can sense things before they happen?" Naomi stood next to the flame, unafraid of the heat.

Tamara shuffled over gravel to stand beside me. "It's hard to explain because I don't know exactly what I can do. I sense intense heat or cold when I feel something is off, kind of like having a sixth sense. But I'm very good at hitting targets, too. Knives are my specialty. I didn't tell anyone until now, but it's bizarre. I see lines of color from point A to my target. Kind of like what the Taser does for us. Sometimes blue or green but invisible to others. It's how I never miss my mark."

"Hmmm ... Ava says she sees colors, too. But I don't see what you both see. I can only ..." Naomi reached into the flame, then raised her hand, a ring of fire around it.

Tamara screamed. Her heart must have jumped out of her chest like mine. Tamara dove for Naomi but I yanked her back in mid-advance.

"I didn't mean to scare you." Naomi slapped her hands together and dissolved the flames.

"Jesus. Don't give me a heart attack, girl." Tamara placed a hand over her forehead, her chest frantically rising and falling.

She had seen Naomi produce heat from her hands on that rooftop, but not put her hand into a fire. I'd almost flipped out, too.

Then the three of us burst out in squealing laughter. Tears of mirth gathered in the corners of my eyes. Despite the sadness, it felt good to let it all out. For the moment, we were three ordinary friends enjoying each other's company.

"Okay ..." I wiped my eyes and smacked my palms together to get their attention. "Before we start, I want Tamara to cut my hair as short as hers."

"What?" Tamara's eyes widened.

Naomi raked her fingers through my long hair. "You want to cut this all off?"

160

"I've been thinking about it ever since I left ISAN. I want to look different. I need a change." I spoke in a gruff tone.

"Okay then. Let's do this." Tamara took out her pocket knife.

"Wait. You're not going to cut my hair with a knife, are you?"

"No. There are small scissors inside this pocket." She tugged on a sliver of metal, and sure enough, it extended. "See?"

I sat on a small boulder near the flame. "Cut it before I change my mind." I didn't mean to sound demanding, but I wanted anything that reminded me of ISAN gone.

As she worked, long strands of hair dropped. I already felt lighter, but also naked somehow. I wondered what Rhett would think about my new look.

"It's not perfect, but nobody will know it's not." Tamara snipped a bit more and came around me. "You look hot, Ava."

"Dang girl, you look kickass." Naomi hiked an eyebrow. "I love it. No one will want to mess with you."

I snickered and shook my head.

"Here. You can see for yourself." Tamara took something out of her back pocket and flipped open a small mirror. "What?" She shrugged when Naomi arched her eyebrows. "I like knowing I'm presentable."

It was difficult to get a clear picture of what I looked like but it was enough, and I loved it. Something new and refreshing. I couldn't wait to see the expression on Rhett's face.

"Okay. Time to get serious." I got up and pointed. "I'm going to stand here. Tamara, gather rocks and throw them at me from a distance. And we're going to step up the training. Naomi, stand in the dark area and throw them at me, too. My goal is to stop them before they hit me."

Tamara's eyes were disapproving. "Are you sure? What if I hit you on the head?"

"Then I'll hit you right back, harder. Just kidding."

Tamara let out a fake nervous cackle and took a handful of the stones. "O-kay," she sang and sauntered to her mark.

Naomi had already disappeared. She had been looking forward to training with me again.

"Ready, Ava?"

"Ready, Tams." I breathed, willing the strange yet familiar energy that had been my friend and foe since I was in my mother's womb.

"Okay, I'm going to throw one right now," Tamara shouted. *Not so loud.*

The flames became a brilliant crimson. I heard Jasper and Stella talking in the kitchen with Momo and Coco. A smell of ginger and honey tea floated to my nostrils. Helix had intensified my senses.

"Don't tell me you're going to throw—*ouch*!" I rubbed the side of my skull. A pebble had hit my head.

"I'm so sorry. But why didn't you—"

"Ouch. You hit my boob, Naomi. What happened to the below-the-chest rule?"

"There are rules?" Tamara bellowed. "Nobody told me.?"

"Stop making excuses, Ava. Admit it, you're scared."

Naomi was only trying to help me, but her words hit home and knocked me breathless. I *was* scared. So scared Brooke would not survive the remedy and I would never see her again. So utterly mad at the world for giving me an insane brother. So pissed at my father, who had created HelixB77, and … and …

A new thought crossed my mind. Gene said his blood helped to formulate HelixB88, and I'd overheard my father was still working in ISAN's lab. But had Father realized it was his son's blood?

He had to have known, right? He'd experimented on us and probably looked at our DNA hundreds of times in the course of his research.

If Father had taken his blood, then their paths would have crossed, and he must have known his own son. Had Gene seen Father without realizing it?

Another stone from Tamara hit my arm, but I kept quiet and let the pain ripple down. Then a few more from Naomi hit my legs.

"Come on, Ava. What are you waiting for?"

I vaguely heard Naomi's taunt as more pebbles pelted me.

"Maybe she needs more time, Naomi. Go easy on her."

Tamara's voice seemed to come from an increasing distance as my mind slipped into a zone.

Anger. At my mother, my brother, and especially my father and ISAN. As fury stewed in my veins at the thought of Gene and the things he'd said, the burning sensation intensified from my head to my toes, as if fire had washed over my bones.

I became a living flame inside the shell of my body, fueled by rage, revenge, and—*Be resilient,* my mother had said, as if she'd known somehow what fate had laid for my future.

You should have told me, Mother! You should have told me.

Then thoughts of Brooke and our happy time together, even though we'd been in ISAN, played through my head.

Brooke. She's in there, unconscious. Brooke. She may never wake up. Brooke. She may never know we made it out. We made it out. She should be enjoying this moment, too.

Then, as if a water balloon had filled to the max, something exploded inside me.

Red, blue, green lights flashed from my peripheral vision, but they weren't a hallucination. No, they were the rocks coming at me.

I raised my hands, palm out and whispered to Helix. *Stop.*

Tendril-like waves of energy stretched from my body like invisible hands. These wisps stopped every rock, inches from impact. Then five more launched. I coaxed more Helix and halted them midair.

Ten more. Flying at me all at once.

Twenty more.

They stilled in mid-air. Mesmerized, I stared in awe. As if they were bubbles, I poked them one by one. Each plopped to the ground.

"Ava," Naomi breathed, standing in front of me. "You did it." Her eyes gleamed bright crimson.

Was that her doing or was Helix still active and alive in me, making me see what others couldn't?

Tamara came into the circle of light, her brown eyes bigger and brighter. "You're my idol."

My friends' words faded as I shifted my focus to the dancing campfire. Red, orange, and yellow fingers of flame illuminated, and I could see where each color began and ended, their twists and turns.

Extending my hand toward the flames, I murmured, "Rise."

The inferno shot up higher and higher the more I willed it, reaching for the ceiling panels. It blazed like a giant torch, smoke hovering overhead.

I jerked and jumped back when the heat became unbearable. The fire shrank to its original size, but I couldn't believe what I had done.

With more practice, I would be faster and find other hidden abilities.

"Ava?"

I spun and almost bumped into Rhett. Sweat gleamed on his

forehead and he smelled like citrus. He must have had some oranges before he came to see me.

Rhett had changed into his form-fitting training outfit. I knew he was fit and toned, but his outfit served him well. My smile grew so wide my cheeks tugged.

"What did you do to your hair? I mean, you cut your hair? I mean, I love it. You look beautiful."

Rhett's hasty rambling made me giggle. "I asked Tamara to cut my hair short like hers. I needed something different."

Rhett ran his fingers through my strands, his amber eyes warm and tender. "I'll have to get used to it, but I love anything you love."

"Even if I buzz my hair off, you'll love it?" I said playfully.

"Sure." His tone spiked up, not convincing. "Anyway, I came to see if you ladies were okay. I thought the fire shot up almost as tall as the ceiling." Rhett squinted and sniffed, waving at the lingering smoke. "I smell something fishy. What are you girls up to?"

"Oh, stuff. Just practice." I bobbed a shoulder with a cynical smile. "They were throwing rocks at me."

"What?" Rhett scrunched his eyebrows, incredulous.

"Naomi hit my boob." I snorted.

Rhett's eyes darkened and leaned in. "Would you like me to kiss it and make it better?"

I flushed with a different kind of heat, sure my cheeks bloomed flaming red.

Naomi and Tamara smiled. Whether they'd heard Rhett, I had no idea. Our flirting ended when a shrill whistle shot through the air.

"Hey." Ozzie waved at us from the top of a debris pile with a grin brighter than it had been in days.

"What?" Rhett shouted.

Ozzie raised both fists to the sky. "Brooke is awake."

CHAPTER TWENTY-ONE – WELCOME BACK BROOKE

AVA

Brooke is awake. She's awake. Awake. Awake. Awake.
I raced to the medical room, my friends behind me. Panting, I skidded to a stop and nearly collided with Zen.

Reyna and a few others were there, waiting. I dashed to the open casket, but no Brooke.

"Where's Brooke? Oz said she's awake." I frantically searched the room.

Ozzie would have told me if something was wrong, but maybe he'd just been the messenger and didn't know anything either.

"Now, Ava, Brooke is—"

I didn't like Zen's tone, like a parent about to tell a child bad news.

"Where is she?" I shoved my face to his. It wasn't Zen's fault, but he was taking too long.

"You cut your hair?" Zen crinkled his forehead, backing away.

I didn't answer. I wasn't sure if it was a question. Was he afraid of me? He knew what I was capable of, but I would never cause harm—unless he gave me a reason.

"Brooke is with Dr. Crumb. I asked him to come to check up on Brooke. She's getting all her vitals checked. But there is something you should ... we all should be aware and speak carefully. Brooke is a bit confused. When I asked her what she

166

remembered last, she couldn't recall. I didn't want to rattle her, so I stopped asking questions. She's asking to see her mother. Brooke was brought up by foster parents, right?"

It took seconds for me to register his words. Every nerve-ending in my body went into panic mode. "Yes," I finally replied. "She had many because of her dysfunctional behavior. Brooke didn't go to online school like most kids did. She went to a special needs school for behavioral disorders. Brooke did poorly in classes and got into fights, and then finally she ended up in juvie. I don't know what she did to warrant that. I wished I'd asked her. We didn't talk much about our past."

"That's okay. I only meant for you to see her first. I didn't realize Ozzie was going to rally the whole gang." Zen tossed a scowl at Ozzie.

"Oh." Ozzie's cheeks flushed. "You told me to get Ava. I suppose you meant only Ava, then."

"So, Brooke didn't ask for me?" A worried lump caught in my throat.

"No. Like I said, I didn't want to throw names at her in case the distress causes her to have a meltdown. Why don't the rest of you stay here and let me take Ava to see Brooke first?"

Zen and I tracked over the uneven dirt ground, past the kitchen area, and then to another small nook. Not quite a room, but secluded and private nevertheless.

I didn't breathe as I tiptoed inside. Dr. Crumb watched the dial as he released the air in a blood pressure cuff. Brooke, out of her uniform, wore baggy brown pants and a loose sweatshirt. When Dr. Crumb turned away, her eyes landed on Zen, and then me.

Brooke shuddered a breath.

"Brooke?" I swallowed.

Heat flushed through me, burning as I waited for her to respond. Brooke's hand went to her mouth. She trembled and a squeak left her throat.

"Ava?"

Her question was hardly audible, but I heard it as loud as my own beating heart. She knew me. It was good enough. Perhaps seeing me triggered her memory.

Brooke stood, a hand anchoring herself to a table. With her legs wobbling, dragging her feet step by step, she came toward me. I didn't hesitate. I leaped and embraced her with all of me.

"You're alive. You're okay?" She hiccupped between sobs. "We made it out. We did it. We really did it."

Tears of relief streamed down my face as we held each other for what felt like eternity. Forever could come and go, I didn't care. That moment was all about Brooke, for her, for us.

She trembled in my arms as she wept. Then she released me. Wiping our cheeks, we stood face-to-face.

"I didn't know it was you at first. Your hair is shorter. A lot shorter. I thought you were dead. I got so scared when I only saw Zen. I froze up. I asked to see my mother, but it was the only thing I could think of to say. Even when he told me who he was, I didn't believe him. I thought it was another of ISAN's tricks."

I laughed, a full belly laugh. Leave it to Brooke to say something crazy.

"Well," Zen said, chuckling. "Now I don't have to worry about you, Brooke. We still need to do more testing, but all vital signs look good so far. I'll leave you two alone. If you feel any different, please come see me."

"Thank you. I didn't mean to act all crazy," Brooke said. "I was just protecting myself."

"Noted." Zen raised his index finger.

"Thank you, Zen," I said. "I don't know what to say. I'm in your debt." Stupid thing to say perhaps, but my gratitude was bigger than a simple thank you.

"No need, Ava. We are all working together. You can thank Councilor Chang. The formula made a difference."

"Councilor Chang?" Brooke's pitch rose sharply.

"I have so much to tell you," I said.

"Well, I'm finished with Brooke, so I shall be on my way." Dr. Crumb gathered his medical bags. "If you need me, Zen, you know where to find me."

"Thank you," I said.

When Zen and Dr. Crumb left, I gave my attention to Brooke.

"You." I stroked her hair, my lips tugging upward. "I'm so happy you're okay. You gave us a big scare."

"I'm a bit weak, but I feel fine. Zen explained I was injected with HelixB88, which put me in a coma. Mitch? Did he do this to me? And how about you and Tamara?"

"Tamara is fine, never got the 88. I had 88, too, but my body fought it off. And Mitch didn't do it. Novak tried to get rid of you to teach me a lesson."

I dipped my chin, feeling horrible and guilty. She wouldn't have been in this predicament had it not been for me.

Brooke snarled. "I'm going to kill him."

"Get in line. I'm first."

She tilted her head and pinched her eyebrows together. "Wait. If you kill him first then how do I kill him next?" She giggled— music to my ears. "Never mind. I'm not making sense. I've been in a coma, did you know?" She laughed again. "Okay, but serious now. You first. 'Cause I'm too chicken to even look at him. After you shoot him down, I'll take over. I talk like I have no filter and pretend to be all tough, but when it comes to Novak, I might pee my pants if I had to face him."

I let out a belly laugh again. The Brooke I knew and loved—I couldn't believe she was standing in front of me as if nothing had happened to her.

I thanked the heavens she was fine.

She snorted. "So, what's been happening?"

I heaved a breath. "Oh, lots. Where do I begin?"

"Let's sit."

Brooked eased into a chair and I grabbed Zen's rolling stool and placed myself in front of her.

"What do you remember last?" I asked.

Brooke's nostrils flared and her lips twitched. "Justine. She's Novak's little girl. Right? Or did I hear things?"

"No, it's true. You heard right."

"No wonder. It makes perfect sense. She's just as crazy as he is."

"Well, like they say, the apple doesn't fall far from the tree. So what else?"

"I remember ..." Brooke pressed the heel of her palm on her head, groaning. "I remember things that don't make sense to me."

"Like?"

"My mom."

"Your mom?"

"Yeah. I was told she died when I was a toddler, and I was sent to a foster home. But, I have memories of her being taken away by force. Men wearing black. And I only recall one foster home, not as many as I thought I had. And, I keep picturing a face. A guy's

170

face. I think he was my boyfriend. So strange. I can't connect anything together. It's like my past and my present are jumbled up in a messy pile. I'm not absolutely sure about anything."

"It's okay. It will take time. Once you get familiar with everything, things will come to light. Maybe HelixB88 gave you access to lost memories."

Brooke drew back, her features twisting in confusion. "Lost memories? What are you talking about? Are you sure you're okay?"

I'd forgotten she didn't know about those details, so I explained what Zen had discovered.

She shrank in her seat. "That's so messed up. Wow. And I'd thought I heard the worst of ISAN."

"I know, right? Good thing we escaped. Who knows how else they would mess with our minds?"

Brooke offered an affable smile and socked my arm lightly. "I can't believe we're here, though. We actually escaped that God-awful place. What about Tamara? Where is she?"

"She's here with us. She's waiting for you."

Brooke sighed with relief. "Oh, good. I can't wait to see her, too. But I have to tell you, even though this place sucks, it sure beats being at ISAN."

"What do you mean it sucks?"

She peered up to the ceiling and then glanced about the walls. "It's run down."

"You'll get used it. You're going to like it here and the people."

"Anyone is better than Novak and Justine. So what about you? Rhett here, too?"

"Yes. Let me tell you what's been happening and then I'll take you to meet the rest. They're all anxious to see you."

Brooke slapped my thigh. "Woohoo. I'm a celebrity. Almost

a dead celebrity who semi-came back to life. With reverse amnesia. Wait. Did that even make sense?"

I cracked up with her. "Did I tell you how much I missed you?"

"Not enough." She poked my forehead.

I lightly poked her stomach. "That's for making me worried sick."

"Yeah, well, I'm good at that. It's my talent. So, you going to fill me in or do I have to guess?"

"Get ready. It's going to be information overload."

"You know me. I'm ready." She patted her skull rapidly. "My brainy head will be filled with gossip and all things sexy. I hope you have something juicy to tell me, especially about you and Rhett."

"Brooke," I squealed, my face heating.

"Awww, you're blushing," she cooed. "The look of a girl in love. Hey, is that new?" She pointed at my necklace. "It's beautiful. Who gave that to you?"

"Rhett," I said. "We have a matching tattoo."

"What? When? How? Girl, you better start talking."

There was no hiding from her. So I told her everything.

CHAPTER TWENTY-TWO – CONFUSED BROOKE

AVA

Brooke's jaw slackened and she almost keeled over. "No way. You just dumped a whole load of soap-opera fantasy crazy shit. I can't wait to meet everyone. I think I love the kids the most."

"They are adorable, brave, and they act their age." I rolled my eyes. "Do you need help standing?"

"Nope." She slowly slid off her butt. "I got this. I'm an ISAN assassin." She put up a finger and halted. "No, not ISAN. I'm a kick-ass rebel soldier now. I need to get back in shape so I can go out in the field with you all. I'm not going to be happy sitting around waiting."

"Let me help you." I linked my arm with hers and accompanied her to the medical room.

Brooke dragged her feet at first, but when her legs became steadier and her steps more confident, I released her.

"Tamara." Brooke's happy voice ricocheted under the alcove.

"Brooke." Tamara raced toward us and almost knocked Brooke over, holding her tightly with tears in her eyes. "You gave us such a scare. We almost lost you."

Brooke pulled back and rested her hands on Tamara's shoulders. "I know. I'm sorry. But you should know me by now, it's what I do best."

They both giggled.

"Come. Meet the others. They're waiting for you." Tamara tugged Brooke along.

"I'm such a superstar. I love all this attention." Brooke's excitement was infectious.

You are *a superstar, Brooke. Don't you ever forget it.*

Rhett waited by the entrance and gave Brooke the warmest smile. "Hello Brooke. I'm Rhett."

Brooke's cheeks colored slightly pink. "Oh, hello there. You are Rhett. You are my hottie Rhett," she said as if she couldn't believe he stood in front of her. She shoved a hand to her mouth. "I meant not my hottie, but Ava's hottie. It's so nice to finally meet you."

"Same here." Rhett's smile grew wider. "We are so relieved you are well." He squeezed his arms around her briefly and let go.

Brooke, all smiles, pointed at Rhett. "I think we're going to be friends."

I snorted. Such a Brooke thing to say. "Stop gawking at my man. Meet our squad." I pointed as I named them. "This is Naomi, Cleo, and this is Reyna."

Naomi smiled and shook Brooke's hand.

"It's nice to meet you, finally." Cleo gave her a hug.

"Hi. Glad to see you on your feet." Reyna gave Brooke a once-over.

Not as friendly as I'd hoped she would be, but Reyna had a reserved personality. She had been that way with all of us at the beginning, so I didn't judge her.

Ozzie stood in the corner with his hands behind his back and his head lowered almost as if he were shy or trying to avoid us.

"Oz. Remember my friend Brooke?" I escorted Brooke to Ozzie.

Ozzie slowly lifted his head. When Brooke and Ozzie locked eyes, neither of them said a word. They stood there, lost in each other. No one else existed, it seemed.

Then Ozzie's chest rose and fell with a soft sigh. His eyes twinkled and his lips tugged at the corner. Brooke, on the other hand, went from mesmerized to a cold glare—colder than I'd ever seen her wear.

What's going on?

Ozzie's face whipped to the side with a whack. Brooke had slapped him once, and then twice.

We stood there, shocked.

Ozzie blinked, the only reaction he showed.

Brooke backed away, baffled, a hand going to her mouth. "I'm so sorry. Oh, my God. What am I doing? I know you, don't I? You said you would come back. How do I know that? I'm so confused. What's happening to me? Am I going crazy?" Brooke looked at me for guidance.

Ozzie's red cheeks glowed brighter. "I feel like I know you, too, but I don't know why. I'd only seen you once in ISAN when Mitch brought me in as a prisoner."

"I feel the same way." Brooke took a step toward him, her shoulders relaxing and her tone softer. "I don't remember much, but I know your name is Ozwald. I remember your blue eyes, and you have the softest hair. You and I were in a foster home together. There were other children, too, but we fell in love ... I think. I'm not sure."

"I think you're right."

I had always known Ozzie to be shy and reserved, but what he did next shocked me to my core. Well, not just me. Everyone gasped.

175

Ozzie coiled his arms around Brooke's waist so fast she sucked in a breath. She made a *whoomph* sound as Ozzie pulled her against him and kissed her with feverish passion.

I blinked, feeling myself hot all over.

I hadn't realized I was standing right beside them until Rhett gently pushed me back to his chest and whispered, "I think I need to kiss you more often if you can't keep your eyes off them."

I elbowed his side, gawking at the two love birds. Rhett and I had secretly wished Ozzie and Reyna would get together. We'd even tried to get them alone by setting up meetings and then bailing. But for some reason, Ozzie never took interest.

Now I knew why. His heart had been somewhere else, and even he hadn't known it. He'd stayed true to his promise, waiting for Brooke.

Brooke pulled away, knees buckling. Ozzie caught her before she fell.

"Well, that sure made up for lost time." Brooke smacked her lips and thumped her head into Ozzie's chest when she noted we were all watching. "I think I'd like to try that again soon, but when I'm not so drained. I just woke up from a coma so I'm not sure if I'm doing the kissing thing at full strength."

Brooke being shy? That was a first.

"Oh, sure. Of course." Ozzie's neck reddened. "We should take it one day at a time. When you're ready, I'd like to know what you remember of our past. I have no recollection at all." He pulled her back to meet her baffled gaze, his knuckle under her chin. "We have a chance to get to know each other again. This time, I won't leave you. I swear it on my life."

I fought the sting in my heart as I leaned back into Rhett's arms. Moments like this were rare. We had to take all the good offered to us. No one knew what would happen tomorrow, or even an hour later.

"So, what should we do next?" Reyna dabbed the corner of her eyes.

"We should eat. Brooke must be hungry." Ozzie looked at her to confirm.

"I guess I should eat, then," she said, smiling.

"He always thinks about food," Tamara grumbled.

"I had some fresh pastries delivered," Cleo sang, shuffling to the exit.

"My favorite." Ozzie extended a hand to Brooke. "May I carry you?"

Brooke's mouth distorted into a dorky grin, looking delighted and embarrassed. "He wants to carry me. He's a prince. Eeek."

I jerked my head, smiling. "Let him."

"Sure?" Her answer came off like a question, but she squealed happily when he scooped her up.

"Ozwald would love to," Rhett teased. "Ozwald. Ozwald. Ozwald."

Ozzie flipped up his middle finger. "Shut up." Then he cradled Brooke to his chest and fled.

While everyone followed, Rhett and I stayed behind.

Rhett cupped my face. "Wow. I did not see that kiss coming."

"Neither did I."

"Everything go okay back there with Brooke?"

"Yes. Couldn't have gone better. Brooke is fine. I'm grateful."

"Good. Because when you're good, I'm good."

I lowered my arms and shoved my hands inside his back pockets. "And when you're good, I'm good. See how that works?"

"I like your hands inside my pockets." He did the same with

his hands.

"And I like your hands inside mine, too."

"Would you like my hands in other places?"

"Rhett," I squealed, yanking back.

He caught my hands in midair and snatched me into the circle of his arms. "You have a dirty mind, Ava. I meant a massage. You know, how I loosened your muscles the last time."

"You're such a liar." I stuck out my tongue.

"Stick that tongue back out again and there will be consequences."

"Oh, really? And will I like them?"

"Let me show you."

Rhett gave me a toe-curling kiss that would have me thinking about him all day. "You are so bad," I murmured when he let go.

"You love me bad." He draped his arm around my neck and led me out.

Everyone was seated around the campfire near the kitchen, drinking something warm and eating fruits and pastries— chocolate and strawberry-filled doughnuts, twisted bread sprinkled with powdered sugar, bread baked with cranberries and nuts, and homemade chocolate chip cookies.

How I missed baking cookies with Mom—peanut butter, snickerdoodles, oatmeal, and sugar. Mom would coax me to the kitchen when she felt guilty for snapping at me when I asked questions about Dad she refused to answer.

Sweets always made things better then, but nothing was sweeter than Rhett. He sat beside me, always touching me, my back, my arm, my shoulder, and any available part of my body, as if we were linked together and he couldn't have enough of me.

It was strange to see Ozzie and Brooke sitting together,

bashfully ogling each other. Who would have thought they had a history?

Sometimes in the craziest moments, something wonderful transpires. Those were the best kind of revelations. Their story was not complete, but they would slowly sew their love back together.

When I was at Abandoned City for the first time, I'd wished Brooke was with me. I'd gone back for her because I could have never lived with the guilt of leaving her behind. Seeing her happy with Ozzie and the company of others reinforced my decision. I'd gotten my wish, and having Tamara with us made it even better.

My heart hammered with bliss as I watched my friends, new and old, enjoying themselves and each other's company. In ISAN, a moment like this would have seemed impossible. And if I died right now, I would die happy.

Rhett planted a soft kiss on my cheek, his face glowing by the firelight. The heat from the flames and his body tucking closer to mine gave me all the warmth I savored.

I took a bite of a chocolate-stuffed doughnut and gave Rhett a bite, too. Then Rhett peeled an orange and fed it to me. There were plenty of pastries and fruits, but we shared to leave more for the kids.

"I'm never going to forget this moment. These times are precious." His lips brushed my earlobes.

I leaned into his touch, licking chocolate off my fingers. "You think they'll miss us if we leave?" My voice was seductive, an invitation.

"Is this a request or a summons, my queen? Or perhaps you're teasing me?" Rhett kissed the back of my neck and then wrecked me with a slow lick.

I quivered and melted into a puddle. "Whatever you want to

call it, I don't care."

A soft growl escaped Rhett's lips, a promise of what he had planned for me. But for the time, we were there to celebrate Brooke's awakening.

My friend. The sister I wished was mine instead of that monstrous brother.

I would have to tell Brooke about Gene, but not yet. Today was all about Brooke. And I thanked God, the stars, and the universe, whoever would listen, for this moment. I prayed to keep us safe while we fought to bring down ISAN one step at a time.

The crowd got bigger as Jo, the southern rebel kids, Jasper, and Stella joined us. As I looked around to all the people who had graced me with their kindness and made my life fuller and richer, I also thought about what it would mean to me if they died in the coming battles.

It was a morbid thought, but in ISAN, I had killed efficiently and with no remorse. Though I was sad about those we had lost, I hadn't known them. I hadn't cared for them like I did for this group, those who were smiling, eating, and laughing like a family.

God help me. Keep us safe.

CHAPTER TWENTY-THREE – PREPARATION

AVA

The next morning, we cremated Bobo and had a small, touching ceremony. The wasted life was a tragedy. A reminder how precious life was, and how at any given point one of us could be next.

Anything was fair game in war.

Afterward, our group held a meeting. Zen told everyone Gene was my twin and he was to remain in his cell for not cooperating. He had left out Gene was a lunatic.

Everyone had the shock of their lives. Thankfully, they hadn't asked me how I felt or I might have told them the truth.

The southern rebel troop mostly kept to themselves after they helped with their chores. The atmosphere seemed oppressive, but we kept up a good front. Zen, Rhett, and I interrogated Gene, but nothing new came out of the visit.

Gene began civilly, and then his irritation grew into a full shouting meltdown. Though Gene insisted Novak would find him, Zen reassured us that wouldn't happen. Like before, Gene royally pissed me off and I wanted to chop his head off.

Sibling rivalry was an understatement.

Zen halted when we arrived at the center of a massive edifice where the tower of debris almost reached the ceiling. "I'm getting a crew to clean up this mess. This was to be our temporary home, but it seems we'll be staying here a lot longer than I had anticipated."

Good. I was going to suggest we clean up the past and move forward. Besides, inhaling this junk couldn't be good for our lungs.

"Where are we going to put all this?" Rhett waved a hand.

I looked over my shoulder as if I could see the other side of the wall. "Nowhere to put it but outside with the rest."

"Good idea." Zen gave me a thumbs up. "I'll let you lead the cleaning crew."

I said nothing and acted the perfect picture of a grateful person but secretly, I was cursing. *Great.* Next time I planned to keep my mouth shut. I had seen how Zen manipulated others into new duties. I hadn't learned, apparently.

But of course, I had another thought. I would suggest to Jo to round up the kids to keep them busy.

Perfect plan indeed.

At a chirp from Zen's chip, he pulled up a hologram message.

"Councilor Chang, good afternoon."

Pause.

"Good news."

A longer pause.

"Please ask your guards to back away and do not engage when my team arrives. Yes, I got the coordinates."

A short pause.

"I'll keep you informed. And Councilor Chang, the formula helped. Brooke is well. I have several vials of the remedy in my possession. Hopefully we won't need them." A pause. "Yes. Frank and his men are from the North as well. They were separated during the escape. I'll have my crew keep searching for others." Another pause. "Yes, I agree, we need to regroup." A pause. "Yes.

Yes. Have a safe, wonderful day."

Zen glanced between Rhett and me wearily, like he had a lot to share.

"What's the bad news and the good news?" I tried not to sound eager.

"Get ready." Zen rubbed a finger over his chip and gave a false optimistic grin. "I'll brief you, and then you assemble your team. The bad news—it's all over social media. A group of girls used their abilities for financial gain. They went missing, but we all know who took them."

"ISAN," I whispered.

"They're probably dead." Rhett frowned.

"Perhaps," Zen said somberly. "But the good news is, Chang has eyes on two other girls. We should hurry."

"Why can't I go?" Brooke followed me into the meeting room, yapping away.

Frank, Hansh, Miguel, and Owen nodded in greeting as I shifted my eyes to the team already seated at the table waiting for me. Convincing Brooke she couldn't come with us had taken longer than I'd expected. If she asked me one more time, I might ram her against the wall.

God help me. Give me patience.

"I feel fine," Brooke said for the hundredth time.

I poked her chest. "You just got out of a coma. I get you're not used to being left behind, but you can't just spring back into action. Your body has been through the wringer. You need rest. You also need to train and be in top shape."

"I haven't been in a coma for that long. Besides, I feel great."

"Why don't you ask the team?" I waved a hand to them with a mask of cool composure. "If they all agree, then fine."

Rhett rubbed at his chin, his eyes trained warily on Brooke. "What's this all about?"

Ozzie's neutral expression drew into a frown. "Brooke, I already explained to you. You can go next time."

Brooke shifted her weight to one hip and crossed her arms. Her intense glare seemed to intimidate the rest of my squad members. Cleo, Naomi, and Tamara turned away without a word.

Fine. Make me the villain.

"I agree with Ava, Brooke," Reyna said. "You need to rest this one out. You'll just get in the way." Reyna, who spoke her mind like Brooke, picked up a Taser from the arsenal displayed on the table.

Brooke's eyebrows arched so high, they looked like they might fly off her forehead. "In the way? I'll show you *in the way.*"

Had it not been Tamara's fast reflexes, Brooke would have jumped on Reyna. Tamara held Brooke back, who snarled like a wild animal on a leash, her arms flailing.

"Calm down, Brooke, or I'll make you." Tamara's threat calmed Brooke. Then she gave Tamara a resentful stare.

Brooke's face reddened. "For your information, Reyna, I have super hearing. Yeah, so I heard you tell one of your friends you *used to be* Ava's best friend. Of course you would never side with me."

I stared at her, slack jawed in disbelief. One, I'd guessed Brooke had super hearing but she'd never confirmed it. Two, Brooke was a better person. Something else was up with her.

Zen had said the remedy serum would likely mess with her hormones, and her actions seemed to prove it. I was most surprised

Reyna hadn't thrown any punches back. She didn't take crap from anyone, drugged up or not.

"Sorry, Reyna. She doesn't know what she's saying." I felt the need to intervene, especially since I had practically ignored her since Brooke had awakened.

I still cared for Reyna. She had been my bestie once, but time and ISAN's technology had changed a lot of things—for all of us.

"HelixB88 remedy is—"

Reyna rolled back her shoulders. "It's okay, Ava. You don't need to apologize for Brooke. She's acting like a jealous, spoiled brat."

There it was. Reyna's claws had come out, though less sharp than usual. Her retort could have been worse, but she'd tamed herself.

Brooke shuddered. "Jealous, spoiled brat—"

"Let's go for a walk." Ozzie seized Brooke's shoulders and took her out of the room.

Zen rushed out as well. He'd likely give her a sedative or something to help her calm down.

"Anyway ..." Rhett shook his head and tapped the monitor. A hologram of a city in the south materialized. "We're going to take Councilor Chang's glider here when the sun goes down." He raised a slim metal pointer, and a laser beam touched the image at a skyscraper's roof.

Frank pressed his knuckles on the table and leaned in. "So then what do you plan to do after? You do realize that building is not our destination, right?"

Rhett crossed his arms, tipping back in a cool relaxed manner, not at all fazed. "Of course I do. I'm all about staying off the radar. So, we fly."

Frank swore. Hansh snickered. Miguel nodded with a grin,

like he couldn't wait.

"I've always wanted to use the flying apparatus," Drew said.

"Well, that's not all," Rhett went on. "We'll have to ditch the glider and go on foot. When we return home, we'll have to take the hydro glider."

Frank cursed.

"Say what?" Hansh tilted his head back.

This just gets better.

Frank parted his lips, closed them, and then parted again but said nothing when Zen and Ozzie walked in.

I straightened in my seat. "Where's Brooke? She okay?"

"I gave her something to lessen her anxiety." Zen scrubbed his six o'clock shadow. "I think her past is colliding with her present and she's getting confused. It's making her agitated."

"To say the least," Reyna murmured.

"You think HelixB88 gave her memories back, then?" Cleo winced with a shrug.

"I don't know, and I don't want to test that theory. Not just yet. I need to gather more facts. So, we all good?" Zen glanced between Frank and Rhett.

Naomi, who hadn't said a word since I'd arrived, raised a hand. "One question. What if the girls are gone when we get there?"

Zen pulled out a rickety chair and sat. A heavy, tired sigh escaped him. "They'll be there. Councilor Chang set up a fake sweepstakes win. All expenses paid to the Crystal Tower Casino. The girls are being treated like queens with a set itinerary. They are at a restaurant as we speak. When you arrive, they will be heading to their reservation at the spa. Reyna, Naomi, and Tamara, you'll be on standby. Frank, Hansh, Miguel, and Drew—I have another assignment for you. You'll drop off the team as planned but I need you to meet up with

Chang. She gave me the coordinates to the meeting point. I have no details on this assignment. She'll let you know once you arrive."

"Sure thing," Frank said. "Whatever you need us to do."

Zen continued. "Rhett, Ozzie, and Ava, you'll have access to the spa room. All your uniforms and changes of identity will be inside a storage room. It can only be opened with a numeric code on the fiftieth floor. I sent the code to Rhett's chip. Do you have any questions?"

Cleo pinched her lips together, scraping her boot on the ground. "Yes, I do. What about me? Did you forget to say my name?"

"No. You're not going this time."

Cleo exhaled a terse breath. "Why? The mission doesn't seem dangerous. Easy in and out, right? I'm going, and you can't stop me."

Zen rose ever so slowly, his mouth tight, eyebrows angling downward. "Yes. The mission should be simple, but we're dealing with girls with unknown powers. You are not special like this unit."

Ouch. Way to stick it to her, Pops.

Cleo brought her eyes downward and then raised her chin. "Rhett and Ozzie aren't special. What can Reyna do? I haven't seen anything special about her either."

"Reyna trained at ISAN for a reason. She has the DNA marker for enhanced senses at the least. What she can do is none of your business. Rhett and Ozzie are expert agents. The party has been assembled, and you're not part of it this time. I need you to help Jo. End of discussion. Does anyone have a question?"

Cleo, who usually fought her father to get her way, said nothing else.

When no one spoke a word, Zen said, "Then let's get to it. Bring the girls home."

CHAPTER TWENTY-FOUR – OTHERS

JUSTINE

Payton pivoted on his heel and ambled ahead. "Stay behind me. We don't want them to get suspicious."

Like they weren't already suspicious-looking—clad in all black with Tasers in their hands, they were walking among the citizens in daylight in full gear. They looked like council guards.

Justine's father had demanded her team capture the two teen girls who had exhibited Helix powers. They had been last spotted at a clothing store, having the time of their lives, and had walked out with a bunch of stolen goods.

From what they'd gathered from the media recordings, the first girl turned invisible and the second girl shot electricity out of her fingertips. How were they able to manifest those abilities without Helix? Justine had thought only she could.

Justine understood why her father would want them on their team, mostly to help them quash the anti-ISAN rebels, but then he would have to train them. What if they didn't want to join? Would he just let them leave?

The first set of girls they'd heard about with powers robbed a bank. They had literally huffed and puffed their way in and out like big badass wolves. Justine laughed at her own joke, but her uptight father hadn't. Though Russ and Mitch had snickered behind his back.

"There." Payton pointed to the northwest. "They are headed to the parking garage. I'll tell our girls to corner them up ahead."

"Are you sure they're headed there? You've been wrong before." Justine couldn't believe she was going to say this but ... "Don't you have a mental map like Ava, or something close to it?"

Payton leveled his irate gaze at her, and she didn't want to know what he was thinking, so she preempted the question she expected.

"No, I don't miss her. You're a much better leader than her."

Liar. I'm a big fat liar.

Payton sucked at leading missions. Justine should have gotten the job.

"Sure, whatever, but we should go now." He went up the walkway, lengthening his strides to pick up speed.

Justine threw up her hands and prayed this mission would be over soon. Payton was an idiot, and the newbies on their team were no fun. They didn't want to talk about boys or girly stuff when they had free time. In fact, they didn't want to socialize with her at all.

Something was wrong with them. Jealous, probably. Justine was the popular girl since Ava had left. Yes. They were jealous of her. That had to be the reason.

I don't miss Brooke. I don't miss Tamara. And I certainly don't miss Ava.

As Justine rushed ahead, an unobservant woman with a child bumped into her. The lady tumbled down with her daughter. Justine's strength had thrown them both several feet, and it seemed like she had pushed them on purpose.

"What's wrong with you?" shouted a man who was helping them up.

Justine swore to herself and moved on ahead. She didn't have time to apologize or help them, and she didn't feel like being a good person either.

If Justine could avoid being among civilians during missions, she would gladly do it. They only got in the way.

Justine almost rammed into Payton when he skidded to a halt on the first level. As she silently cursed, she rounded the corner with him. Then she used her chip to switch on her contact lenses, showing the hologram bodies.

"There." Payton pointed and ran toward the escalator.

They kept their heads down and rode in silence. A few men dressed in suits had stepped in with them. They kept their heads forward, never said a word to each other, and when they got off on the eighth floor, their shoulders relaxed.

Yes, Payton and Justine looked intimidating, but they looked like C-guards, too. Or close enough so no one screamed and ran away like they were assassins ready to blast everyone in sight.

They got off on the tenth floor. Justine's contact lenses confirmed two girls holding shopping bags, giggling as they walked toward their parked aircraft. It was a quiet afternoon and most people were at work, leaving the garage empty of citizens.

Payton sent a message through his chip to their girls in hiding. *"We're on level ten. I see you at the far back corner. Wait for my mark."*

"Confirmed."

Justine scanned the area, and then they advanced to the girl with short hair and a nose piercing standing by her glider.

Payton cleared his throat. "Excuse me. Can I have a word with you?"

Serious? Couldn't he have come up with a better line?

The girl's eyes rounded in alarm. She clearly hadn't heard

Payton coming, so his appearing behind her must have scared the bejesus out of her.

She sized up Justine's teammate, curled her lips a bit as if liking what she saw, and then her eyes landed on Justine.

"No. We're in a hurry." The second girl jerked her head at her friend. "Nina, get inside."

Payton rested his hand on the glider. "We just want to talk. We know what you can do and how you filled up the bags. I'm not here to arrest you. We're not council guards."

The girl with the nose ring, Nina, raised her chin. "And if we refuse?"

Justine stepped in front of Payton. "You won't. Either make this easy or face the consequences."

Nina snarled. When Justine seized her arm to keep her from leaving, the girl gripped Justine's wrist with her other hand and sent an electric shock up Justine's arm.

Justine didn't know how long it lasted. Two, three, four seconds, but a nanosecond was too much. Her skin blazed like she had been set on fire.

When the girl let go, Justine smacked into the transport parked across from theirs. The ground tilted when she stood, wobbling. White lights dotted her vision.

Justine's reflection stared at her from the glider's silver, shining body. Her hair stood on end like a halo. Helix numbed some of the pain, or it would have been a lot worse.

"You little …" Justine bolted toward her.

"Watch out Nina," the second girl alerted her friend.

Nina's eyes grew wide and then she laughed. The girl struck Justine with her sparks without touching her. She zapped Justine so fast, she didn't see it coming.

Mocking laughter rang in Justine's ears as she soared backward into another aircraft. She trembled with the anger bubbling inside her. This time, her body left a huge dent in the hull. Shaking off her daze, she got to her feet.

"Cora, run," Nina shouted.

Justine's girls scooted in closer.

Red beams streamed from Tessa, Bethany, and Alice as they ran toward them, but none hit their targets. After a second effort, finally, Tessa managed to Tase the pest. She dashed over and held Nina upright before she fell.

Payton was just standing there. Justine had no idea why he hadn't stopped Cora, the second girl, until Justine remembered Cora could turn herself invisible.

Where had she gone?

Payton extended his Taser out to aim and—his eyes darted, narrowed—fired. Target claimed. He shot Cora by the pole. Justine assumed Cora had run toward it to hide.

"You're not laughing now, are you bitch?" Justine whacked Nina's face so hard, a bone snapped.

The girl spun one hundred and eighty degrees out of Tessa's arms and collapsed.

"What's wrong with you? You didn't have to break her." Payton glared at Justine and shoved his Taser back in its holster. "Let's get them in the glider. One of us will have to fly this thing."

"I'll fly with Tessa. You take Bethany, Alice, and the idiots, and I'll meet you back at the base."

Justine didn't wait for his permission, nor did she help drag the girls inside. But she did get a copy of both handprints from their scanner to input onto the glider. Justine didn't know whose aircraft it was, so she took both of theirs. The transporter had belonged to Nina.

The ride back home was pleasant. Tess didn't say a word.

No one spoke to Justine. No one asked her questions. She flew into the clouds and became lost with the universe.

Sometimes Justine wondered what her life would have been like if she wasn't an ISAN soldier. Yes, she wanted to be the top leader, be the best, make her father proud. But there was also a side of her that wished she had a normal life.

Justine talked the big talk and acted like she didn't care, but the truth was, she desperately wanted her father to love her, especially since her mother had left them. Justine's father had told Justine her mother had some kind of mental breakdown.

Justine's mother had left without a word. No goodbye. No note of explanation. What mother does that? So Justine had worshipped the ground her father walked on. She had believed in everything he believed in. Because ... he was her father.

Justine wanted his attention. His love. His loyalty. Now, she wasn't sure of anything anymore, and it hurt every time he saw her without acknowledging her.

I'm not his daughter. To him, I'm just another assassin, one who will never meet his expectations.

ISAN guards carried the girls to their prison when they arrived at the station.

Justine's father met them at Russ's office after an hour of interrogating the girls. Mitch and Lydia were there, too.

Justine's father stood, his hands hidden in his front pants pockets. He rarely sat in the meetings. "I have the analysis of their DNA and it's nothing I've ever seen before."

"Well, that's obvious from their abilities." Mitch sat taller and adjusted the lapel of his button shirt when Justine's father shot him a daggered glare.

Nobody spoke down to Justine's father. Mitch should know better.

"I mean, it's one thing to have such gifts, but they didn't need Helix," Mitch went on.

"Do you think it's a possibility that maybe, perhaps, we don't need Helix?" Justine winced, shrinking in her seat. She already knew she could access abilities without it, but she wasn't sure about her teammates and other assassins. "Maybe we can test the theory with us?"

"Nonsense," Justine's father snapped. "It has already been tested and the results have been the same since the beginning of ISAN. These girls' DNA makeup is different. Though they show tremendous talents, their neurons fire at a rapid pace, fueling a need to destroy or break rules. Aggression seems to release the tension. To simplify, they produce their own Helix compound, but they can't shut it off until they release the energy. They have no self-control. I'm afraid there isn't anything we can do for them."

"What do you mean?" Russ tilted his head, frowning. "Shouldn't we do more tests? Can't the lab create some form of remedy, or at least an interim solution until we do? You going to just kick them out on the streets?"

The look on Justine's father's face told her neither Russ nor she would like what he had to say.

"Of course not. Whenever the news exposes females with such powers, it could stir up the others in hiding. This could expose ISAN, and I can't let that happen. And we certainly don't have the time to wait around. We have a war to prepare for."

"War?" The word came out louder than Justine had intended. "I thought we were helping the government. You know, capturing the bad guys and fighting the rebels. Is there something I'm not getting here?"

Justine's father flinched. He only flinched when he made a mistake, which was almost never. He smoothed his hair back and stood in front of her. His height and domineering sneer made her feel even smaller.

"You are missing the point, *Justine*. We are constantly at war. Within ourselves, our society, and against corruption, to make this world a better place."

Justine hated the way her name rolled off his tongue, as if she were the most dimwitted person on the planet. She wanted to shout at him and maybe jab him in the throat, but that would be unwise.

Would he kill his own daughter like he was suggesting he would do to those girls? She questioned what had really happened to Roxy.

"What Justine is trying to say—"

Justine's father shot a silencing look at Lydia. Justine appreciated Lydia for speaking on her behalf, but she shouldn't have. Justine's father would not tolerate anyone's opinion.

Justine's father sighed and rubbed along his jaw. That perfectly shaved jaw. Never once had she seen him with stubble.

"As I was saying," he continued. "The girls are not cooperative and thus are not ISAN material. We have no use for them."

"So, what does that mean, exactly?" Justine was sure everyone was thinking the same.

Lydia tensed, not making eye contact. Neither did Payton. Ever since Ava had left, he seemed to have checked out.

Yes, Payton did his part during training and in the field, but he looked like he didn't want to be there. And to make things weirder, her know-it-all father always looked at Payton as if he had the answers.

Justine's father ever so slowly craned his head to her—his eyes so cold he could turn her into an ice sculpture. He parted his lips to reprimand her or give her a snide remark perhaps, but instead—

"Why don't I speak to them, Mr. Novak?" Mitch rubbed something off his button-down shirt, but she knew there was nothing there. He was on edge, too.

"You?" Justine's father pivoted to Mitch, his eyes wider, intrigued. "Why do you think they would cooperate with you when they didn't with me?"

"Because, sir." Mitch rolled up the cuff of one sleeve, and then the other. Looking suave and self-assured as her father, the way he lifted his brows and met his eyes. "I'm closer to their age. And I'm very convincing."

After what seemed like a long time, Justine's father said, "Fine. But if you can't, then you'll have to deal with them my way."

Justine swallowed. She had a clear idea what he meant.

"I have a meeting late this evening. I don't plan on coming back until tomorrow morning. You have until then to convince the girls."

"Will do, sir. They will comply."

Justine's father stood in front of Mitch, staring him down. Creepy. Then he turned and walked out. Not even a look over the shoulder to acknowledge his daughter.

When he looked at her, did he see a daughter or a weapon? A weapon he didn't trust enough to make a leader. And sometimes she wondered if he saw any of them as human or just a means to an end. The war he talked about.

CHAPTER TWENTY-FIVE – CRYSTAL TOWER CASINO

AVA

Brooke had been sleeping in the room she shared with Naomi and Tamara when I'd left. Poor Brooke. I could only imagine what she must be feeling.

Rhett went to check up on Jo and the kids. We even checked the back of the gliders for surprise guests.

Following Bobo's death, Momo seemed a bit distant from the older crowd, and stayed close to Jo. It was better that way. Battle was no place for kids, even super-powered ones.

We flew when the sun dipped lower, when the sky cast a stream of pink and violet into the clouds. So peaceful. My shoulders eased, tension almost gone, and I forgot for a moment where we were headed.

From above, the mesmerizing sight took my breath away. For hours, the view was priceless. We punched through cloud after cloud, and then our transporter dipped lower as we neared the South quadrant.

Nothing but flashing lights of red, green, blue, and gold surrounded me. The city came to life with music, water fountain shows, and dancing strobe lights in the night sky, comparable to Las Vegas of the days before—flashy and loud.

People were out and about into the late hours. South quadrant was not a place to raise a family it seemed, but rather a place for young ones wanting to live a fast-paced life. It had been hit the hardest by the meteors, and all their commercial buildings and skyscraper apartments had been built on water.

Frank landed the transporter across from the Crystal Tower Casino and left us as planned.

Icy, punishing wind whipped across the rooftop—strong and heavy. It took all my effort to stand steadfast against the vicious breeze.

I adjusted Naomi's jet pack. I had already given her instructions on how to use it inside the glider, but I worried since it was her first time.

Out of habit, I checked Tamara's, too. A silent moment of understanding passed between us. We had been a band in ISAN and now we were together for a better cause.

The distance between two buildings hadn't seemed like such a big gap from above, but perching on the edge, I wanted to vomit. I had flown from roof to roof before, but this distance was much greater. My nerves fired up. The constant slapping from the current didn't help either.

"Reyna and Ozwald, go," Rhett barked out the order, snagging my attention.

"Ozzie. My name is Ozzie," Ozzie hissed lightheartedly and jumped.

Reyna crept closer to the ledge. She never complained about heights. In fact, she reveled in flying. She pressed a spot on her suit, and the jet pack came to life.

"See you later." Reyna gave a salute and leaped.

A faint squeal of delight echoed with the draft. She even soared backward and then flipped like an aerial acrobat.

Show off.

Tamara and Naomi went next.

"Want to go together?" Rhett tugged at the strap on my suit.

I gave him a sardonic smile. "No. But I'll race ya." Being that we weren't on a life-threatening mission, I felt a bit playful.

"Getting brave, are we?"

No, I was deathly afraid, but competition was what I knew best. It lessened the fear and gave me a new focus.

"Are you afraid, Sniper?"

"Sniper? You calling me by my nickname now?"

"Only when I feel like throwing you a challenge," I said. "The person who reaches the other side first gets to collect on a bet. Whatever we want."

"Anything?" His tone dipped low and playful.

And so did mine. "Anything."

"You're on."

"I'm counting to three. One …"

At the edge, my knees buckled. The moon seemed almost in reach. The world spun when I focused on my target. Our squad gathered near the edge of the other roof. They knew I was afraid of heights.

"No jumping on two, Ava. But if you are, let me know now."

Don't look down. Don't look down.

I couldn't help myself. With the colorful buildings, it was like being in the center of a rainbow. Flashing lights shouted at me, beckoned me to look, to admire.

"Two." I held up my hands. "See. No jumping on two. But you never said no jumping on two and a half. See you on the other side."

Before Rhett could catch on, I dove.

"Ava!"

My stomach dropped as I fell. With the hologram screen in front of me, I used the navigation on my chip.

Focus on Tamara. Focus on your team. Anyone.

The current propelled me forward as I soared like an eagle. The twinkling city lights below filled me with a sense of serenity. I was one with the air, the stars, and the night.

After the initial jump, I loved the flight. I loved being up in the sky.

Halfway there.

Then something flashed at the corner of my eye. No, not something, someone.

Rhett?

Rhett!

How had he passed me?

Rhett had free fallen, giving him more momentum, something I would never do. Then he used his navigator to guide him the rest of the way. He landed a second before me.

"You cheated." I stomped toward Rhett, but recoiled when the breeze shoved me back.

"Ava." Rhett snickered, holding up his hands and taking a few steps back. "You cheated first. So, what're you going to do about it?"

"What's going on?" Naomi sounded confused.

"You'll get used to it," Reyna said dryly. "Some strange competition they have going between them. It's what they always say to each other. We just ignore them."

"Some things never change," Ozzie murmured. "But I'm glad to see them back together."

Before I could give Rhett a mouthful, he took long, swift strides forward and kissed me.

Rhett cupped my face and gave me a smug grin when he released me. "I won. You owe me."

I blinked, coming out of my daze. "That was ... totally unexpected."

"Can you feel that, Ava?" He placed my hand over his heart.

"Yeah." I was sure my smile shone bigger and brighter than the moon. "It beats only for me. Don't *ever* forget it."

The building could have crumbled and we wouldn't have cared. In that moment, we shared something profound, something extraordinary—a memory. Something warm had tugged at my gut the night Rhett and I had flown together on that ruined building when he'd wished me happy birthday. This experience brought us full circle.

We had come so far. We had fought the odds and had made it. *We* were together.

"Hey guys, the casino guards are coming. Can you see them on your map, Ava? We need to go." Tamara sprinted toward the door that led to the stairs.

I had switched off Helix when gliding through the air, afraid of stimulation overload from the dazzling bright lights on the surrounding buildings.

My map confirmed a dozen guards were in the elevator soaring to the roof. I wasn't worried about them. The guards were expected, especially when they spotted intruders. They wouldn't be able to find us once we got inside.

Though Tamara had entered the stairwell first, the Helix pumping through my veins propelled me faster and harder. I raced, beating everyone else as we descended the stairs.

When we finally reached the fiftieth floor, everyone was panting except for me. Reyna opened the door and we entered.

"Couldn't we have taken the escalator?" Naomi plopped down, her chest rising and falling. "You're all so fit. I need to catch up."

Rhett smeared sweat off his forehead with the back of his hand, punched in the key code to the storage room, and we entered.

"Here." Rhett tossed a bundle of fabric at me. "Our uniforms."

I caught the bundle, handed one out to everyone, and put mine on.

"I'm glad Councilor Chang came through." Tamara shoved her arms through the sleeves and buttoned up her cream shirt. Then she pulled up jumper pants and tucked her shirt inside. "There. Do I look like a housekeeper?"

"Yup, and so do I." Naomi retied her hair and bumped into Reyna, who glared.

"I hate this. It's too tight." Reyna tugged on her straps. "Let's go get them and make it quick."

Ozzie and Rhett buttoned up their long, sleek, white coats, and I did the same. I shoved my hands inside the front pockets and fished for the key to open the door. It was so small—about the size of a chip.

"I have a key, too." Rhett held it up and placed it back inside.

"Me too." Ozzie tapped his front pocket.

Tamara held up one to examine. "I have one, too."

"This is so itchy." Reyna rubbed at her chest.

Naomi and Tamara giggled at her.

I jerked when my chip chirped. Our contact had sent a message.

"Room 5011. Ready?" I looked to each of my team members.

When each gave me a nod, Rhett, Ozzie, and I swarmed out after I unlocked the door with a swipe.

Room 5020, 5018, 5016, even on the left, and odd on the right. Finally, we reached 5011. I swiped the key over the scanner and the door slid open.

The scent of lavender and vanilla hit me first. Soft instrumental music filtered through the dim room.

When we walked in farther, we found electric candles around the built-in bath, which was filled with rose petals. Oil bottles and fluffy sponges had been set on a wooden tray next to the tub.

To the left hung plush white robes in a small waiting space with red leather sofas, a metal tea table, and a zebra-striped rug. Not my taste in furniture, but oh well.

To my right were four massage tables with heavy padding and a face cradle, allowing the client to breathe easily while facedown. Behind the tables were cabinets and high-tech equipment. Each massage table had a monitor in front of it.

Ozzie scanned the room for cameras or listening devices.

"Wow. This is amazing." Rhett gave a wolf whistle and whispered in my ear. "Too bad we don't get to use this facility. I would give you a sponge bath."

"I would let you if we could." I waggled my eyebrows at him.

Ozzie sighed as he continued to survey the room. "Gross, you guys. Not now. It's bad enough I feel like the third wheel."

"You don't have to," I said, and dropped my tone playfully. "You could join us."

Ozzie blushed crimson and pretended he didn't hear. He turned off his chip after he finished searching. "All clear. So what do we do, just stand here? What happens when they come in? I'm not a masseuse or masseur or whatever you call it."

"Relax, Ozwald." Rhett squeezed Ozzie's shoulder. "It's all good. Just stand to the side all pretty, and Ava and I will take care of everything. If you'd read your itinerary, you would have known. But I understand, you were busy taking care of Brooke."

I loved how Rhett never made anyone feel like an idiot. He could have put Ozzie down for not knowing, the way Mitch would have, but he didn't.

"Oh, okay. And you're right. I was preoccupied. You know I don't stray from our focus—it's a straightforward mission. Nothing dangerous, right?"

"Right." I gave a thumbs up.

"Then why do I feel so nervous?" Ozzie flapped his robe fervently as if needing air. "My heart is pumping so fast." He patted his pockets and mumbled to himself. "Taser. I'm fine. All is fine. Rhett and Ava are here. The girls are waiting out there."

"Oz, did you take something?" Rhett studied Ozzie's face, giving his cheek a light slap.

"No, no, no. But I wish I had." He paced near the murmuring water fountain.

Ozzie never acted like this. He'd also never cared about anyone before. Yes, he cared for his friends, but caring about someone romantically was all new to him. Well, not new, but he needed to figure things out.

"I know why you're anxious, Oz." I bent lower next to him.

"You do?" Ozzie looked at me. His sad, sky-blue puppy eyes radiated brighter under the fluorescent light.

"Yes. You're worried about Brooke. About how she's doing and you're scared you might not make it back to her. Once you love or care for someone, you see differently, feel differently. Whereas before, the mission was more important. You have someone else to live for now. Because you matter to Brooke and she matters to you. You are not just one person." My eyes met Rhett's. "We are two halves of a heart beating as one. If half a heart stops beating, the other half does, too. Whatever one half feels, the other one does. So, yes, I understand."

Ozzie let out a long breath, as if a brick had lifted from his chest. "You're right. You're so right. Now that I'm processing these emotions, I feel better."

"Good," I said, my eyes still locked on Rhett's.

Rhett's heated gaze extended from across the room to mine. I felt his invisible hands on me and that phantom kiss—the kind that made me feel like I could rocket to the stars.

CHAPTER TWENTY-SIX – THE GIRLS

RHETT

We are two halves of a heart beating as one.

Sometimes Rhett got so lost in Ava, he forgot his own name. Like right then as they stared into each other's eyes as the world slipped away.

"Rhett ... Rhett. It's time."

Rhett flinched back to attention at Ava's warning. Somehow, he'd missed Tamara's signal through his transmitter. He readied next to his girl to greet their clients while Ozzie got situated in the back of the room, acting as an assistant.

"Something's wrong. She's alone and she's wearing a white coat." Tamara's warning sent a chill down his back. "She shouldn't be assigned to this room. Maybe she's just checking the supplies. I don't know. She's entering."

Rhett gripped his Taser inside his pocket. The door slid open, and a woman with short blonde hair entered.

She froze when she saw him, and then her lips curled, and her cheeks flushed pink. Her smile died when she noted Ava.

"You two must have the wrong room." She wrung strands of her hair over her ear. "What's your name?" Her voice became flirtatious when she gave Rhett all her attention. "I don't recall seeing you here before."

Wrong move, lady. Don't piss off Ava.

Rhett had to admit, he enjoyed Ava's jealous side. She crossed

206

her arms, glaring, her feet tapping in a steady beat, faster when the woman fluttered her eyelashes at him.

"I just started here. My partner Fiona, and that's Fletcher in the back, my assistant. I'm expecting clients very soon. They seem to be running a bit late."

"Strange." She pulled a handheld TAB from her white coat and scrolled through it. "You know, you didn't tell me your name." She stole a glance from the corner of her eye and then went back to her screen.

Ava was right. *Whatever one half feels, the other one does, too.* Because Rhett felt Ava's burning rage.

"Jonas," he said. "And you didn't tell me yours."

"Sandra." Her smile grew wider. "Well, Jonas, something is not right here. I'm definitely supposed to be in room 5011." She scrolled again.

"I'm pretty sure we have the right room, *Sandra*. Maybe you need to check yours again." Ava's tone did not match her stellar fake smile. "Maybe *Jonas* should get this over with and Tase you before I do."

"What?"

Before Ava or Rhett had a chance to pull out their Tasers, a red laser beam focused on the woman's neck and a pellet hit its target. Sandra convulsed and dropped to the ground.

"You were taking too long." Ozzie stood before the fallen body. "And Ava looked like she was going to kill her."

"I was not." Ava played with the buttons on her coat, feigning innocence. "Well, *Jonas* shouldn't be so playful."

"I was only trying to get more information from her." Rhett snickered at Ava's pout.

"Hey guys," Reyna snorted. "Someone's mic was on so we

heard everything. Thanks for entertaining us. We're bored out here."

"Great." Ava's face brightened a shade.

"Just doing my job, babe." Rhett winked at Ava.

She stuck her tongue out at him and wrinkled her nose.

Adorable. If Ozzie hadn't been here, he would have taken her and jumped into the bath.

"You do remember what I said about sticking out your tongue at me, right?" Rhett hiked an eyebrow.

Ava's eyes shot open wider, and then she slowly backed away as her expression dared him to come and get her.

"Hey guys." Tamara's voice this time. "The eagles have landed. Get ready."

No more fun and flirting. Ozzie and Rhett carefully placed Sandra inside the closet and went back to their stations.

"Good evening." Rhett gave a curt nod and Ava did the same when the two girls strolled in.

Their profiles matched those on the itinerary he had diligently memorized.

"Mia," Rhett said to the tall girl with dark, shoulder-length hair and heavy makeup. "Please have a seat. We need to go over some details before we get started."

"Sure." Her elation showed on her face as she practically threw herself on the red sofa. Her crimson dress, which looked pasted on her skin, blended in with the upholstery.

"Ella. That means you, too. Please sit next to your friend." Ava gestured to the sofa, her voice smooth and friendly.

Ella seemed hesitant from the way she took her time examining them, even Ozzie, and then carefully sat beside Mia— prim and proper. Not even a strand stuck out from her straight, glossy red hair.

"Oh, the guy back there is our assistant. He's in training." Rhett flashed a quick grin, trying to ease her nerves. "He'll just be observing."

"Cool." Mia bounced on the sofa and lounged against the back comfortably.

Mia acted more like a child than a woman in her early twenties. She seemed way too excited to be here, but Ella was a different story. Tension tightened around her body, and she hadn't eased up since she entered.

Gain her trust.

Ella peered at the ceiling, and then back to Rhett. "I thought, well, I was expecting a female masseuse."

"Don't worry. I'm a masseuse, too," Ava intercepted, her tone clear and reassuring. "I'm not leaving."

Mia caressed her friend's shoulder and eased back with her legs crossed, showing too much skin. "It's fine, Ella. The cute guy can take care of me."

"Not again." Ozzie's grumble reached Rhett's ear.

Rhett clapped once, rubbed his hands, and sat on the knee-high metal table. "Let's get this done, shall we?" The words were more for his squad than for the girls.

Ava slid next to Rhett and started her speech.

"Ladies, we know who you are and what you can do. I want you to know you're safe, but we suspect someone may intend to harm you. If you listen and do as I say, we can protect you."

"Who are you?" Ella shot up from her seat.

"Sit down," Ava snapped.

Ella plopped down and folded her hands.

"What do you want with us?" Mia scooted closer to Ella and

clutched the hem of her dress.

Ava directed her attention to the bouquet of flowers on the table and inhaled. "Just listen, please. And don't ask questions until I'm finished."

"Okay. Fine. You don't have to get all prissy about it," Mia said.

"She's a real winner." Reyna's voice carried through the transmitter.

Rhett almost laughed when Ozzie made a sound like he was spitting.

Ava clenched her fists and offered a don't-mess-with-me expression to Mia, but remained calm when she continued.

"We used to belong to an organization that used people like you with special abilities. I'm not going to go into details, but they are evil. They will literally strip away your identity, give you a new one, and make you think you are fighting for the greater good. This network is looking for you and we are here to protect you."

More than Rhett thought Ava would say, but she had caught the girls' attention.

"We're here to take you somewhere safe," Ava added. "There, you will have a choice. We will also explain what is happening to your body."

"Why can't you tell us now?" Ella intertwined her fingers together and twisted her neck toward the door, and then back, as if deciding on whether or not to bail.

"We don't have time. It's best if we talk somewhere safe. The organization may be on their way. You have already shown yourselves to the world. That's how we found you. Come with us so we can help you start over, or face the consequences. Prison or worse. I know you get the picture. You're not the airheads you profess to be, so cut the bullshit."

"Wait," Mia paused, her eyes narrowing. "This was a set up?" Her pitch crept higher. "We didn't win anything. You set this up."

"What do you know? The ditz has brains after all."

Rhett wished Reyna would stop commentating, but she had taken the words right out of his mouth. He wondered if Mia's actions were a pretense.

"Listen." Ava jolted up when Mia did. She placed her hands out, an offer of peace. "You have to understand. We couldn't just walk up to you and say hey, you know what, guys?"

"No, you couldn't have I suppose," she spat with sarcasm. "But this ... this is all lies. My friend and I belong with no one. Get out of my way, bitch. I'm outta here."

"Maybe we should—" Ella never got to finish.

"Ava, she called you a bitch. Don't take crap from her." Tamara's voice squealed through his ears.

"Stop," Rhett said, louder than he had anticipated.

Mia scoffed like Rhett had offended her. "Come on." She yanked her friend's arm and dragged her toward the door.

When Mia got close enough for the sensor to detect her heat, nothing happened. The door remained closed, as had been planned. Reyna was to tamper with the sensor from the other side.

"You'll regret you double-crossed me. Now, release the door." Mia's eyes grew freakishly silver.

Rhett had seen magical shimmer in Coco, Naomi, and recently in Ava's eyes, though Ava's were brighter when Helix grew stronger.

Ava planted herself on the massage table with her legs crossed, checking out her nails like she had no care in the world. "I don't think so. And just so you know, nobody calls me a bitch."

Mia inhaled a deep breath and blew.

Ava leaped from one massage table to the next as the air from Mia's breath pushed everything in sight. His girl seemed resistant to the new power. Ozzie and Rhett weren't as lucky.

Ozzie smashed into the cabinet, and Rhett somersaulted and flattened against the back wall. Rhett must have accidentally touched a switch in the process, for the wall behind him was no longer white. Palm trees, white sand, and the ocean appeared. Even the room sounded like the beach, with crashing waves and a soft breeze.

"Stop." Ella's voice was hardly audible in the tornado wind circling and stretching bigger.

Water from the tub lifted, floating, as if the space were its rightful domain.

"Do something!" Ozzie hollered. "I don't want to get wet or die."

Too late. The body of water, one massive lump of liquid, swirled around the room. Water showered Rhett and then Ozzie. At least it was warm. The room looked like a thunderstorm had passed right through. Even Ava and the girls were wet.

"What's going on?" Tamara asked. "Do you need us?"

Rhett answered, telling her they needed help, but the violent gust swallowed his voice.

Ava held up her arms, fighting, pushing through the gale while Mia raged on. Ella stood behind her friend, looking flabbergasted.

"Stop this," Ava shouted. "You're going to hurt yourself."

"Like you can stop me."

Mia's power had cabinets opening and slamming closed, but Ava took advantage and used her telekinetic gift. Towels and bottles of oils and cosmetics flew at Mia. They bounced off her, giving pause to the madness.

The tornado slowed as Mia grew weaker, but Ozzie and Rhett were still glued against the wall. It must be good to be a girl with such power.

"How … did you do that?" Mia asked. "And how were you able to resist me?" Mia panted out of breath, fuming in anger.

"I'm like you. Well, better. Now tell me you're sorry for calling me a bitch."

"Or else what?"

"I don't give second chances, girl. I feed on rage, so don't mess with me."

If Ava could see herself, the sight would have stopped her cold. Even Rhett was afraid. The hair on his arm rose. His goosebumps had goosebumps.

Ava had absorbed Mia's energy. Blue light zapped and crackled not only through her, but around her like an electric storm. She became the lightning and wind, uplifting everything around her. The ground shook, walls trembled, and lightbulbs popped like gunshots. Centered in the brilliant phenomenon, she was Mother Nature about to unleash her wrath.

"Holy mother of all mothers." Ozzie's jaw slackened. "Do you see what I see, Rhett?"

"Yes," Rhett said with a grim smile. "That's my girl. I hope she gives them hell."

Mia stood her ground. Rhett gave her credit for courage but she was a fool. Rhett knew Ava would make the right choice, so he didn't try to stop her.

"Well, what's it going to be, *Mia*?" Ava's voice sounded as grand as her display of powers.

Rhett was learning something new about Ava every time she pushed herself, though he worried she might burst. He had no idea how her ability worked.

"I'm not going to apologize, you freak."

Oh, no. She did not just say that.

"Uh oh." Ozzie crouched lower. "Ava hates that word."

Four massage tables zoomed across the room at a flick of Ava's finger, boxing in the girls.

"Like this is going to stop me. Pathetic," Mia spat.

Mia didn't know when to quit. Ava didn't want to hurt her, but she kept punching Ava with insults. Rhett had to do something.

Ava's hands trembled. Her body was shutting down.

"No, they weren't intended to hurt you, and they certainly won't hold you in." Ava shook her thin shoulders. "That was a distraction—this will do the damage." Ava flicked her index finger. A metal tray flew off the counter like a rocket and collided with Mia's face, knocking her head to the table. "The table is to break your fall, idiot. I was being generous. What about you, Ella? Want to walk with me or be carried out like your friend?"

Ella blanched and softened her stance, giving the impression of compliance. Her voice squeaked like a frightened mouse. "I was going to cooperate. I swear I was. I'll walk."

Poor girl. She shook with her arms crossed over her midsection.

The door slid open.

"Why are you all wet? What happened here?" Naomi cursed, her eyes darting around the wrecked room. "Are you guys okay?"

Ozzie pointed to Ava, gawking at her as if she was a goddess. "She did it. It was pretty awesome."

Tamara laughed. "I should have been here earlier to see it all. The sounds did not do it justice."

Reyna smoothed a hand over her face. "We're in so much trouble. Zen's not going to like this. It's a good thing this room had no windows."

"Well, at least we're all going down together." Rhett planted a kiss on his girl and supported her with an arm around her waist. When she'd stopped the bullets at Mitch's apartment, she'd fainted. "You okay?"

Rhett gripped her shaky hand. So cold. All the warmth flushed out of her when Helix had diminished or had burned out. Or however her power worked.

"Yeah. Just a little lightheaded. At least I didn't black out. I got a little carried away."

"A little. Just a little." Rhett chuckled to lighten the mood.

"Are you and Oz okay?" She examined him. "You're wet."

"Oz and I are fine. Do you want a change of clothes? We could try to find—"

"No. Let's get out of here."

Rhett was worried about her. How much could her body take?

Ava had practiced every spare second. Anyone else would be wiped out, but maybe someone like her didn't need a lot of time to recover. If Helix could replenish her quickly, then perhaps it was all good.

"Come on. Someone want to help me drag this lunatic?" Ozzie's shoes squeaked and squashed through two inches of water as he headed toward Mia. "Yup, Zen is going to flip out. Can we pretend it didn't happen? Or do one of you girls have the power to put everything back together? Why can't I have that kind of power? Why am I talking and nobody is answering me?"

"'Cause you talk too much, Ozwald." Rhett grabbed Mia's other arm and hauled her up with Ozzie's help.

Ozzie's mouth scrunched together into a pout. "Ozzie. It's Ozzie or Oz."

How Rhett loved to mess with him, and Rhett knew Ozzie liked it, too, since he did the same to Rhett. It was the way they were.

215

CHAPTER TWENTY-SEVEN – MY LIFE

MITCH

Mitch hated being a spy.

Although the former United States had pulled itself back together, or at least most parts, they hadn't improved anything besides a huge leap forward in technology.

Greed and the thirst for power never went away, and thus a formidable network like ISAN had evolved. He'd bet his life other shady organizations had existed during his grandparents' generation, and they had probably been just as ruthless.

They were supposed to learn from their mistakes, learn what their forefathers did wrong, but they repeated them instead.

As soon as Novak left for the clandestine meeting, Mitch arranged to have the two girls sent to Lydia's room. Somewhere safe and homey. Mitch had one agenda in mind and he had to get it done. No room for failure.

Mitch had asked Lydia to speak to them first. If they were approached with someone kinder, like a sister figure, they might lower their guard enough to listen. Besides, he figured they would trust a woman more easily than a man.

"Girls, this is Mitch, the gentleman I spoke to you about," Lydia introduced Mitch when he entered. Her voice had a way of soothing him.

The tension that had spiked when he'd first walked in

dispersed.

"You checked your room for bugs?" Mitch scrutinized about the space, inhaling the scent of roses. The roses he'd gifted her.

"Yes. We're all clear."

"Good. Nina. Cora." Mitch said their names with a polite nod and then sat on the sofa across from them.

Lydia shuffled closer to him but kept her distance. "I told them about ISAN and offered them a chance to join us on a special, secret unit, working together for the good of our society."

A big fat lie, but good enough.

"Yes, Lydia is right." Mitch leaned closer to the edge, his hands resting on his knees. "We need girls with your talents. Mr. Novak spoke to you earlier, right?"

Nina crinkled her pierced nose. "Yes. He gave us two options. Live or die. What kind of group is this?"

Mitch didn't blame her. There had been no tenderness in either Novak's words or manner, he was sure of it.

"Lydia and I are not like Novak, and we would like to help you. Live or die are his words, not ours. But I'll tell you this, he will stick to his word, so if you don't do exactly as I say, he will have you killed."

"This is bull." Nina shot up, frightened. "He can't make us do anything. We're out of here."

Cora stroked a hand down on one of her braids and vanished. *Incredible.*

"Sit down, Nina. And Cora, no using your power in front of me unless I tell you to do so."

The girls bristled at his harsh tone. Nina didn't act on her threat, and Cora reappeared.

No more Mr. Nice Guy. Mitch had to lay it out to them. He

normally would not expose himself, but he saw an opportunity that would help the rebels and help him. Secret weapons of his own.

Mr. Novak hadn't been sharing his plans. Not knowing what he had up his sleeve drove him insane. He had to prepare for the unknown. So, he planned to create a team of his own behind Novak's back.

"Now, listen to me carefully and listen well. Novak will carry out his threat, I kid you not." Mitch shifted toward Lydia, giving her the stage. He needed the girls to see he told the truth. When Lydia nodded, he continued.

"Mr. Novak runs ISAN but I run this quadrant. Yes, there are more ISAN locations. When he comes back tomorrow, I'm going to tell him you're willing to join our force. You will train. You will be fed. You will work with kids your age and you will not cause trouble. Do you understand?"

The girls swapped glances, their baleful expression turned apprehensive, then they faced him. Their attitudes were checked.

"I will do everything in my power to keep you alive, but in return I need your absolute loyalty over Novak."

Nina placed an elbow on the armrest and rubbed the side of her face. "You mean be like a double agent?"

"Yes. I'm putting my life on the line by helping you, because now you know I am one, too. You have put your trust and faith in me, and I must do the same with you. But if you tell anyone, I will kill you myself. All I have to do is make a phone call or give you the wrong serum and you are gone. As long as the two of you understand this, we will be fine."

"You're working with the rebels?" Cora's face lit up, her eyes darting from me to Lydia. "You're working with Sniper?"

Sniper? Then Mitch recognized the name. He rolled his eyes.

"Yes, I know him." His tone dulled, flattened. She shouldn't know that name. "How do you know Sniper?"

"It's a long story but we were homeless," Cora said. "We traveled with the black market to different quadrants. We tried to steal food from this old Chinese man, Mr. Lee, but instead of turning us in, he gave us free food. When he noticed we were … different, he told us about Sniper. He told us to wait around and he would come by, but we didn't want to stick around. We helped the old man with errands, but he couldn't pay us—"

"So you used your powers to get what you wanted," Mitch finished, and there was nothing light about his tone anymore. "Do you know how irresponsible your actions were? You not only hailed attention from the media, you got Novak's, too. It's why you're in this mess. And this is the reason you will do exactly as I tell you."

The girls cowered. It was then Mitch knew he had them.

"Do we have a deal, ladies?" Mitch met each of their resigned gazes.

"Seems like we have no choice." Nina sighed and rubbed under her chin.

"Yes," Cora said and pressed her lips together so tight she looked like she was constipated.

Mitch spread his arms wide. "Sorry, but just remember you got yourselves here. You did this. And let me remind you—do not show off your powers under any circumstances unless I tell you. It's forbidden. Lydia will go over the rules with you. If there is any problem or if you see anything suspicious, or if you feel like your life has been threatened, contact me and only me. One more thing before I go—Lydia was not here at this meeting. She came after I was done. Is that clear?"

"Yes." The girls flashed a glance at Lydia and then back to me.

Mitch gave a curt nod and prayed his tactics would not backfire, or he was good as dead. It was not just his life he had put out there. Mitch gave a knowing smile to the woman he had come to cherish and left.

No one knew about Mitch and Lydia's relationship. It had bloomed slowly after Rhett and his crew had escaped. On one of their encounters, Rhett had said, "You love danger, Mitch. It's your downfall. One day you'll get it when you love someone as much as I love Ava."

Mitch finally got it. He really did.

Rhett didn't know about Lydia. Mitch would never expose them. Rhett and Ava were idiots. They hadn't been overt when they first met, but everyone could see the attraction. You had to be blind not to.

Rhett and Ava were safe, but Lydia and Mitch were a different story. Mitch would shelter Lydia from Novak, no matter the cost.

Lydia knew Rhett was his half-brother, as did Novak, but in front of everyone, Mitch made it clear he despised Rhett. Sometimes he did.

Others might have done things differently, perhaps not switched on the alarm during the big escape, but it was the right call. One of the guards had seen Mitch with them, talking in a civil manner, and he hadn't tried to stop them.

Mitch felt horrible, but he was the one left behind. He had to stay alive and be their only guardian from this end. What a surprise when he found out Lydia had been sent by Councilor Chang long before they were there.

Lydia and Mitch had bumped into each other at a restaurant, and they both looked like they had been through the wringer. After too many drinks, they had confessed their roles.

They had each other to rely on, and it kept Mitch from going insane. There were days when he wanted out of here, to join Rhett and his rebel team. At least there he wouldn't have to watch his back, though he might have to cover his ass from Ozzie.

There were times when Mitch wondered if Novak knew about him. But if he did, he would shoot him on the spot.

Mitch headed to his room and waited for Lydia. He had spoken to her about his plan, and so far all seemed to be going well. Lydia liked his idea of preparing the girls by using Novak's facilities but keep them loyal to them. It had better work, or they were screwed.

Lydia shouldered through the door about thirty minutes later. For a brief moment, Mitch soaked her in. The lavender dress she wore framed her hourglass figure nicely. He took her into his arms, releasing the stress, and was engulfed by her flowery scent that always calmed him.

"Hey. All good?" Mitch cupped her cheeks and gave her a kiss.

"Yeah. I took them to Diana and asked her to show them their rooms and get them started on lesson one."

"Good idea." Mitch led her to his bed.

They sat side by side and then simultaneously fell back with a thump on the mattress.

Lydia kicked off her heels and propped up an elbow. "That was so stressful. I didn't know if you could convince them."

Mitch mimicked her pose and caressed her arm. "I wished you would have stayed out of it. I didn't want you involved. If something were to happen to you—"

Lydia waved a hand. "Like I'm not in this deep already. I've been in here longer than you, remember?"

"You remind me all the time." He sounded annoyed.

"I'll keep reminding you. And ..." She ran a slow hand across his chin, where the stubble barely showed. "You, my dear, need to stop sending me flowers."

Mitch traced a hand over her shoulder and made idle circles on her neck. "How else am I to show you how much I care about you besides sneaking you into my room?"

"I like sneaking around with you more than flowers. Besides, the roses are too expensive." She bit her bottom lip, hiking up her leg to anchor around his, exposing her skin.

Indeed, they were, but she was worth it.

Lydia had softened him. Where he might have punched someone before, he more often yelled at them instead. There was a *we* in their team, and he didn't feel so alone. Through their relationship, he understood Rhett and Ava's.

Before, he'd wondered why anyone would want to be attached to someone but not now. Lydia made it all bearable. She brightened his days and gave him hope. A reason to live.

Mitch's hand went to her leg. He trailed up ever so slowly. She moaned and moved closer.

"Do people ask you about the flowers?"

"Most students don't. One time, Novak asked me about them, and I told him I sent them to myself."

"Good thinking. And you were able to get the remedy to Chang?" Mitch might have broken the mood, but these questions were important.

"I did. I hope I got it to her in time to save Brooke. She's a good girl. She doesn't deserve—"

"I know." He smoothed her hair away from her face. "But whatever happens to Brooke won't be your fault."

Lydia sat up and crossed her legs, playfulness all gone. "There's something I don't understand. You administered the serum to them. Couldn't you tell it wasn't the right serum?"

The question sounded accusatory, and Mitch needed to clear the air. "No, I couldn't. The serums had names on the vials, which I'd thought was strange, but I had no time to ask questions. We were at the battlefield. I figured the girls needed different dosages."

"I see." Lydia dipped her head, focusing on the blanket, her expression unreadable.

"What is it? You don't believe me?"

His heart lodged up his throat. Had he said something wrong? He'd dated many women, but Lydia was special to him. She alone had the power to break his heart.

"Yes, of course I believe you. Sorry, I was thinking." Lydia folded his hands into hers, and she looked like she needed to tell him something important.

Her chestnut eyes drew him in, and her dimples deepened when she smiled even slightly. Mitch sat there like a love-sick fool. She parted her mouth to speak but he rushed in.

"You're so beautiful." Mitch loosened her hair clip, and dark hair cascaded down her face. "I don't think I've ever seen anything more beautiful than you."

Lydia blinked, and her face beamed hot red. Seeing her flushed was the sexiest thing.

"Thank you." She took a moment, and then her expression turned serious. "There's something I need to tell you."

"What is it?" Mitch straightened his spine and released her hand.

"I might have some information. I haven't told Chang yet. It could be nothing, but it could be something to look into." Lydia inhaled a shuddering breath as if it took much energy to speak. "I found out through a source, Roxy was sent to a facility."

"Well, I knew that. Novak wasn't about to send her to another foster care system. I'm surprised he didn't kill her."

Mitch might have spoken too soon, which he tended to do. Lydia narrowed her eyes at him.

"Go on." Mitch motioned with his finger to encourage her to speak faster.

"I'm certain Roxy was sent there to be experimented on. And get this … Gene, the one that was kidnapped by the rebels—"

"Yes?" His interest piqued.

"Well, he's been going to the same facility. My question is, why does he get to go in and out when Roxy didn't? Also, my source told me there are numbers on a data log. Many numbers. I think each number identifies a human being."

"Novak doesn't want to use names, so he's using numbers." Mitch stared at the gray wall. "So, then maybe …" He met her eyes again. "Where and how did you get this information? Who is your source?"

"She's one of the guards and she travels to the facility. The guards are stationed outside and are never allowed in. When they are taken back and forth, they are blindfolded."

Rhett's mind spun, wheels turning a mile a minute. "I need that list. Or better yet, I need to get inside. Maybe I can find out where my father was taken."

Lydia placed a hand on his arm, her expression sympathetic. "Mitch, you don't know what happened to your father. You can't assume he's alive."

"You know how much my father means to me. He wouldn't have taken off and never returned, especially when my mother left without a word. He was a responsible parent. He would—there has

224

to be an explanation. The ridiculous amount of money deposited into mine and Rhett's account, how I got that letter from ISAN the day after, nothing about it makes sense. He was kidnapped. I'm on the right track. I've come this far and done many things I'm ashamed of, but if it leads me to my father, then it would have been worth it."

"I know." She released a breath. "I'll see what I can do. Not just for your father's sake, but something is happening there, wherever there is."

"Does Novak go there often? Do you know? None of us ever question where he goes or what he does."

She shook her head. "I don't have answers for you. He'd probably suspect something if I asked."

"Were you able to get Gene's profile?"

"No, not yet. It's strange, though. He's not in our system. Everyone is listed—their background, their blood type, even the breakdown of their DNA, but not Gene. Why?"

"I don't know, but we need to get it as soon as possible. I don't feel right about Gene being locked up in the rebel base. You heard Novak. Gene has instructions to carry out. Tamara grabbed him so it wasn't like he manipulated them, but he just happened to be at the right place at the right time. It doesn't make sense why he was there and his unit was elsewhere. You don't abandon your troop unless you know something and want to witness it. I don't have anything but guesses right now but I need his profile. It might tell us what Novak is up to."

"Sure. I'll do what I can. Perhaps Sabrina might have something."

"What are you going to tell her? I don't want her running to Novak. Fingers will be pointed at you and I don't like it."

"I could say I'm worried about him, being locked up, and that I would like to study his profile to see how I can help."

"It might work. Okay." Mitch rubbed his temples. His head throbbed. "But be careful."

Mitch rose from the bed and stood in front of the small mirror on his desk. He brushed back his hair, smoothing a strand in place.

Their time had expired. They had teams to see and places to be. When he looked presentable, he paced to Lydia, who was off the bed, adjusting her dress and shoving her feet into her heels.

"Be careful with your source," Mitch said, planting a gentle kiss on her forehead. "You can't trust anyone. For all we know, it could be a trap."

"I will. And you too."

Mitch headed to the wall next to his hand scanner, told the door to open, and peeked to see if anyone stood outside. At his all-clear signal, Lydia rushed out. After a few minutes, he strutted out of his room toward Russ's office.

Mitch's bad mood was going to suck for the next squad. He needed to burn some energy and frustration—lots of it. When he pulled up his chip to see the schedule, he grinned with satisfaction. Payton's team was next on his agenda.

CHAPTER TWENTY-EIGHT – PAYTON'S TEAM

MITCH

Mitch had lost count of how many girls he had trained, but among all of them, no one had ever come close to Ava's time on mental mission, and no one had her spunk in the field.

Justine might be the next best, but all she cared about was winning. Working as a team came behind victory, the glory under her name.

Mitch missed Ava, Brooke, and Tamara. He hadn't noticed it back then, but they'd made him laugh with their idiotic jokes and their friendliness. They were what he would call the "normal" girls. Girls you could hang with and have a meaningful conversation.

When Novak came back the next day, Mitch convinced him the new girls would be acquiescent. He gave Mitch the green light to not only train them, but to place them under Payton's group.

"Mitch?" Nina called. "We're ready."

Nina and Cora wore ISAN's gray, skintight uniform, but they seemed uncomfortable, shifting their weight and glancing about the room as if someone would jump out at them.

Nina's nose ring was gone. ISAN didn't allow room for individuality.

"Don't be shy." Mitch gestured with his hand. "Come in."

They nodded and offered nervous smiles. Not the same girls he'd seen before. They'd had a taste of ISAN's brutal reality, and

Novak's end-game declaration.

Justine sauntered in behind Payton.

"You're both late," Mitch said, keeping his tone neutral.

"Sorry. I was held up in Mr. Novak's office. He …" Payton stopped talking when he saw the new girls.

Why was Mitch not surprised Payton had been in Novak's office?

"I was waiting for him." Justine poked Payton's back. "So it's his fault."

Mitch frowned at her. "Of course it is. Nothing is ever your fault."

Justine's fists flew to her hips. "What do you mean?"

Mitch leaned so close her eyelashes fluttered from his proximity. "If you don't know, then too bad."

Justine flipped her hair back. Talking to her made him want to punch himself. She was Novak's spawn for sure.

"Wait." She looked across the mat at the new girls. "What are they doing here? Where's Bethany, Alice, and Tessa?"

"Units have been shuffled. If you have a problem, talk to Mr. Novak."

Justine scoffed, her eyes rolling.

After Mitch demonstrated some basic moves and worked with them one-on-one, it was time for the girls to practice with the team. He paired them up and paced about the mat to observe their strengths and weaknesses.

Justine knocked Cora down with a leg sweep. Cora hissed and got back up, fists rounded and legs apart.

"I've been here a lot longer than you, girl. You'll never beat me." Justine squatted lower to dodge a swing and socked Cora in the stomach when she saw a clear opening.

Cora flew back and crashed on the mat, her arms and legs spread.

"I told you." Justine smirked.

Nina left Payton and dashed across the mat. Even knowing what she would do, Mitch didn't stop her. She slammed into Justine. They tumbled together. Justine leaped off her and got back to her feet.

"You idiot. I'm not your partner." Justine grabbed Nina's shirt and tossed her like a rag doll.

Cora, having been partner-swapped, dashed to Payton.

When Cora attacked Payton, he flipped her over his shoulder. Cora landed on her back with a thump and refused to get up.

A scream captured Mitch's attention when Nina tackled Justine again. They struggled, arms flailing with blow after blow.

Mitch should stop this, but it was quite entertaining. Even Payton snickered beside him. Before it got out of hand, Mitch whistled with the tip of his tongue pressed against his teeth.

They didn't stop.

Mitch blew again.

Finally, they halted, their chests heaving and sweat trickling down their temples.

"Get off me," Justine sneered.

Silver light filled Nina's eyes and a spark flashed from her fingertip. Not as big as before, but enough to cause a problem.

Again, Mitch should have stopped Nina, but ...

Justine's eyes grew wide with horror. She dragged herself back, but Nina moved faster and grabbed Justine's leg.

Justine shot across the mattress like a rocket and slammed into the wall. The ends of her hair frizzed out like she'd put her finger in a socket. Mitch should run to check on her, make sure she was breathing, but her chest rose and fell, and hate twisted her face.

She deserved it.

"I'm going to murder you," was all Justine managed to say before she blacked out.

"Well, team. That was productive." Mitch pointed at Nina, who sat with her shoulders slumped. "You just showed us what not to do to our team members. This is your last warning. Do not ever display your power again. Only in the field, and then only when your lead, Payton, or I ask you to do so. Got it?"

Mitch didn't listen to her reply. He clicked on his chip that had been chiming. A message from Lydia opened.

I got it. Meet me. Vague and simple, but he knew what it was.

Mitch clapped once. "That concludes our training for today. I believe you're seeing Russ next."

After everyone was out of the training room, he booked it to his room and waited for Lydia. Mitch paced the length from the desk to his bed until her face appeared on his door screen.

"Open," he said.

The door whooshed and closed itself when she entered.

"What do you have for me?" Mitch greeted her with a kiss on the cheek.

They didn't get comfortable. They stood there, tense with urgency. It had always been like this. Finding time alone was rare. Their relationship could not be discovered. They didn't want to give Novak ammunition if one of them got caught.

Such a dangerous game they played.

Lydia released a long, heavy sigh, but her eyes beamed. "Sabrina sent me Gene's file." A twist of her lips crinkled the corner or her mouth.

"Why do you look so worried?"

"She sent it to me without asking questions. She didn't say anything to me like, I hope we find him soon, or I hope he's okay. Something to indicate she was worried about him, even though he was under her supervision."

Mitch scratched his neck and scrunched his nose. "I've worked with her before, and she's cold. Not as warmhearted as you." He caressed her face. That soft smooth skin of hers. "Maybe she sent it because you're one of the supervisors. If she asked you for the file of one of our girls, you would send it to her, right?"

She nodded, but stared off as if in thought. "Perhaps you're right."

"Have you read it?"

Her eyes glimmered, as if she realized something. "Yes. It's impressive."

Lydia tapped on her chipped arm and a picture of Gene popped up. She shared her file so he could see as well.

"Male. Six-feet. Half-Asian." He read the words under his picture and then flipped to the next page.

What Mitch processed next was unfathomable. He wasn't a scientist, but he'd had to study the basics of DNA and the human genome, and Gene's was remarkable. His DNA was similar to Ava's, but not identical.

Lydia's incredulous expression met his.

"Right? This kid is not only a genius, but—"

"Read the notes." Lydia pointed, but her finger went through the written words.

Mitch found himself reading aloud to Lydia as shock took hold. "Gene's body adjusts to any temperature."

"Incredible. He never gets cold or hot," Lydia said. "Go on."

"His system modifies and rebuilds. What?"

Lydia heard his confusion. "He can heal himself. I'm not sure if he could heal a bullet to his heart, but it says below at the asterisks he can rebuild tissue, muscles, and possibly bones at an accelerated rate."

"He's almost like Superman. Thank God he can't fly. Can he?" Mitch looked at Lydia to confirm. He should read more but he had to know.

"No." She tried to hide her frown but failed.

Her dimples caved inward, and his stomach somersaulted. Then he refocused on Gene.

"Gene's name is an acronym," Mitch said. "GENE. Genetically Enhanced Neo Entity. He was experimented on, and no one is calling attention to this? Novak would know. Sabrina knew, right? She has to know."

"Look." Lydia poked at the hologram. "It could be the coordinates to the facility he was sent to. It's what we've been looking for."

Mitch couldn't believe their luck. "Take a picture of the coordinates for me, will ya? I'm going to send it to Zeke for Rhett. I'll have to proceed carefully and find a way to bring it up with Novak. This is tricky. I'm not supposed to know it exists."

Then Mitch thought of Ava. Rhett had shared what Ava had found out from the journal her father had left behind. Ava had a twin. And Gene's DNA was similar to Ava's.

Dare he hypothesize Gene was Ava's twin? If this was true, could Ava heal herself? He tried to think back on her missions. When she'd cracked the window and landed on top of Thomax Thorpe, he'd injected her right away with painkillers. She had been taken to Dr. Machine.

For every scratch, nick, cut, or bruise, the girls went to Dr. Machine to not only heal them but to cosmetically get rid of any scar tissue. So she'd never had the chance to examine the possibility. And perhaps Novak never wanted her to find out.

Mitch continued to skim, tracking the words faster and faster.

Lydia gasped. "Read this, right here." She pointed toward the bottom, her voice lowering to a harsh whisper. "Gene and Ava are twins. Why weren't we told? Sabrina sent Gene's profile to me so the information is not a secret, but on Ava's profile, there is nothing about her twin."

My God. What else is ISAN hiding?

"Lydia. Transfer the document to me and then get rid of it on your end. I don't want Novak finding out you ever saw it."

"Okay." Her fingers danced along the icons and on hologram keys. "Done. Sent. Look." She increased the size of what she wanted him to read. "He can punch through concrete, glass, and walls, and even the thickest and unbreakable ones. He—my God—can kill someone with a punch to the chest."

Mitch swallowed the rock that had formed in his throat.

"Did you read the last sentence?"

"Getting to it." Mitch lowered his eyelashes, disgusted. He wanted to vomit. His face burned but his body became glacial. Mitch wasn't sure if he was still breathing. "Gene can ... he can ... oh, God. Listen carefully, Lydia. If Novak asks where I am, tell him I had to run some errands at the black market. Also, I need you to ask your source who guards the facility for help."

"Okay, I will. But where are you really going?" The lines on her forehead deepened.

Forget Gene could heal. Forget Gene could break through concrete and glass. What he'd read on the last line had me nearing a heart attack.

"I'm going to the black market. I have to get to Rhett. I have to find him and tell him about Gene or they're all dead."

CHAPTER TWENTY-NINE – GOING HOME

AVA

Inhaling a deep, soothing breath, I allowed Helix to work through me. Warmth bubbled in my chest, and the tingling sensation zapped to every nerve ending, through every vein, muscle, and bone.

Then, electrical lights had sizzled through and around my body. A similar incident had happened when the beat-up glider wouldn't fly, and I had directed the energy from Coco to ISAN guards. Like I had at Mitch's apartment rooftop, I saw the whole building blueprint, every single level, clearly. This time, I was able to ignore the information I didn't need.

My friends glowed like firelight. I saw through their skin and muscles, and the blood pumping through their veins. They had no identity. I didn't know who was who. Only their voices gave me their location.

After we had captured the girls, Helix lingered. The more powerful the Helix, the longer it took to pacify it. I was most surprised by how I had absorbed Mia's energy, used it as if it were my own.

Another new ability, I realized.

Going down the private employee elevator was a piece of cake, though not so easy for Rhett and Ozzie who were carrying a passed-out Mia. I focused on the countdown of the numbers when I started to feel boxed in.

We were standing shoulder-to-shoulder and the space seemed to get smaller. The zoom of the descending elevator reverberated in the quiet, and Rhett's sighs sounded like a whip. Every shift of movement assaulted my eardrums.

I wanted to puke.

I closed my eyes to steady my nerves and the Helix-induced chaos inside my body.

When Mia had attacked us in the massage room, my first instinct had been to protect, but I'd also wanted to fight back. I still hoarded anger and resentment over my mother dying too soon and a father who had experimented on his own children.

Those feelings had become my darkness and fed the Helix in me. Having a cause to fight for, to protect the ones I loved, gave me strength.

A heartbeat, the only one I wanted to hear, broke through the sensations. Rhett's heart, thumping faster and faster.

Rhett, slow down. I'm here.

My eyes opened, coming back to the present. My pulse slowed and Helix slumbered again.

"We're almost there." I squeezed Rhett's hand.

Sweat beaded his temples, and he wiped it away. "There's no air in here."

"We're almost there." I peered up at the floor numbers. "Look. Five. Four. Three. Two ..."

Ding.

I stepped out, checked to the left and right, and raised my hand to give the all-clear sign. We rushed through the back door and onto a bridge, into the frigid air. I pulled up Helix and my map guided me to our destination.

We traveled in our practiced formation with weapons drawn. Tamara and Naomi flanked me. Behind me, Reyna gripped Ella's arm. Rhett and Ozzie, carrying Mia, also followed in a line as water crashed below.

We were about twenty-four feet above the water, but I didn't know how deep the bottom reached.

"This way." I veered around a corner and led them off the bridge and into a dimly lit alley.

"It's freezing." Naomi rubbed her hands together and blew into them.

"Says the girl who can heat up her own hands." I snorted.

She shrugged nonchalantly. "So, is this what you've been doing? Saving girls with super powers?"

"Yes, and more. It's difficult to explain." Out of the alley, I pivoted right and headed north on the sidewalk.

"How far are we?" Naomi examined the boats docked to the left of us.

"We're close."

I admired the biggest yacht, the word *Freedom* painted across the bow, and wished I could sail away. To be able to have your own transport and go where you please … I would love to have that choice one day.

"Are we almost there yet?" Ozzie's breaths came in spurts.

"Yes, son. We're almost there." Rhett chuckled.

Ozzie's grumble was lost in the airstream.

My hologram map showed me a daylight view of the city. Even in the darkest areas, I clearly saw the boats ahead. The hydro gliders were parked and no one was inside. The public transportation had closed for the day.

"We're almost there," I hollered while looking over my

shoulder to ensure my troop had heard. "Not far. Less than a quarter mile."

"You have an awesome gift," Naomi said. "You can see the layout even though you've never been here before. You're like your own navigator." Naomi giggled. "Sorry, I have no idea why I'm laughing."

"It's fine. I've been called worse."

We walked the rest of the way in silence down long wooden planks, keeping our formation tight. The tall solar lamps gave just enough light to see the nearby surroundings. Five minutes later, we arrived.

The privately-owned hydro glider was smaller than I'd expected, but large enough to accommodate all of us. Most hydro gliders were shaped like bullets, but this one narrowed sharply at the front—sleeker and newly designed, it seemed.

Ozzie gave a wolf whistle. "Is that our ride?"

Before I had a chance to speak, something burst out of the water and floated over the waves. No. Not something. *Someone.* And more popped out ... about ten figures dressed in dark wet suits, pointing weapons at us.

Apparently, my map couldn't see through water.

"Stop right there. Don't move," the one in the center said, a high-tech weapon as long as his arm aimed at me.

"What now?" Rhett murmured.

The man had some sort of gadget on his back, like a mini-backpack, and then one around his wrist. I got a better view when he approached closer. A field around him shimmered, reflected by the lamplight, making his face and body hazy.

It was invisible to the human eye, but not mine. Some form of protective bubble encased him. The reason he could travel in or out of water.

"What do you want?" I said.

"I should be asking you that question, young lady. Who do you work for? What is your jurisdiction?"

Do I lie? What do I say?

I could leap for the first guy. Tamara had small knives at her disposal. She could probably take out two. But the shimmering thing protected them, and I didn't know if any weapon could penetrate it. Rhett or the others could help us take down the rest. But their arsenal ...

"It depends, gentlemen." I took a step closer to the ramp like I owned the night. I stopped advancing when their weapons cranked to life. Blue light glowed at the tips.

"Ava. Stop."

Naomi had forgotten not to use our names.

"Okay. I'm not going anywhere." I raised my hands.

I'd thought the man in the center would shoot me, but instead he directed his finger at me.

As his ensemble came closer, I stood there trembling in the unforgivable breeze. The man waved to this team, and they lowered their weapons.

"Ava. Rhett. Ozzie. Reyna. Tamara. Naomi." The man said each of our names as if he was taking a roll call. His helmet must have scanned our faces.

He shouldn't have known our names. Our chips emitted fake names. So that meant only one thing.

"Why didn't you tell me who you guys were in the first place? I'm Vince. People call me V."

Yeah, like I would just tell you my name.

Vince or V didn't register. As far as I knew, this guy was an adversary.

He propelled forward and landed in front of me. When the bubble shield released him, I grabbed my Taser, and pointed it at his chest, ignoring the fact he still held a tank of a weapon. My squad had out their weapons, too.

"Whoa, whoa, whoa. People, we're not your enemy. I'm the head of the northern rebel base. Councilor Chang directed us to assist your unit back home."

I lowered my Taser. Frank was from the North as well. His troop had split up. "Chang didn't tell us. It would have been nice if she had. I appreciate your assistance, but we're fine. You may go back where you came from."

Vince smacked his lips. "Sorry, sweetheart. That's not going to happen. We have our orders to escort you back to the base. Besides, I have another agenda. I've asked Chang to set up a meeting with Zen. So, we can stand here all night and argue about it, or you can cooperate and get in."

Rhett, who had been surprisingly quiet, said, "Fine. But I'll need to check in with Zen first. Got it?"

"Sure. Go right ahead as we waste time." He tapped his foot and glanced about like he was bored.

At first impression, Vince seemed relaxed and amiable, but now he made my blood run hot. He needed to check his attitude.

"You're clear." Rhett shut off his chip. "I've just been informed there was an attempt to assassinate Councilor Chang yesterday. Do you know anything about it?"

"Who do you think rescued her? My men and I were there disguised as C-guards. It happened before she got on her glider. She was on her way to the meeting. I had advised her to use a double. Chang got on the second glider with us, wearing a C-guard uniform. When we took off, the glider her double was in blew up. Fortunately, we were able to keep the incident from media exposure. My guess, Verlot was involved and ISAN assassins from the West or North somehow got through her security system."

Tamara gasped. "This is awful. We just saw her."

"This is a silent war," Vince said. "Verlot sits in his office feigning innocence while he's got ISAN doing his dirty work. I wouldn't be surprised if he stages an assassination attempt on himself."

"Let's talk inside, shall we?" Rhett said, shivering. "Someplace warm. We need to get going."

The wind howled and stole my breath.

"Wait." Reyna squinted. "What's that called?"

"It allows us to fly, too." Vince reached into his bag and took out a few gadgets. "It's called the propeller. It's your lucky day. You get to try it. It's one heck of an experience. Almost like flying. Ava, you first."

Vince placed a gadget around my wrist, which looked like a thick bracelet. After I punched in a code Vince gave me, an invisible layer of *something* engulfed me.

A hologram monitor appeared with a twinkle. An incandescent light flashed once and disappeared. Then the transporter rose, smooth and weightless as a bubble floating in the air.

Rhett went next, and then everyone else followed suit. When I tapped the upper arrow sign, the propeller floated skyward.

"This is so cool." Tamara's voice projected inside my propeller.

"Just letting you know, we are all connected. Whatever you say, we all hear it. So don't say something you'll regret." Vince chuckled, and then gave me a thumbs up when he glided next to me. "Ava, punch it."

I swiped my finger across a green square, and I soared higher and faster. "Why don't we have these?"

"Chang provided this equipment to us first to test it out." Vince's voice sounded as if he was standing next to me.

We sailed across the water like drifting petals. To my left, the city blurred, the colorful lights coalescing. To my right, nothing but the ocean darkness and the pinprick dots lighting our way.

CHAPTER THIRTY – G.E.N.E.S.

AVA

Zen greeted us inside. While Naomi and Tamara took the girls to their holding place, Vince and his ten-man crew held a meeting with Zen behind closed doors.

Rhett and I were headed to the kitchen to get something to eat when kids bombarded us.

"Rhett. Ava." Momo wrung her thin arms around us, sighing. "I'm so glad you're back."

Me too, kid.

Jasper, Stella, and others joined us, their shirts unkempt and grubby. I wondered what they'd been up to. The new group of kids got along well with the others. It had taken a few days for them to adjust, but they had bonded well.

Momo had been worried about us. Losing a loved one could do that to you.

My lips tugged at the corners when I thought of Momo's spunky attitude and unwavering confidence. She was keeping a positive front, despite her friend's death. I admired her courage.

"So, what did you do all day?" I took in each grimy shirt.

"Lots of labor." Stella drooped her shoulders, looking winded. Strands of hair stuck out from her low ponytail, as if she'd just woken up.

Momo hiked a finger over her shoulder. "Remember the pile

242

of shit?" She shot her gaze to the panel on the ceiling, looking sheepish. "I meant, the pile of *stuff*. Well, our team was put in charge of cleaning. Meaning"—she swallowed and fanned her face—"I sweated a lot. We had to carry stuff outside and make another pile. It was a lot of work."

"Yeah," her friends said all together.

"Nah. That was nothing." Jasper waved a hand.

"It took most of the day. What do you mean, 'that was nothing'?" Coco gave Jasper a light shove.

Jasper, always the joker, chuckled. Just listening to the cute sound gave me all the good feels.

My plan in delegating to Jo had worked. She'd kept the kids busy.

"Did you find anything interesting?"

Who knew what was buried beneath it all? All the floor levels and the back of the building had collapsed. The front and side of the edifice was the only thing that had survived the earthquake.

"I found a skull and some skeletons." Jasper's face contorted.

"Shut up. You found no such things." Stella smacked his arm.

"Ouch. Why you gotta hit me?" He massaged his biceps.

"Why do you think?" Stella rubbed her knuckles on his head.

"Anyway," Momo drawled. "I found old things—a computer monitor, a keyboard, and something called a mouse." She used her fingers to outline an oval shape in midair and then curled her fingers like a claw. "Zen said people didn't have chips and holograms back then. Can you imagine that?"

"No." I shook my head, humoring her.

She rambled on about the old items they had found as if they were ancient artifacts.

"You guys did a great job. I'm proud of you for helping out,"

243

Rhett said.

"Well, we did other chores, too." Momo cocked her head toward the kitchen area. "And Zen gave us a tour of the whole Hope City. We went to the other dilapidated building, and even the prison, but we didn't get to see Gene. Oh, look. You'll never guess what we found."

She reached inside her hoodie's front pocket and pulled out a dandelion. Her friends did the same. They each held one.

I choked up thinking of my mother, as I brushed the necklace Rhett had gifted me.

"Here." Momo handed one to Rhett and me. "It's like the dandelion inside Ava's pendant. It's so rare to see things growing in this dry land, especially around waste piles. Don't forget to make a wish when you blow it. Well, we'd better get going. Jo will get mad at us if she sees us taking your time and chatting when it's not our break. Come guys—let's leave the two love birds alone." With a giggle and a shake of her shoulders, she sprinted away.

"Thanks for the—" I didn't bother to finish. They wouldn't have heard.

"Well, look at that. I think this is a sign fate is on our side." Rhett dragged the flower down the bridge of my nose and kissed the tip.

"I hope you're right." I twirled the dandelion and examined it like I had never seen one before. "It's beautiful. Some people don't see the beauty in it, but ever since my mother told me about them, I saw them differently."

"Blow on mine and I'll blow on yours." He brought his inches from my mouth.

I closed my eyes and made a wish. When I opened them, I blew so hard, the seeds stuck to Rhett's sweaty face. My laughter bounced off the walls while I brushed them away.

Rhett chuckled and fanned his face. "What did you wish for?"

"Don't you know the rule? You shouldn't tell or it won't come true."

"Well, in that case, my turn."

I held up my flower toward the ceiling and he let out a breath. The white seeds danced in the air as a gentle breeze carried them away.

"What did you wish for?" I followed the seeds with my eyes.

"You don't follow your own rules, Ava?"

"Doesn't mean I can't ask."

Rhett looked at me with tenderness, and I felt his love to my marrow. I didn't know what I'd done right to have him in my life.

"Mine already came true the day you came back to me." He rested his forehead against mine.

I melted right then and there. My insides ripped a little at the agony of what he had been through, what we had been through. But then I ignited with warmth. Against all odds, we had made it. I was here with him. Beside each other was where we belonged. Our home.

My throat clogged. "My wish came true when I remembered you."

"This is temporary," I said to Ella. "I promise you'll be out of there after we go through a process."

Rhett and I had paid her cell a visit when she had asked for me.

She'd been tossed in a new environment with people she

didn't know. I understood her concerns. When Rhett had kidnapped me and I hadn't known where I was, I hadn't handled it well. Unlike me, Ella was cooperative.

"Okay." Ella sat next to Mia, who was spread out on the mattress.

Mia was still unconscious.

We had taken the girls to the second cell. I hadn't known there were two until Rhett had taken me across the hall, opposite the room from Gene.

"Zen will be here soon." I glanced to the door as if he would walk in any second. "The guards are here to protect you so no harm will come to you."

"Somebody wants to hurt us?"

Ella scrunched her cheeks, apprehension written across her face. I should've kept my mouth shut.

"No." I held up my hands like that would help her understand. "Nobody wants to hurt you. Just, you'll see. I'll be back, okay?"

Ella's eyes filled with tears, and I felt like crap, but there was nothing I could do to make it easier for them. I couldn't promise Zen the girls wouldn't attack. Maybe they wouldn't attack Ella, but her friend was something else.

"Hey, Ava. Are there more kids like us? I mean, what's going to happen to us?"

"I promise you're in good hands. Zen is going to explain everything and what your options are, but I promise nothing bad will happen."

I meant it. No harm would come to those who didn't want to fight in our war. We would not operate like ISAN. These girls hadn't been trained, and there was certainly no time to bring them

246

up to par with the rest of us. If they wanted to help, that would be their choice. But they had the right to choose.

"Okay." She clasped her shaky hands together.

I decided to try to calm her down a bit more. What I really wanted to do was listen to Zen and Vince's conversation. Whatever they were planning to do to bring down ISAN, I wanted to know. I wanted in.

Looking over my shoulder at Rhett, I held up my index finger. "Give me a second." When he nodded, I closed the distance to the glass dividing us. "When did you start showing signs you were different?"

The words came out colder and more uncaring than they sounded in my head, but Ella didn't seem offended.

She tucked her knees to her chest. "The first time I noticed I was different, I was five years old. I blew out my birthday candles. I must have blown too hard. Instead of the flames dying, they somehow spread to the few children across from me. My friend's hair got burned. The boy caught fire on his face. And the other kid, on his neck."

I rubbed my collarbone, understanding her devastation. "I'm so sorry."

"Yeah, I know. Horrible." She offered a humorless laugh. "My parents claimed something was wrong with the candles. I never blew out birthday candles again. I didn't want to rob that bank, but I didn't want Mia to go alone. It's no excuse, but I wanted to protect her. Or more like I needed to put a leash on her. She's overwhelmed and yet fascinated with what she can do. She only found out recently, and she was determined to make the government pay. She wants compensation. She said the councilors did this and they hid the truth from all of us. Something to do with

247

the meteor."

"Well, you'll get your answers. I want to make sure you get the correct information. I'm not the one to tell that story." I didn't want to be the one to explain. Zen was better at it.

"Sure. I'll wait." She raised her chin and looked downward. "I have nowhere to go, anyway."

"Again. I'm so sorry to leave you here, but you can't guarantee me your friend will be friendly."

"I know. It's fine. It's better than being handed over to the C-guards or worse, getting thrown in jail."

"Yes. I agree with you. Anyway, I have things to take care of. I'll be back."

Rhett was already halfway up the stairs when I backed away. This side of the cell looked exactly like the one in which Gene was held captive.

I reached the top and watched the door shut. "Do you have any other surprise rooms you haven't told me about?"

The door swished, thumped, and clicked.

"Maybe," Rhett said. "I'll show you when everyone goes to sleep."

"I see. In that case, I'll wait." My tone did not come off as playful as his.

Rhett had caught on to my effort. I could never hide anything from him. He held me in his arms and we stood there without a word. Even though our mission had been simple and we hadn't been harmed, it could have gone worse.

For a moment, I allowed myself to only feel Rhett's warmth as my chest brushed against his.

Let the stress go. Gone. *Let the worries go.* Gone. Refocus. *Your team needs you.* I hoped one day they wouldn't.

Call it physiological or mental or whatever, but when I had been given a dose of Helix at ISAN, I'd felt invincible. I hadn't let myself fear or have doubts. I hadn't cared if I lived or died, and so much had changed.

"I know you don't want to see Gene," Rhett said. "But I just got a message from Zen. Gene has been asking for you."

Rhett's words lingered in the air, and I pretended to not have heard.

"Did you hear me, babe?"

"Yeah. Do we have to?" I tilted my head, arching my back. "I really don't like him."

Rhett pulled me up, his face close to mine. "We don't have to see him if you don't want to, but I think you should see what he has to say."

"Fine." I sighed.

I veered to the left to the other wall and rested my hand on the scanner. Zen had programmed the sensors so Rhett and I had access to Gene's cell. We went down and greeted the guards, and I dragged my feet closer to the glass while Rhett stood in the back.

Gene offered what looked like a genuine smile, all his teeth showing. "Oh hey, sis. So glad you decided to visit me. And, you cut your hair. I like it."

I wanted to wipe that smirk off his face and knock the legs off his chair. He would be right where he belonged, kissing the ground and begging me to release him.

I wondered who had given him a chair.

"What do you want?" My tone matched my slumped shoulders.

"I haven't seen you in days, it seems. You'll have to excuse me if I'm wrong. I'm not aware what day or time it is."

I hated his mocking words and his sweet voice, but I gave it right back.

"Yes, you are aware, brother. You can count the number of meals served to you."

He crossed his leg and rubbed his chin. "True."

"I see you've cleaned up and changed clothes."

But no shaving. He could take out the razor and use it as a weapon, no doubt.

"Oh, yes. Well, the shower is right over there." He cocked his head to the right. "And the guards were nice enough to bring me fresh but common clothes. They're not as soft as the ones in ISAN, but when you're a prisoner, you can't complain."

I'd had enough. "I have things to do, so let's cut to the chase. Why did you ask to see me?"

He rose and met me at the barrier. "I've changed my mind. I want to be nice. Let me out for a day or even an hour. It's lonely here. I promise to behave."

Liar. I didn't have time for his games.

I pivoted on my heel and strode away wordlessly. Either he would confess the truth or he would throw a tantrum.

Still, a part of me felt guilty. Was he trying to reach out to me? People acted differently under desperate circumstances.

"Ava. My name is Gene, but it's not *just* Gene. That's what Novak said to me. GENES stands for Genetically Enhanced Neo Entity Subject. I've been enhanced and so have you."

Almost to the stairs, I stopped dead in my tracks. Blood ran cold through my veins.

He continued. "Though we should be the same, we're not. I embraced the power and was treated like royalty, while you squealed like a pig and cowered in the gutter. We have similar genes and yet the only thing you can do is that ludicrous map thing in your head." He scoffed. "And people think you're special. Now that's funny."

My insides detonated like a bomb, but I waved off his nasty comment. I didn't want him to think his words got to me. I knew I had been experimented on, but what else was he willing to share? Slowly, I turned to look at the devil's face.

"You don't remember the facility, do you?" he said.

I skirted closer. "What facility?"

"You know, the place where kids get sent if they've been deported."

My instinct had told me kids who wanted to leave ISAN weren't sent back to juvie or back to their foster parents as we had been told. I'd thought they were terminated, but if he was telling the truth, I'd been wrong.

"You're lying," I said.

His eyes grew wider, drawing me in, daring me to believe him. "What if I'm not? Would you dismiss a chance to take the organization down? Don't you want to save those kids?"

I moseyed closer. "How many?"

"That's for me to know and you to find out."

I hissed through my nose and a soft growl escaped me. Helix sizzled to my fingertips. I wanted to zap him out of existence and didn't know if my power could penetrate the wall.

"Ava."

Rhett's cry of warning steadied me, and I rethought my tactics. *Be smarter. Don't let him get to you.*

"I'll tell you this much." Gene raised one finger at a time until he held up four. "Kids from all four quadrants were detained there. How many were shipped out of ISAN on a weekly or monthly basis? Don't you want to find out?"

Even one person was too many. I sought Rhett's gaze, silently asking for his advice. Making this call on my own didn't seem right. When Rhett nodded, I felt better about the decision.

"Fine." I clenched and unclenched my fists on the glass. "I'll take you out for an hour, but you have to tell me where this facility is. And if you're lying to me, you'll be wishing for death."

"It's a deal. You won't regret it. But I won't be giving you any information until I'm out of here."

The sharp curl of his lips into a smug grin gave me chills.

Are you sure, Ava? Are you doing the right thing?

But what was the harm in taking him out for one hour?

He would be heavily guarded. Then Mitch's warning came to mind. Perhaps he should be partially sedated.

I had to know where this facility was located. If there was any chance he was telling the truth, we had to do something. The facility was part of ISAN. Bringing down a limb of the network would be a win.

"You go with your hands cuffed behind you and you'll get a light dose of sedation, or the deal is off." I gestured at the guards to carry out my words.

He scoffed. "You don't trust me, sis? Good. I wouldn't either."

Those words made me want to run. I wished I didn't know him. He was hot and cold. Night and day. Diabolical.

Warm hands on my shoulder let me know Rhett had had enough, too. Then he opened a cabinet to take out the sedative and went to help the guards.

The barrier whooshed open. Something clinked, metal touching metal. Handcuffs.

"Spread out your feet and put your arms on the glass," Rhett said to Gene. "You even so much as flinch, I'll bring your ass down. Do you understand?"

"What if I blink? Is that flinching? I just want to make sure."

Seriously? He was such a pain in the ass.

"Just shut up and do as I say, or I'll repeat what happened the last time," Rhett snapped and administered the dosage.

"Oh, I remember. It wasn't fun, but don't worry, I'll return the favor."

"Rhett." My heart ricocheted against my ribcage, a warning.

Rhett said nothing, focused and careful, taking Gene out of the cell.

"Guards, open the door," Rhett said.

I followed behind, my Taser ready.

Gene's smile was way too big for his face.

Please don't let me regret this.

CHAPTER THIRTY-ONE – LOVELY BROTHER

AVA

Zen looked surprised when he saw Gene, handcuffed, Rhett and me flanking him on either side.

"What's going on?" Zen placed his TAB on the counter and walked away from Vince. He dropped his voice to a whisper when he approached. "Did he finally confess something worthwhile?"

"He is right here. His name is Gene. You do realize I can hear, right?"

Zen stared down at Gene wordlessly. He clenched his jaw, veins on his neck protruding. I understood his frustration. Talking to Gene could make a person want to kill themselves.

"Not yet, but he will." I squeezed Gene's arm tighter, a little reminder.

"Fine. Whatever he has to say, he can say it in front of all of us." Zen went back to his seat next to Vince.

Rhett tugged Gene across the room and shoved a chair behind him. "Sit and speak."

Gene adjusted himself to accommodate his cuffed arms. "Such a wide vocabulary you have."

Rhett glared but kept quiet.

"Is that how you speak to your girlfriend's brother? I mean, after all, you're screwing my sister, aren't you? Or have you not gotten that far?"

I placed my index finger on Gene's forehead as if it were a gun and tilted his head back.

"Look at me," I said calmly. He peered up through his eyelashes. "One more asinine remark from you, you're back to solitude, got it?"

His eyelashes fluttered. "Yes, sis. You've got pretty eyes. They look like mine."

I've been desperately wanting him to acknowledge we were siblings, but hearing it made me nauseous. How I wished he wasn't related to me.

I ignored him. As soon as he talked, I planned to put him back in.

Rhett craned his neck from side to side and rounded his shoulders to stretch. Probably releasing the tension and the need to put a bullet through Gene's skull.

"So, what can Gene tell us?" Vince leaned forward, arms taut.

I should have Vince ruffle Gene's feathers a bit. Just looking at Vince's tank body would discourage anyone from being a prick.

"Gene said he was experimented on, and he isn't the only one," I replied. "Girls are being taken to a facility for that purpose. If we could bring that part of the pipeline down, it could be the first step in winning this war."

"There could be many such places, but it would certainly cause a commotion—and perhaps we could attract media attention." Zen rubbed his chin, contemplating. "Bringing attention to ISAN might somehow leak Verlot's connection to them."

"It's a possibility," Vince said. "So where is this facility located?"

Gene looked up from his shoes and fluttered his eyes open as if coming out of a daze or sleep. "The nice home underground you put me in. It's radar proof, right? No signal can penetrate through the walls, right? But up here is different. I can feel the energy, the electrical currents." He lifted his chin and closed his eyes, as feeling the warmth of the sun. "These currents are like the synapses in your brain, connecting and reconnecting. It has only one purpose, to find the main source of memories. I am that source."

"What is he saying?" Zen frowned.

"Oh, nothing important, *sir*." Gene's tone a mockery. "Just thinking out loud. Something you wouldn't understand. Or maybe you would. You did work for ISAN once. Believed in their cause. You even worked with a genius. I believe his name is Dr. Hunt. What happened to him?"

Zen shot up from his seat, the chair almost tipping backward. "Either he speaks or put him back."

"He will speak," Gene said with no hint of anger, just a perfect portrait of someone in command. "After all, I do need to be fair and keep my end of my deal with my sis." He smiled at me—the kind of smile I would have liked if things were normal between us.

"Stop talking and just say it." Vince groaned, his patience thin.

"Where's Tamara? She's here somewhere, isn't she? She fooled all of us, don't you think? She came across as this innocent and soft-spoken girl, and then she shot Justine and Payton and kidnapped me. I really liked her. Is she going to visit?"

I'd had enough. "No, she's not going to visit you. Tell me now."

"I was just trying to be social. A trait ISAN soldiers need to improve on. But since you don't want my friendship, I suppose it's not my fault."

"Gene," I growled.

"Fine. Only for you, sis. The coordinates are …"

After he told us, Zen sent the information to Frank to check it out.

"How do we know he's telling us the truth?" Vince whispered.

"I can hear you," Gene sang out.

I rolled my eyes and sighed.

Zen peered at the ceiling and locked his eyes there for a second. He lowered them to Rhett and seethed. "Take that filth out of my office before I do something I'll regret." A pause. "Wait. Since he's out and sedated, take him to the lab first. Tell my assistant to get a sample of his blood again. I owe Ava a favor." Zen flashed a quick grin at me.

"Thank you," I said.

Rhett instructed the guards to do what Zen had requested, and then he went back to Zen.

"What's our plan?" Rhett clicked on his chip when it chimed. He checked his message and turned it off.

Zen tucked his pistol behind his waistband and picked up his TAB. "A couple of things, actually. I'm going to place a team and head to south quadrant with Vince. We're going after Verlot's men. We have their location. Hopefully we can keep a few alive. We need information. We're too much in the dark. I've been overloading Jo with information just in case none of us are here. I need someone in command."

He meant if none of us ever came back. Another morbid thought, but we had to face the possibility. Plan for the worst and hope for the best.

Zen gripped Rhett's shoulder in a tender way. "Take a group with you to check out the facility, but do not go in without my permission. It could be a trap. However, if it is as Gene said, then we'll need help. I'll gather a decent sized force. We don't know what we'll be facing."

"Yes, sir. But first, I need to stop by the black market. I got an urgent message."

"Fine. Do whatever you need to do. Keep communication open."

"Will do." Rhett grabbed Vince's arm. "Take care of Zen for me. Don't let anything happen to this old man."

Vince chuckled. "You don't need to worry about Zen. Actually, he'll be watching my back."

I had never seen Zen in action. I only knew he had trained with council guards and he knew a lot about military tactics. I also knew he'd worked with my father. Yes, my father was the genius and though Zen was a scientist, too, he was clearly skilled in multiple ways.

CHAPTER THIRTY-TWO – ONE MORE CHANCE

AVA

Gene didn't complain he didn't get his full hour, nor did he try to persuade us to change our minds. He went quietly back into his cell. No resistance. Simply obedient. Why?

"That was interesting." I stood under the alcove with Rhett. "Gene seemed glad to be back inside."

"Maybe he feels safe there. Zen looked like he was going to beat the crap out of him." Rhett rolled up his sleeve and rubbed the back of his neck. "We all did. I wanted to several times. I kind of get why he's that way, but you turned out so much different. I believe environment plays a huge role in how a child matures. I don't know what he's been through, but you've been through a lot, babe, and you didn't turn out like him."

I shook my head. "I don't know. I wish I could ask him. A part of me wants to know, but the bigger part of me doesn't care. I'm afraid my feelings might soften toward him if I knew and I'm not sure that would be good." I picked at my fingernails as I fought the yearning inside me. "I wish things were different between us. We could help each other. Grieve for our mother. Find our father together. We should be swapping stories. I should … " Anger spiked fast and hard, and I felt the urge to get what I needed to say out of my system. "I should go and tell him how I feel."

"Ava. Wait."

His words went in one ear and out the other as I stormed back to Gene's cell.

Rhett's footsteps thudded behind me. "Are you sure you want to do this? So far, talking to him gets you nowhere except frustrated."

I whirled and gripped Rhett's shirt in trembling hands, my eyes stinging. I didn't want to have a breakdown but I just might.

"I have to try one last time, Rhett. I have to. I have to." I blinked and angled my face to the ceiling, pushing back the disappointment and hurt. "It's the only card I've got left. I have to do it for me. For my mother. She would want me to try. I don't want to hate my brother. I don't. I hate this feeling."

"Okay." Rhett embraced me and caressed my back. "Okay Ava. Just don't expect him to be different this time. I don't like it when your heart is broken. I'll go in with you, but I'll stay in the back. Just …" His warm breath brushed against my ear. "Go pour your heart out. I'll be here."

I descended the stairs and went straight to Gene, who stood near the glass, smirking.

"Back again so soon, sis? Did you miss me?"

I crossed my arms in the center and tapped my foot. "I don't want to hate you, Gene. You're my brother. I want to get to know you better. I want to know about your past, what you've been through, and I want to tell you my story. I'm willing to start over if you want to."

Gene dipped his head lower, rubbed his forehead as if deep in thought, and then peered up. "I think I can try. I've always wanted a sister. But what do you want from me?"

"Nothing." I shook my head, lightheaded at the thought our relationship could be mended. "I don't want anything from you. I want to tell you about our mother. You never got the chance to meet her. But you see, she never knew you existed. Our father told her you had died at birth. She never got to hold you. But I already told you all this."

He looked confused. "Oh, I remember you telling me your story when you spewed your guts to me the first time, but I did get to meet her. I knew you were my sister when I first met you at the ISAN West compound, by the way. Whoa, that feels better. It was bothering me."

I shuddered with rage. *Calm down. Calm down. Calm down.*

"You knew?" Any once of softness was gone. "You knew I was your sister all this time?" I banged my fist on the barrier. "Oh, this is …. You know what, never mind." I wasn't going to give him the satisfaction of seeing me all worked up. Besides, he'd said something that mattered more. "What do you mean you met my mother? How could you meet her when she's dead?"

He cocked his head. "You mean *our* mother, sis. Oh, you don't know. But of course you don't know. If you go to the facility, you might run into her."

"What? Run into who?"

"Run into Mother, silly."

"What?" My breaths turned into gasps. "Mother is dead. How can you see her?"

"I have seen her. She told me she was sorry. She didn't know I was alive. She doesn't understand why Father did it for science."

"Stop. I don't want to hear your lies. Stop messing with my mind. Mother is dead."

"No. Mother is not dead. I told you there were others in the facility."

I took a quiet moment to process his words. Of course he was messing with my mind, but I wanted to know more. If there was even the slightest possibility Mother was alive, I had ... no. She wouldn't have let me think she had ... She would have never left me.

Had she been kidnapped?

"When did you know about Mother?" I asked.

"I met her when I turned thirteen. They lied to *you*, not me. Mother never died, Ava. What kind of daughter are you not to know that?"

I had been thirteen when she'd fallen ill, and then she had been taken from me. I had been told she'd passed away from a rare disease. Being underage, I'd had no rights. Grieving for her, and not having family or resources, I'd accepted what I had been told. I'd had no choice.

"Stop it. You're lying." The walls spun around me. Dizzy. So dizzy. I didn't know if it was from anger or the possibility he could be telling the truth.

No. He's lying. He's lying.

"Am I? Think about it. Why would I lie? You should feel lucky I'm telling you this. I could have kept my mouth shut. Granted, since it seems you're so desperate to have some kind of connection, even to a brother who doesn't give a damn about you, I feel like giving you something. So maybe I am making this up." He traced a line on his palm and looked back at me. "Or maybe I'm not. Maybe you'll have to go to the facility and find out."

I wanted to punch the glass—no, I wanted rip out his heart.

"Why?" I hollered. "Why are you like this? Why can't you be a normal brother? Why do you play games with me?"

Gene didn't look at me when he spoke. Instead, he drew an X on the glass like the last time. "I'll see if I can answer your questions. I am what I am. Normal is too boring. I only know how to be what I am. One day you'll understand, but not today. No, I don't think today is a good day. I don't think I'll tell you anything, especially when you're acting childish."

"You know what? I take it all back. I do hate you. I wish you weren't my brother. I wish I'd never met you."

Gene flinched. Perhaps I had stung his heart a bit, if he had one.

Yes, I acted like a child, but I could only handle so much from him. The possibility of my mother being alive ate at my soul.

What if she was? What was she doing there? Was she a prisoner? Would ISAN experiment on her because of me? No, Gene had to be making this up. He thrived on playing with my mind.

"Are you done with sharing time now? I'm tired of listening." Gene pinched the bridge of his nose and rolled his eyes back.

I gave him my back. People who crave attention or think they are in control can't stand to be ignored. Like Justine. It drove her mad when I disregarded her, so I figured I would do the same to Gene. I was right.

"Are we done?" He sounded like a spoiled brat.

I kept walking.

"I'm talking to you, sister." His tone grew deeper, a bit louder.

Making eye contact with Rhett, I tilted my head to the stairs.

"Fine. Ignore me." Gene pounded the barrier. "You're going to regret it."

Though I continued to hike up the stairs with Rhett by my side, I dared to take a glimpse from the corner of my eyes. Gene's eyes followed me, and he smiled when our gazes met.

"Boom." He threw up his arms in a circle. "Boom. You're all

dead. They're coming for you."

My skin crawled, my chest tight. I should have taken his words seriously, but I had written him off as a lunatic. He was crazy, but that didn't mean he wasn't a threat.

My heart broke. I had gone down there hoping I could convince him to meet me halfway and start anew, but he'd crushed a sliver of hope.

And I kept punishing myself for it.

I had given up on him for now, but a part of me never would. There had to be something of him worth saving, some part that had once been good.

CHAPTER THIRTY-THREE – TOO LATE

AVA

Thankfully, the black market hadn't moved yet. The shops hadn't been switched around either, the way they sometimes were, so we didn't have to waste time looking for Mr. Lee.

Rhett had received a message from Zeke when we had taken Gene to talk with Zen. Hopefully, the coordinates Gene had given us were good, but it could be a trap. Regardless, we had to take a chance.

Mr. Lee had customers, more than the last time. We filed into line and surveyed the perimeter.

"I thought we had to check in with Zeke and not his uncle." The dumpling aroma made my mouth water.

"We do and we are, but first I'm getting us a xiaolongbao." Rhett slyly leaned back to take a peek at the next shop. The customers' loud voices caught his attention.

Ozzie smiled immensely, not taking his eyes off the food.

"Vito never let us have any when we went to the black market." Naomi glanced behind her, always on alert.

"Don't worry," I said. "Vito is in jail. Councilor Chang took care of him and his men, thanks to you."

Naomi shrugged bashfully. "He needed to be put down. He's caused so much damage. People like him deserve a death sentence."

"I agree," Tamara said.

The conversation between us became minimal as voices filled my ears. Thanks to Helix, I eavesdropped on people bargaining as I followed footsteps, the hum of gadgets, the beeping of transactions, and even drops of rain leaking through the dilapidated roof.

"Sniper. Welcome back." The old man's grin was infectious. "You brought more friends. Good, good, good. I just made some fresh dumplings."

"I'll take five orders of xiaolongbao, and you have to let me pay this time. I got a message from Zeke. We're on our way to see him."

Mr. Lee passed recyclable bowls to Rhett filled with not just xiaolongbao but chicken feet as well.

I cringed and gripped my cloak. I'd just lost my appetite.

"I love chicken feet." Tamara took one and sucked on it.

Nauseated, I focused on the shops below.

"You don't give me money. I don't want it." Mr. Lee shook a pointed finger at Rhett. "Your payment is coming to see me. I don't know many good people. My nephew ..." He shook his head. "I don't know what to do with him."

Rhett bowed to thank him and passed the containers to us. "He's a big boy. What he does is out of your hands."

"Sniper ... Never," he said softly, defeated. "I promised my sister to look after him and I will. Even on my death bed, I'll be looking after him. Perhaps I will even in the afterlife."

"He's lucky to have you. Not all parents have your patience."

"I get older faster because of Zeke." He pointed to his head. "He gave me gray hair too fast. He needs a good woman to take care of him." He chuckled and tipped his head to the side. "Eat. Enjoy your meal. Zeke is still in his tent doing God knows what business." He paused, his eyes focused straight ahead. "Wait a moment." He reached behind the electric store, disappeared for a few seconds, and came back. "I have something for the pretty girls. Here."

On Mr. Lee's palm were three flat, green objects as long as my pinky with a sharp point at the end, looped with sliver-plated chain. It looked like an arrow pendant, similar to Zeke's. I narrowed my eyes and looked back at him.

"It's made from jade, which cannot be detected through any type of metal scanners. They are a symbol of good luck, and you can also use it as a weapon. The tip is sharp, so be careful. You remind me of these teenagers I used to know. Their names were Nina and Cora. I don't know what happened to them." He dipped his head. "I hope they are well."

When I hesitated, he cupped my hand and placed the cool stone in my palm. "Please. It's for your protection. I see a lot of danger and bad things happen to young pretty girls like yourselves. I see you cut your hair, Ava. I like it," he said with enthusiasm. Then he handed Naomi and Tamara the other two pendants.

He had no idea I was an assassin—ex-assassin—but it was thoughtful of him. I'd always wanted a grandfather. Mother had told me my grandparents had died young from the radiation and her generation had been the first to outlive the effects with the aid of medications derived from the meteor.

"Thank you. I will always keep it with me." I slipped it around my neck. It would make a perfect hidden weapon.

"Rhett, I need a moment with you," Mr. Lee said.

As Rhett exchanged words with Mr. Lee, Ozzie continued to stuff his face. He loved eating more than anyone I'd ever known.

"Hey Einstein, I think I'll call you Ozzie Bear," I said,

enjoying my meal.

He frowned and swallowed a piece of dumpling. "Why?"

"Because you love to eat like a bear and bears are cute."

He shrugged. "Fine by me."

"You should be glad she's not calling you Fuzzy Wuzzy." Naomi finished her dumplings and wiped her hand on her cloak.

"Huh?" I said.

"You know, Fuzzy Wuzzy was a bear. Fuzzy Wuzzy had no hair." When I shook my head, she added, "Never mind. It's an old nursery rhyme."

"I have hair." Ozzie squinted, running his hand down his skull.

"Like I said, never mind." Naomi snickered at her own joke.

"Those chicken feet were delicious." Tamara licked her fingers, not following what we were talking about. She ate mine as well when I offered.

I spied Rhett and Mr. Lee having an intense conversation. I wondered what they were talking about. We had to hurry. Rhett had told me Zeke had told him the message from Mitch was urgent. But everything seemed urgent to Mitch.

After we said our goodbyes, we went straight to Zeke, sans a special coin. No Eben and his guards this time. Where were they?

When we slipped into the tent, a pleasant scent caressed my nostrils.

"It's about time. What took you so long?" Zeke rose and his girls scampered away. He slipped on a button-down shirt, the spear-shaped jade and onyx cross pendants swinging with his motion.

No asinine remark from him. Straight to business and no bantering.

Rhett crossed his arms. "You think I just sit around and do nothing?"

"I don't know what you do all day and I don't care, but I have things to do. So excuse me if I sound annoyed."

"Just give me Mitch's message." Rhett's voice, still irate. "You're so lucky Mr. Lee is your uncle."

"And you're lucky you're not alone." Zeke smirked, brushing his curls to the side. "I see you brought a new girl."

I linked my arm around Rhett when he twitched a muscle. "Steady," I whispered, and then to Zeke. "Hurry, so we can get out of here."

Zeke pressed his chip and Mitch's body appeared like a phantom. "Don't worry. You may not trust me, but Mitch does, and so does Zen, don't forget. What I hear stays with me."

"It better. Press play." Rhett jerked his chin.

Mitch's hologram spoke.

"I'll make this quick." Hologram Mitch stood with his legs apart and arms behind his back, ISAN assassin stance. "Three things you need to know. One, my source told me it is highly likely our father is being held captive at this facility, along with many others. I sent Zeke the coordinates. The source's contact will be there today, guarding the door. She will let you in. Please do not miss this opportunity. Second, I can assume Zen took Gene's blood sample and did a thorough examination of his DNA. If he did, he would also have found out Gene is Ava's twin. Third, Gene is dangerous. Gene is capable of punching through walls, even the ones thought to be unbreakable. He can heal himself, among other things, but I'll cut to the chase. This is most important. You need to get everyone out. I mean everyone. Mr. Novak knows your exact coordinates because of Gene. Mr. Novak implanted a liquidized beacon in him so no metal scanner can detect it. Rhett, did you hear me? The strike unit is on their way now. Get out. I repeat, get out now."

The message died, the hologram gone, but Mitch's desperate plea lingered in the air.

Dead silence. Only the pounding of my heart reverberated through my ears. I wasn't sure if I was breathing.

When I'd taken Gene to see Zen, Gene had said he could feel the energy, the electrical currents. He had said they had only one purpose, to find the main source. And he was that source.

I'd thought Gene was rambling, talking nonsense. But he had been giving away his secret. How could I have missed it?

A vicious snarl snapped me out of my reverie.

Ozzie pounced on Zeke and grabbed him by the collar. "Why didn't you get this to us earlier?"

"Oz." Rhett yanked him aside. "He doesn't know what's going on. It's not his fault. I'm going to make a call to Zen now."

The calmness in Rhett's voice didn't surprise me. ISAN had trained us not to panic. I had the same training, but I panicked anyway.

Calm down. Rhett will make the call to Zen and they can escape. Escape to where?

We should be there helping evacuate.

Brooke, Reyna, the kids … everyone. Oh God.

"My chip is not getting through." Rhett tapped his arm.

"Let me try mine." Ozzie fiddled with his own. "Something is wrong with the reception here." His voice became desperate, angrier.

"Something is wrong with mine, too," Tamara said.

"I got a signal."

They huddled around me.

"Zen. Zen. Can you hear me?" Rhett said.

"Rhett. I can. What's wrong?" Zen replied a few seconds later.

"I don't have time to explain. Gene is a tracker. ISAN sent a strike team. You need to get everyone out to safety."

Silence.

"Zen? Zen? Did you hear me?" Rhett tapped at my arm, cursing.

"Rhett. I'm not at the base. Vince, Frank, and I left already. You have to call Reyna. I'll abort this mission, but I don't know if I can reach them in time. This is—"

Rhett scrubbed his face. "Zen? Zen?" He clicked on my chip and called Reyna.

Ozzie paced in the small space, making me more nervous. Naomi covered her face.

"Reyna. This is Rhett. Can you hear me?"

I froze, my heart thundering. Even a second delay was too long. What if we were too late?

"Rhett? What's up?" Her face popped up.

Oh, thank God.

A breath left me at her jovial voice. They were alive. They had a chance to escape.

"Listen carefully, Reyna. This is urgent. Get everyone to—"

Screams drowned out Rhett's voice.

When Reyna ducked, the hologram tilted sideways. "The front door just blew up. Zen isn't here. What do I do?"

"Listen, Reyna. Get everyone out now. Novak sent a strike team. Get people to safety. Do you hear me?"

More screams. Chaos. I got a glimpse of kids running past Reyna. Then a small bomb exploded and sunlight filtered through

271

the giant gap.

"Rhett. Drones. ISAN drones are here shooting at us," Reyna shouted "I have to go. I have to—"

"Reyna. Reyna. Reyna. Shit!" Rhett bellowed when the screen went dead. He clutched his hair and whirled about.

"It's okay." I had to be the voice of reason, the voice that calmed us down, because if I didn't, we would fall apart. "Reyna knows what to do. Gene is one person. He can't … but the strike unit. Zen has been teaching Jo all the escape routes and …"

I had no idea what to say. My voice of reason sucked. But Zen's soldiers and the rebel kids were prepared for such an attack. They practiced emergency evacuation drills. They were smart and had survival skills.

"Sorry, man," was all Zeke said, his tone genuine for once. He rubbed at his cross pendant as if in prayer.

Shocked, stricken, I made no effort to leave.

Get going, Ava. People need you.

I couldn't be at two places at once. So I formed a plan. It might not be ideal, and Rhett might shoot it down, but I had to say something.

"Okay. Rhett and Oz, since you two know the rebel base well, it only makes sense you two go back. Naomi, Tamara, and I will go to the facility."

Rhett regarded me silently for long heartbeats, and then shook his head. He opened his mouth to retort. "No. Absolutely not. We stay together."

"I don't want to split up," I said, my voice frantic. "But we'll miss the window of opportunity to get into the facility if we don't. Who knows how long we'd have to wait for another chance? Every day, every hour we wait is a delay that might set us back. Your father might be there and my mother, too. We need to find a way to bring down ISAN, or this will never end. Novak bombed our base. We don't know …" I couldn't finish.

Rhett shoved his fingers through his hair as a frustrated growl escaped him. After taking a few steps back, he cupped his face as if he needed a second to think and then opened them.

"How are you going to get there? We only brought one glider," he said.

I rubbed at my forehead.

Think. Think.

A small movement of someone retreating gave me the answer. "Zeke. He'll take us."

Zeke froze. "Whoa. Wait. I'm just the messenger. I deliver messages. I'm no fighter. I have no beef with ISIN or IZAP or whatever you call it."

With one swift kick, I brought him to his knees. It was aggressive, but I was desperate and out of time.

I pointed a Taser between his eyes. "You have no choice if you don't want to die."

I wouldn't act on my threat, but he didn't know that.

Tamara took out her pocket knife and laid the tip on his jugular when he didn't oblige. "Knives are my best friend."

He raised his hands to surrender. "Okay. Okay. I'll take you there and leave."

I pushed the Taser harder on his skull. "No, you take us there and you stay there until I tell you to leave. Got it? Because if you don't listen, I know where you work. You don't want to mess with me. I will ruin you and your business. But Tamara might beat me to it and cut you up piece by piece. She will drain you dry."

An exaggerated image for him to think about.

"Fine." He sighed.

I kept one eye on Zeke, who didn't move a muscle. "Rhett. Oz. Go. We'll be fine. Please be careful and give me an update when you get there."

Rhett's eyes were filled with anticipation and worry as he caressed my arms. Then he leaned his forehead to mine. "I hate this. We were supposed to do this together."

"I know. It's okay. Whatever it takes, remember." I tried to sound strong for the both of us, but my voice cracked.

"I love you." Rhett held me tightly as if I was his lifeline, and then he kissed me with desperation. When he pulled away, he didn't let go of my arms. "Compare Mitch's coordinates to the ones Gene gave us. If it's different, let me know. The three of you look after yourselves. Please do not go inside until backup arrives."

What backup? There would be no backup now. Our backup might be … I didn't want to remind Rhett or he might not go.

"I will," I said.

Ozzie embraced me next, a tight bear hug, making me lose a breath. "Don't do anything foolish."

"I won't. I promise. Brooke is fine. She's a survivor."

I said it for the both of us. He worried about her, but he didn't single her out. So many lives were on the line.

"Go." I pushed Rhett, who couldn't take his eyes off me.

With one last kiss and a breath, he was gone.

Zeke rose from his knees. "Would you ladies like to—"

"Shut up." I rammed the Taser in front of his nose. We had no time for small talk. "It hurts like a bitch when you get stung on the face. Now, take us to your ride."

CHAPTER THIRTY-FOUR – TIME TO RISE

GENE

Gene couldn't stand any more of Zen and Ava's boring questions and grueling lectures. But he had to play his part. Gene playacted helplessness as he waited patiently, half-listening.

A tiny part of Gene, just for a brief moment, imagined what it would be like to have a sister who cared about him. He could have sent Novak his location as soon as he'd arrived, but he wanted to get to know his sister. She was his twin after all. And then he had been locked up.

Sometimes his temper got the best of him. Novak told Gene he had to learn to control that fire blazing inside him. His father even sent him to a therapist. That didn't go well. He'd killed her. His father found him another therapist. Gene had killed him, too.

Novak said his anger issues got worse when his body produced too much HelixB88. Technically, it wasn't his fault. Gene didn't *try* to get angry. It was usually triggered by something trivial, and then it grew. Gene was GENE—Genetically Enhanced Neo Entity—after all.

Gene had his chance to fulfill his mission when they'd ushered him to see a man named Zen. Zen had met Gene when he was young, but Zen hadn't put two and two together. Besides, Zen had deserted, so Zen was no friend of his.

Nobody would ever know how Gene alerted Novak of his

whereabouts.

Gene was his property, Novak had told him once. That word didn't bother him. Gene had no one else.

Time to rise, Gene.

Just as Gene was about to punch through the so-called unbreakable glass, a figure emerged from the stairs. She acknowledged the guards with a wave and approached him, inquisitive.

She looked familiar. Pretty thing. Too bad he had to kill her.

"Who are you and what do you want?" Gene said.

"I'm Ava's friend, Brooke. We were on an assignment together. Don't you remember me?"

She had her hair tied back, the reason he couldn't recall her face. And the dim lighting obscured his view.

"Ah. Yes. I remember you. You didn't like Drew."

She frowned, likely wondering what that had to do with her. Funny how Gene recalled inconsequential things about people.

"Yeah, well, that's not the reason why I'm here," Brooke continued. "Your sister doesn't know I'm here. Ava is like a sister to me, so I wanted to meet you."

Shoving his hands inside his front pockets, he released a sigh of boredom. "You must not mean much to her if you had to come and introduce yourself to me. Where is Ava, by the way?"

She bristled. "None of your business. She has her reasons and it isn't what you think. And from your comment, I see what she means."

"What do you mean?"

Rubbing his stubble with his thumb and index finger, he examined her closer. The lighting made him see his own reflection. He really needed to shave.

She stepped closer. Her gait, more like a swagger, and her height, reminded him of his sister.

"You don't need to know. You only need to know you made the mistake of your life. Ava searched for you. Risked her life to find you. When she finally did, you turned out to be a disappointment. Don't you care you have a sister? Doesn't family mean anything to you? You've been alone for so long. How could you not?"

Gene tuned out Brooke's rambling, but one word stuck out like a sore thumb—disappointment. Slowly he rolled up his sleeves, preparing to use his power.

"No. I don't care I have a sister. I only care about science and how the world can benefit from research. I have no use for emotions and feelings. They only get in the way. Sister is just a word. I don't owe her anything and she owes me nothing. I didn't ask to have a sister or ever want one, so why should I start caring? It's so inconvenient."

"What?"

Brooke's eyes grew so wide, Gene imagined them popping out of her sockets. He must have looked amused because she snarled.

"What's so funny?" Brooke asked.

"Everything will be, sweetheart, when this place turns into a giant hole."

"Don't call me sweetheart." She batted her eyelashes as if she remembered something. "What did you say?" Her face nearly touched the glass.

Gene focused back on his duty. Soon, Novak's team would be here, and no doubt West ISAN as well. Leisurely, he made an X on the glass over the smudged one he had drawn before. It was about the size of his hand, right over her nose. Her perfectly cute bunny nose.

So pretty. She had beautiful eyes and a pretty face.

"Soon, nothing will matter. An ISAN strike unit is coming. Unless you want your face smashed in, I suggest you step aside."

Brooke stared at him as if he had spoken a different language. Then she laughed or spat or maybe both at the same time, but it made him furious.

"You." She choked on her cackle. "You think you can break through the …" She knocked on the glass. "This is unbreakable, for your information. For a semi-intelligent guy, you don't know squat. HelixB88 messed with your mind."

You have no idea. Helix didn't mess *with me. It made me who I am.*

"You don't believe I can? Watch me."

Gene concentrated on his mark and drew Helix. Every nerve ending in his veins warmed and got hotter as power grew. He had been born with HelixB88. Ever since his gift first showed at the age of thirteen, Novak had trained him and molded him to be the perfect ISAN assassin.

Rumors had spread about Ava. Little did people know someone more powerful lurked behind her. Novak had planned to let him shine when the time was right.

That time was now.

Brooke recoiled and retreated. She must have seen his energy crackle like lightning around and through his body. Gene's eyes should be silver and sparkling. He must appear like a waking raging storm ready to unleash.

Gene slammed on the center of his X with the heel of his palm. The glass splintered and spider-webbed. The guards readied their arsenal, cursing, while Brooke stood there mesmerized.

"Run." Gene gave a mocking grin and punched the center again and again.

By the fifth time, the glass burst outward and smashed into the monitors. The two guards came at him and fired their pistols, but he stopped the bullets in midair with a wave of his hand.

Gene rammed his fist inside the first guard's chest. His keen ears heard the sound of ribs cracking and muscles tearing. He yanked out his heart and tossed it like it was trash.

With blood dripping between his fingers, he gripped the second guard by his neck, lifted him, and tossed him across the room. The guard rammed against the wall so hard his spine broke.

Brooke, behind the monitor, frantically touched everything in her sight to open the door leading out of this room. Poor girl. She shook like a scared deer.

"Something wrong, Brooke?"

The sound of her swallowing resonated in his ear. Sometimes Helix overpowered him.

Then something clicked. A weapon perhaps, in her possession.

"Don't move, prick." She pointed a gun at him as he suspected.

What Gene didn't expect was the size. It was small enough to go undetected, the kind ISAN used during missions. She must have taken it with her when she'd left.

Gene smirked. "You did see me stop the bullets, right? Stop this nonsense and come with me. I'll treat you like royalty. You'll have the best of everything. Why stay in this dump?"

"You have got to be kidding me." She kept touching the monitors with her other hand with no luck.

"No, I'm not kidding." Gene extended his arm. "I'm running out of time. Either you come with me or I kill you. Hurry and make up your mind."

She scoffed and pulled the trigger five times. Five bullets came at him, but he saw every single one of them in slow motion. He stopped them in midair, then rotated the bullets around.

Brooke swore and ducked. Then to his surprise, she closed her eyes.

Gene had thought she would be an easy kill. Wrong. She didn't need Helix. Girls at ISAN weren't aware—the girls here would find out the truth. No protein drink here, nothing to inhibit their ability.

Brooke sprang, graceful as a feline, and landed on all fours. She fired her gun again. This time, Gene allowed the bullet to penetrate through his palm. The excruciating pain rippled through him as blood dripped on the floor.

It was worth getting shot to see her smirk and then watch her expression drastically change when she witnessed his flesh stitch itself back up.

"What? How?" She didn't hesitate and continuously fired her gun.

When she was close enough, she dove for him. They tumbled, skidding across the sleek floor, until his back jabbed the table leg.

Brooke pushed off Gene, but he caught her ankle. She twisted at her waist and fired again. Gene stopped the bullet inches before it impacted his chest and spun it back to her. Brooke jerked aside, and the bullet missed her by a hair.

An equal opponent. Gene would've had fun with her, but he had no time to play. He had to leave.

Then the ground shook violently, the wall cracking.

It had begun.

Brooke managed to free herself and scrambled away in the

process, her arms and knees dragging frantically. Gene could have left without her, but he wanted Ava to suffer. Brooke's death would destroy her. And why not?

Another boom rocked the earth.

Brooke was at the top of the stairs, trying to push her way out. When Gene closed the distance and ascended halfway up, she flipped over him. He leaped. She threw a punch. Gene blocked her blow and socked her in her gut. She flew across the space and collided against the back wall.

With her face down, she groaned, trying to lift herself up.

"You had your chance to live and come with me. Too bad the deal is over."

No more fooling around. Gene should have been out by now. He was not going to be stuck here when ISAN blew up a joke of a base. Not only would the bomb obliterate everything on top, but it would penetrate the surface. There would be no survivors. Only a huge gaping hole.

Brooke pressed her back to the wall and dragged herself upward. "I would rather die than go with you. Such a disappointment."

Disappointment. There was that word he detested again. A word that triggered him to destruct.

Fury burned through Gene, causing HelixB88 to burn hot in his veins. He had no mercy. Gene only wanted to release sensations clawing to get away. The only way to fix it was to let it run its course.

Gene released his tight fist. Instead of contacting Brooke's face, it went through the wall. Every jab he threw, she dodged. So he pushed harder and moved faster. This time, she couldn't keep up with his blows.

Brooke's head punched through the wall. Her nose bloody and broken, blood dripped down her chin. Gene went lower and broke at least a few of her ribs, or more.

Bones crunching was music to his ears.

Brooke swayed, continuing to throw lazy, sloppy punches. She fought hard. Gene gave her credit for not giving up.

Now for the killing blow.

The whoosh and the thump caught his attention. Someone had opened the door from the outside. Multiple footsteps let him know there was more than one. He had to get out of there.

No time to kill Brooke. She would probably die of internal bleeding anyhow. Gene had really messed her up.

Brooke collapsed, and Gene used most of his strength to punch through the plaster. The hole led to another room, identical to his. He went up the stairs and blasted through the door into smoke and mayhem.

CHAPTER THIRTY-FIVE – BOOM

GENE

No one dared to stop Gene or challenge him in the pandemonium. Rebel soldiers exchanged bullets with ISAN guards and ISAN drones while kids scrambled to safety.

One side of the building had been blasted away. Gene ran toward it, but an airstream forced him back. Then, as if he had been hit by a tornado, he soared across the space and landed on someone's tent.

A crude, pathetic home.

Gene wrenched up to see a girl in front of him with short hair. She must have been the one to blow him fifty yards. Impressive. After the initial stare down, believing he wasn't a threat, she shifted her attention to ISAN guards coming at her.

"Mia, watch out," her friend bellowed and shot a drone firing at her.

"Ella, I got them. Stay behind me."

Mia inhaled a long deep breath and exhaled with all her might. Men went flying like Gene had. Then the ground shook again, and something fell from the ceiling—a small chunk, and then a broken solar panel. Section by section, the ceiling began caving in.

"Watch out!" someone shouted.

Ella and Mia created an invisible barrier with their breaths. The debris would have crushed everyone under it. The fragments dropped when people moved out of the way. Even the ISAN guards were safe, and those outside of the perimeter froze in awe for a second.

Then battle resumed.

Gene spotted Drew and his party on the opposite end. His squad was there as well, along with Payton's. He almost shouted at them but thought better of it.

ISAN teams chased down the young ones. Novak must have told them to bring them in unharmed. They were easier to train.

When a little Asian girl disregarded Gene and took off, he seized the opportunity to find his group. Gene dashed over the fresh debris from the ceiling and found them in hand-to-hand combat with the rebel soldiers.

Gene was quite thrilled to see children everywhere, to witness their power.

A shiver coursed through him when one of the girls feigned to surrender. Gene believed the rebels called her Coco. When a guard came close in contact, she gripped his wrist. Tendrils of electricity shot through him. Coco was unharmed, but the guard went limp, faint steam rising off her body.

"Don't come too close, Momo," Coco warned her friend as she attacked the next several guards at once.

Momo swooped in dodging bullets and moving faster than Gene had ever seen anyone move before. Mind-blowing. Even he wasn't as swift as her. Then she climbed higher, somersaulted in the air like an acrobat, and kicked at a drone. The drone split in half, its insides splintering apart.

Another youngling dropped to her knees and placed her palm on the dirt. The earth rumbled and split, drawing a line to her target. The guard wobbled and was sucked inside the crack.

A thin girl with long hair brought a guard down with a swipe of her leg to the back of his knee, and when she touched him, he turned to stone. Gene swallowed. For the first time, fear slithered down his back. Then her friend next to her karate-chopped him in half and whirled in time to transform a guard's arm to ice.

Gene shivered in ecstasy at what he'd witnessed. The miracle of science. The vision and dream of a better world, sophisticated people and their gifts. How many girls had such gifts?

The S in ISAN stood for Sensory. These girls' powers were all about the sensory realm. Gene would bet there was much more to their abilities if they tested their limits.

"Gene," Drew said. "I looked for you everywhere. Come on. Let's go. What are you standing around for?"

Drew caught Gene's attention from behind a boulder. Coward. Drew had purposely avoided the younglings. Gene knew Drew had no chance to defeat a group of such strength and force.

"What about them?" Gene gestured at the kids still battling the ISAN guards.

"Leave them. We got what we came for. This whole place is about to blow." Drew looked at his timer, projected by his chip. "I'm leaving with my team, now." He bolted, his crew behind him.

Gene tailed him into the sunlight. Drew would lead him to the transporter. Just before Gene stepped inside the glider, he swung to peek at the mess he was leaving behind.

A girl with dark skin—*Reyna*, he thought—and another girl, carried a limp Brooke to the opposite end of the destruction. Why bother to save her? She was good as dead.

Someone was hollering, directing them to get out.

Just as their glider took off, a blinding light shot through the air when the bomb impacted the earth. Thunder ricocheted around

Gene.

"Boom, boom," Gene said with such joy and satisfaction. "I told you this would happen, sis."

Then the ground dropped like a landslide and everything crumbled onto itself.

A splendid vision indeed.

CHAPTER THIRTY-SIX – NIGHTMARE

RHETT

"Oz. Wait for me. There might be—"

Ozzie didn't listen. As soon as they landed, Ozzie dashed out of the glider. With Rhett's weapon aimed, he stepped out. His pulse raced as he anticipated the devastation.

Steady, Rhett. You're a soldier.

Smoke from the blast still lingered. Ashes and soot blanketed the ground. But Rhett couldn't fully make out the destruction until he neared.

And what he saw …

Rhett had pictured what the damage might look like on the way here, but who was he kidding? Who was he freakin' kidding?

The ground had caved in with their home, as if a giant meteor had landed. This was the picture of what the generations before him had endured.

There couldn't possibly be any survivors.

Rhett dropped to his knees. Loss of breath robbed him of his screams. Rhett wanted to let out the anguish and fury inside him, but it kept growing and expanding. He gasped and panted and beat his fist against his chest, cries escaping his mouth.

Reyna. Brooke. Momo. Coco. Rebel soldiers. The kids. The innocent people. Faces flashed in his mind. He couldn't breathe. He couldn't move. So many dead in a matter of seconds.

Too many. Like when he'd escaped, so many had died. Their faces. Their cries. Their bodies.

How was Rhett to tell Ava? Her brother had done this. She would blame herself. They couldn't have known *he* was the tracker. This wasn't her fault. It was his fault. Rhett had encouraged her.

No matter, the guilt alone would crush her.

Rhett squeezed his eyes shut. Even though he could see the destruction in front of him, his mind refused to believe it. It felt like a dream. A dream from which he was desperate to wake up but couldn't.

Ozzie.

Rhett looked for him, but he was nowhere in sight. Where had he gone?

"Oz," Rhett shouted and rose.

No answer.

"Oz?" Rhett stopped searching for him and listened for his footsteps.

Then it dawned on him. Rhett looked to the right. There were two parts of Hope City. No one knew except for those who lived here. The second building was where families lived, those who had not been trained to fight but who wanted to support the cause. Some had loved ones who fought, and some had lost someone to ISAN.

The second building had not been touched.

Rhett sprinted toward it and halted next to Ozzie. He would have gone straight in, but Ozzie seemed to be in a daze. Ozzie stood like a statue with arms to his side, never taking his eyes off the edifice.

"Oz. What are you doing?"

Ozzie didn't look at Rhett. He seemed a world away. Even his tone came off as nonchalant. "Do you see, Rhett?"

"What am I supposed to see?" Rhett worried he was drowned in denial.

Ozzie cared about everyone, but Reyna and Brooke meant the world to him. He'd recently found Brooke again and now this. They hadn't gotten their time to figure things out.

"This building is still in one piece. You think Reyna and Brooke are in there? You think they managed to escape before ..."

So much pain laced his words. Rhett took a second to collect himself so he wouldn't fall apart. One of them had to be strong.

Rhett's father's words came to his mind. *Survival is an instinct. You take care of your needs first. Emotions come second.*

"Do you want to go in together? We can."

"I can't go in." Ozzie's eyes became glassy, his voice cracking. "I just can't. Our friends, they were innocent. They wanted to have their own lives and not be a part of what he stood for. Why can't he leave us alone? Why did Novak kill them?"

There were a lot of reasons, and Rhett's explanation wouldn't matter.

"Listen. I'm going to go in. You stay out here. Please, do not wander off by yourself. Do we have a deal?"

Rhett had never seen Ozzie so indecisive before. The fear of finding the truth had a vise grip on Ozzie. Rhett understood though.

"Yeah. I'll wait right here." His voice was flat and uncaring.

Rhett swallowed, forced his muscles to work. Ava was expecting an update, but he couldn't call her until he knew for sure what had happened here.

The metallic tang of blood nearly overwhelmed Rhett when he entered. Many people were gathered toward the front. Their

Hope City family, women and men, attended to the wounded. Some were on cots or on mattresses, but most were on the ground, bleeding heavily.

Dr. Crumb was not here. They didn't have doctors on-hand, but Zen had trained a group of women and men in basic first-aid. He'd also taught them how to administer medication and drugs to lessen the pain.

"Rhett. Thank God you're safe. What happened?" asked a woman he barely knew.

"I—I don't know."

It was an odd question since she had been here and not him, but she wasn't a soldier. She wouldn't know an ISAN strike team had done this.

Rhett couldn't peel his eyes away from the wounded. Searching for his friends in the sea of so many wasn't easy, especially when they were scattered about. If he could just find one, he could get answers faster.

"Have you seen Reyna?" Rhett asked.

She would know who he was talking about since Reyna liked to come visit this part of Hope City more than anyone of them did.

"No. She was in the other—" She shook her head. "She didn't come here. A group of soldiers went to help but they never came back. Who would do this? I don't understand."

"I don't either," was the only explanation he could give her. "Zen is on his way. He will explain to all of you."

"Okay. I should go help." She gave him a tight-lipped smile and went back to whatever she'd been doing.

"Rhett."

A hoarse, low voice sounded behind Rhett. He got down on

his knees next to a cot where John, one of the soldiers, lay. His eyes had been closed a minute before, and he didn't want to bother him with questions. He had a blood-soaked length of fabric swathed around his head.

"John. What happened?"

John scrunched his features as if in pain. "I don't remember much and I don't have much to tell. A section of the wall went down from a blast and then another. Small bombs at first. It happened all too fast."

"Do you know if Gene escaped?"

"Yes. I saw him. Reyna asked several of us to help her get Gene. He not only destroyed the unbreakable barrier, he punched through several walls. But ..." When he swallowed, he gripped his neck. "But Brooke ... poor girl. Gene messed up Brooke."

"What?" Rhett heard himself say the word, but it sounded like someone else had spoken. "What do you mean? Is she okay?"

"Reyna and Jo found her, and I carried her out. Brooke was unconscious but her nose, her face ... and I can only image what damage Gene did to her body. I don't think she ..."

Rhett scrubbed his hands over his face with a defeated sigh. "What happened next?"

John closed his eyes and then opened them halfway. "There was another blast. We got thrown in different directions. When I came to, I found myself here. I prayed she was here with me, but when I asked the person attending me about Brooke, they didn't know who I was talking about."

As Rhett had thought. Brooke hadn't been brought to this section.

"What about Reyna, Jo, Stella, Jasper, and the rest of the kids?"

"They stayed to fight until the very end to ensure the soldiers without superpowers got out first. I saw them in action. They're incredible. Brave. Even Mia and Ella helped. We made a mad dash just as the final bomb exploded. But I don't know what happened next. I'm so sorry, Rhett. If they're not here, then, I'm so sorry. I'm so sorry."

Blood rushed to Rhett's head and then seemed to drain away, leaving him lightheaded. He lost the will to move. How was he supposed to tell that to Ozzie? To Ava? To Zen?

How could he come to terms with this?

War always had causalities. But to have this many people he cared about wiped away at once was unfathomable.

This had to be a joke.

John had fallen asleep. He didn't know for sure what happened, so a part of Rhett still had hope. He'd given up on a lot of things in his life, but meeting Ava had changed him.

His friends had thought Ava would never remember him. They'd thought she might not join their company. He'd never given up.

Don't ever give up on hope. If you do, there is nothing left. Hope is life.

Rhett wove around the wounded one last time in search for any of his friends. Fruitless endeavor. As he prepared himself to get back to his friend, he told himself to think like a soldier. Rhett refused to believe they had all died in the blast. If John had made it out, then others had, too. He needed to search harder.

But where?

When Rhett came out, he found Ozzie on his knees, his head pressed to the dirt. At the crunch of Rhett's boots on debris, Ozzie jerked up. His eyes begged Rhett to give him the answers he so desperately wanted.

"Oz, come with me." Rhett jogged toward the rubble of building one.

"Rhett. Wait. Did you find out if our friends survived?"

The hope in his voice crushed him. Rhett ran faster to the other side of the ruin. He had missed something.

Think like the kids.

Sometimes, children were smarter than adults, more resourceful, cunning, and witty. Rhett didn't know much about the kids' powers or their training, but he did know one thing: they worked as a team. He had witnessed it when they'd first met, and again when Bobo had died. He'd definitely seen it during their training with Jo.

"Rhett. You didn't answer my question. Where are you going?"

Ozzie's voice had changed from hopeless to angry.

Good. Rhett needed him to be determined. He needed the old Ozzie back.

Rhett gripped Ozzie's shoulders when he finally caught up to Rhett, panting. "I need you to think like Momo. Think like a child, okay?"

"What are you talking about? Did you find out if our friends were in—" Ozzie looked over to the second building as if he could see the inside of the place and then frowned at Rhett. "They're …"

"Look." Rhett cupped Ozzie's face and forced him to bend his neck lower. "Do you see those?"

Ozzie shoved him away. "So what? They're footprints. There are footprints all over."

"Look." Rhett almost sobbed from happiness as he pointed to a trail of overlapping prints leading to a pile of debris, next to the bigger one.

One of the kids' duties was to clean up the mess inside. They bragged about how hard they worked. In a short amount of time, they had done their job well. They even seemed to enjoy it. Rhett had suspected they were up to something mischievous, but they were just being kids and having fun.

"So what? It proves nothing." Ozzie's nostrils flared.

Ozzie wasn't thinking like Rhett because hope had left him. He only saw death and obliteration.

"Come on, Ozwald. I'm going to need your help."

Ozzie followed, swearing and kicking things in his way. Rhett had never heard so much foul language leave his lips. There were words he'd never heard, some he thought Ozzie might have made up. But the despairing anger in his voice made the meaning clear.

Rhett halted when the prints diverged instead of continuing together. Smart move. Someone had wiped away the evidence.

"See. That's it. It leads nowhere." Ozzie threw up his hands in defeat. "Why are you still smiling?"

"You need to stop being a grouch and be a kid. Think like a child."

"You make no sense. When is Zen arriving?"

Ozzie rambled as he trudged behind Rhett, but at least he followed.

Rhett nearly applauded when he came face-to-face with what the kids had built. From afar, it looked like a pile of junk. A person passing by would've thought so. But on the side, the side facing the bigger debris that had shifted and somewhat collapsed, the entrance narrowed.

It was big enough for one person to squeeze through. It was darker on this side, but light filtered through dimly in the passage between the piles.

"I'm not going in there. It's—"

Before he could continue, Rhett tugged at Ozzie's shirt to snatch him in with him.

"Momo. Coco. Reyna. Stella. Jasper. Jo. Mia. Ella. Can anyone hear me?"

Ozzie's laugh squeaked to the right of Rhett, almost crazed. "You're losing your mind. You think they're inside a pile of rubble?"

Rhett glared at him and then called their names again. These kids were intelligent, resourceful, and imaginative. They hadn't been randomly throwing junk out here. They'd been creating their own hideout. That's what Rhett would have done with his friends at their age.

Come on. Come on. Answer me. Please, answer me.

If they didn't, Rhett wasn't sure what he would do next. He might punch the remains of the building until his fists bled. Staring hard at the wall as if that would make the kids appear, Rhett groped for an opening or any crack he could get a grip on as he shouted their names again.

Come on. Answer me.

Calling their names might have sounded ridiculous, but Rhett needed to release the extra adrenaline, anyway. They *had* to be in there.

What Rhett was about to do next would look even more outlandish to Ozzie the skeptic. Rhett knocked on the construction like it was a front door, using the pattern Momo had made when she'd taken them to meet Jo and the rest of their team at their hideout.

Tap. Pause. Tap. Tap. Pause. Tap. Tap. Tap.

Silence.

"What are you doing?" A crease deepened on Ozzie's forehead.

For a second, Rhett doubted himself. What was he doing?

No, stay on course. Don't give up. Don't give up on them.

Rhett rapped on the dusty wooden panel again, using the same pattern. Tap. Pause. Tap. Tap. Pause. Tap. Tap. Tap.

When no response came, his hands trembled, then the rest of him. Rhett slumped on the ground, covering his face. Hope had played with his mind. Anguish. Rage. Despair ate him alive.

A series of thumps from above Rhett interrupted his grief.

Rhett peered up, his heart swelling with joy, but deflated when it wasn't a return response. Ozzie had smacked a wide metal panel, realizing what Rhett tried to do.

Ozzie moved farther down and hammered again, the same rhythm. When there was no reply, he climbed higher and struck with his first three times. Jolting up, Rhett moved the opposite way and beat the pattern on a flat spot with his fist.

Then …

Bang-bang-bang came the response.

Rhett pressed closer to the sound, wondering if he'd heard correctly or if he had imagined it, until …

Thump. Thump. Thump. Another response.

Rhett's heart thundered with joy. Ozzie jumped down with wide, stunned eyes and waited.

A sound like a saw cutting into steel vibrated the debris near them, while white sparks flew. Then a large chunk of metal flew off to the left of Rhett.

CHAPTER THIRTY-SEVEN – AFTERMATH

RHETT

A mop of dark hair poked out, followed by an alert figure with a gun aimed to the right, and then left. When Reyna spotted Rhett, she covered her mouth.

Soot and white ash dusted her like snowflakes, but other than that, she looked fine.

"Reyna," Rhett breathed, relief washing over him.

She waved behind her through the opening, letting others know it was safe, and then crushed her body to Rhett.

"Rhett. Oh, God. It's so good to see you." She trembled in his arms.

Rhett couldn't think of anything to say. She held him longer than she ever had. How scared she must have been. She slowly released him and ran to Ozzie.

While she embraced Ozzie, tears streamed down her face. Rhett shuddered another breath of relief as Jo, Cleo, Mia, Ella, Momo, Coco, and more climbed out one by one.

White ash dusted their clothes and hair, and grime and dirt smudged their faces like they hadn't washed in weeks.

Momo crushed Rhett in a hug first, and then the rest followed. He held them tightly, grateful.

Alive. They fought the impossible. A miracle.

"I'm so proud of you," Rhett said. "You're safe."

"You—you know our code." Momo lifted a shaky smile.

"I didn't know if you would come out if I just knocked."

"We heard the knock, but it was faint," Coco said. "But when we heard it the second and third time, we knew it had to be one of us and not ISAN. We were debating whether to open the door at first. But when we heard it again, we voted to take a chance. We thought it could have been one of us who had been injured, but we never expected you. I mean, we're glad it's you, but—"

"And I'm glad you did. I'm just so happy to see you well." The relief in Rhett's voice drew a few smiles.

Not enough, Rhett thought as the last group of kids clambered out.

"Jasper? Stella?" Rhett checked the faces around him. He hadn't seen them. Where were they? "Jasper. Stella!" Maybe they were at the other structure, unconscious or out of view.

"Rhett." Reyna gripped his shoulders, forcing him to meet her stern gaze. "I'm sorry. I couldn't save them." Her tears streamed down harder.

"Couldn't save who?" Rhett glanced about, calling their names again.

"Rhett. Stop." She flattened her hands on his cheeks. "Jasper and Stella didn't make it out."

Rhett blinked, unable to process her words. "What do you mean?"

Reyna shook her head, choking on her words. "I tried, but I was too late. They ..." She turned toward the destruction.

"No. No. No." Rhett murmured, stumbling back a step. "Maybe you didn't see them. You know how they are." His hope shattered even as he tried to deny it, even as he was telling Reyna she was wrong.

When Cleo sobbed into her palms and Reyna embraced him, Rhett closed his eyes, taking a moment of silence as he allowed himself to come to terms with their deaths.

Rhett already felt disconnected to his body but it kept getting worse.

"I'm sorry, Rhett." Momo enclosed her thin arms from behind him, and he welcomed her comfort and warmth.

Rhett had to snap out of his grief. Grieving was for later. He had to be a leader and take care of the situation at hand. The kids hadn't fallen apart. He couldn't either. They needed him.

Rhett released Reyna and took Momo in his arms. "Thanks, kid. We have to count our blessings."

"Where's Brooke?" Ozzie's voice was calm but brittle, and he was going to fall apart if he didn't get the answer he wanted.

Rhett turned to Reyna standing next to Ozzie, thinking she would speak up, but Cleo cleared her throat.

"I want to let you know Brooke is alive, but ..."

Ozzie sucked in a breath and clasped his hands together as if his prayer had been answered. "But what? What happened to her? Let me see her."

"Let me take you to her. Let's all go inside and I'll explain everything." Cleo slipped back in first.

The kids filed in line behind her, and Rhett went in last after he looked over his shoulder for anything suspicious.

The first thing that stood out was the cleanliness on the ground, and then the low ceiling. The blueprint was similar to their hiding place when they escaped ISAN.

In the left corner were blankets and extra clothes. The right corner held neatly arranged weapons. Small makeshift tables were scattered about. Had they been sleeping here before the bomb?

Perhaps they met here when they wanted their own space. After all, they had been a unit once.

Rhett couldn't fathom how they'd built this place in such a short amount of time. It was nothing elaborate, but still—to stack the debris into another stable unit was amazing.

"I'm here." Ozzie lowered to his knees beside Brooke, who was sitting upright against the wall.

He reached for her, his trembling hands hovered over her face, and then he brought his arms to his side. Ozzie squeezed his eyes shut, but his taut features showed rage and anguish.

"Oz …" Brooke croaked, cringing, as if it hurt to speak.

Her nose, her face, the soldier had said. She didn't look as broken as he had described.

Brooke was unnaturally still. Her nose seemed fine, but her eyes were swollen, bloodshot, and she looked like someone had brutally beaten her.

"Who did this to you?" Ozzie asked, his fingers digging into the dirt.

Brooke blinked and tears escaped down her cheek. "I tried to stop him. I tried so hard, but he was too strong."

"Who?" Ozzie clenched his jaw, his fists so tight his knuckles paled. "Who did this to you?"

"Gene."

Ozzie swore, and Rhett cursed under his breath. Crazy, diabolical trash. Even though John had told Rhett, hearing it from Brooke sounded a lot worse.

"Where is he?" Ozzie growled.

"He escaped," Jo said.

"How?" Ozzie kept his stone-cold tone, so foreign on him.

Jo told us what had happened, starting with Rhett's call to

Reyna. A couple small bombs had been deployed at that point. When Jo and Reyna had gone down to get Gene, they'd found Brooke pretty broken up.

When Jo paused, Reyna added, "John carried Brooke out of there moments before the compound collapsed. ISAN guards, drones, and assassins entered when a second bomb exploded. Then the showdown happened and chaos broke out all over. Just before the last bomb detonated, Mia, Ella, and I used our power to put up a shield around our group as we ran for cover. We were separated at the last impact when we got out."

Amid many casualties on both sides, they'd managed to get out before the building fully came down.

"We ran to the shelter the kids had made," Jo continued. "Ava had assigned me the task of getting them to clean up debris. It worked out since they'd wanted a place of their own, and Tamara had encouraged it to keep them busy. When we talked about it during a meal, she suggested building it sturdy and fast because we might need it one day."

Tamara had sensed something catastrophic would happen. She had told Rhett that was her power, but he'd only half-believed her. A flash of warning here and there. Her nonsense mumbo jumbo that was too vague to be useful half the time. But … she had warned Rhett about Ava.

Something's wrong. I didn't tell Ava, but I feel cold around her. Something powerful and strong is coming.

Tamara's words had just been a warning, not a premonition, Rhett reminded himself. A warning, that was all, right?

"I need to call Ava and give her an update, but I wanted to get all the facts first. Oz and I thought you were all … We didn't think there were any survivors."

"Well, if it weren't for Reyna, Mia, and Ella, we would be underground," Cleo said.

It had been a while since Reyna had used her gift, a powerful shield that created a bubble-like space around her. The shield was expandable and durable, able to handle even a bomb explosion.

She had sworn off her power on the day they'd escaped ISAN, but had gone against her own promise to save lives. Sometimes Rhett forgot what she was capable of.

"The destruction looks like a massive landslide." Momo dipped her head low. "Some of our friends didn't make it and others were taken."

"I'm so sorry." Rhett wanted to hug all of them, to let them know everything was going to be fine, but that would be a lie. The truth—this was just the beginning.

"I'm thankful to Marissa," Brooke said. "She saved my life. She healed my broken nose and a few of my ribs."

That explained why Brooke looked better than Rhett had expected. "Who is Marissa?"

"What do you mean she healed you?" Ozzie inquired.

Jo wrapped her arms around a girl, bringing her closer to them. She had been standing behind her friends. A petite, shy little thing.

"She has the ability to heal people with her touch," Jo said. "She had to stop to rest because it takes a lot out of her, but she still needs to heal Brooke's right side. Gene cracked all of her ribs."

They had a healer? Maybe she could have helped Brooke when she was in a coma.

"Marissa can heal wounds as far as we can tell, but not disease or something like a poison," Jo said as if she could hear Rhett's thoughts. "So she couldn't have helped Brooke before, but she can and has now."

Impressive.

Ozzie gently placed his head on Brooke's lap, as if asking for her forgiveness. "I'm so sorry, Brooke. I'm here now. I'm going to take care of you. I swear I'll make him pay."

"It's not your fault. And revenge is not your forte. Karma. He'll get what he deserves one day." Brooke raised her shaky arm and rested it on Ozzie's head. "I shouldn't have gone to see him. I didn't know he had such strength and I didn't know we were going to get bombed. I shot him. He bled, but healed himself in seconds. I saw the wound stitch itself back up. If he is Ava's brother, wouldn't they have similar powers?"

"I don't know." Ozzie rubbed Brooke's hands as if to warm them. "ISAN suppressed Ava's gifts for so long she might not be able to figure them all out."

Rhett scratched his chin and sighed. Sooner or later they would have to deal with Gene. He could kill any one of them with a single blow. Who would defeat him? Ava? Rhett didn't want to think about it.

"Do you think after Marissa heals Brooke, she can help the injured in the other building?" Rhett didn't want to give such a task to a little girl, but they were desperate.

"Sure. Zen told me about the other structure. He had asked us to stay in the main building, but this would be for a good reason."

"He will understand." Rhett nodded to reassure her.

"What do we do now?"

"We wait for Zen."

303

CHAPTER THIRTY-EIGHT – NEXT PLAN

RHETT

While they waited, Rhett messaged Ava. She was on her way to the facility. Rhett reminded her not to enter the building without Zen's permission.

Rhett knew Ava. She would feel empowered to act because Naomi and Tamara were with her. But she wouldn't risk their lives, would she?

Before they hung up, Rhett asked her several more times not to engage. She agreed, but his gut told him to worry.

Their conversation had been cut short, and he couldn't reach her again. They must have been going through a no-reception zone. Waiting for her reply would be hell.

Rhett needed the coordinates Mitch had given Zeke. Rhett had asked Ava to compare them to Gene's and let him know. But could they trust any of the coordinates? Mitch could have gotten the wrong ones and Gene would likely send them to a trap. Rhett's worries compiled.

Tamara's words played in his mind. *I feel cold around Ava.* Rhett wished he had asked her before this mission if she still felt that way. He would have made Ava come with him, but what was done was done.

After Zen, Vince, and Frank greeted the survivors, they wordlessly took what remained of their base. Zen turned from

Rhett with his fist over his heart, and then he wiped at his face.

Zen could hide his tears. He could hide the tornado of pain he must feel. But he could not hide his bloodshot eyes and the fracture in his voice.

After he collected himself, Zen faced Rhett. "I thought we were safe here. There's always a possibility of discovery, but the percentage was slim. I certainly couldn't have predicted someone like Gene. Novak wanted no survivors. It's a miracle anyone escaped."

"It could have been worse." Frank kept his gaze on the gaping massive hole. "They could have taken down the other building."

"I agree with Frank." Vince kicked something by his foot. It flew into the bombed-out pit.

"Novak didn't know Reyna, Mia, and Ella, had such gifts," Rhett said.

Zen rubbed his nape. "I guess it goes both ways. I don't understand. We were so careful."

"Nothing could have been done. It was Gene. It was all Gene." Rhett started shouting, kicking rocks, kicking anything in his way. "It had to be when we were most vulnerable. When you, Ava, and I left. He—"

Zen placed a hand on Rhett's shoulder. "Tell me from the beginning. Tell me everything."

Rhett began where Jo had begun, starting from Brooke's encounter with Gene.

Vince arched his eyebrows. "Ava is Gene's sister. Do you think she's capable of the same strength and the ability to heal?"

Zen tilted his head to the smoky sky and then focused on his feet. "They do have similar DNA, but even with the test, I didn't see anything significantly different with Gene. I missed something."

Rhett's turn to place a hand on Zen's shoulder. "You couldn't have known. A DNA test doesn't list their powers. And it wasn't his power that alerted ISAN. It was the liquid, an injectable tracker ISAN techs put inside him. And Tamara got unlucky when she kidnapped him. We didn't know."

But couldn't she have sensed something about him? If she'd told Rhett she felt cold around Ava, couldn't she have sensed it on Gene, too?

"Wait. What?"

Rhett didn't like the accusation in Vince's voice.

Vince frowned. "Tamara kidnapped Gene. Is this a coincidence? Where is she now? I would like to speak to her."

"She's with Ava and you don't need to worry about her loyalty." Zen's voice deepened with authority. "I recruited her. I trust her."

Vince, his tank size and all, flinched, and looking offended. "How? Tell me about Tamara."

Good. Rhett was glad he'd asked.

Zen glared at Vince. He didn't like to be challenged. "This happened before I met Rhett. While I was working for ISAN, I was also working for Councilor Chang. My men and I had been searching for girls, particularly around the ages of sixteen and seventeen, to build our resistance. I wanted to find girls who might have special gifts. I stumbled upon Tamara's case. Tamara was on trial for killing her boyfriend."

Vince's eyes grew wider. "Did she?"

"Yes, but it's a little bit complicated. The poor girl had a black eye, and her cheeks were black and blue and swollen. I would have killed her boyfriend myself. Anyone could see she'd been beaten up. But Tamara didn't deny it or even claim self-defense. She told the court she had an intuition her boyfriend was going to kill her. The court had delivered a life sentence and marked her as insane. I didn't agree with their decision so I decided to take a chance. I helped her escape."

"Escape from jail?" Frank breathed. "How? That's almost impossible."

"I arranged the rendezvous with Councilor Chang. I had told Chang we had to snatch Tamara or ISAN would."

Rhett should have known Councilor Chang had a hand in it. Zen and Chang's relationship went far back.

"We made it look like a suicide," Zen continued. "Chang had a talk with her privately in her cell. When Tamara agreed to our arrangement, Chang gave her a pill to make it seem like she had a heart attack. She was carried out in a body bag and sent to get cremated."

"No one questioned her death or did a thorough examination?" Frank rocked on his heel with his arms crossed.

"No. She was nobody to them. Tamara lived with her grandmother, who had died shortly after Tamara was taken to juvie. As soon as she was in my hands, I trained her. She had natural talent. She's an excellent markswoman like Rhett, with an exceptional talent for knife throwing as well. So after I thought she was ready, I sent her to ISAN to keep an eye out for Ava."

"And it backfired."

Rhett was just about to give Vince a piece of his mind when Zen spoke.

"No, it didn't. Tamara helped in a lot of ways. If it hadn't been for her, the situation could have been worse, especially when Ava escaped. But I'm not going to stand here and explain. We have important matters to discuss. If I tell you Tamara can be trusted, I hope you respect my judgment."

Silence fell, a breeze the only whisper of sound.

Zen looked somewhere in the distance and then back to them. "We need to find a place to live. We can't all fit in the first structure, and I don't want to put their lives in jeopardy. Got any suggestions?"

Rhett crossed his arms to gather warmth. The brisk wind shifted cooler in the waning daylight. "I have an idea. We can go to the base in the mountain. It will be crowded, but we can make room."

"I think that's a good plan. I hate to impose, Rhett, but we have no options. We need to move as soon as possible."

"What about the wounded soldiers?" Vince hiked a thumb to the other building. "We can't move them."

"The ones that need more time will have to stay behind. We'll come and get them when they are ready. The sooner we move, the better."

"How about the girl who can heal?" Frank asked. "Does she stay or come with us?"

Zen looked at Rhett, allowing him to make the call. Under pressure, Rhett didn't know what to say. He had to do right by all.

"Marissa will stay behind. I'll ask Jo and a few of her closest friends to stay as well. I don't want to separate her from her friends. What happens next?"

Zen gave Rhett a taut grin, his way of letting him know he agreed. "Rhett, I want you to take them."

Unsure of what he was asking, because he'd better not be asking Rhett to go to the mountain base just yet, he said, "What do you mean? Take who and where?"

Zen scrunched his eyebrows in confusion. "Take our team to

the mountain base," he said slowly as if he was unsure.

Rhett shuffled his feet in the dirt, stalling. He didn't want to be the one. He wanted to get to his girl.

"No," Rhett said with conviction. He didn't care if he was being rude. "What about you? Can't you take them? I need to get back to Ava."

"Your ensemble in the mountain follows your orders. You'll need to get them settled. This is not negotiable. I need to head back to my appointment, and then I'll meet Ava at the secret facility. Contact her and tell her to stand down and wait for me. If we miss a chance, then so be it. We'll find another way, another time. Too much has happened. I don't want to lose anyone else."

After Zen took off to the other building, Rhett contacted Ava. It was bad enough they were separated, but when he couldn't get hold of her again, he couldn't breathe. Exasperated, Rhett kicked a pebble and spat out curses.

Zen needed to hurry and get to his girl. Rhett prayed Gene's coordinates were the same as Mitch's. Rhett fished out the picture of Ava he had taken with him, the one Ava had found in their room, and he stared at it as if he was talking to her.

Please wait for backup, Ava. Don't do this alone.

With a long sigh, Rhett went back to his team to get them ready for departure.

CHAPTER THIRTY-NINE – THE FACILITY

"**N**ow, Zeke. Move it."

I had half a mind to let him feel the sting of my Taser, but that would only be a waste of time.

"Don't get all pushy, princess. I can't just take off."

"Why? We need to leave *now.*"

"Tiana," Zeke called, exasperated.

Beside me, Naomi clenched her hands into dimly glowing fists. When I tapped her arm, she relaxed her fingers and the fire died.

I've had enough of Zeke. Time to act.

Zeke clapped his hands fast twice before I could nudge him again. A woman appeared from the flap behind him, dressed like a warrior. Wearing all black, she had weapons on either side of the holsters.

Swords were crisscrossed on her back. Her short, dark hair tied in a tight ponytail accentuated high cheekbones.

"Yes, Master Zeke." She bowed.

"Keep an eye on things while I go run an errand. If my men show up, tell them I'm off for a couple of days. I'll message you when I can."

Tiana examined us. "Be careful. You trust these—"

Tamara yanked on Zeke's ears. "The question is, can we trust him? Come on, Zeke. We have things to do."

"I would like to do things to you." He waggled his eyebrows, taking in Tamara's body.

310

I rolled my eyes. "If I find out you're keeping women as sex slaves, you'll find yourself unable to walk. Got it?"

I flashed a glance to Tiana to see her reaction. When she glared at me, I assumed at least she was there by her free will, but I didn't know about the others.

"They can't resist me." He flashed a coy grin.

I shoved Zeke. "Shut up and get to your glider."

As Zeke led us down the empty hall, we flanked him with our weapons drawn. About five flights down, he exited through a narrow, dark path.

Sunlight penetrated through cracks in the side of the building when we rounded the corner. A cool-looking glider was the only thing parked on the entire floor. The transporter was nothing short of elegant—sleek, polished, and silver.

I had never seen one like it before. Not on the highways and not even on the net. I supposed a criminal like Zeke could afford the best.

Tamara blew a wolf whistle and ran a finger along the wing. "This is one awesome glider."

"Hey, don't touch that, love." Zeke extended his arm to stop her, but thought better of it.

"It's just a glider. Geez. You can wash my cooties afterwards. And I'm not your love."

"It's not an *it*. It's a *she*. She's special. I had her especially designed for me. Get in before I change my mind."

The smell of leather from the plush chairs came first, and then I took in the sophisticated details. The dark, polished-wood panels covered the entire dashboard and metallic silver side trim extended all around the aircraft.

"What is this?" Naomi stuck her hand through a ring attached to the chair.

Zeke angled his brow. "It's a drink holder. Haven't you seen one before? Did you live under a rock?"

"Hey watch what you say." I shoved him lightly, more like nudging him to get to his seat. "We didn't have privileges like you. Stop chattering and get us to the destination."

"Fine. But don't touch anything."

When he carefully slid into his chair, front, back, and side view holograms of the aircraft popped up. Monitors and panels shifted, and knobs and buttons emerged from secret compartments.

"That is the coolest thing I've ever seen." Tamara fluttered her eyelashes, taking in the high-tech gear.

"You haven't seen nothing yet." Zeke howled like a wolf. "Where to, princess?"

I'd almost told him not to call me that, but he would ignore me, anyway. Instead, I said, "Punch in the location Mitch gave you."

When I had compared the two coordinates, they were nowhere near each other. My blood had run cold. I decided to go with Mitch's first since I trusted him more than my psycho brother.

If my intuition was right, then Gene had lied to me. I would tell Rhett of my decision when he contacted me. It was a simple fix.

When Zeke pushed back something that looked like a stick, the glider sped down the long, empty floor and soared out into the world.

My stomach dropped. I figured this aircraft would move faster than any other I'd been in, but I couldn't have predicted *how* fast.

Rhett would love to fly one.

I didn't know how long had passed, but we flew among the clouds in silence for at least an hour. My mind wandered to Rhett and everyone at the rebel base.

My chip dinged with his smiling image, but then it faded.

"Rhett?"

"Babe, are you there?" He sounded worried.

"I'm here. Did you see Brooke? Reyna? The kids? What happened?"

"You're breaking up. Remember do not engage without Zen—that is his order. Zen will be on his way soon. Promise me you will wait."

"I promise."

"Wait for Zen. Swear it."

"Okay. I swear it," I said halfheartedly.

"I mean it, Ava." His voice was stern, the tone he used when he worried I wouldn't listen. "I need you to send me—"

A buzz sound shot through my eardrums.

"Rhett. Rhett? Are you there?"

No answer.

My chest caved in. I wanted to ask him why he wasn't coming, too. Something was wrong, and a part of me didn't want to know. Had he purposely cut me off to avoid giving me the worst news?

When I peered up, Naomi gaped at me.

"Are you okay? What did Rhett say?"

"I'm afraid not much. We got cut off. I didn't get the chance to give him the coordinates."

Naomi slouched into her seat.

Tamara looked out the window, caressing her arms.

What was wrong? What did she know?

"Ava," she said softly. "I need to tell you something and please don't get mad. I should have told you earlier, but I was hoping this feeling I'm having would go away. It hasn't, and it's getting stronger the closer we get to the facility."

"What is it?" I failed at my attempt to not sound annoyed. I didn't need another thing to worry about.

Tamara tensed and then hesitantly said, "I sense danger around you. I'm afraid for you. Maybe we should go back to the base."

"What?" Naomi angled her eyebrows. "You can feel that? I think we're almost there, though. What if we miss this opportunity? If you don't know for sure what the danger is, it would be silly to leave now. But it's Ava's call."

"Did you feel something around Gene?" I asked.

It was unfair to get upset at her, but if she knew there was a danger, she should have told me. I wish people would stop trying to protect me and just tell me the truth.

"No." She closed her eyes and opened them. "If I had sensed something, I would have told you. Do you"—she swallowed— "you don't blame me, do you?"

"No." I didn't mean to raise my voice, but the thought was ridiculous. "Of course I don't blame you. I blame myself. He's my brother. How could I make that kind of mistake? We had other warnings about him—we just didn't know what we were looking for." I lightly socked the side panel.

"Hey. Don't hurt my baby," Zeke hissed.

Naomi cleared her throat. "No one should blame anyone. You don't know what happened. Everyone could be fine."

Tamara shook her head, her lips a thin line. "Didn't you hear the explosion when we were talking with Reyna? You don't know ISAN. You've never been there. You really don't know."

GENES

A fast beat blasted in the space with an annoying voice and a screeching melody.

"Can you turn the music down, please?" I had half a mind to throw Zeke in the ocean, especially when he ignored my request. "What's the matter with you, are you deaf?"

Zeke bopped his head to the music and obnoxiously sang along—out of tune but having fun. I counted three seconds before I lunged off my seat.

I took five long steps and pointed a Taser at the back of his skull. Tamara's warning had put me in a foul mood. "Turn it off."

"Okay, okay, okay." He touched his screen and silence filled the cabin again. "I got tired of hearing you ladies yapping about senses and touchy feely stuff. It got boring."

"I don't care what you think. Don't ever do that again. It's rude."

He scoffed. "You're the one pointing a gun at my head. Who's the rude one?"

"It's a Taser. At least I didn't plan on killing you."

"You're killing me by being in my baby and forcing me to take you to some uninhabitable, dangerous place. Have you heard of radiation?"

"That was ages ago." Tamara's dismissive tone did not match the worry in her expression.

"You're impossible. Just shut up." I socked his headrest.

"Hey. My ship. I do what I want."

I lost the chance to retort when the glider began a descent. A dumpster-looking place materialized. Nothing but debris and trash covered the landscape. Farther out, craters pocked a wide, desolate plain.

"Whoa, do you see those?" Tamara pointed through the front

window. "Are those meteor craters?"

"Possibly." I moved to the other side and saw no crater dents, but snow-covered mountains.

I didn't know where we were headed, but the horrid place exceeded my expectations for an ISAN torture palace.

"Are you sure this is the right location?" I tapped the window for emphasis.

"I'm using Mitch's coordinates, princess, like you had told me to. I'm never wrong. You might want to double check, though. I can't imagine this would be a safe place for you ladies. I'm going to cloak my baby for all of our sakes. Let's hope they haven't spotted us."

I appreciated his concern.

"There." I pointed to the left of what I suspected was the entrance. A few aircraft were parked to the right of a gray dome.

That dome had to be our way in. I assumed this facility was underground. There were no buildings, homes, or people as far as I could see.

When we landed, Naomi and I got out to inspect the surroundings. Tamara stayed behind to ensure Zeke didn't take off without us.

A gust of wind not only brought a horrible smell, but made it difficult to breathe. I covered my nose with my hand.

We moved swiftly across the dry, cracked earth, from one trash pile to the next. The dome was about ten yards away. Two figures wearing black ISAN uniforms and masks flanked the alcove, standing like statues.

So, Gene had given me the wrong location. I should have known better. No matter how many times he disappointed me, I kept hoping he would do something right.

I tapped on my chip to speak to Tamara, but I couldn't get through. The reception was still horrible. I wondered if there was any at all. But who would be crazy enough to come here?

"Naomi. Tell Tamara to go back and send Rhett these coordinates. I need you to go back with her."

Her eyes went wild. "What about you?" Then understanding showed on her long face. "No. I'm not leaving your side. You always planned to go in by yourself, didn't you? You only let us come because you knew Rhett wouldn't let you go by yourself. So you agreed and then planned to send us away."

"I—there's no service." I sucked at lying, to my friends at least, but it was true. We had no reception.

She crossed her arms. "I'm staying right here. You go tell Tamara yourself. I'll keep watch and look out for our contact. Now, go."

I swore under my breath. Naomi's tone told me she would hold her ground and more so when she shoved me. I dashed back to the glider and pounded the door.

The ramp dropped.

Zeke scowled. "Hey, you don't need to abuse her. Just give me a ring." He pinched his nose. "It reeks. What's that smell?"

Zeke closed the door after I stormed in.

"Tamara, I tried to reach you via chip. Did you get any of my messages?"

She stopped flipping her throwing knife, rolled up her sleeve, and looked at her arm. "No. I'm so sorry. Did you need me?"

"Yes. I'm not sure what to do." I drummed my fingers on my crossed arms. "I can't get ahold of Rhett. This is bad. There's no service. Rhett is going to freak out."

Tamara rose from her seat, worry contorting her features.

"What should we do?" When I didn't answer, she continued. "We should go back. I don't feel right, Ava. Remember my warning?"

Her intuition had been correct so far, but the one about me sounded vague. Danger followed me wherever I went, especially now.

We were *all* in peril.

This was war.

No one was safe.

Tamara, you're wrong this time. I'm going to be fine.

I shook her shoulders, forcing her to meet my gaze. "Listen carefully. I need you to go back with Zeke and tell Rhett I couldn't reach him."

"No." Tamara backed away. "What about you? What about Naomi? Don't make me do this. If something happens to you, I ... please, Ava. You have to believe me." Tears glistened in her eyes.

I couldn't look at her. I don't know why, but I just couldn't. It felt like I was saying goodbye, or betraying her.

Get a hold of yourself. You're just scared. This is unknown territory, so of course you would be cautious.

"Naomi and I are staying," I said. "I need you to go because Rhett trusts you. You can lead a team back here, okay?"

"I don't like this." She shook her head and gripped me like her lifeline.

"Tamara, you looked after me in ISAN. I appreciate everything you did for me. But we're not in ISAN anymore. You don't need to watch over me all the time."

"I know. But—"

I raised my chin and sharpened my tone. "This isn't a request. I hate playing the leader card, but that's who I am. I'm ordering you to go."

Her shoulders slumped and she opened her mouth to retort, but closed it again. "Okay, but promise me you won't go in? At least give us that peace of mind."

I pivoted to Zeke, who hadn't moved. "Please take Tamara back to where she needs to go." I inched closer. "If you take her anywhere else or if you do anything you're not supposed to do, I swear to you, I'll find you."

Zeke gave me an exaggerated bow. He could have kissed the ground. "Don't worry. I don't ever want to see you again." Then he slapped the button to release the ramp.

I faced Tamara to say goodbye but she beat me to it.

"Wait." Tamara took three long fast strides and crushed her body to mine. "I'm normally not this emotional, but I just want you to know that you're a good person. You were good to me in ISAN even though I lied to you. You didn't make me feel bad. You've been a good friend. Well, you and Brooke were my *only* friends. So, please, be careful. I haven't allowed myself to care about people after my grandmother passed away, but I care about you and Brooke."

My eyes burned and I squeezed her tighter. "You and Brooke mean the world to me. We are friends for life."

"Friends for life." She sniffed.

I drew back. "Can you tell Rhett something for me?"

"Sure. Anything."

"Tell Rhett ..." I swallowed a hard lump. "Tell him ... I love him. Tell him he means everything to me." My voice cracked. "Tell him my favorite place in the world is next to him. He's my reason. Even when I didn't remember him, I always knew a part of me was missing someone. Tell him ... my heart is my map, and it leads me only to him. It always has and always will."

I repeated Rhett's words to me, but those words went both ways.

"No, Ava. You tell Rhett yourself." Tamara drew forward, reaching out to me. "Please. Don't go in without backup. Please."

I shuddered a breath to keep my emotions at bay and became an ISAN soldier I was trained to be—cruel, cold, and without feeling. "Novak will kill anyone and everyone to get to me. I have to stop him. I think he's there."

"We can do it together. You don't have to do it alone."

"We can't miss our opportunity. My mother is in there."

"You're going by what Gene said. You can't trust him."

Her pleading voice put a hole in my determination, reminding me of Rhett's reasoning. I would not let her stop me. If I got any indication my mother was in there, I would still go even if I got caught.

"This time, I have to. I have no choice," I said with conviction.

I embraced her again tightly as if I would never see her again, and ran out with a mask on this time, plus one for Naomi, before I could change my mind.

Be brave, Ava. Be someone important. My mother's words resonated in my mind, giving me courage.

Hold on, Mother. I'm coming for you.

CHAPTER FORTY – THE SOURCE

AVA

Naomi jerked when I slipped next to her, her hand going to her mouth to suppress a scream. The mask covered my nose and mouth except for my eyes. She didn't recognize me at first.

"You nearly gave me a heart attack, Ava."

"Sorry. Here. Put this on." I handed her the mask.

"Thanks." Naomi groaned quietly, placing it over her head.

"Do you have any update?"

"No. The two guards have been standing there, looking out to … nothing. How can they stand it? It would drive me nuts. So, what do we do now?"

"They don't know we're here. I think—"

Before I could say another word, a glider materialized through the cloud of dusk. Then a form stepped out, clad in an ISAN uniform.

Naomi pushed me farther down into hiding.

How was I supposed to see what the heck the person was doing from this angle? I needed to get closer. "Stay right here. I'll be back."

Naomi grabbed my arm when I got off my knees and whispered harshly. "Are you crazy?"

"We can't see anything. Stay right here. That's an order." I gave her an unyielding look.

She blinked, hurt crossing her features, but she nodded.

I hated pulling rank, but whoever had exited that glider must be our ticket in. Mitch had said someone would let us in, but we had to be there at a specific time. We'd arrived earlier to ensure we would have plenty of time.

Carefully, I moved to the closest pile of debris, but it wasn't close enough. I lifted my hand to Naomi to signal *wait here*. She frowned but nodded.

I rose and headed toward the three guards now, who were talking among themselves. I hoped they would ask questions first and shoot later. Thanks to my assassin stealth, I got close enough to hear them. They were in a heated conversation and didn't notice me until one of the guards pointed a Taser at me.

"Stop right there. Who are you?"

"I'm an ISAN assassin. Who are you?" There was no hesitation or fear in my voice.

"How did you get here? What territory are you from?" the second guard asked.

"She's with me," the new person answered—a female I realized.

I knew for sure then she was our contact.

"What? No one told us our shift was over." The first guy kept his weapon on me.

"Put your Taser down, Gunter. You know who I am. This girl is new. Either get out or we're going. You can take the next ten-hour shift, too." When they didn't answer, she added, "Suit yourself. I'm outta here."

"She's telling the truth." The second guard closed a message from his chip. "Janine is taking the second shift, but there's no other name."

Janine made an exaggerated sigh. "She's new. They probably forgot to put her name on the list. I'm training her."

"Where's Steve?" Gunter lowered his weapon. "Steve usually takes the second shift."

"How should I know? I'm not his keeper," Janine said.

Gunter examined me, his eyes lingering, making me nervous. "She's not wearing the right uniform."

"Seriously? You're questioning me about recruit protocol? I don't know why her uniform is different. Like I told you, she's new." Her tone became sarcastic as she leaned closer to him. "Maybe she'll get an upgrade on her uniform when she graduates out of training."

Gunter scowled. Then he left with his partner to the glider.

"Don't talk. Don't move. Assume the ISAN stance like me and face the front."

Janine's brief orders made my pulse race faster as I waited for her next instruction. I had no idea who this person was. I had no choice but to trust her. Only when the transporter left with the other two guards did she finally look at me.

"What's your name?" she asked. "Tilt your head slightly lower and twist your neck to the left when you talk. The camera won't be able to pick up the movement of your lips."

One of the rules in the ISAN manual—never disclose your name. She should know that.

When I didn't answer she added, "Sorry. I shouldn't have asked. That's not important. We are allowed a bathroom break, so when you are ready, let me know and I'll let you in."

I angled my head as she instructed. "What will I see when I go inside?"

Pulling my map would be easy, but I didn't know what else awaited me. Naomi tried to get my attention by waving her hand, but I ignored her. My plan was to leave her out there.

There seemed to be one way in and one way out. I would not have her trapped in there with me if things went south.

"Listen and watch carefully." Janine bent down. "The squares represent rooms. There are stairs to the basement level."

As she pretended to retie her boots, she drew five squares. Three at the top and two at the bottom. She drew two big Xs on the top middle square and the bottom right one. Then she rose.

"What is that?"

Using her feet, she erased the evidence of her drawing. "When you enter, the restroom is on the left. We never go farther in on guard duty. We're not allowed. However, I've accompanied a few prisoners to the squares I marked X."

"Prisoners? You mean—?"

"Don't ask. I don't know who. They're usually drugged or unconscious when they're brought in on gurneys. I wouldn't be able to tell you if they were male, female, adult, or child. In the boxes with the Xs, guards are stationed. Maybe about five. I'm going to assume you can take them down on your own. You're going to have to, since you have no backup."

Good. She hadn't spotted Naomi.

"I'm on my own and yes, taking down five on my own won't be a problem."

She gave me a curt nod. "You should skip the other rooms to save you time. I don't know who you're hoping to find, but this is suicide. Are you sure you want to go through with this?"

"Weren't you the one that told—"

"Don't."

Her tone was so cold I flinched.

"Don't what?" I gave her the same irate tone back.

"Don't say the name. Just go quickly and come out. And make sure you don't get caught. Since I've vouched for you, I'm in it just the same as you."

324

"Don't worry. If I fall, you won't fall with me. I would never disclose you, but what about the other guards?"

"I'm not worried about them. I'll deal with them if necessary."

"Again, you don't have to worry about me. I appreciate you putting your life on the line."

"I know you won't rat me out."

I frowned. "And you know this because ..."

"I was told you were in one of the groups that escaped ISAN. Your group was one of the lucky ones. Our group was found out, and guards stormed the halls. I pretended to be dead when they shot and killed my faction. When the guards were out of sight, I slipped back into my room. How pathetic was that? I was a coward and I didn't know what else to do. Soon after, they transferred me to another location. I thought I was good as dead, but I found myself with a new position. I swore if I could help the rebels I would."

"Oh, I'm sorry," was all I could say.

"It's fine. At least I'm here and I can help. What would you like me to do?"

I hadn't known she would offer to help, but I also wouldn't ask her to come inside with me. That would be too risky.

"I'm going to go in to snoop around first, but if the second rebel troop comes before I'm out, tell them to wait. I'm going in to get a general idea of the place."

"You're ..." She dropped her voice lower, but it was filled with elation. "Ava, aren't you? That's what you meant by getting a general idea of the place because you can map out the whole area."

"Yes."

"I'm so sorry. I didn't know it was you because of your mask."

"It's fine. I need a favor, though."

"Yes, anything." Her attitude toward me had changed—even

her tone was more respectful.

"Are you allowed to move out of your spot?"

"Yes."

"I have a friend who's hiding behind the junk area to my right. Do you see it?"

She got on her tiptoes and searched. "Yes. I see a bit of black material poking out."

"Good. When she sees me go in, she's going to freak out. So please go there and tell her something for me. Her name is Naomi. Tell her I told you her name and she's not allowed to disobey my order. That way she will trust you. Tell her I went in to look around and that I will be back out. Can you do that for me?"

"Yes."

I rested a hand on her arm and lightly squeezed. "You're not a coward. Don't ever think that. You did the right thing by saving yourself when everyone around you was dead and there was no way out. You're here now, sticking out your neck to help me. Not just me, but if there are people in there, you will be helping them. Bravery comes in all forms. You just have to know which suits you best."

Her eyes became glassy. "Thank you. Your words mean a lot to me."

"You're welcome."

I felt a sting in my heart as I thought of Rhett and my friends and prayed to anyone who would listen that they'd be fine.

No, not now. Get it together, Ava. It's time.

I shut down my emotions. No room to feel. No room for fear. I inhaled a deep breath.

"Now, let me in." I rubbed the jade pendant Mr. Lee had given me for good luck and the necklace Rhett had gifted me. Then I handed her my mask and entered.

CHAPTER FORTY-ONE – INSIDE FACILITY

AVA

Cool air and a sterile scent accosted me when I entered. The corridor was wider and brighter than I had expected.

I veered to my left with my head dipped lower when I spotted a few guards walking my way. I rushed into the restroom and waited inside, counting my breaths until my heart steadied.

When the coast seemed clear, I eased out and pulled up my map. A few more guards waited to the left, so I shuffled down to the right and tiptoed down the stairs. Like the first floor, it was expansive and bright.

I shouldn't go any farther. I should do a mental layout and go back out, but the guards had moved by the stairs. I decided to investigate a bit more until I had a clear path to exit.

Keeping my head low, I walked cautiously down the hall. Doors lined the walls on either side of me. My map showed me a detailed outline—small, square rooms with a toilet and a cot, but no people.

I thought something was wrong with my map. Why have quarters with no one inside?

Go back, a small voice whispered. But there were no guards down here.

I curved right and followed another long corridor, housing more identical small rooms. When I walked farther inside, there were no more chambers, but instead a larger space. Must be one of the X rooms. Then about twenty hologram bodies appeared in a sitting position with a few others moving among the rows.

These people ... were they kids? I had to know. I contemplated what to do. If I barged in, I would have given myself away without an exit plan for myself or any of them. I tossed that thought out.

Think. No. Go back. You can't do this on your own. What if there are cameras? Go, now! But I had come this far.

I ignored my little voice and decided to draw more on Helix. When I did, the hologram images became sharper, but I couldn't see their faces clear enough. I didn't need to. The height of these subjects told me enough.

What was ISAN doing with grown-ups? *My mother?*

Unable to see through walls, I drew out more Helix, pushing more and more. My effort gave no result. Something was blocking me.

I pressed my back against the concrete surface and focused behind the door and listened. Feet shuffled. The sound of a finger tapping on a TAB, perhaps. Then a female voice.

"Dr. Hunt will be pleased with the results."

"Are you sure?" A male voice. "I'm not seeing the same mutations as in Gene's DNA. We don't know the subject will have the same abilities."

"It's close enough."

"Close enough is not good enough. Send the rest back, but keep X410. Give her HelixB200. See if that makes a difference. If not, increase the serum."

"That's not a good idea. You could kill her."

He gave a forced-sounding laugh. "She wouldn't be the first.

You know this. Don't start caring now."

"Please. Stop this." A woman's voice—soft and fragile. "Why are you doing this?"

I slid down the wall at the pain in her voice. Why were they doing this? I wanted to break in and kill the male first and then the other two, and free everyone. And then what?

"Please. Let us go," the woman whimpered.

"Listen X412," the male began with a mocking tone, and then paused. "How is she awake? Let me see her results." Another pause. "What is this? How is she even here? Get rid of her. She's done."

"What? No. You can't make that call." A new voice—the third person finally spoke.

I quivered with anger, my fingernails scraping across the floor.

"Mr. Novak gave me the go-ahead. If you have any problem, you can bring it up with him."

"Please. I won't tell anyone. Please let me go. Please."

The desperation in her tone made me leap up, my fingers inches from opening the door.

Ava, get back. You can't do anything. Your cover will be blown. But that woman.

She was someone's daughter, or someone's mother, or someone's wife. Then I thought about my mother, and about Rhett's mother and father who had gone missing.

I stiffened when I heard light footsteps. *Crap!* My cover would be blown. Pulling my Taser from the back of my waistband, I prepared to shoot. The steps faltered, and a woman in a long, white gown looked down the hall at me, and then continued on her path.

My heart leaped out of my chest and I lost my breath.

Mom?

I rubbed my eyes and ran toward the woman to get a better

329

look. If she was my mom, she would have recognized me, right?

Maybe not.

She'd died when I'd turned thirteen. That had been six years ago, and I had changed so much. My uniform would have thrown her off as well. Or they could have erased her memory of me.

Right?

Gene said Mother is alive. Could he have been telling the truth? He lied about the coordinates of this location, so why not about Mom?

I didn't want to believe him. I didn't want my hope to burst and have her die all over again. Regardless, I had to be sure, the reason I'd risked my own life.

Why would they let a woman roam around the hall by herself? I doubted they would allow prisoners that kind of freedom. Perhaps she'd escaped somehow and was reaching out for help? Or I had to consider she might be with ISAN.

Every gut instinct told me this was a trap, but if she was my mother, I couldn't leave.

"Mom?" I whispered, trailing her.

She rounded the corner, feet padding along the floor faster. I caught a better glimpse of her face. Her hair was shorter, but I knew that heart-shaped face—her perfect angled nose and those beautiful eyes that always seemed like they were smiling.

"Stop. I just want to talk to you."

I shouldn't be speaking so loudly—I shouldn't be speaking to anyone at all. When I realized my mistake and that I'd lost her, I raced back to the stairs instead of pulling up my map. But I couldn't leave.

Naomi and Janine must be wondering what was taking me so long.

It's not right to make them worry, Ava.

I took my first step on the stairs, intending to get back to Naomi. Then perhaps after I gave her the details of what I had seen, we could come up with a better plan. Hopefully my backup would be here before Janine had to leave.

"Ava." A soft voice reverberated down the hall.

At first, I thought I was hearing things, but when I heard my name again, I stopped.

Get out. This time Rhett's voice uttered the warning inside my mind.

"Ava. Help me."

My breath hitched. Hearing my mother's voice for the second time impaled me. She appeared again and then disappeared around the turn.

"Mom." I followed the sound of her footsteps.

"Ava. Come. This way." She moved faster.

"Mom. Stop."

It was like a maze, more complicated than Janine's drawing.

Of course she didn't listen, and of course I was making the biggest mistake of my life. But what if she was leading me to the others who needed my help? What if Rhett's father and mother were here? What if there were kids on the other side being experimented on, just like the adults on this side. I had to get to my mother.

My mother. Gene had been telling the truth.

I spun right and entered the nearest room. I had no intention of losing her this time.

"Mom? Is that you?"

I nearly choked on my words and crumpled to my knees. All these years I'd thought she was dead. How could I have not known?

"Ava?" She shook her head frantically, tears dampening her eyes.

Then the strangest thing happened. She mouthed the words. "Get out."

What? Confusion held me immobile.

When she reached out her hand to me, she disappeared. Vanished. Gone.

A hologram?

A hologram.

Not my mother, but a stupid, stupid, freakin' hologram.

White vapor leaked from the ceiling like clouds sinking. I ran to the door, but it was no longer there. I slammed it again and again. Dents marked the walls, but I couldn't break through.

My eyes burned. The room spun. My last thought was of Rhett before darkness engulfed me.

CHAPTER FORTY-TWO – GOODNIGHT

AVA

"**H**ello, pumpkin. I'm here to tuck you in. You have a book for me to read?"

My dad's voice, but I couldn't see his face. My mattress slumped a bit from his weight. He smelled like the sterile floor of his lab.

I was dreaming. I knew because I'd had this dream before.

I didn't want to be dreaming. I tried to make it go away, but then I thought perhaps I could find some answers. Maybe I would see my father's face this time.

I encouraged my dream to continue.

The dream yanked me back with invisible hands. I grabbed a book from the nightstand and handed it to him.

My father read the title. "*Goodnight Moon* again?" He chuckled.

I smiled, showing all my little teeth. "It's my favorite," I said and lowered my blanket, nestling my head on the pillow.

"I know. How was your day?"

"Good," I said eagerly. Spending time with my dad warmed my heart. "How was yours, Daddy?"

"Very good. You know why?" He turned to the first page.

"Why?"

"Because you're here with me." He tapped my nose.

I giggled and crinkled my nose. I loved it when he told me how much I meant to him. "I'm happy you're here with me, too."

He caressed my cheek and read to the last page.

My eyelashes fluttered and I inhaled a deep, satisfying breath. "Goodnight, Daddy."

The mattress shifted, the weight of him lifted. "I love you, pumpkin." He kissed my forehead.

I tried to kiss him back, but he was gone, and flowers surrounded me instead. The sun heated my body. I saw my mom on her knees planting roses and smiled.

"Mom?" I dropped beside her and pulled out a dandelion. "Look what I found."

"Ava. Do you remember what I told you about dandelions?"

"Yes. Dandelions are strong. You told me to be the same. Be resilient. Be resilient like dandelions."

"Yes. Even when you feel like hope is gone, you must remember. You must. Ava, do you hear me? You must be resilient. You must. You must. You must. You must. You must. You must. You must."

"Stop!" I covered my ears, my mother's voice sounded like a robot's and she wouldn't stop.

The noise faded and the dream continued.

"Ava. Make a wish and blow," she said.

I stared at the white, feathery seeds. "I wish … I wish for …"

I wished silently to keep my secret safe and blew. The dandelion seeds drifted upward and then crashed on my face, burning my skin. I swatted at them, but they stuck to my skin.

"No, no, no. Please stop." I shifted and stirred, but I couldn't wake up.

Something clinked, metal on metal. My wrists. They hurt.

Then a cool breeze brushed my face, replacing the blazing heat. I sighed with relief.

I shot my eyes open. The mattress shifted at the bottom edge. I jerked back. Gene sat inches from me, a wicked grin on his face.

"Hello, sister. Did you miss me?"

My stomach somersaulted. "Get out. Get out of my dream."

"Who says I'm in your dream? Maybe you're in mine."

"You would say that, wouldn't you?"

He leaned closer. "Maybe it's not a dream." Then he was gone.

Dim light filtered through. I opened my eyes. The ceiling spun and the panel lights cleaved into one. I moved my hands to cover my eyes but I couldn't. My right hand had been cuffed to the bed.

Am I dreaming?

I yanked at it and whimpered from the pain. Okay, not a dream then. I should have been able to easily break the cuff. So I reached for Helix within, but I felt nothing.

Sometimes Helix came fast and easy I didn't feel it, but this time I knew something was wrong. I tugged at my cuff, but pain ripped through.

What to do now?

I sat up, but I had to scoot toward the wall because of the chain. "Is Mr. Novak there? Who's watching me? Coward. Show yourself."

As bold as I tried to be, saying the name *Novak* made my skin crawl. He not only gave me the creeps, he'd tried to kill me. Here, unable to pull up Helix, I'd never felt so vulnerable.

The door slid open. A woman with dark, shoulder-length hair and a long white gown entered. She was the woman I'd followed. She ...

"Mom?" I swallowed, my pulse out of control. "Mom?" I rose to my knees.

The woman peered up, looking straight at me, but she didn't seem to see me. She seemed to be drugged or in a daze. Getting a full view of her face, I shuddered a breath as my heart lunged to my throat.

The woman standing in front of me was my mother. My mother. My mother who I had been told had died from a rare disease. They had lied to me. They were ISAN. ISAN had lied to me. ISAN had stolen my mother. ISAN had stolen my life.

ISAN is going to pay.

I wanted to run to her but I couldn't.

"Mom. Look at me," I said frantically.

She stared but said nothing. She didn't even blink.

Why was she here? There were so many questions. I needed to get to her before she left.

"Come sit with me, Mom. Look at me." I raised my voice, saying anything I could to get her to break out of her stupor.

When she began to back away, I panicked and rattled my chain to make that awful sound. She didn't even flinch. My heart deflated and then I second guessed myself.

Maybe she wasn't my mom and just looked like her. Maybe I didn't remember her as well as I thought. Maybe it was another hologram.

The door slid open for her. *No. Don't leave.* Even if she wasn't my mom, her presence gave me comfort.

Footsteps echoed.

I watched the woman retreat another step, but she stopped when an arm nestled around her shoulder.

"Well, hello, sister. Seems like we've switched positions."

Blood drained out of me. Gene being here only meant … what did it mean? How had he escaped? What had happened? What about the rebels? My friends? Rhett?

"How are you here? Let me go." I wanted to tear that smirk off his face.

"Sorry, I have orders."

Prick. I said nothing. I wasn't going to play his game.

"Well, I see Mother has found you." He looked at her fondly and stroked her hair.

I focused on Mom and my insides quaked. Emotions I didn't know how to process flushed through me. I opened my mouth to speak but closed it instead. What could I say? There was so much to say, but I didn't want Gene here.

"What's wrong with her?" I said.

All these years. All the time lost.

I wanted to scream but I had no voice. I wanted to sob from the happiness of finding Mother, but I had no tears to shed. Utterly shocked, I couldn't process any of this. It felt like a dream. Perhaps it was.

"Let me talk to her," I said, my voice calmer.

"You can try, but I don't think she can hear you right now."

The mockery of his tone made me want to wring his neck.

The door opened. I knew those clicking steps as if they were my own.

I held my breath when a man in a tailored, dark suit walked in. He was debonair and polished perfection from sleeked-back hair down to his spit-polished shoes.

"Ava. It's nice to see you again."

Mr. Novak, despite his warm tone, sent shivers down my spine.

337

His lips spread into a smirk. "The family is finally together at last. Exactly how I planned it. Though I'm afraid I have to cut the family reunion short, but I promise, they'll be back soon. Right now, it's bedtime."

Breaths left me in short spurts. He couldn't ... how did he ... *no!*

Before I could say another word, a tiny needle popped out of the wall and stung me. All three faces blurred. My body weighed a ton, but I felt light as dandelion petals, drifting away. It all seemed to happen so fast, and yet somehow slow.

My back hit the mattress. I desperately fluttered my eyes to keep them open but it was hopeless.

Mr. Novak's face appeared over mine, shining with adoration. His smile appeared genuine, but it was all a ruse with lies and promises to do his worst.

He had me now. Right where he wanted me. I'd fallen into his trap ... so he thought.

No, Novak. You fell into mine. I will find out what you are doing here—all of it.

"You. Had. My. Mother." It took all my effort to get the words out.

Novak caressed my hair, his lips tugging into a smirk. "You will understand soon, but for now, you must sleep. You've been a naughty girl, Ava, but don't worry yourself. I forgive you."

I wanted to break his every bone. "What. Did. You. Do. To. Me?"

"Just feeding you all the protein drinks you missed. You will be submissive. You will do as I say, or there will be consequences. But I know you will cooperate. I have so much to tell you. So much I have planned."

GENES

I will never I wanted to say, but darkness loomed around me. And just before my body shut down, Novak leaned closer and whispered.

"Goodnight, pumpkin."

About the Author

Mary is an international bestselling, award-winning author. She writes soulful, spellbinding stories that excite the imagination and captivate readers around the world. Her books span a wide range of genres, and her storytelling talents have earned a devoted legion of fans, as well as garnered critical praise.

Becoming an author happened by chance. It was a way to grieve the death of her beloved grandmother, and inspired by a dream she had in high school. After realizing she wanted to become a full-time author, Mary retired from teaching after twenty years. She also had the privileged of touring with the Magic Johnson Foundation to promote literacy and her children's chapter book: No Bullies Allowed.

Mary resides in Southern California with her husband, two children, and two little dogs, Mochi and Mocha. She enjoys oil painting and making jewelry.

www.ISAN.Agency
www.TangledTalesofTing.com